Midnight Louie's
Pet Detectives

Also by Carole Nelson Douglas from Tom Doherty Associates

MYSTERY

MIDNIGHT LOUIE MYSTERIES
Catnap
Pussyfoot
Cat on a Blue Monday
Cat in a Crimson Haze
Cat in a Diamond Dazzle
Cat with an Emerald Eye
Cat in a Flamingo Fedora
Cat in a Golden Garland
Cat on a Hyacinth Hunt
*Cat in an Indigo Mood**

IRENE ADLER ADVENTURES
Good Night, Mr. Holmes
Good Morning, Irene
Irene at Large
Irene's Last Waltz

Marilyn: Shades of Blonde (editor of anthology)

HISTORICAL ROMANCE
Amberleigh‡
Lady Rogue‡
Fair Wind, Fiery Star

SCIENCE FICTION
Probe‡
Counterprobe‡

FANTASY

TALISWOMAN
Cup of Clay
Seed upon the Wind

SWORD AND CIRCLET
Keepers of Edanvant
Heir of Rengarth
Seven of Swords

*forthcoming
‡also mystery

Midnight
Louie's
Pet Detectives

EDITED BY

Carole Nelson Douglas

A Tom Doherty Associates Book
New York

MIDNIGHT LOUIE'S PET DETECTIVES

Copyright © 1998 by Carole Nelson Douglas

Art by Ellisa Mitchell

A Forge Book
Published by Tom Doherty Associates, Inc.
175 Fifth Avenue
New York, NY 10010

Forge® is a registered trademark of Tom Doherty Associates, Inc.

Library of Congress Cataloging-in-Publication Data

Midnight Louie's pet detectives / edited by Carole Nelson Douglas. — 1st ed.
        p.   cm.
     "A Tom Doherty Associates book."
     ISBN 0–312–86435–3 (acid-free paper)
     1. Cats—Fiction. 2. Detective and mystery stories, American.
     I. Douglas, Carole Nelson.
     PS648.C38M53   1998
     813'.01083629752—dc21   98–12431

First Edition: October 1998

Printed in the United States of America

0 9 8 7 6 5 4 3 2 1

For my husband, Sam Douglas,
whose idea it was to let Louie loose with a blue pencil,
and for Bambi, Onyx, Galadriel, Dido, Shadow,
Dione, and Rynx,
and everyone's furred, feathered, and scaled friends
who have crossed the Rainbow Bridge

CONTENTS

EDITOR'S NOTE

Allow me to introduce myself.

I can do exactly that, for I am a literate cat and a literary lion as well, it so happens. I *should* introduce myself first, for I am the first feline to edit a collection of short stories, each one of which I will introduce in turn.

I am a self-made soul and something of an autodidact. "Autodidact" is one of those impressive words certain humans like to toss around like dead mice to showcase their prowess, and it means self-taught. "Street-smart" was the expression in the alley-cat lingo I grew up with before I stumbled across the abandoned Funk and Wagnell's I cut my canines on.

There was no room in the inn, so I was born behind it: Dinah's in Palo Alto, California, in the early seventies. It is still there. My clan were "motel cats," dumped or abandoned in litters, living on lizards and the occasional manna left outside closed doors on room-service trays: chocolate cake and sometimes even coffee cream.

Most of us were doomed to two or three feral years before we died of disease, untended injuries, cruelty, or cars. I alone survived.

Maybe it was because I was black and good at camouflage. (They do not call me Midnight Louie for nothing.) Maybe it was because I was particularly bold, and discovered the carp café in the motel pond. Maybe I had what they call in the shelters "a good personality" and could always con any female—on stilettos or off, furred or non—into providing a warm and cozy place to sleep.

I was always too smart to be totally feral. It can get cold at night, even in California, but on chill nights I often found a welcome mat when I ankled up to human females patronizing the soft-drink machines before bedtime. One, name of Jackie, flew me coach-class to my first real home: an apartment in St. Paul, Minnesota.

Son of Bastet, but it is cold in that clime! And apartment living was way too confining for a free spirit of my sort. Even though Jackie was nice to cuddle up to, her lawyer husband had other ideas. Said I was a lowlife (I *am* short) and a nogoodnik (they talked like that in the seventies). So I was put on the auction block in the local rag's classified section. For one buck!

This rank insult attracted the attention of a sharp-eyed reporter with a nose for a hot story: my current biographer and collaborator, Miss Carole Nelson Douglas. Luckily, she had the smarts to realize I was a black diamond-in-the-rough, and after introducing the facts of my finding, let me tell my story in my own words.

I was not an overnight sensation.

So I was sentenced to years of bucolic obscurity in Moo World (doing time on the farm) until Miss Carole Nelson Douglas left the newspaper to write novels and hired me as the part-time smart-sass narrator of a quartet of romances with mystery, *Love Boat* in Las Vegas, if you will. I was to provide local color, but I soon discovered Vegas was my kind of town: all-night action; crime and punishment; dolls, dudes, and shady dames; moolah and murder; neon and nefarious doings. But Midnight Louie is not a part-time kind of guy, and I found my literary voice, which is a whole lot of Damon Runyon with a little generic gumshoe and Mrs. Malaprop thrown in. And the occasional French phrase for finish.

To make a long story short, my first novelistic outing was a bust. I was supposed to debut in 1986, but the romance editor didn't think much of a black-cat house detective at a Vegas hotel. Let us call her the Lizzie Borden of the literary world: she cut my lines by forty percent, and when the job was done, she cut the books by forty-one.

I have to credit my collaborator for recognizing that I had been axed untimely, and for resurrecting me as the leading man of my own mystery series. I debuted as the first first-person feline PI in the mystery world with *Catnap* in 1992.

Feline fiction was a tough sell even then, but the animal kingdom has risen triumphant in a host of new mystery series. Dogs are coming up strong on the inside, as well as other species, but I am happy to report that the cat is still king, and queen, when it comes to mystery. This collection showcases a variety of beasts up to their ears in crime, from elephantine palm-leaves to hamster mini-mouse ears; any creature that man or woman can use, abuse and, miracle of miracles, domesticate, care for and love. Of course, not all of us domesticate. Ahem. And you will see some of those in this collection, too.

Midnight Louie, Esq.
Las Vegas

INTRODUCTION
Lawrence Block

This is a book with cats.

It is also, to be sure, a book with dogs and hamsters, raccoons and elephants, lovebirds and owls. All of these other furred and feathered friends will do a great deal to enrich your reading pleasure, but their presence is essentially beside the point when you're trying to figure out where on your bookshelves this volume belongs. You see, this is not merely a book with cats. It is a Book With Cats.

Some years ago, Mystery Writers of America was in the midst of a flap of the sort that animates that worthy organization every now and then. While memory mercifully dims the details, the gist of it was this: one faction wanted the Edgar Allan Poe Award to be divided, with not one but two best novels singled out (well, doubled out) each year. One would be the best book of one sort, while the other would be the best book of the other sort.

The problem lay in the impossibility of saying what exactly each of the two sorts was. Hard-boiled versus cozy? That came closest to the distinction people were trying to draw, but it raised as many questions as it answered. Where did you draw the line? How could you say for certain which book was eligible for which award?

I pondered the point, giving it about as much serious thought as I give anything, and inspiration struck, as it sometimes does. What I realized was this: Just as there are two kinds of people in the world, people who divide people into two classes and people who do not, so are there two kinds of mysteries.

Books with cats and books without cats.

I wrote a piece for *Mystery Scene,* a modest proposal for the categorization of mysteries, in which I expanded upon this observation. It was, I stressed, remarkably clear-cut. A book either had a cat in it or it didn't. With a cat, it was eligible for the Best Book With Cats Edgar. Without it, it wasn't.

In the end, MWA left the Edgars undiluted, and went on to explore other areas of dissent and ill-feeling. That's for the best, I would say, but I still think in the terms I raised in that essay. "It's a book with cats," I'll say of one novel. "It's a book without cats," I'll say of another. And people generally seem to know what I mean.

In 1994, I resumed writing about Bernie Rhodenbarr. The seventh book of the series, *The Burglar Who Traded Ted Williams,* represents not only the return of the eponymous bookselling burglar after an absence of eleven years, but the debut of Raffles the Cat, the neutered, declawed, tail-less gray tabby whose job it is to keep Barnegat Books free of rodents. Most readers found Raffles quite charming, but a few saw his appearance as shameless pandering to the legion of ailurophilic mystery readers.

Au contraire, mon cher. What struck me was the certain knowledge that the Burglar books were, in every respect but one, perfect examples of Books With Cats. All they lacked, in fact, was the sine qua non, the cat itself. By installing Raffles in that little used-book store on East Eleventh Street, I was merely supplying the series in fact with what it had always had in spirit. Raffles has appeared in all the books since *Ted Williams,* as well he should. Bernie would be lost without him.

But that's more than enough from me. It's time now to yield the floor to Midnight Louie himself. He has brought together a rich menagerie of tales. Enjoy!

—Lawrence Block
Greenwich Village

Lawrence Block

Lawrence Block's work ranges from the urban noir of PI Matthew Scudder to the urbane effervescence of burglar Bernie Rhoden-

barr. He has won a slew of awards, including the key to the city of Muncie, Indiana, and has been named a Grand Master by the Mystery Writers of America. But he hasn't let it go to his head. His new Matthew Scudder novel is Everybody Dies. *As the title might suggest, it's unquestionably a "Book Without Cats."*

Because he and his wife travel relentlessly, their only animal companions in recent years have been the stuffed bears and rabbits pressed upon them by fans. In years past, however, the indefatigable author has shared his life with dogs, cats, turtles, tropical fish, rabbits, a sheep, a pony, goats, geese, donkeys, and a charming but willful raccoon.

dor, all of her. But she doesn't put on any airs. I sometimes wonder if perhaps she doesn't know.

We all sang as we went down the road. We usually do. The beach is a marvelous place. I don't care much for water myself, but the sand is wide open and full of wonderful smells and things to chase.

On this occasion Mother Perry was out for one of her walks. I've heard it said that she goes out every day. She is Friend's mother and is very old indeed. If she were a dog she'd be about fourteen, or even more. She lives down in the village. I haven't been to her house, but Tara has, and so has Bertie, who is one of our cats. We have more of them than I can count, although I know them all, of course! Every time the Boss goes to the vet and they have a homeless kitten she brings it back.

Bertie is black, and likes riding in cars. He does it whenever he gets the chance. I hate it, except to go the beach. But there's no accounting for cats. I don't know how the Boss expects me to keep so many of them in order, stopping them from going where they shouldn't, sharpening their claws on the furniture, and eating things that don't belong to them which are left on the top of benches. But she does! It's "Daisy, stop Isadora!" and "Daisy, get Freddie off the stairs!" I was the first here, so it's my job. I've been with the Boss since I was two weeks old. Now and then she will show people embarrassing pictures of me as a puppy with a towel around my chin, being fed porridge on a teaspoon.

Anyway, this day Mother Perry seemed to be very upset. All three of them stood together on the sand talking quietly and shaking their heads. They completely ignored Tara digging up stones and barking at them, and Willow dancing around in the water and shivering. I don't know what is the matter with her sometimes. She's peculiar about water. I don't even like the rain, but she only has to see a puddle in the drive, and she sits in it.

Casper was tearing about in circles as usual, just for the sake of it. But I could see that there was something seriously wrong, so I went over to listen. I need to know things. That is part of my job also.

"It is really very sad indeed." Mother Perry shook her head.

I may be the master of American Alleycat Noir, but when it comes to Victorian Noir, there is only one contender, Miss Anne Perry. But this time she is not offering one of her intense, dense, and dark stories of blighted life—and death—in dear old Blighty of yore. For the first time she sets the scene in the present-day, in the very own northern Scotland village in which she resides personally, and "peoples" the tale with domestic pets, all of whom are well-known to her. She reports that she loves writing about my four-footed kith and kin, and plans more of it. I applaud her conversion to crime most furry. In this case, human failings are detected and righted by a quartet of quadrupeds.

—M.L.

Daisy and the Silver Quaich
Anne Perry

THE MATTER OF the silver quaich began without any warning. When the weather is good and the Boss feels like it, she starts up the Woofer Wagon and takes all four of us down the hill to the beach. "Us," is me—Daisy—a smooth-haired, black-and-white collie ... well, more or less; my half-sister, Willow, who is heavily influenced by spaniel; and Casper, who is very young and all legs ... I've never seen a dog with such legs before! When he lies down he folds up like a deck chair. He says his mother was a collie and his father a pointer, but I find it hard to believe. He's nothing like any collie I ever saw. The fourth is Tara who lives over the driveway with the Boss's Friend. She's a yellow Labra

"Now this has happened it looks like spoiling everyone's holiday, and they saved up so hard to come here. They don't have a lot, so they won't be able to come again. I wish I could do something to help, but unless Mrs. MacKinnon declines to press the matter, it's going to become most unpleasant."

"Is there any chance she won't?" Friend asked.

"Not at all, on past knowledge of her," Mother Perry replied, looking miserable.

It was a lovely day, full of sun and wind and I wanted to join the others, or mooch about to see what I could find, but this was obviously more important, so I couldn't leave it.

"What can we do to help?" the Boss asked.

"Nothing at all," Mother Perry answered her. "I am afraid it is a tragedy which is just going to run its course. Several of us have tried reason and persuasion, going back over everything that happened that day, but none of it serves except to make her angrier. They are cousins, and their relationship goes back a long way."

"Who are cousins?" Friend asked. "Mrs. MacKinnon and Mrs. MacPherson."

"Yes."

"Oh . . ." Friend sounded as if she could see how that explained everything. I couldn't.

"Have they told the police?" the Boss asked.

Mother Perry looked very miserable. She was leaning on her stick as if she needed it to hold her up. As I said, she is terribly old.

"Not yet," she said, biting her lip. "But I am afraid they will, if it is not solved within a day or two."

At this point an elderly man came into sight along the beach and Casper started out at a gallop to investigate, shouting as usual. The Boss started to call after him, and they all said goodbye, and we were herded back into the Woofer Wagon and went home again.

The matter bothered me all day. After all, if it is the Boss's business, then it is mine. I thought about it a lot, and asked everybody else what they knew, but they didn't have any ideas. Cats wander around rather freely; they have their own doors for coming and going. They might have heard. They do know things sometimes. I even found an opportunity first thing next morning to ask Thea, Friend's Siamese cat. She is lilac point, whatever that means, and has a pedigree what goes back to the Ark, and when she is annoyed she uses a tone of voice that hurts my ears. All she could tell me was that Friend was very bothered about it too, and had been switching the light on and off when she should have been asleep, in order to telephone Mother Perry and talk to her. By that I presume Thea meant that she herself had been asleep and didn't like being disturbed. She is allowed to sleep on the bed, and is thoroughly spoiled, like a few other people I could name.

After breakfast I had a word with Bertie and suggested that at the next opportunity he should get into the car—the blue one, not the Woofer Wagon—and go with the Boss down to see Mother Perry. I of course didn't *tell* him to. There's no point in telling cats, they do what they please, but I thought I might spur his curiosity. Apparently I succeeded, because he did agree. He's really quite a good fellow, for a cat.

He achieved it that very afternoon. The Boss took Mother Perry a bunch of flowers, and Bertie nipped into the car. I think he was quite keen on the idea because Mother Perry thinks he is rather special, and tells him so. He likes all the attention. Anyway, he was looking very pleased with himself when he came back. Not that this is unusual, he has that kind of face, all black and smiling.

"Well?" I said, as soon as he came into the kitchen. He was purring fit to burst and winding himself 'round and 'round the chair legs, so it was difficult to have a sensible conversation.

"It is missing," he replied.

I am a very patient dog; with all the responsibilities of my position I have to be. "What is missing?" I asked.

"The silver quaich," he replied, jumping up onto the table to see if there was anything edible left out by chance. "Mrs. Mac-Kinnon's silver quaich."

I hate appearing ignorant—it undermines my authority—

but on this occasion I had to know, so I asked quite casually, "What is a quaich? And why is it so important?"

"I don't know," he admitted frankly. Cats can do that without losing face, because they always look as if they don't care.

He was not being clear. "What don't you know?" I demanded. "And don't touch that biscuit! It's not yours!"

"I don't eat biscuits," he said disdainfully. "I don't know what a quaich is, or why it matters. Lots of things go missing without causing this kind of fuss."

That is perfectly true. Friend is always losing things and calling up the Boss to ask her if she knows where they are. Remarkably often she does.

"Is there really a fuss?" I asked Bertie. I wasn't sure if he was exaggerating to make himself sound important. Cats do that.

"Terrible," he answered quite seriously, looking at me again, and forgetting what might be on the table. "Mother Perry said people are beginning to take sides, some for Mrs. MacKinnon and some against, some blaming Mrs. MacPherson because she is her cousin and that is what Mrs. MacKinnon is saying."

"What is?"

"That Mrs. MacPherson took it, of course!" He hopped down onto one of the chairs, so I could see him face-to-face. "Others say it is boys, like when the cigarettes went from the shop. I should think somebody's probably buried it in a safe place, and forgotten where. Mother Perry does that herself. She did it with pepper before the war, whatever that means. She never found it, so she says."

He's quite right. Casper is always doing it with bones. He never knows where he's put anything.

"Somebody dug up bones down in the field near the village, when they were putting pipes in," Bertie went on. "But Casper doesn't usually go that far. He said they weren't his. But he forgets."

"They weren't his!" I told him tartly. "They were Pictish, and two thousand years old!"

"Perhaps they were Mother Perry's?" he suggested. "Like

the pepper. She likes to dig. She's always burying potatoes and then digging them up again later."

Bertie is only two, and he hasn't much sense of time. I didn't bother to explain to him. He had been very helpful and I thanked him. Actually I think he was rather pleased to be involved, although of course he wouldn't admit it.

"We've got to do something about this," I said to Willow later in the day. She was on the landing, digging herself a place in the duvet and turning 'round and 'round. I've never seen anybody sleep as much as she does. She curls herself up in that thing and disappears.

"I'm very good at finding things," she said, finally making the place she wanted and winding up into a ball.

"You can't find it if you don't know what it is," I pointed out patiently.

"That's right," she agreed with her eyes closed.

"Wake up, Willow!" I poked her sharply. "This is no time to be going to sleep! We have to do something about it!"

"It's a very good time." She pushed her nose into her paws and kept her eyes shut. "It's nearly night."

Since she'll sleep all day as well, if she's given the chance, that was irrelevant, and I told her so. "Think!" I ordered.

"I've seen a quaich," she said absently. "But I can't remember where. It was very beautiful," she added after a moment, and then went to sleep.

A little while later I encountered Humphrey on the stairs. He is a very large white cat with ginger patches and a ginger tail. I have not yet decided whether he is confused but lucky, or cleverer than he looks. He does not seem to be sure whether he lives here or next door with Friend. He comes and goes, and always seems to be present at meal times either end.

I was about to make some casual remark when I suddenly realized that if Willow really had seen a quaich then it must have been either here or at Friend's house. She hasn't been anywhere else where there would be such a thing—probably.

"Do we have a quaich?" I asked Humphrey.

He looked a bit nonplussed. Perhaps he's not so clever after all, and he only gets two breakfasts and two dinners by accident.

"No," he said after a moment. "The Boss gave it to Friend . . . for Christmas."

I misjudged him. At some time I shall apologize, but not now. Now there are far more urgent issues in hand.

"What is it like?" I asked quickly.

I can never tell if he is surprised or not. He has that shape of face.

"It was in this box," he answered. "Friend was very pleased. She kept taking it out to look."

"Describe it!" I demanded.

"I can't." He still had that round-eyed look. I think he can't help it. "I wasn't interested. You can't eat it and it isn't any use."

I was getting exasperated. "Is it still there?"

"Of course it is," he replied.

"Well go and look at it!" I said urgently. "Then come back and tell me what it is!" I would much rather have gone myself, but I cannot get in and out through the cat door, and Humphrey can, which is why he ends up sleeping on other people's beds and having two or three breakfasts. Actually he is a very agreeable creature, and he went off to comply immediately. Perhaps he was curious, or he may even have understood the importance of it all. One never knows with cats. They pretend they don't care when they really do. It all has to do with saving face. It's a cat thing.

He must have slept over there because he wasn't back until after second breakfast, and looking for a third, but he did have the information I needed. Even Willow woke up enough to be pleased, and Casper was so excited he ran 'round and 'round the table. Apparently a quaich is a kind of silver cup with two handles, and very beautiful indeed. It was made of solid silver, and that is why Friend kept it in a blue box.

Humphrey told me with a very casual air how clever it had been of him to knock it off the table and get it open enough to see. It is obviously precious, and if Mrs. MacKinnon's has disappeared, I can see how the whole village is upset. I understand all about property. I know exactly what is mine, and who can touch what and who can't, and where people are allowed to go. Puppies are a bit lax about such things, but not a good dog who knows her job. I have my own dish, and my bed, and my toys. Especially I know my bones and my biscuits. It seems quaiches are like that for people. We must definitely learn more about this. It matters.

The opportunity came the next morning. The Boss was out in the garden burying plants, or at least burying half of them. She always leaves half sticking out so anyone can see where they are. Then she gets cross if people dig them up . . . which wouldn't happen if she buried them properly. I dug a few holes to help, then sat and watched. The man came who delivers the gas bottles for the sitting room fire, and I heard him say that the trouble in the village was worse: there are accusations all over the place and people are talking of the police coming.

Then a few hours later Willow had disappeared without my noticing, and she came back from Friend's garden whisking her tail like a propeller. She'll fall over one of these days.

"I know where it is!" she said with tremendous glee.

"How do you know?" I asked.

"I've been over with Roddy," she explained.

Roddy comes and works at Friend's garden sometimes . . . when he feels like it. He can make anything grow. Willow loves him because he talks to her or throws things for her—sticks and that kind of thing. Personally I prefer to find my own sticks and carry them, like walking sticks and broom handles. But there's no accounting for taste.

"You know where the quaich is?" I could hardly believe it.

Willow gave me a look as if I were foolish. "Not exactly, no, of course not!" she said sharply. "But I know where it went from, and where anyone would bury it, if we can just take a proper look."

"Where?"

"In one of those four gardens along the beach," she said, still pleased with herself.

"That is very clever," I said generously. After all, she is my sister. "Why is it there?"

She looked at me witheringly. "If you are going to hide something precious that you shouldn't have, and that you might want again some day, then you are going to bury it in your own garden, aren't you? Otherwise somebody else is going to dig it up! Even Casper knows that!"

I forbore from mentioning that Casper actually does bury bones in Friend's garden, and other people do dig them up, but he's only a puppy and he doesn't know any better . . . even if he has got legs like a horse. Actually Willow's idea was very sensible.

"You are quite right," I agreed. "In fact it is elementary, my dear."

She looked at me oddly. She goes to sleep instead of watching television, and she had no idea of the allusion. It did seem more patronizing than I had intended. "You have done very well," I added. "Now we must make a plan."

"Who with?" she asked.

"Everybody," I replied.

"You mean Tara and Casper?"

"And Bertie, if necessary, and anyone else who might be useful."

She sneezed loudly at the notion of any of the cats being useful, but she didn't say anything.

We explained our plan to the others and put it into action the next time we went down to the beach, which was early the following day. Tara and Willow exploded out of the Woofer Wagon and raced down the sand and straight into the water, barking for all they were worth. Casper was so excited he nearly forgot what he was supposed to do, then he remembered and started running in ever-increasing circles, making sure both the Boss and Friend were watching him, until he disappeared altogether, and they were obliged to go after him, in case he got into real trouble.

Then Tara and Willow came back up the beach and the three of us set about the real business of the day. When you are looking for something that has been buried recently there are lots of signs to follow: freshly turned earth, broken bits of leaves and twigs, damp patches, smells that are different. If you are paying any attention at all, you can't miss it. We separated and went to work. I was already aware of the Boss shouting my name in the distance, but this was no time to pay attention.

There was nothing even remotely interesting in the first garden, so I squeezed, with difficulty, through the fence into the second. I had just begun to explore, although it was in such neat orderly rows it didn't look at all promising, when I heard Willow yapping with excitement from behind the next wall.

I scrambled over it and landed with less dignity than I would have wished—and there she was shivering from top to toe with anticipation and her face and front feet covered with earth. I went to her immediately.

"What have you got?" I demanded. "What is it?"

She did not reply, but began to dig again, sending earth flying all over the place. I barked to let Tara know what had happened, then started to help. A moment later she arrived and went at it like a bulldozer—she's built that way—and in minutes we had a hole big enough for an entire skeleton. She is a little overenthusiastic. Labradors are like that.

Then Willow struck it! Silver! There was a clang of claws, and through the dirt a bright sheen. In moments we had it up. It was a small, polished cup with two handles, just as Humphrey had said. We all barked as loudly as we could.

The first one to arrive was Casper, with Friend and Boss close behind. Then as they were examining the quaich and realizing what had happened, two or three other people arrived, including a little woman from the house whose garden we were in. She looked sleepy and not very well. She proved to be Mrs. MacPherson, and from then on it all got very unpleasant. There were words like "theft" and "police." Mrs. MacKinnon was sent for, and she came with grim satisfaction and swore that, yes, that was her quaich, and no, she had not given or lent it to Mrs. MacPherson. Even being family as she was, but she'd had her doubts about her before, and now . . . well . . . facts were facts. She would have to think what she was going to do.

I thought we had all been extremely clever, but nobody told us so, and we went home feeling pretty miserable. We had solved the problem, found the missing quaich, and everything was worse than before.

We spent all evening thinking about what to do next. The Boss and Friend went to see Mother Perry, and came back even more convinced that somehow or other there must be another explanation, but now Mrs. MacPherson was too upset to think clearly. Being a widow, she was all by herself, and it seemed no one else was on her side. As Mrs. MacKinnon had said, facts were facts. There was no denying where we had found the quaich.

In the morning I heard the Boss call Friend on the telephone and suggest that they take Mother Perry to the lighthouse. It is one of her favorite places. But they don't allow dogs, which is very narrow-minded of them, so there was no chance of any of us going along and overhearing what they might say.

Once again it was Bertie's turn to be useful. He popped into the car very quickly, and I suspect nobody noticed him until it was too late. He came back two hours later, completely exhausted. He says it is an enormously long walk, but he was even more than usually pleased with himself. He sat washing his sore feet and telling us about it. Some of it he heard from Mother Perry, who seems to have befriended Mrs. MacPherson, and some of it he overheard while he was sitting in the car parked outside the shop. Naturally people were talking.

"It goes back a very long way," he said, examining his feet ruefully. "It seems when they were young, Mrs. MacKinnon was the prettier, but Mrs. MacPherson was the nicer. They were neither of them married then. I have two broken claws on this foot."

I sympathized, but told him to get on with it.

"They used to be quite good friends," he continued. "But not very. Sort of like neighborhood dogs. It's all right as long as everybody knows their place, and keeps to it."

"Go on!" Willow said impatiently. "What about it?"

"What about it?" Casper echoed.

Bertie deliberately washed all the rest of his feet, carefully, before continuing.

"Then Mrs. MacKinnon met a young man and fell in love with him . . . but he married Mrs. MacPherson."

Casper looked puzzled. "I don't understand."

"Neither do I," Boswell added.

He's a black kitten. He's only seven months old and nobody even knew he'd been listening.

"Somebody took something that was hers," I explained it as simply as I could. "At least that's what she felt."

"Whose?" Boswell asked.

"Mrs. MacKinnon's."

"The silver quaich." Casper nodded.

"No—not the silver quaich!" I said. "Mr. MacPherson!"

"Who's Mr. MacPherson?" Boswell was now thoroughly confused. "I thought you said Mrs. MacPherson!"

Sometimes I despair of kittens.

"It's revenge," Bertie put in, washing his tender feet again. "Mrs. MacKinnon is getting her revenge on Mrs. MacPherson for something that happened a long time ago."

"It must be," Willow agreed. "Mrs. MacPherson doesn't need any revenge. She won . . . that time."

"She isn't winning this time," I pointed out. "And we've got to do something about it."

Everybody paid attention, but nobody had any helpful ideas.

"I'll go and talk to them over the road," Bertie offered. "See if they can think of anything."

He came back several hours later, his sore feet forgotten. He was gracious enough to admit that the plan was at least in part Thea's. I could very easily believe that devious Siamese thought of it. She has that kind of mind behind her sky-blue eyes.

"We'll bury something else," Bertie began when we were all assembled in the kitchen. "Something precious."

"What good will that do?" Willow was puzzled. "They might blame her for that too!"

"Not if we bury it in Mrs. MacKinnon's garden, and then dig it up for everyone to see!" Bertie explained. "And everyone will think she buried it herself, just as they did with Mrs. Mac-Pherson."

I thought about it hard, and it seemed to be the best idea we had. No one else said anything. They were all looking at me.

"Yes," I agreed at last. "We'll do that."

"What shall we bury?" Casper said, looking interested.

"What about that china cat?" Willow suggested, looking at the shelf. "I could carry that easily."

"It's the Boss's," Boswell chipped up.

"That's right," Bertie agreed. "We need something they won't blame us for, if possible."

"Something out of Mrs. MacPherson's garden," I hit on the perfect thing. "Something precious she wouldn't want to lose."

It was agreed unanimously, although I think several of the kittens didn't really know what we were talking about.

Tara also thought it was a wonderful plan. We didn't tell her it was Thea's. I'm not sure how she feels about Thea.

It wasn't as easy down on the beach as when we were sitting in the kitchen. To start with, both the Boss and Friend were watching us rather too closely. The first time I wandered off to see what I could find, I was called back very smartly and told I would be shut in the Woofer Wagon if I did it again. That would be most unfortunate. They couldn't possibly manage without me. It's all hands on deck! Especially the captain!

Then Casper tried. He went off at a gallop, but the threats that followed him were so dire that he came back with his tail and ears down and a very alarmed look on his face.

I was getting desperate when Willow saved the day. She was in the sea, as usual, and she just started swimming out as if she had intended to go to the horizon.

The Boss said she would never do anything so silly, and I think she mostly believed it, but Friend got very agitated. While they were standing down by the tide edge deciding what to do, Casper and I took advantage of their preoccupation to disappear. We could have used Willow's excellent nose—it's the best—but she was bravely risking her life in the cause. Tara stayed with them, just in case she really did get into trouble. She's by far the strongest swimmer. Anyway, if we'd all gone, it might have been noticed.

We went straight up to Mrs. MacPherson's garden and started to rummage around to see what there was. She must have heard us, because she came out to look. Considering the trouble we had got her into, she was surprisingly nice. I stayed and made polite overtures to her while Casper shot into the house, and within five minutes came out with a very fine jam spoon in his mouth, jam and all. But it was a perfect choice.

I beat a hasty retreat, and together we raced over to Mrs. MacKinnon's garden.

"Well done!" I said with heartfelt praise.

Casper said nothing because of the jam spoon in his mouth.

I dug a hole and Casper reluctantly dropped the spoon into it.

"I like jam," he said with feeling.

We covered the hole, then I sat guard while he went to see where Boss and Friend were. Actually I was a trifle concerned for Willow, so I was greatly relieved when he came back to say they were all very angry indeed, and on their way over. That was good, because there was no saying how long we had before Mrs. Mac-Kinnon might come to the door and all would be undone.

The Boss and Friend appeared at the garden gate and ordered us to come out instantly.

I sat down.

Casper looked at me, then sat down, too. He was rather nervous, but he stood his ground magnificently, metaphorically speaking, if you can stand while sitting.

"Well done," I said under my breath, trying to appear innocent.

"Daisy! Come out, now!" The Boss was furious, and worried. I could see Willow dripping all over the place. I've never seen her so wet. Tara jumped over the wall and came to join us. It was a very noble gesture of solidarity, all things considered.

Friend shouted at her, but she, too, stayed put. Actually by the time they had shouted and we had barked, there was quite a little collection of people gathering, including an extremely angry Mrs. MacKinnon.

"Get your wretched dogs out of my garden!" she commanded, her face very red. "Or I'll report you, and have them dealt with!"

Mrs. MacPherson appeared behind the people, keeping quiet.

It was definitely time to start digging. I gave the word, and we all three went for it. It was only seconds before Casper emerged triumphant with the jam spoon and dropped it at the Boss's feet.

She picked it up and looked at it curiously.

"It's beautiful!" she said with surprise, looking at Mrs. Mac-Kinnon. "How did it get into your garden?"

"It looks like real silver," someone else remarked.

"It is," Friend agreed, taking it and turning it over to look at the back. "And it isn't tarnished at all. It hasn't been there long." She regarded Mrs. MacKinnon with disfavor.

They all swiveled to look at Mrs. MacPherson and Friend held out the spoon.

"It's mine," Mrs. MacPherson said in amazement. "I . . . I thought I still had it!"

"Well, it rather looks as if it was stolen," the Boss said meaningfully. "The dogs just found it . . . here. We all saw them!"

"Oh, dear!" Mrs. MacPherson was totally confused, but there was no spite or satisfaction in her. "How sad." She looked at Mrs. MacKinnon. "Really, Mabel, you didn't need to do that! I didn't take your quaich, you know."

"I didn't take your wretched spoon!" Mrs. MacKinnon was furious, and profoundly embarrassed. But there was a look of awful guilt about her, like Casper when he's eaten the cat food, so I knew perfectly well she'd put the quaich in the garden herself, hoping to hurt Mrs. MacPherson. People are just like us, sometimes . . . so easy to read.

"That's as may be," someone muttered, and put his arm around Mrs. MacPherson.

"Good," Tara said in my ear. "I think we're terribly clever."

I nodded. "And Willow's very brave," I agreed. "Or incredibly stupid."

"I like jam," Casper repeated, licking his lips.

Actually it was very satisfactory all around, and the Boss and Friend both told us we were extremely clever. They had no idea how much! But then people don't know half as much as they think they do.

Anne Perry

Anne Perry is the very model of the modern historical mystery novelist, almost single-handedly accounting for the form's surging current popularity. Her two multibook series, one featuring Thomas and Charlotte Pitt and the other amnesiac Inspector Monk, provide a cumulative picture of the culture, style, and mores, as well as the dark and complex social sins of the mid-Victorian English period. She lives and writes in a seaside village in remote north Scotland, and was delighted to address lighter and more parochial problems in her story here.

Although dogs dominate her story's cast of characters, in real life the opposite is true. She provides a home for a yellow Labrador, Tara, eight; a black-and-white cat, Pansy, fifteen; a three-year-old lilac point Siamese cat, Thea; a silver angora named Sandokhar, and two "move-ins"—Humphrey, a very large white-and-ginger cat, and Archie, a ginger-and-white cat. She confesses to developing "a taste" for animal stories and plans to do more. Her latest books are Brunswick Gardens *and* Bedford Square.

What is as high as a house, carries its own baggage, and plays in the brass section of the local orchestra? It is one big trunk-totin', trumpetin' mama of an elephant, name of Hermia, and the subject of this story by Toni L. P. Kelner, whom I am almost afraid to call "Miss" in my normal effusion of courtesy, as I am intimidated by all those initials. But I *should* be afraid of Miss Toni L. P. Kelner. She tells an informative tale of what happens when an animal is too big for its own good, and too big a clue to see past to a murderer.

—M.L.

Where Does a Herd of Elephants Go?
Toni L. P. Kelner

"**WHICH ONE WAS** it?" I asked, looking at the four elephants grazing in the paddock.

"That one," Deputy Sweeney said, pointing.

"Hermia?" I said. "That *is* Hermia, isn't it?"

Crabby, the handler who'd worked with my father, spat and said, "Of course that's Hermia, you stupid townie. But she didn't do it."

I wanted to believe him, just like I wanted to believe that Pop was still alive. How could he have been trampled by one of his own elephants? He'd loved them nearly as much as he loved me, and knew them better. There was no way he could have made the kind of mistake that would have gotten him killed.

But here I was at Fox's Old-Fashioned Circus while Pop's

body was in the tiny North Carolina town's morgue. "You're sure it was Hermia?"

"We found her next to your father's body, May," said Chris Fox, the show owner. "There was blood all over her feet."

At Deputy Sweeney's firm suggestion, I'd forgone viewing Pop's body since Crabby had already made the formal identification. Sweeney had danced around it the way only a Southerner can, but I knew Hermia must have had a lot more than blood on her feet.

"Why do elephants have round, flat feet?" I said.

"I beg your pardon?" Fox said.

"It's an elephant joke. Pop gave me a book of them one year for my birthday. Why do elephants have round, flat feet?" None of the others answered, so I answered myself. "To walk on lily pads."

No doubt they all thought I was nuts, or maybe just grief-stricken. In addition to Sweeney, Fox, and Crabby, there was Mr. Waterson, who owned the lot where the show was set up, and Madame Cassandra. It was Cassie who put her arm around me, but I didn't respond. It wasn't that I didn't appreciate the gesture, especially when she must have been hurting too, but I just couldn't tear my eyes away from the girls.

I was surprised they hadn't hobbled Hermia and staked her, but the only ones who would have known to do that were Crabby and Pop; obviously Crabby was in no mood to help. So they were relying on a member of the big-top crew to watch and make sure she didn't go rogue. Not that it looked likely, as the girls blithely scratched up dirt with their feet and used their trunks to toss it onto their backs and keep flies away.

In traditional circus lingo, elephants are called bulls, even though most circus elephants are female, but Pop called them his girls, or, if he was talking with me, his other girls. Maybe I should have been jealous, but I loved them too, and waited impatiently for the rare visits my mother allowed so I could see them again. There was imperious Titania, the leader of the small herd; flirty and mischievous Juliet, who would toss hay at people when they walked by if they didn't stop to say hello; loving Portia, who cuddled as much as an elephant can cuddle; and docile Hermia, who never seemed bothered by the one-night stands, long road trips, and horrible weather a circus elephant lives with.

Like many elephant men, Pop supplemented his paycheck by giving elephant rides, and Hermia was the one he always used. He trusted her not to move too quickly and scare the kids or run off with them on her back, because her temperament was as even as her pace. What could have happened?

I asked the one person left who should know. "Crabby, has Hermia been sick? Did that abscessed tooth come back?" Pop always doctored the girls himself, saying that the vets in the small towns where the show played wouldn't have the first idea of how to help his elephants. All I could think of was that he'd accidentally hurt her, and she lost control. It only takes a second to get hurt when you're dealing with something as big as an elephant.

"Does she look sick? Even you should be able to tell that she's healthy as a horse—you can see it by looking at her. I don't care what this townie cop says—she didn't kill Leo! I was in my camper all night. I'd have heard if she'd gone after him."

Unless he was drunk again. It was early afternoon, but his breath was already enough to make me high. No doubt he'd been mourning Pop in his own way. Crabby had been with him since before I was born, and he loved the elephants nearly as much as Pop had.

Deputy Sweeney sounded apologetic as he said, "The injuries were consistent with trampling, and none of the other elephants had any blood on their feet. It had to be Hermia."

"I know that elephant better than I know myself," Crabby said. "She wouldn't do it. If you kill her, I'll—"

"Kill her?" I said. "Who said anything about killing her?"

Deputy Sweeney looked uncomfortable. "I'm sorry, but I thought you understood that we'd have to destroy the elephant. It's town law."

"You have a law about elephants?" I said in disbelief.

Sweeney colored slightly. "No, ma'am. The law was written for dogs, but it's been applied to cougars, snakes, and so on. This is the first time anybody here was killed by an elephant."

"What are you going to do?" Crabby demanded. "Electrocute her? Poison? They hanged an elephant once, you know."

"Actually, we're still researching the most humane method. The chief has been in contact with the state zoo at Asheboro."

Crabby's face was dark red, his fists clenched. "She didn't do it!" he said again, sputtering in his indignation. Then he glared at me and said, "Your father would never have let anybody hurt one of the girls."

"But Pop's not here," I said evenly.

Crabby looked over at Hermia again and stumbled away, muttering about townies. I knew he was going back to his drinking, but for once, I didn't blame him.

"Y'all aren't going to do it on my land, are you?" Waterson asked, looking a little sick. "I'd never have asked you people here if I'd known this was going to happen. I just wanted a little publicity for the antique fair."

Fox went into action, still as smooth as he'd ever been as ringmaster. "I assure you, Mr. Waterson, there's no way to predict an incident like this. Mr. Solano knew the risks, and he was a careful man, but there's no guarantee when working with wild animals. Though elephants look friendly, they are at heart creatures of the veldt." With Fox laying it on so thick, I figured he must want to book the lot again next season.

"Should we cancel tonight's show?" Waterson asked.

Fox looked shocked. "Never! That's the last thing Leo Solano would have wanted. Like all circus people, 'the show must go on' was the creed he lived by. To disappoint the children who've been dreaming of tonight's show would be an insult to his memory."

I heard a tiny snort from Cassie, and turned to see the twinkle in her eye. I wanted to laugh too, thinking of how Pop would have reacted to Fox's spiel. Then I suddenly wanted to cry.

As always, Cassie knew what I was feeling. She said, "Gentlemen, if you'll excuse us, there's things May needs to attend to."

"Of course," Mr. Fox said. "May, later this afternoon, we should meet and discuss your plans for the elephants. Other than Hermia, of course."

"Oh, right." How could I have forgotten that I was going to have to make arrangements for the girls?

"Later," Cassie said firmly, and pulled me toward her trailer, with its ruffled curtains and shiny exterior. The inside was just as pristine, everything as neatly arranged as a pocket sewing kit. On a shelf over the couch were the crystal ball and tarot cards Cassie used to make her living before taking over the ticket booth. Some people still called her Madame Cassandra, but these days she preferred Cassie.

"Sit," she said, pushing me toward the couch. Then she conjured up a mug of hot coffee with two sugars and put it into my hand. If I hadn't lifted it to my lips, she'd probably have done that for me too.

"It will get better, May," she said.

I nodded, knowing she was right, even if it didn't feel that way. "How about you? I mean, you and Pop were . . . You two were very close."

"We were lovers, sugar. This is 1998. You can say it out loud."

I smiled sheepishly. "Sorry."

"Anyway, I'm doing all right." She reached over and touched my hand. "May, I meant to tell you about Leo myself, but Fox had the phone tied up. I'm sorry you had to hear about it from a stranger."

"It's okay, Cassie. Deputy Sweeney was very kind." Not only had he broken the news to me as gently as possible, but he'd picked me up at the nearest airport and brought me to town.

"Good. He seems pretty nice, for a townie. Did Fox tell you about the memorial service?"

I shook my head.

"We were planning a little something to honor Leo tonight. If you don't mind, that is."

"Of course I don't mind." I'd be taking his body back to Massachusetts, but of course the people from the show wouldn't be able to attend a funeral up there. This way, they'd have a chance to say good-bye. "That's just what Pop would have wanted."

"I think so, too." She paused. "Does your mother know?"

"I called her as soon as I heard. She said she'd tell Gram and Papa." Pop's parents had never liked him being in the circus. Neither had Mom—that's why they'd divorced. I suspected the three of them had wagged their heads over Pop not heeding their warnings all those years ago, but even they couldn't have guessed that he'd end up this way. "Cassie, how did it happen?"

"Sugar, you know as much as I do. Crabby came out of his camper to take a leak late last night and saw Hermia messing with something on the ground. He went to see what it was, and once he realized it was Leo, he let out a yell that woke the whole lot up. By the time I got there, he had his arms around your father, blubbering like a baby. Crabby has his faults, but he loved Leo."

"I know." Despite Crabby's personality and lack of hygiene, he was devoted to Pop and the girls. In fact, they were apparently the only ones he cared about. He had little use for the rest of the circus people, and none at all for me or any other townie.

"Anyway, we called the police, and they called you. That's all there is."

I wasn't sure if I had the right to ask the next question, but I couldn't help myself. "Have you consulted the crystal?" I didn't know if it was because of all the years she'd been a fortune-teller or from something inborn, but Cassie did seem to know things she had no other way of knowing.

"You know I don't call on the departed, sugar. Leo is gone—there's nothing we can do to bring him back."

"I don't mean that. I mean, have you tried to find out more about what happened?"

She looked at me as searchingly as she did the crystal. "You don't think Hermia did it?"

"No. I mean, yes, I guess I do, but there must have been some reason. You know how Hermia is. Something must have spooked her or . . ." She was still looking at me. "I just want to know why."

"People die, May. There isn't always a reason."

But she was reaching behind me for the crystal as she spoke, and she held it out in front of her. Fortune-tellers on television have elaborate pedestals for their crystals, but Cassie prefers holding the ball herself.

I stayed quiet as she stared into it, her brow slightly furrowed. Then she sniffed several times. A moment later, she shook herself all over and put the crystal back on the shelf.

"What did you see?"

"Not much," she admitted. "It was dark last night. New moon. But I smelled something."

"The elephants?" They do have a pungent smell, but I loved it, just as Pop had. Even the dung isn't bad when you get used to it.

She shook her head. "Not that. It was marijuana."

"Pop didn't smoke pot, did he?"

"Not that I ever saw, but that's all I got—the smell of pot. Most likely I smelled some when we found Leo last night, but didn't notice it until now."

Cassie never claimed to have any special powers. She said the crystal was just a way to focus her thoughts, and that her tarot readings depended more on the body language of the customer than on which cards she laid out on the table. Whatever it was, she was right more often than not.

"Maybe Pop caught somebody getting high and trying to bother the girls," I speculated. "Or maybe somebody thought it would be funny to give some to the girls." I'd met people who thought it was funny to get a dog stoned. Why not an elephant?

She shrugged her shoulders.

I finished the last of my coffee. "I suppose I better go on over to Pop's trailer and start sorting. And I've got to decide what to do with the girls."

"Don't rush yourself, May. You've had that long flight down from Boston, and there's the memorial service tonight. No matter what Fox says, there'll be time to make up your mind tomorrow. Go for a walk, take some time to think. Check out the antique fair—they've got some nice things."

"Maybe you're right," I said noncommittally, meaning to get to work anyway, but once I gave her a quick hug and went outside, my feet led me away from Pop's trailer almost of their own accord.

I spent the next hour or so wandering through the outdoor antique fair. I didn't know if the circus had helped drum up business or not, but there were plenty of people out there, enough that I had to concentrate on not running into anybody. I didn't have any room left to brood about Pop.

I'd stopped to look at a display of brightly colored, iridescent dishes, wondering if Mom would like one of them, when I saw a whole shelf full of elephants. There were china and onyx figurines, brass ashtrays with elephants dancing around the edge, an umbrella with an elephant for a handle, lacquered boxes with designs of elephants on the lid, and right in the middle, a porcelain circus elephant with a bright red plume. My first thought was that Pop would love them. My second was to remember.

"Damn, I'm sorry," a voice said.

I turned and recognized Mr. Waterson. He started grabbing elephants and shoving them into a box. "I shouldn't have left these out, under the circumstances."

"Don't worry about it," I said. "Pop loved elephant stuff. If he could have, he'd have bought every piece he saw." Pop started sending me elephants the day I was born, much to Mom's dismay.

He stopped, not sure if he should keep putting pieces away or if he should return them to the shelf. So I reached inside and pulled out the circus statue and placed it back in front.

"Your father was here yesterday, as a matter of fact," Waterson said. "He mentioned that he might come back to get that one for his daughter. I guess that's you."

I nodded. "It's a nice one."

He picked it up, looked at it for a second, then pushed it at me. "Here, take it."

"No, I couldn't."

"I insist. I feel responsible for what happened. After all, I arranged for the circus to come here."

Looking at his face, I relented. It would make him feel better, and the fact that Pop had wanted it for me meant something. "Thank you."

"It's the least I can do."

A woman came over then to ask about an umbrella stand she'd seen the day before, and I used that as an excuse to leave. Cassie had been right about my needing a break, but I really did have to start taking care of Pop's business.

There were more people out and about on the circus lot, performers rehearsing, animal handlers cleaning out pens and cages, concessionaires making sure they had plenty of popcorn, and workmen toting equipment in all directions. This time I didn't stop to look at the elephants, just went straight to Pop's trailer. Deputy Sweeney had given me the key they'd found in Pop's pocket, and since nobody had been inside since they found him, everything was just the way Pop had left it. In other words, the place was a mess.

One corner of the living room was filled with a pile of harnesses waiting to be mended, and another was stacked high with magazines, books, circus programs, and yellowing newspaper articles about elephants. The coffee table was covered with files and antiseptics for taking care of the girls' nails, and the kitchen counter was piled with bottles of the concoctions Pop used to supplement their diet. Pop lived with the elephants. He only slept in the trailer. And with Cassie around, he didn't always do that. I wasn't looking forward to going through it all.

First things first, I decided, which meant the girls' food. Elephants go through roughly a hundred pounds of feed a day, not counting peanuts, so I needed to make sure there was enough to keep them satisfied until I decided what I was going to do with them. Fortunately, Pop had always been meticulous about keeping supplies on hand. I found his ledger in the kitchen drawer, and ran my finger down the rows until I saw that he'd just bought hay, fruit, and vegetables two days before, a load of timothy the day after that. That should hold them a while.

I closed the ledger and was putting it back in the drawer when an envelope slipped out. Inside, I found two hundred dollars, which surprised me. Pop didn't like to keep cash on hand. A drifter had joined the show a few years back, and stayed just long enough to find out where everybody kept their money. Then he robbed them during a matinee. That's when Pop got an ATM card and started paying for everything with checks.

I started to slide the money back into the envelope, but I thought I smelled something. I held a twenty to my nose and inhaled deeply. Marijuana.

Maybe Pop had started smoking pot, no matter what Cassie thought. Naturally, he'd want cash to pay his dealer. That could even explain his death. A stoned elephant handler was an accident waiting to happen. It made more sense than anything else I'd thought of, but knowing Pop, it didn't make any sense at all. Even though I'd never seen him smoke, on those rare occasions when he'd drunk more than he should have, he knew to stay away from the girls. Why would he start smoking now, and then break his own rule by going around the girls while high?

I briefly considered calling Deputy Sweeney to see if they'd found any signs of marijuana on Pop, but decided it wasn't something I wanted to ask a stranger. Maybe I could talk to Crabby later. He should know, and he might be convinced to tell me.

I put the money and ledger away, and spent the rest of the afternoon going through the trailer, filling four garbage bags with the trash nobody could possibly want. I found a box for the things I thought Crabby could use, another for keepsakes for Cassie, and a third for things I wanted to take home for myself, including the circus elephant statue Waterson had given me. That still left an enormous amount of elephant harnesses, medicine, and assorted stuff, but I decided that I could include it when I found somebody to take in the girls.

That's how I tried to think of it, like I was putting them up for adoption rather than selling them, but mostly, I worried about them. Fox would want them for the rest of the season, of course. What was a circus without elephants? Large parts of the show, especially the opening and closing spectacles, were designed with them in mind. What I didn't know was whether he'd want to buy them or just lease them. If I had to sell them to somebody else, would I be able to keep them together? Titania was used to being in charge—what would happen if I had to sell her to a show with another boss elephant? How could I be sure that the new owner would care for them properly?

My last Christmas gift to Pop had been a book about an elephant named Modoc. This one man had handled her, but then moved on to another circus or something. Years later, he found her in dreadful shape from being mistreated. I couldn't bear the thought of that happening to the girls.

Was there some way I could get them to Massachusetts? Obviously I couldn't afford to keep them myself, much as I wanted to. Marketing pays well, but not that well, though it might have been worth going into debt to see my mother's face if I showed up with them. Still, there were zoos nearby, and at least I'd be able to see them once in a while. Of course, it would cost a fortune to transport them, even if I found someplace. Besides, they were happy in the circus. Would they like living in a zoo?

Then there was Crabby to think about. What would happen to him? Though he was wonderful with the girls, he wasn't personable or completely reliable when it came to working hours. Pop himself had paid him, not Fox, so I didn't know if he even had a job anymore. Or if he could get another one.

And I kept worrying about Hermia. I just couldn't be angry at her. No matter what had happened, I didn't believe she meant to hurt Pop. None of the elephants had ever hurt him, not on purpose anyway. True, Titania had gotten in a snit once because Pop gave her stale hay, and knocked him over, but that was different—she'd only used a fraction of her strength. It had to have been some sort of accident, no matter what the police thought, and it didn't seem right that Hermia had to die too.

At least Pop was going to get a funeral and a memorial service. The best poor Hermia would get was a quick death. I didn't know what would happen to her then. I remembered Pop telling me about a so-called elephant man who'd put down an elephant who'd gotten too old to perform, then butchered her, selling her head to be put on somebody's wall, her hide to make boots, and her body for meat. Pop said he'd have ground her tusks for an aphrodisiac and made her feet into umbrella stands if he could have gotten away with it. The whole idea sickened me.

I was nearly in tears when I heard a tap on the door, and Cassie stepped in, her arms full of paper bags. "Don't just sit there," she said. "Take something before I drop it!"

Whatever she was carrying smelled wonderful, and I realized I hadn't eaten since that bagel on the plane. I didn't know whether it was just luck or something else that brought Cassie to me just then, but I was happy to join her in an enormous meal of pulled-pork barbecue, hush puppies, cole slaw, and syrupy iced tea. After we ate, I tried to get her advice for what I should do about Crabby and the girls, but she kept telling me that every-thing would be clearer in the morning. Then she'd tell me an-other hilarious story about Pop or one of his terrible elephant jokes, like why elephants have trunks and how do you make an elephant float. I'd heard them all before, but maybe she'd spiked the iced tea, because I laughed so hard I forgot to worry.

I realized later that Cassie must have gotten a replacement at the ticket booth so she could be with me, because we talked right through the night's show, hardly noticing the music and distant applause. I hadn't wanted to go to the show anyway. Seeing the girls go through their routine without Pop would have upset me, and I wasn't sure if it would bother me more to see Hermia in the act or to know she was wondering why she'd been left out.

About the time the townies were heading for their houses, Cassie told me it was time to get ready for the memorial service. I'd left my suitcase at her trailer, so we went over there to change. She wouldn't let me put on the dress I'd brought, because she said it would be too formal. Instead I wore a pair of khakis and a white blouse, while she wore one of the vivid caftans she liked.

Mr. Fox had said we'd be gathering in the main tent, and when we stepped inside, I saw men pulling chairs from the grand-stand seats to arrange them in the center ring. I had to grin. Like most circus folks, Pop had a thing for the center ring. What bet-ter place to say good-bye to him?

It looked like everybody from the show was there: per-formers, animal trainers, concessionaires, even the kitchen crew. As Cassie had warned me, people were wearing everything from their costumes to blue jeans to shorts and T-shirts. Deputy Sweeney had come, and Mr. Waterson was there too, looking uncomfortable and overdressed in a black suit. The only one I didn't see was Crabby. I'd have to ask Cassie if we should check on him later.

Fox got things started, and I have to admit he did a nice job. Sure, he made it sound like Pop had been a mix of Gunther Gebel-Williams, Gandhi, and Ozzie Nelson, but as far as I was concerned, he had been. Fox even had a handful of telegrams from other elephant men, including Gebel-Williams and the legendary Woodcock family. There were plenty of tears, probably more than there'd be at Pop's funeral, especially when Cassie spoke about him. Pop would have been proud.

One of the clowns was eulogizing Pop when there was a commotion from the side entrance to the tent. It was Crabby, and the girls were walking behind him, trunk to tail. Seeing the surprised faces, he shouted, "They deserve to be here, damn it!" The man who'd been left to watch them was following, looking helpless. Which he was, really. Like Pop always said, "Where does a herd of elephants go? Wherever they want."

This being a circus, people might have accepted the tribute the way Crabby meant it if he hadn't brought Hermia, too. There was dead silence when we saw her, and everybody stared as she came toward us. For the first time since I'd known her, she looked menacing. Then the whole line stopped, with Titania in front just a few yards from us.

In a determinedly calm voice, Deputy Sweeney said, "Sir, I think you should take the elephants back to their paddock."

"Why? Are you going to kill all of them?" Crabby was crying so hard I didn't know how he could see, and he stumbled over his own feet. Titania, sensing the tension in the air, trumpeted loudly, and a couple of people started to edge toward the other entrance. "They won't hurt you! They wouldn't hurt anybody!" Crabby sobbed.

Normally, he was right, but the situation was anything but normal. All of the girls were showing signs of nervousness, and I was afraid someone would panic and run, which would only make things worse. Crabby was leaning up against one of Titania's front legs, barely able to stand.

I carefully stood up, and started walking toward Titania with deliberate steps. A couple of hands grabbed at my sleeve, and I heard Deputy Sweeney say something, but I ignored them all. My attention was on the boss elephant.

Despite the myth, elephants do forget, but their memories are as good as the average human's, so I thought Titania would remember me. Whether she'd follow my orders was another question. Pop had taught me that the best way to approach an elephant you're not sure of is from the left rear, so I walked past Titania, making sure to stay out of trunk range.

Watching to see how she was going to react, I moved closer to her. When she didn't move, I got close enough to slap her on the shoulder, letting her know I was there. Still no reaction, so I got closer still and patted her on the back of her ear, her favorite place for attention. She seemed to relax a bit.

Crabby was still leaning against her, holding the bull hook. Pop never used the hook much, preferring to use his voice, but I knew I'd feel better if I had something in my hand. All I had to do was convince Crabby to give it to me. I said, "It's okay, Crabby. They've paid their respects—it's time for them to go to bed. I'm not going to let anybody hurt them."

He didn't hand me the bull hook, but when I reached for it, he didn't fight me.

Feeling a little more confident, I said, "Titania! Turn."

Titania looked at me. I'd never given her orders without Pop there to back me up, so she wasn't sure if I had any authority over her or not.

I used the hook to tug at her leg. "Come on, lady. Turn." Elephants can move quickly, but most times, they don't. I had endless seconds to wait until she finally started turning and heading back the way she came.

I had to use the hook to get Juliet and Portia going too, but Hermia was perfectly willing to follow along. I stayed with them, moving back and forth along the line to make sure they stayed together until we reached the paddock. Once each one filed inside, I carefully closed the gate behind them. Later on, they'd need to be hobbled in the menagerie tent for the night, but the paddock would keep them contained for the time being.

Then I took a breath, inhaling the scent of elephant and feeling a little like I'd been drinking with Crabby. At that moment, I knew exactly why Pop had wanted to spend his life with elephants.

Deputy Sweeney must have been following, because he was suddenly there. "Are you all right?"

All I could do was nod.

"Ms. Solano, I've never seen anything like that. You could have been killed."

I had been as scared as I'd ever been in my life, but no elephant handler likes to admit that she's afraid of her own elephants, so I said, "I've known these elephants since I was a little girl. All they need is a strong hand, and they'll do just what they're told. Hermia doesn't even need that—she'll follow anybody."

That's when it struck me, and the buzz from handling the girls melted away. Hermia really would follow almost anybody. "Deputy, what if somebody murdered my father, maybe drugged him or shot him or hit him with something. Then he led Hermia back and forth over the body. Wouldn't that make it look like she'd killed him?"

He shook his head. "No, ma'am. There were no drugs in your father's system, and the coroner couldn't find any injuries that aren't consistent with an elephant's foot."

I looked over at the girls' feet. There's nothing to compare with an elephant's foot, in size or shape. Except another elephant's foot, of course. That's when I figured out how Pop had been killed, and from that, it was easy to guess who had done it.

By now, most of the other people from the tent were gathered around. Fox was trying to soothe Mr. Waterson, probably still worried about next season. I pointed at them. "He did it! He killed my father!"

Fox just looked surprised, but Waterson went white as a sheet and jerked into a run. Before I could say anything, I heard Cassie yell, "Hey, rube!" That's the traditional circus cry for help, and Waterson didn't get a dozen yards away before he was dragged back by a trapeze catcher and a concessionaire.

"Ms. Solano, would you care to explain that?" Deputy Sweeney said, using the same careful tone he had with Crabby.

"He used an elephant-foot umbrella stand to either kill Pop or knock him out, and then got Hermia to trample the body. Search his store, and I'll bet you'll find it. They used to be popular, but you only find them in antique stores now."

"She's crazy," Waterson sputtered. "I sold that stand yesterday."

"Prove it!" I snapped.

"Ma'am, he doesn't have to prove anything. We do. Why would he have killed your father?"

Crabby was standing nearby, looking dumbfounded. "Crabby," I said, "was Pop selling Waterson elephant dung?"

"Yeah. He said he wanted it for fertilizer."

"That's right. For fertilizing marijuana," I said. That's why the money in Pop's ledger had smelled of it.

"Sweeney, you're not going to believe this old drunk, are you?" Waterson said.

But Sweeney was looking intrigued. "The fact is, there's been rumors that somebody around here has been shipping out a lot of weed, but we haven't been able to pin down who it was. Waterson, you don't mind if we search your land, do you?"

Waterson slumped in the arms of the men holding him.

I said, "I bet Pop figured out what you were using the fertilizer for, and told you he wouldn't sell you any more."

"I was afraid he'd tell the police," Waterson said. "I'd have lost everything—the DEA could have taken the land, my house. This land's been in my family for generations. I had to keep him quiet."

That's when I saw red. Pop had died because of a few worthless acres of dirt? If I'd been Titania, I'd have trumpeted and charged at him. "Do you really think Pop gave a damn about your little pot patch?" I said in as scathing a tone as I could manage. "No offense, Deputy, but Pop wouldn't have wasted a dime to call you. All he wanted was to stay out of it." I gave Waterson a moment to realize that he'd destroyed himself. Then I said, "Only a townie would be that stupid."

I expected to have to testify, but a plea bargain preempted the trial. In return for the names of his distributors, Waterson pleaded guilty and avoided the death penalty. That was good enough for me. But I swear, if Hermia had been put to death before we found out that Waterson was guilty, I'd have done everything I could to make sure he followed her to the grave.

As for the girls, all four of them are still with Fox's Old-Fashioned Circus, being looked after by Crabby and doing fine. I'm there to make sure they stay that way. Mom said I was crazy to waste a college education and that I was too old to run away to the circus, but she finally resigned herself to the fact that I'm Pop's daughter. She even promised to come see the show when we get closer to Massachusetts.

Of course, Cassie had known all along that I was going to stay. I asked her if it was the cards or the crystal, but she said it was nothing more mystical than the expression on my face when I looked at the elephants.

It's not much of a joke, but do you know why the marketing director joined the circus? Because she liked working for peanuts.

Toni L. P. Kelner

Though this is Toni L. P. Kelner's first fictional trip to the circus, she visits the real thing as often as she can. A member of the Circus Fans Association of America, Toni's circus reference collection includes over sixty books. She has a particular weakness for elephant acts, and celebrated the completion of this story with a ride on Carol, a talented pachyderm who is part of the Royal Hanneford Circus.

Toni's personal version of a three-ring circus is trying to tame her ferocious two-year-old and defying death in Boston traffic. Her fictional milieu is perhaps even more exotic than the circus: the mill towns of North Carolina. In Tight as a Tick, *the fifth in her mystery series, protagonist Laura goes undercover to find out who killed a back-stabbing flea market dealer by stabbing him in the back.* Death of a Damn Yankee, *due out in May 1999, has Laura investigating the Northern investors who are dead-set on buying the town mill, even after one of them ends up just plain dead.*

She is the Mother of All Animal Mysteries and the uncontested First Lady of Feline Felony Fiction. Since the 1960s, Ms. Lilian Jackson Braun has elevated the feline presence in mystery novels from the object of occasional background interest to front-and-center crime-solver. The clue-sniffing cats in her series of mystery novels about Jim Qwilleran, a newspaperman-turned-millionaire who keeps running into murder most cozy, are Siamese, if you please: Koko and Yum Yum. This story, "The Dark One," first appeared in *Ellery Queen's Mystery Magazine* in 1966. It is notable not only for using the cat's third-person point-of-view, which paved the way for my own first fur-person incarnation two decades later, but for an unsparing look at a current issue seldom examined in fiction thirty-some years ago: domestic abuse. Of course domestic pets, as my kind are sometimes called, often suffer also in abusive situations. And sometimes we are not as small and helpless as we might seem. . . .

—M.L.

The Dark One

Lilian Jackson Braun

ONLY DAKH WON knows the true reason for his action that night on the moonlit path. It is not a cat's nature to be vengeful—or heroic. He merely does what is necessary to secure food, warmth, comfort, peace, and an occasional scratch behind the ears. But Dakh Won is a Siamese, a breed known for its intelligence and loyalty.

He has always been called "the dark one," because his fur is an unusually deep shade of fawn. Between his seal brown ears and his seal brown tail, the silky back shades hardly at all. Only his soft underside is pale. He is a husky cat whose strength ripples under his sleek coat, and his slanted eyes are full of sapphire secrets.

During his early life at the cattery Dakh Won enjoyed food, warmth, comfort, attention, and—most of all—peace. Then one day after he was full-grown, he was handed over to strange arms and exposed for the first time to hostility and conflict.

Before he was placed in a basket and carried away, a gentle and familiar voice said: "Dakh Won is very special. I wouldn't sell him to anyone but you, Hilda."

"You know I'll give him a good home, Elizabeth."

"How about your husband? Does he like animals?"

"He prefers dogs, but I'm the one who needs a pet. Jack's away from home most of the time. All his construction jobs seem to be halfway across the state."

"Honestly, Hilda, I don't know how you stand it in the country. You were so active when you were a city gal."

"It's lonely, but I have my piano. I'd love to give lessons to the farm children in my community."

"Why don't you? It would be good for you."

"Jack doesn't like the idea."

"Why on earth should he object?"

Hilda looked uncomfortable. "Oh, he's funny about some things. . . . I hope Dakh Won likes music. Do cats like music?"

Elizabeth studied the face of her old friend. "Hilda, is everything all right with you and Jack? I'm worried about you."

"Of course everything's all right. . . . Now, I'd better leave if I'm going to catch that bus. I hope the cat won't mind the ride." Dakh Won was sniffing the strange pair of shoes and nibbling the tantalizing shoelaces; he had never seen laces with little tassels. Hilda said: "Isn't that adorable, Elizabeth? He's untying my shoelaces."

"Let me tie them for you."

"Thank you." There was a sigh. "Aren't these shoes horrible? The doctor says I'll never wear pretty shoes again."

"That was a terrible accident, Hilda—in more ways than one. You're lucky to be alive."

"It wasn't really Jack's fault, you know."

"Yes, you've told me that before. Do you still have pain?"

"Not too much, but I'll always have this ugly limp. That's one reason I don't mind hiding away in the country."

Then Dakh Won was handed over, making a small verbal protest and spreading his toes in apprehension, but when he found himself in a covered basket, he settled down and was quiet throughout the long journey. Occasionally he felt reassured by strong fingers that reached into the basket, and he amiably allowed his ears to be flattened and his fur gently ruffled.

Dakh Won's adopted home was a small house in the country, overlooking a ravine—a fascinating new world of fringed rugs, cozy heat registers, wide windowsills, soft chairs, and a grand piano.

He soon discovered the joys of sitting in this elevated box with half-opened lid, but it proved to be off-limits to cats. After lights were turned out for the night he was welcome, however, to share a soft bed with a warm armpit and reassuring heartbeat. That was where he slept—except on weekends.

"Hilda, I'm telling you for the last time: Get that animal out of this bed!"

"He isn't bothering you, Jack. He's over on my side."

"I don't want him in this bedroom! Lock him up in the basement."

"It's damp down there. He'll howl all night."

"Okay, if that cat's more important than me, I'll go down and bunk on the sofa."

"Don't bother. I'll sleep on the sofa myself."

"Thanks."

"I knew you'd like the idea."

"Don't slam the door."

Dakh Won jumped out of the warm bed and followed the bedroom slippers as they moved slowly down the stairs, one careful step at a time. His ears were laid back, and his fur was sharply ridged. He disliked loud voices, and the tension that he sensed made him vaguely uncomfortable.

Quarreling was not the only discomfort on weekends. There was the onslaught of feet. Nowhere on the floor could Dakh Won feel safe. He liked to sprawl full length in any patch of sun that warmed the rug. The floor was his domain, and feet were expected to detour. But on weekends his rights were ignored.

One Saturday he waked with a snarl of anguish when a crushing weight came down on the tip of his tail, and the next day he received a cruel blow to his soft underside when he was stretched trustingly in the middle of the hallway.

"Damn that cat! I tripped over him! I could have broke my leg. *Hilda, do you hear me?*"

"You should look where you're going. Have you been drinking again?"

"You think more of that stinking beast than you do of me."

"He smells better than that cigar you're smoking."

"It's my house, and I'll smoke what I like and walk where I like, and if that flea bait don't keep out of my way—"

"You're beginning to talk like those trashy people you associate with."

"If he don't keep out of my way, I'll drown him!"

"He doesn't have fleas, and you're not going to touch him. He's mine. I'm not going to die of loneliness in this godforsaken place. You don't know what it's like to be isolated all week—"

"What's wrong with you women? You want all kinds of labor-saving gadgets, and then you gripe about having nothing to do. Why don't you bake some bread or something instead of buying everything ready-made, if you're so bored?"

"Stop pacing up and down—or else take those clumsy boots off. You're ruining the floor."

"Try scrubbing clothes with a washboard, if you're so bored."

"I'm a pianist, not a laundress. You seem to forget that I gave up a career to marry you. One of these days I'm going to start giving lessons—"

"And let people think I can't support a . . . a sick wife?"

"If you'd stop pacing the floor and listen—"

"And have a lot of dirty farmers' kids tramping through the house? Over my dead body!"

"Look out! You almost stepped on his paw!"

"Fool cat!"

Dakh Won soon learned to keep out of sight on weekends. Most of the time he stayed outdoors. He liked high places, and the path that ran along the edge of the ravine was a balcony overlooking Dakh Won's universe. At the bottom of the rocky slope there was a gurgling stream with woods beyond it and mysterious noises in the underbrush.

Dakh Won could sit on the ravine trail for hours, entertaining his senses. He watched a leaf being tickled by the breeze, smelled wild cherries and the toasted aroma of earth warmed by the sun, tasted bitter grass and the sourness of insects that he caught with his paw, heard the whispers of the soil as a root reached down for moisture.

His ear was also tuned to sounds from the house—the loud and jarring voices, the slamming doors, the stamping of the cruel boots. High-laced, thick-soled, blunt-toed, they made him feel like a small and vulnerable creature.

When the weekend was over, he again felt safe. As if he knew he was needed, he stayed close, sitting on the piano bench while fingers danced on the keys and a foot tapped the pedal. The shoes were tied with leather tassles that bounced with every move.

Afternoons he followed the bobbing tassels down the ravine trail. The path was a narrow aisle of well-trodden clay, bordered on one side by wild cherry bushes and on the other by clumps of grass that drooped over the edge of the ravine. The tassled shoes always walked haltingly down the ravine trail, stopping to rest at a rustic bench before continuing to the wire fence at the end. There was a gate there, and another house beyond, but the tasseled shoes never went farther than the fence.

One day following the afternoon walk, the big round table in the kitchen was set with a single plate and a single cup and saucer, and Dakh Won sat on a chair to watch morsels of food passing from plate to fork to mouth.

"You're good company, Dakh Won. You're my best friend."

He squeezed his eyes.

"You're a big, strong, brave, intelligent cat."

Dakh Won licked a paw and passed it modestly over his seal brown mask.

"Would you like a little taste of crabmeat?"

With guttural assent Dakh Won sprang to the tabletop.

"Oh, dear! Cats aren't supposed to jump on the dinner table."

Dakh Won sat primly, keeping a respectable distance from the cream pitcher.

"But it's all right when we're alone—just you and me. We won't tell anyone."

For the rest of the week, meals were companionable events, but when Friday night came, Dakh Won sensed a change in the system.

There was a brown tablecloth with brass candlesticks and two plates instead of one. Alone in the kitchen he surveyed the table setting. The spot he usually occupied was cluttered with dinnerware, but there was plenty of room between the candlesticks. He hopped up lightly, stepped daintily among the china and glassware, and arranged himself as a dusky centerpiece on the brown tablecloth.

At that moment there were ominous sounds outdoors. A car had pulled into the yard, crunching on the gravel, and the heavy boots that Dakh Won feared were stamping on the back porch. He made himself into a small motionless bundle. Bruising boots could not reach him on the table.

The back door opened and banged shut, making a little flapping noise at the impact.

"Hey, Hilda! Hilda! Where the devil are you? What's happened to this door?"

"Here I am. I was upstairs, dressing."

"Why? Who's coming?"

"Nobody. I thought it would be nice to—"

"What the devil have you done to the back door?"

"That's a cat-hatch. I had it installed so Dakh Won can go in and out. It's hinged, you see—"

"A cat-hatch! You've ruined a perfectly good door! Who made it? Who cut the thing?"

"A very nice man from the farm down the road. It didn't cost anything, if that's what you're worried about."

"How did you meet this man? Why didn't it cost anything?"

"Well, I was taking my walk along the ravine—the way the doctor said I should—and the farmer was mending the fence around his property, so we started talking. Dakh Won was with me, and the man said we ought to have a cat-hatch. So he came over with a box of tools—"

"And you had this man in the house when you were alone?"

"Jack, the man is seventy years old. He has thirteen grandchildren. One of his grandsons wants to study piano, and I'm going to teach that boy whether you like it or not."

"How old is he?"

"What does that matter?"

"I want to know what goes on here when I'm away."

"Don't be silly, Jack."

"You're not interested in me, so I figure you've got something else going."

"That's insulting—and crude!"

"You don't appreciate a real man. You should've married one of those long-haired musicians."

"Jack, you make me tired. Are you going to change clothes, or ruin the floor with those stupid boots?"

"That's a laugh. You cut a hole in the door and give me hell for scratching the floor!"

As the voices grew louder, Dakh Won became more and more uncomfortable. He shifted his position nervously.

"Hilda! He's on the table! . . . Scram! Beat it!"

A rough hand swept Dakh Won to the floor, and a ruthless boot thudded into his middle, lifting him into the air.

"Jack! Don't you dare kick that cat!"

"I'm not having no lousy cat on my table!"

Dakh Won scudded through the cat-hatch and across the porch, pausing long enough to lick his quivering body before heading for the ravine. In the weeds alongside the trail he hunched himself into a pensive bundle and listened to the buzzing of evening insects.

Soon he heard the car drive away with more than the usual noise, and then he saw the shoe with bobbing tassels limping down the path.

"Dakh Won! Where are you? . . . Poor cat! Are you hurt?"

Strong hands lifted Dakh Won and smoothed his fur. He let himself be hugged tightly, and he flicked an ear when a drop of moisture fell on it.

"I don't know what to do, Dakh Won. I just don't know what to do. I can't go on like this."

The evil boots stayed away all weekend, and the next, and the next, but strange feet started walking into the house. The visitors came through the gate at the end of the ravine trail, bringing pleasant voices and laughter and small treats for Dakh Won, and they were careful where they walked.

One night, after an evening of music, the visitors went back down the trail, and Dakh Won stretched full length in the middle of the living room rug. Suddenly he raised his head. There was a menacing sound in the darkness outdoors—the familiar rumble of heavy boots on the back porch. They stamped their way uncertainly into the house.

"Jack! . . . So you decided to come back! Where have you been?"

"Whazzit matter?"

"You've been drinking again."

"I been drinkin' an' thinkin' an' drinkin' an'—"

Dakh Won heard something crash in the kitchen.

"You're dead drunk! You can't even sit on a chair."

"I wanna find the cat. Where's Stinker? I wanna drown 'im."

"Jack, you'd better leave."

There was another crash, and Dakh Won streaked through the house—a brown blur passing through the kitchen and out the cat-hatch. Under the back steps he hunched and listened to the anger of the voices.

"I'm warning you, Jack. Don't give me any trouble. Go away from here."

"You tryin' to throw me outta my own house?"

"I'm all through with you. That's final."

"Whaddaya mean?"

"I'm filing for divorce."

"Whoopee! Now I can have some fun."

"You've been having plenty of fun, as you call it. I know all about that camp trailer you live in. I know what goes on when you're away on a job—you and your tramps!"

"Go on—getta divorce. Nobody wants you. Nobody wants a—wants a cripple!"

"You and your drunken driving made me a cripple! And you're going to pay—and pay—and pay."

"You witch!"

"You won't have a dollar left for tramps—not when the court gets through with you!"

"You crippled, ugly witch! I'll smash your fingers!"

"Don't you touch me!"

"I'll kill you—"

"Stop it!... *STOP*..."

Dakh Won heard the screams and the scuffling feet. Then he saw the tassled shoes limping hurriedly from the house into the night. They headed for the ravine faster than he'd ever seen them go.

Bounding after them he heard sobs and moans as the feet hobbled unevenly along the trail toward the gate. The clay path was white in the moonlight, winding between the dark cherry bushes and the blackness of the ravine.

Back in the house there were crashing noises and a bellowing voice. Then Dakh Won saw the brutal boots staggering across the yard toward the white ribbon of pathway.

Ahead of him, the tassled shoes hurried on in panic, and behind him the boots were coming. The cat's ears went back, and his sleek tail became a bushy plume. He stopped in the path and arched his back.

Then unaccountably, with a sudden languor, Dakh Won sprawled on the path and lay there, motionless. Where he happened to stretch his dark body there was a streak of shadow across the moonlit path, cast by a wild cherry bush, and in this puddle of darkness Dakh Won was an invisible mound of dark brown fur.

The boots lumbered closer, the voice roaring. "I'll get you, you witch! I'll kill you!"

Dakh Won closed his eyes. The feet bore down, and the boots tumbled over him, plunging deep into his unprotected side. With a snarl of pain he sprang to his feet—just as the evil boots sailed over him and disappeared. There was a rumbling of loose rocks in the ravine and then only the splash of the rushing stream down below as the cat licked his wounded side.

Only Dakh Won knows the true reason for his action that night on the ravine trail. It is not a cat's nature to be vengeful—or heroic—but Dakh Won is a Siamese, and when people talk about the fatal accident in the ravine, his sapphire eyes are full of secrets.

Lilian Jackson Braun

The history of Lilian Jackson Braun's The Cat Who *series reveals that the publishing industry is as mysterious as her novels. From 1966 to 1968, she published three novels to critical acclaim:* The Cat Who Could Read Backwards, The Cat Who Ate Danish Modern, *and* The Cat Who Turned On and Off. *In 1966, the* New York Times *labeled Braun "the new detective of the year."*

Then the market for mysteries dried up. Not until 1986 did an original paperback, The Cat Who Saw Red, *reintroduce Braun's protagonist Jim Qwilleran and his Siamese partners-in-crime-solving, Koko and Yum Yum, to the mystery scene. Within two years, Berkley released four new novels in paperback and reprinted the three mysteries from the sixties. G. P. Putnam's Sons has since published thirteen hardcover originals. The most recent,* The Cat Who Sang for the Birds, *brings the best-selling series' total to twenty. Lilian was the "Good Living" editor of the* Detroit Free Press *for twenty-nine years and now writes mysteries full-time. Short stories, she says, are a favorite form. She lives with her husband, Earl Bettinger, and two Siamese cats, Koko III and Pitti Sing, in North Carolina.*

Now Miss Nancy Pickard does not scare me, and she should. This lady packs an awesome number of mystery awards for a peace-loving soul. Some of her stories, like "Afraid All the Time," peel back the skin to show the contemporary violence and fear pulsing beneath the surface. Others, like "It Had to Be You" from *Marilyn: Shades of Blonde,* edited by my co-conspirator in a solo moment, celebrate contemporary transcendence, as when Marilyn Monroe's image appears on Mount Rushmore. That story has been selected for inclusion in *The Year's Best Fantasy and Horror Stories.* Miss Nancy Pickard's story here is in her more gentle mode. But do not be deceived; there is always a touch of loss beneath the surface in Miss Nancy Pickard's works.

—M.L.

Dr. Couch Saves a Bird
Nancy Pickard

"**WHAT'S THE MATTER** with him, Grandpa?"

"I don't know, my dear."

If there was anything that Dr. Franklin Couch hated to do, it was to disappoint his ten-year-old granddaughter and namesake, Frankie. "As much as I know about dogs and cats," the retired veterinarian was forced to admit to the child, "that's also how much I don't know about birds." As they peered into the roomy, well-tended cage of her new pet, he sensed her dismay and disappointment, and he felt awful about it. To his knowledge, he had never previously let her down, not as he had her mother and his other daughter. For them, he'd been often absent, taking care of other people's pet emergencies. But for Frances, known as Frankie, he'd tried so very hard to be there always when she needed him. It hurt his old heart to detect the budding disillusionment the dear child was kindly attempting to hide from him.

She was terribly concerned about her new blue parakeet, and rightly so, was the old vet's unvoiced and inexpert opinion. He hadn't the heart to tell her that, however. He also hadn't the slightest notion what might be ailing the poor bird, but he knew a sickly looking animal when he saw one, even if it was wearing a beak instead of a muzzle and had wings instead of paws.

"You really don't know?" Frankie asked, in whispery disbelief.

Her grandfather was supposed to know everything there was to know about animals; everybody in town believed that about Dr. Frank, and when it came to small, furry domestic creatures, that exalted evaluation was very nearly true. But this tiny blue avian, staring lethargically back at him out of the one dull eye which was open, was another species altogether. It might as well have been a creature from Mars, Dr. Frank thought unhappily, for all he knew about birdy ailments and birdy complaints. Obviously it couldn't be suffering from distemper, or feline leukemia, or canine rabies. He knew that birds got viruses; he wondered if they caught colds or the flu, as warm-blooded animals did. Back when he had gone to veterinary school, they didn't get even a day's worth of lectures about the avian world, he recalled to his regret.

"No," he told her, "I wish I did, but the fact is, I don't."

"He won't eat." Frankie's sturdy voice trembled on the verge of tears. "He won't come out and fly around the room, either. He just sits there, like that."

That description struck a familiar chord with Dr. Frank, both personally and professionally, and suddenly he thought he knew exactly what might be sickening the little fellow. There was a time when those symptoms that his granddaughter had just voiced might well have described himself, though he didn't say so to the child. But there was another time, when they might have described a bird of a different feather.

"Is he going to die, Grandpa?"

Dr. Frank looked from the listless bird to the brimming brown eyes of his adored and only grandchild. "No, child," he said, with sudden and happy conviction. "I may not know enough about birds to fill a hummingbird's beak, but I do think I know what's wrong with this little fellow. Have I ever told you the story of the lovebird who solved a murder?"

"Really? I mean, no!"

"I haven't? Well, I'll be. And it just happens to have a direct bearing on the sad case of your little friend here. It may even hold the solution to his misery. Would you like to hear about it?"

"Oh, yes, Grandpa." Tactfully, urgently, she asked, "Can you tell me quick, so we can save Percy?"

"I'll tell you while we're on our way to the rescue. We'll catch two birds with one thistle, so to speak. Come with me, Frankie. We're going for a ride."

"Should I bring Percy with us?"

Dr. Frank started to decline her generous offer of avian company, but then had second thoughts about it. "Why, yes, I think he absolutely must come with us. This rescue mission might not work successfully without Percy."

The little girl was jumping up and down with hope and excitement now, although she calmed down long enough to grasp the top handle of Percy's cage with a steady little hand. Her grandfather, taking the cage away from her to carry out to the car in his own big hands, found himself suddenly hoping that he wasn't promising a salvation that he wouldn't be able to deliver.

"Should I ask my mom, Grandpa?"

"No," he advised her, after a second's thought. "We'll just slip out the back door and take my car. We'll be back so soon, your mother won't even have time to worry, although just to be on the safe side, we'll leave a note."

The note, quite illegibly written in the veterinarian's hand, did not happen to mention their destination, or the purpose for it. "Gone out," it said, if anyone could manage to read it. "Back soon." He signed it with two big capital "F's," which stood for Franklin and Frances.

On the way, with Percy clinging to his perch in his cage on Frankie's lap, her grandfather distracted her from her worry with his story of a murder mystery from long ago.

"This happened, oh, golly, back in the dark ages of the 1950s," he began. "Our town was much smaller then, you know, and everybody knew practically everybody else. I was still the only vet in town, so they naturally called me whenever there was a problem about any animal, whether it was a squirrel that got hit by a car or a lovebird that flew onto somebody's porch one day."

"Did that really happen?"

"The lovebird? It certainly did, Frankie. Of course, I didn't know it was a lovebird, not at first, anyway. I only knew I got a call from Mrs. Tommy Alexander one fine day, and she was so excited about some strange bird that had showed up on her front porch that she could hardly get the words out to tell me. It's pink! she said, first, and I said, well, it's probably a house finch, I think they have a reddish, pinkish head and chest. No, no, Mrs. Alexander said, you don't understand, Dr. Frank, it's green! Oh, well, then it's someone's escaped parakeet, I told her, but then she got quite rightly impatient with me, since I was still a young fellow who thought I knew it all and wouldn't give her a chance to finish. No, Dr. Frank, listen to me, she pleaded, it's pink and blue and green and it has a prominent beak and big dark eyes and it makes the loudest bird call you ever heard. I'm a bird-watcher, she said, and I know that it's not a finch, and it's not a parakeet, but I can't find it in any of my bird books. I don't think it's a parrot, either. What can it be, and where did it come from?"

He glanced over at his grandchild, then returned his gaze immediately to the street ahead of him, for her safety and his. He knew that an eighty-year-old driver couldn't risk an accident, for fear the powers-that-be might take his license, and his liberty, away from him.

"I am embarrassed to tell you, Frankie, that I was tempted to ask Mrs. Alexander what she had been drinking."

As he had hoped she would, the child giggled at that.

"She begged me to come see the bird for myself, as it appeared to her to be taking up lodging in one of her drainpipes. She wanted to know how she might catch it, what she should feed it, all that sort of thing. I tried to tell her that I wouldn't know, even if I saw the bird, but she wouldn't listen to that sort of discouragement, she just begged me to come quickly, saying that if it were her schnauzer that needed help, or her fine old tabby, I'd have come in a flash. That was true, I couldn't deny it. I saw I could do no less for the bird."

"Good for you, Grandpa."

"Thank you, although I don't know that I deserve any particular credit, considering how grouchy I was about it. Well, on the way over to Mrs. Alexander's house, I stopped in at the library and checked out every book I could find on exotic birds. There was only one, actually, and I took it with me. Luckily, it had photographs, so I hoped they would help me to identify Mrs. Alexander's exotic stranger. To tell you the truth, I still expected the bird to turn out to be something ordinary to which Mrs. Alexander had applied a heavy dose of imagination."

Frankie laughed again, and stroked the thin metal bars closest to her parakeet, as if to pet and comfort him.

Percy didn't respond.

To Dr. Frank's eye, the bird appeared to be feeling worse. It would be terrible if Percy died before they reached their destination, he thought. Dr. Frank stepped on the gas pedal, risking a speeding ticket in the name of love.

Quickly, he related to Frankie the story of arriving at the Alexander home, and of hearing the bird's call before he saw it.

"She was right," Dr. Frank said, "that wasn't the call of any finch or parakeet. If it was, it was a ten-pound parakeet! No, this was a much larger bird I heard, and then it peeked out of the top of the drainpipe, and I saw that it must be about six or seven inches tall, as big as a cardinal, only with a shorter tail. Oh, it was the prettiest bird I ever saw, Frankie, I just fell in love with it on the spot. It was obviously accustomed to people, because it began to scold both Mrs. Alexander and me."

"Really?" Frankie asked, laughing again.

"Yes, as if it was hungry and wanted to know where its food had got to, and what were we going to do about it."

He told her about sitting on the porch with Mrs. Alexander and thumbing through the book about exotic birds until they came to a lovely little picture of a bird with a rosy head and chest, a green body, a hooked yellow beak, big dark eyes with a white ring around each of them, and bright blue on top of its tail.

"That's it!" Mrs. Alexander had said, pointing in excitement.

It was, indeed, a peach-faced West African lovebird. From the description in the book, this one appeared to be a male. They learned from their quick reading, that in its native habitat, it lived in small flocks, near water, and that it stuck very close to its mate, to whom it remained attached for life.

"As you may imagine, West African peach-faced lovebirds are not indigenous to this area," Dr. Frank told his granddaughter, in a dry tone that made her laugh again. "Do you know what indigenous means?"

"It means they're not from here."

"Bright child! No, not anywhere close to here. About thousands of miles from here, that's where they're from. And suddenly, I realized why Mrs. Alexander was so wrought up, apart from the thrill of seeing such an exotic bird on her porch. It was the second week of November, Frankie. What does that suggest to you?"

The child sat in thought while Dr. Frank navigated a stoplight, and then she said, "Oh, gosh, that meant that winter was coming on, doesn't it? It was going to get cold and the lovebird might die?"

"It might, indeed. The library book said that some lovebirds could live at heights of over five thousand feet above sea level, but they certainly were not suited to the sorts of subzero temperatures and freezing rain that we get in our winters."

He paused to negotiate a tricky turn in the road.

"And there was something else worrisome, Frankie."

"What, Grandpa?"

"I don't want to upset you, but I have to tell you that as I looked at that beautiful bird, I saw that its chest was a darker red than the photographs suggested it should be. And I said to Mrs. Alexander, Mrs. Alexander, I think that bird has blood all over it."

"Oh, my gosh!"

"Now don't worry, Frankie, it wasn't the bird's blood, although we didn't know that, at first. I was afraid it was mortally wounded, that perhaps it had been attacked by a cat, although it seemed awfully feisty and healthy and loud for a bird that was dying."

Frankie's hand paused on the top of the cage.

Dr. Frank could have bit his tongue for saying those last words. He hurried on with his story, trying to distract her from her immediate concerns.

"If it wasn't its own blood, Frankie, whose blood do you suppose it might have been?"

"The cat's?"

The old vet laughed out loud. "The cat's? That's very good, Frankie, but it wasn't cat blood. Who else's might it have been?"

The intelligent child thought only for half a block before saying, "Somebody who had owned it?"

"Ah, that's it. And you see, you figured that out before we did. We didn't know that until much later in the story. At that moment, the only thing we were thinking about was how to capture the bird and get it out of the cold, and take care of it, especially if it was hurt. And while we were sitting there discussing this, a terrible thing happened."

"What, Grandpa?"

"It flew away!"

"Oh, no!"

"Yes, it did, it just flew straight away from that house."

"What did you and Mrs. Alexander do?"

"Well, what would you have done?"

This time, the child thought about the question for a good long block, before coming up with a most intelligent reply. "I would call the animal shelter, to see if anybody had reported a lost bird. And if that didn't work, I would call all the vets in town . . . oh, I guess you were the only vet, weren't you? Okay, then I would call the cops, to tell them to be on the lookout for a beautiful, bloody bird. And last, I would call the newspaper, to get them to print a big story about it, so everybody would keep their eyes open in case the bird showed up on their porch."

"Excellent ideas. We did contact the animal shelter and we did ask the cops if anybody had called to report a lost bird, but what really worked best was when Mrs. Alexander's neighbor came over to find out why I was sitting on a married woman's porch. This was a smaller town then, remember, and everybody knew practically everybody else. So when we told the nosy neighbor lady what was going on, guess what happened next?"

He glanced over to see a grin on his granddaughter's face.

"The neighbor lady called up all her friends?"

"That's right! And they called all their friends, and before the day was out the whole town was on the lookout for that West African peach-faced lovebird."

"But, Grandpa, if the whole town knew about it, wouldn't the owners find out about it and come forward and say it was their bird they lost?"

"Yes, they would have Frankie, if they could have."

They drove in silence, before the child took in a shocked breath. "Oh, my gosh. They couldn't, because they were dead! It was their blood on the bird, wasn't it? Were they dead, Grandpa?"

He nodded solemnly. "And we found out about that, because their neighbors wondered why they didn't step forward to claim the ownership of the bird that everybody was talking about. The neighbor lady went over to ask them if it was their bird that was lost, and when she knocked on the door, it opened and she saw their bodies inside, lying on the living room carpet."

Frankie's mouth was hanging open with astonishment.

"They had been shot, Frankie, at close range."

"How'd the bird get out of their house?"

"That," he said approvingly, "is a very good question, on which the whole rest of the story hinges." He pulled carefully into a parking spot between two big vans. "But first, we're here. Let's take Percy and go inside."

But his granddaughter was staring at the storefront before

them. "The pet store, Grandpa?" Frankie burst into tears, and in a voice full of the pain of betrayal, she cried, "Are we going to take Percy back to the store?"

Her grandfather was appalled at the obvious mistake he'd made in not confiding his whole plan to her. "Oh, my word, of course we're not, child! Heaven's no! Why, we're here to get a friend for Percy! I think that's what may be ailing him, he's feeling heartsick for the friends he left behind."

Frankie couldn't stop crying for several minutes, as if all of her concern for her pet were pouring out all at once.

Helplessly, her grandfather patted her back.

Finally, she wiped her face with the back of her hands and smiled at him as they sat in the car. "I was so scared when we got here. I thought I was going to have to give him back. I'm sorry I made such a fuss."

Dr. Frank patted the top of her head. "Percy is worth a fuss, Frankie, all animals are, and don't you ever feel bad for feeling bad about them. It's perfectly all right, especially with me." He apologized profusely to her for frightening her so badly, and then they went into the pet store to look for a friend for Percy.

Of course, the pet store people were surprised to see them coming back in with Percy, and they assumed he was being returned.

"Oh, no," Frankie exclaimed, self-confidently, "we're here to find him a friend."

The little blue bird visibly perked up at the sight and sound of the chattering cagefuls of parakeets at the back of the store. Not twenty minutes later, Dr. Frank was fifteen dollars poorer and ten feet taller, in the esteem of his grandchild, for Percy was already happily nuzzling the beak of his pretty new playmate, who also appeared content with the arrangement. They had seemed to pick each other out, by each clinging to their separate cages as if they were trying to get closer to each other. That had been the sign that Dr. Frank and Frankie were watching for, and they found it confirmed by the affectionate manner in which the two birds were now getting acquainted. (Or, perhaps, reacquainted,

Dr. Frank suspected.) Of course, the main purchase had also required the acquisition of a second cuttle bone, more seed, and an extra swinging perch, but Dr. Frank considered it money well spent. He thought, privately, that there was something a little sad about having to pay only fifteen dollars for something so beautiful and precious as a living creature.

"Thank you, Grandpa," said Frankie, for the umpteenth time, once they were back in the car. "Thank you so much. Now will you tell me the rest of the story, about the lovebird that solved a murder?"

She was already excited and happy; this, he knew, was mere icing.

"When the neighbor walked into that house and saw that poor couple on the living room carpet, that is just about all she saw, Frankie, because there was nothing else there! Now it turned out that these were a man and woman in their late seventies who had lived in that house all of the fifty years of their married life, but there wasn't even any furniture there. No television, no sofa, chairs, beds or tables, not even a refrigerator or a stove. There wasn't even a bird cage to show a lovebird had ever lived there." He glanced expectantly at her. "What do you think it all means, Frankie? Just from the little I've told you, can you figure out anything about the crime?"

"They got robbed!"

"Indeed, they did, and not only that, they got robbed of every single thing they owned. But what kind of robbers would take everything? Even their papers and their clothes? And how would the robbers gather all of those things up, and carry them out of the house without being noticed? Even if it happened at night, wouldn't somebody see that house was being emptied of all of its belongings, and wonder if something criminal was going on?"

As the child frowned in concentration, Dr. Frank quietly navigated the streets and tried to think up more obvious clues in case she didn't get it right away.

"Did I tell you they were an old couple?" he asked her, hoping that was a clue which would steer her in the right direction. "And all of their children were grown and gone? And that it was a big old house which must have been a lot for them to take care of, at their age?"

She stared at her two parakeets, who were twittering away like an old married couple themselves, and then she said, hesitantly, "Remember when Grandma was still alive, Grandpa?"

The question startled him, though he hid his reaction to it.

"Yes," he answered, gravely, without any irony, "I do."

"And you guys used to live in that big old house of yours?"

He smiled at the term "you guys" to describe himself and his late wife, and he also smiled because he saw that Frankie was already on the right track.

"Yes?" he encouraged her.

"And Grandma got tired of keeping it clean and she said you were going to fall off the roof and break your fool neck if you kept climbing up there to fix the ... the ..."

"Shingles."

"Right. And so you guys sold that house and you bought the one you have now, remember?"

Every detail, he remembered ... of how he hadn't wanted to move to a much smaller place, but Emma had insisted, and how right she had been, for the saddest of reasons. Within the year she was gone, from a terrifyingly fast cancer, and he knew he would have rattled around their big house like a lonely old dog. At least the new house didn't haunt him with memories. Dr. Frank glanced at the parakeets; he knew what it felt like to pine away in loneliness. If the dear child seated beside him hadn't been around to enchant him, he might have stopped eating and caring, himself, just like her little pet.

"Grandpa?"

"I remember," he said, after clearing his throat.

"Well, was that old couple moving into a retirement home, or something? And was it the movers who killed them and robbed them?"

"Brilliant detective work!" he lauded her, and was rewarded by a glowing look on her small, sweet face. "That's exactly right. They had hired a fly-by-night outfit of men they didn't know anything about. And the one fact I didn't tell you was that the couple was very wealthy, with many valuable belongings which they had all packed up in boxes, ready for the movers to take."

"Did the cops catch the murderers, Grandpa?"

"The cops did, and quite easily. I wonder if you can imagine how they did it. Remember, I told you, it was the lovebird who solved the murders. You see, the robbers didn't realize that the lovebird was also valuable, and since they didn't want to fool with him, they let him out of his cage. He escaped from the house while they were moving the furniture. So, Frankie, if you were a police officer, and you located some suspects, and you knew those men might have stolen things from a couple who kept a bird, and you knew that bird had gotten out of its cage while the suspects were still in the house, what telltale sign might you look for, on them, or their clothes?"

Frankie thought for a minute, and then her hands flew to her mouth and she giggled behind them, before she exclaimed, "Bird poop!"

"Yes, Frankie, on a jacket one of them had worn."

They laughed together about that, until the really important question occurred to his granddaughter and she became very serious again. "What ever happened to the lovebird, Grandpa?"

That lovebird, he told her, was sighted all over town for the rest of the week. Everybody was getting really worried about it, the whole town seemed to take a personal interest, and reports were coming in that its loud chirp was growing fainter, that it was looking thin, and that it had stopped scolding the people it encountered.

"And then somebody got a great idea," he said. "They obtained a second lovebird and put it in a cage on Mrs. Tommy Alexander's front porch. And before the day was out, the first bird had heard the second bird calling, and had flown right up to the cage. When we brought the cage into the Alexanders' living room, the bird came, too, and it lived happily ever after with its mate, and with Mrs. Alexander to look after them very well for the rest of their days."

"Was it your great idea?"

"Well," he admitted modestly, "I suppose it was."

She patted her cage. "And this was your great idea, too."

They had the cage all set back up in its spot before her mother even knew they'd been gone. But eventually, she did come in to ask if they wanted cheeseburgers or grilled cheese for their lunch.

Nervously, Dr. Frank watched his daughter glance at the cage, do a double take, and then walk over to stare.

Behind her, a large old man and a small girl held hands and their breath.

When Frankie's mother turned around, she merely said, "It's amazing how much better he looks, isn't it?"

"Can I keep it?" Frankie pleaded.

"Yes, you may. Thank you, Dad."

But on her way out of the room, his daughter leaned over to whisper in his ear, "I'm sure glad we didn't give her a *horse* for her birthday."

After his daughter had left, Dr. Frank asked, "What are you going to name your new bird, Frankie?"

"Lovie," she said, promptly, "after the lovebird who solved a murder." She gazed up at her grandfather in a way that caused his heart to ache pleasurably within his chest. He suddenly felt as if his own sorrow over his wife's death had been redeemed, because it had helped him to recognize loneliness when he saw it in another of God's creatures.

"Lovie," he told her gratefully, "is a very good name, indeed." As he settled back into an easy chair, and Frankie climbed happily onto his lap to wait for lunch, he said, "For some reason, that reminds me, have I ever told you the story of the horse that put out a fire?"

Nancy Pickard

The hailed creator of the Jenny Cain mystery series, Nancy Pickard lives near Kansas City with her son, two-long-haired miniature dachshunds, and two nine-month-old cats, all of whom get along blissfully. Their names, starting with the son, are Nick, Ducky, Lucy, Jimmy, and Cloud. Nancy has won the Agatha, Anthony, Shamus, and Macavity mystery awards and her short stories frequently appear in collections of the year's best. She says that when she cleans the bathroom all of the animals line up at the doorway to watch, causing her to wonder if perhaps their standards are higher than hers.

Oh, that Miss Dorothy Cannell! Only she of the current mystery-writing crop can lead the reader on the giddy chase one expects from the classic age of British mystery. One would never know Miss Dorothy Cannell is now a Yank-in-residence. As one follows the adventures of Dickie, Foof, and Fetch, one would hardly know from the names which was the mere animal, and which was the superior human. In fact, this story suggests that the only superior humans may be as much in service to humanity as man's—and woman's—best friend, the ordinary dog. But Fetch is no ordinary dog, or he would not be in my anthology.

—M.L.

Fetch
Dorothy Cannell

"I'M SORRY, OLD bean, but every once in a donkey's age a husband has to take a stand, and what it comes right down to—putting the matter in the proverbial nutshell, so to speak—is that I will not have a notorious thief under this roof." Mr. Richard Ambleforth, aged twenty-five, but looking more like an earnest six former home for the hols, felt rather good about this master-ful speech addressed to his bride of two days.

"Honestly, Dickie! How can you be so stuffy!" The former Lady Felicity Entwhistle, known to her intimate circle as Foof, tossed her silky black bob, stamped her dainty foot, and flounced over to the window seat. There she sat balefully eyeing the ceiling and addressed the crown molding. "Your mother was right.

You should never have married me; I was bound to let on sooner rather than later that I prefer hobnobbing with criminals to having afternoon tea with the vicar."

"I say." Dickie glanced nervously over his shoulder as if expecting his formidable parent to materialize and clasp him to the maternal bosom. "Shouldn't bring the mater into this, tempting fate, don't you know! Before we can duck behind the curtains there'll be a knock at the door. And in she'll march with a list of all the foods I'm not supposed to eat on the honeymoon."

"Oh, the more the merrier!" Foof gave a hollow laugh. "After all, we are taking Woodstock with us. Heaven forbid he should be left behind looking sadly at his bucket and spade!"

At this less than propitious moment a large man with iron-gray hair, in unequivocal butler's garb, entered the book-lined sitting room of what had been Dickie's London bachelor digs. Despite his size he moved with a lightness of step that verged on the ethereal as he placed a silver tray with a decanter and two glasses on the table behind the worn leather sofa.

"Oh, jolly good fun! It's time for sherry!" Foof sat swinging her lengthy rope of pearls in an arc that threatened to lasso the clock off the mantelpiece. "How about a toast, Dickie? To life on the streets for that miserable miscreant I so regrettably brought home because"—her voice broke—"I'm sure Woodcock followed your orders and turfed the poor fellow out onto the fire escape."

"I must confess to having fallen short in that regard." The butler addressed the sherry glass he handed to her. "After forty years in the service of Mr. Ambleforth's family I am wont to take the occasional liberty of making certain modifications to the instructions bestowed upon me, when I deem it in the best interest of continued harmony within the household. If in so doing on this occasion I have transgressed beyond the bounds of leniency, then I shall respectfully hand in my notice and repair to my room to pack my travel bag."

"I thought it was already packed for the honeymoon." Such was Dickie's state of alarm that he could pick up only on this trivial point.

"I stand corrected, sir." Woodcock's austere demeanor was belied by the twinkle in his eye and Foof sprang to her feet, dribbling sherry down the front of her elegant frock to bestow a kiss on his cheek.

"You treasure of a man! How horrid of me to think for a moment that you would not see the matter precisely as I do. Haven't I always been certain that Dickie only got up the courage to propose to me after you told him what to say and prodded him out the door with one of his mother's hat pins? Now, if you can only persuade him"—Foof put what was left of her drink down on a table and clasped her hands imploringly—"that it is his Christian duty to help reclaim a wayward soul, I will be an exemplary wife to Dickie, and the perfect mistress to you, darling Woodcock."

"Sorry, Foof! But I refuse to budge on this." Dickie wandered over to the sofa table and picked up his sherry glass. "If I allowed my heart to soften and agreed to let the fellow remain here, we'd be letting ourselves in for the most beastly time. Before we'd know it not one of our chums would be willing to set foot inside the flat for fear of having their coat pockets picked or their handbags raided."

"Fiddlesticks!" His bride returned to the window seat in a swirl of skirts. "I explained to him that he was lucky not to be in prison with the wicked man who got him into a life of crime. Had you seen the remorse in his soft brown eyes you would know that he has truly seen the error of his ways and is intent on becoming a pillar of society."

"Even the most hardened of hearts do, upon occasion, see the light and henceforth embark upon lives of unblemished spirituality." Woodcock proffered this pronouncement along with a plate of wafer-thin almond biscuits which he had procured from the interior of the sideboard. "I am thinking, Mr. Ambleforth, most particularly of my cousin Bert who led a ribald youth consorting with women of an unsavory nature. He had not attended a church service in many years until one Sunday morning, when feeling the effects of the night before, he entered a Plymouth Brethren meeting hall. Merely in search of a place to sit down. But whilst there he came to realize in a blinding flash—as he described it to me—that his previous life had been nothing but wickedness and sin."

"What a lovely story," enthused Foof. "I suppose he was embraced back into the bosom of the family."

"An attempt was made," responded Woodcock, "but resentment was felt by some at his attempts to dissuade them from engaging in such unholy practices as walking down to the village green to watch Sunday cricket matches. However, such a complete and sustained conversion is not, from what I have gleaned of life, in any way uncommon. Such was my thinking, Mr. Ambleforth, as I prepared a light repast for the personage presently in the kitchen. And sensing a willingness on his part to rethink the manner of his days, agreed to add my voice to Lady Felicity's in pleading his cause."

"Oh, bring him in here! It's clear I'll have no peace until you do." Dickie flopped back down in his chair, refusing to meet his bride's eyes while Woodcock retreated out into the hall and seconds later wafted back into the room with what looked like shamed humility itself tiptoeing in his wake.

"Darling, Dickie! Does he look like a cutthroat cur?" asked Foof in her most wheedling voice.

"No, I suppose not, but he wouldn't have been much good at his job if he did. Oh, very well, let's hear what he has to say for himself."

"Woof!" came the ingratiating response.

"There," cried Foof, dancing across the room to scoop the small black-and-brown dog with a face like a floor mop into her arms. "Fetch is saying he's ever so sorry that he got into bad company and was led wickedly astray. But if you will be his new master, Dickie, he will never again steal so much as a matchstick. Isn't that so"—kissing the furry forehead—"my adorable precious?" The animal looked over her shoulder and woofed with a great deal of conviction.

Dickie wasn't entirely mollified. "Yes, he sounds sorry, old bean. But we can't lose sight of the fact that he's a confidence trickster."

"Very true, sir," concurred Woodcock. "Were such not the

case, Lady Felicity might have been less sympathetic when she found him in an alleyway, after being informed by her milliner that he had been rendered homeless when his master, Lord Bentbrook, was recently made a guest of His Majesty. But one should perhaps bear in mind, Mr. Ambleforth, that in all walks of life, four-footed or otherwise, there are those who are induced to live by their wits because life's contrivances against them."

"Miss Honeywell pined to take Fetch in herself but she could not risk getting dog hair on her adorable hats. And anyway, darling Dickie, I am sure he will be much happier with us. A honeymoon is just what he needs to help banish the past and—"

"Now there I do draw the line," protested Dickie, "that dog is not, I repeat not, coming with us."

His words were still ringing in his ears an hour later when he, Foof, Woodcock, and Fetch sat in a train heading out of London Bridge Station for Little Biddlington-on-Sea. They had decided against driving the car and had selected a third-class carriage because Dickie harbored the not unvalid fear that his mother might have instructed her innumerable acquaintances to be on the lookout for them. And at the first report of a sighting she would be on their track. Possibly even waiting for them when they arrived at the honeymoon suite. Because what mother worthy of the name would allow her son to go off on his very first honeymoon without her being there to make sure that he did not fail to attend to his health by eating regular meals and getting a good night's sleep?

"Little Biddlington-on-Sea sounds absolutely topping!" Foof looked delectable in a slim brown suit, buttoned shoes, with one of Miss Honeywell's demurest hats cupping her face. Fetch sat beside her like a small furry package as she gazed dreamily out the window at the rows of sooty faced houses whizzing past on the embankment.

"Yes, it should be perfect." What Dickie meant was that it was the last place on earth his mother would look for them. It was known to be a pretty resort, but one favored by working-class people who wanted to enjoy a quiet holiday without crowded promenades, fun fairs, and young people belting out songs as they came wavering home from the nearest pub. He was still feeling a bit glum about Fetch's presence, but he had to admit that so far the dog had not misbehaved an inch. True, the little beast kept glancing at the communication cord as if considering the possibility of leaping up and giving it a tug. But Foof's soothing hand upon his wiry back kept him in place. Until, that is, the train pulled into a station and a woman entered the carriage which so far they'd had to themselves.

She was a nondescript person of medium build in a gray flannel coat and a serviceable hat secured to the bun at the back of her head with a small-tipped pin. Foof, who was wondering aloud how much farther it was to Little Biddlington-on-Sea, barely looked at her. But Dickie had the uneasy feeling that he might have seen the woman somewhere before. Could she be one of the mater's spies, cleverly disguised to look like somebody's housekeeper? Woodcock, who had been perusing a periodical providing advice on the proper maintenance of a gentleman's wine cellar, rose and placed the woman's small suitcase on the overhead rack. He resumed his seat at the opposite window from his employers. She took hers across from him and, as the train rumbled back to life, opened her handbag, withdrew a darning bobbin, and was just about to pull a black sock over its mushroom-shaped head when Fetch leaped into action. Scrambling across the floor, he attacked the woman's shoes in a blur of brown-and-black fur, tearing at her laces while barking out the side of his mouth.

Dickie's mother would have denounced it as a common bark, definitely cockney. But there was worse to come. When the woman bent down, dropping her darning in the process, Fetch leaped with the speed of light onto the seat and was rummaging inside her handbag when Woodcock, rising to ominous proportions, hauled him up by the scruff of the neck. And continued to dangle him in the air.

"I trust the animal did not inflict an injury, Madam." This was Woodcock at his most butlerish, concerned but unflustered and Foof silently vowed that she would never go on a honeymoon without him.

"It's all right, he hasn't hurt me." The woman looked down at her tangled shoelaces. And Dickie, who wasn't known amongst fellow members of his club to be uncannily astute, got the odd feeling that she did so to avoid meeting Woodcock's eyes. Almost as if she were the one to feel embarrassment.

"It was frightfully naughty of him." Foof still had her hands clapped to her face—which was as white as Dickie's was red. "I should have had him on his lead. My husband and I are most awfully sorry."

"More than we can possibly say," croaked Dickie.

"Fetch I want you to apologize to the lady," instructed Foof.

A decidedly hangdog woof resulted. Woodcock returned the animal to its appropriate seat and handed the woman's darning back to her.

She replaced it to her handbag, saying, "I think I'll have a sleep. That'll help me get over the scare." Whereupon she proceeded to sit with eyes resolutely closed for the next hour and a half. At which time the train chuffed into the station displaying a sign reading Little Biddlington-on-Sea. Instantly, the woman became alert, and took down her suitcase before Woodcock could help her with it. Foof and Dickie voiced renewed apologies as she stepped down onto the platform ahead of them. The evening was cloudy, but they felt considerably brighter when she disappeared from view. Even Fetch displayed a renewed perkiness as he trotted alongside them on his lead. Woodcock located a porter to assist with the suitcases and they soon found themselves outside the station, looking hopefully around for their taxi.

"My profound apologies, Mr. Ambleforth and Lady Felicity. I telephoned to arrange for one to be waiting for us upon our arrival." Woodcock shook his head. It was rare that his organization skills did not meet with impeccable results and beneath his imperturbable exterior he felt the matter keenly.

"I think I can guess what happened, sir," offered the porter. "Smith was here with his taxi, fifteen minutes ago. Likes to be ahead of himself when possible and have a cheese sandwich and a cup of cocoa from his Thermos. We had another train come in, the three-fifty from Nottingham, and just one gentleman got out. Anyways, to cut a long story shorter he talked Smith into taking him where he needed to go."

"Well, of all the cheek!" said Foof.

"Always one to make an extra five bob, is Smith. But I did hear the man say he was feeling poorly, so it could be Smith's heart was touched and he wasn't just thinking about the tip he'd get out of it." The porter was sympathetic to their plight, but unable to come up with a solution to the problem of transportation. There wasn't another taxi service or a bus that went to the Sea Breeze Guest House. It seemed they would have to walk.

"It can't be far," endeavoring to console Woodcock, Dickie picked up a suitcase before he could be prevented.

"One would assume not, sir. When I telephoned to make inquiries into the nature of the premises I was informed that they are located not five minutes' walk from the railway station, and within a stone's throw of the sea."

"Exactly what I was told by my friend Binkie Harbottle, whose landlady always comes here on her holiday. Chin up Woodcock! Never say die, Foof. Let's be on our way. We can even sing Ten Green Bottles to help pick up the tempo."

Dickie, having manfully decided that he wouldn't let Fetch's lapse ruin things, began to hum as he strutted forward along the road that rose into a hill. A hill that shortly began to seem part of a mountain range. Up and up they puffed, afraid to stop unless they slid backwards to the bottom. Had they perhaps misunderstood the porter's directions when he told them to turn right on leaving the station and continue straight ahead until they reached the Sea Breeze? It was a chilly evening for June, but Foof had never felt hotter in her life. She was gasping for a cup of tea.

They passed no one, although a couple of times Dickie thought he saw a figure a considerable distance ahead of them making the same interminable trudge. Then, just as Foof whispered that she couldn't go on, she would have to lie down and die, they saw a gate. It bore the sign SEA BREEZE GUEST HOUSE and stood blissfully open. With renewed energy they all, includ-

ing Fetch, who long ago had looked as though his paws had given
out, hobbled down the short path to the door. While Woodcock
rang the bell Dickie strove to regain his voice.

"Old Binkie's landlady told a whopper about the Sea Breeze
being a short walk from the station, but she didn't misrepresent
about it being a stone's throw from the sea. We're on top a
beastly cliff. I expect that if we go around the back we'll be able
to stand on the brink of the precipice and toss pebbles into the
surf to our hearts' content."

"The Sea Breeze had better have other attractions or I'm
leaving first thing tomorrow morning." Foof sagged against the
door just as it was opened by a cozy-looking woman in a hair net,
who ushered them into the dark varnished hall with a strip of
Turkish-red carpet and bade them welcome. As Mr. and Mrs.
Ambleforth. Woodcock, in accordance with his employers' desire
to avoid an excess of bowing and scraping, had not mentioned
Foof's title when booking them in.

"I'm Mrs. Roscombe. Leave your cases here and the hubby
will bring them up. Me and him have run this place for years. So
we know how to make our guests comfortable. Had a pleasant
journey did you? Well, isn't that nice! And already feeling the
benefit of our good salt air from the looks of you." She dug into
her overalls pocket for a bunch of keys and hurried ahead of
them up a flight of steep narrow stairs as Dickie and Foof produced incoherent replies. Woodcock and Fetch vouchsafed nothing at all.

"You young marrieds are to have this room." Mrs. Roscombe
unlocked the door and handed Dickie the key. "There's a basin
and wash jug, but you shouldn't have to wait over long to use the
bathroom. We've only got three other guests booked in at the
moment. There's Mr. and Mrs. Samuels, that comes from the midlands, two doors down from you. They were here last year. And
her cousin Miss Hastings is at the end of the hall. She just arrived.
We often gets families here." Mrs. Roscombe beamed with pride.
"We make things easy. That's what they like. The front door's always open so you never have to worry about taking a key out
with you. And we don't fuss if people come down late for break-

fast or get back late for the evening meal. You can have yours tonight as soon as you're ready."

"You don't object to our dog?" Dickie asked her.

"Not a bit! The hubby and I are proper softies when it comes to animals."

Fetch showed his appreciation by woofing in a manner that would have done credit to Uriah Heep. And Mrs. Roscombe pronounced him a dear little fellow, before saying she would show Woodcock to his room, which was directly across the hall from that of his employers. Foof and Dickie went inside to study their surroundings with determined cheerfulness. It wasn't what they were used to, but it was spotlessly clean with a mock-silk bedspread in the same dusky rose as the curtains, two elderly wardrobes, and a decent sized dressing table whose mirror made the room look a little larger than was actually the case. Moments later a stooped but smiling Mr. Roscombe appeared with their suitcases and the instant he departed Woodcock tapped and, upon entering, suggested that Mr. Ambleforth and Lady Felicity might wish to go downstairs while he unpacked for them.

"I expressed to Mrs. Roscombe my belief that you might not be adverse to a pot of tea, my lady."

"Dearest Woodcock!" Foof stood up from removing Fetch's lead. "You are a paragon among men."

"I've always known that," said Dickie, "but what I don't know—and what has my mind in a tweak, Woodcock, is who was that woman in the train? I'll be blowed if I haven't seen her somewhere before, and from the glint in your eye when you looked at her you were wondering the same thing."

"Her identity was not what had me in a quandary, sir. I recognized her when she entered the carriage. She is a Miss Hastings. Housekeeper to Sir Isaac Gusterstone. When he is in town, which is not often of late due to his advancing years, he resides in one of the flats across the street from your own. You have possibly noticed the woman at one time or another upon her entering or departing the building."

"I say!" Dickie exclaimed. "You're spot on, Woodcock! I have seen her. Passed her in the street a couple of times. Remember thinking she looked like someone who'd always lived a confoundedly dreary life, without a spark of happiness to call her very own. But if you weren't trying to remember who she was, Woodcock, what was it about her that had you puzzled in the train?"

"Only, sir, that she showed no sign of recognition on seeing me. And, although we are not well acquainted, we have spoken upon occasion."

"Perhaps she was startled to the point of confusion at seeing Dickie and me in a third-class compartment," suggested Foof.

"That is possible, my lady." Woodcock trod soundlessly across the floor to the suitcases. "However, I do not intend to repine upon the matter, especially as it is always possible that I may discover the reason during the course of our stay at the Sea Breeze."

"And just how is that likely?" Dickie asked him.

"Because, sir, as Mrs. Roscombe informed us Miss Hastings is also staying here. She is certainly a fast walker to have moved so far ahead of us up the hill. Of course, it is also possible that factors unknown to us lent wings to her feet. And now if you and your ladyship will excuse me, I will not further delay the unpacking."

Taking the hint, the honeymooners departed the room with Fetch at their heels. But when they reached the bottom of the stairs and Foof turned to remind the dog to be on his best behavior, meaning he was not to get any ideas about silver teaspoons, they discovered that he was gone. Racing back to their room, Dickie found Woodcock placidly stowing shirts in the gentleman's chest of drawers. The butler had not readmitted Fetch to the room, and he voiced the conviction that the door had been closed until Mr. Ambleforth reappeared. Even so, he searched under the bed and behind the curtains along with every other place where it was remotely possible that the dog might be hiding.

Woodcock then accompanied Dickie out into the hallway. All the other doors were shut except for the one at the far end. Assuming, correctly, that here was the bathroom, they went inside to discover a likely solution to Fetch's disappearance. The window overlooked a veranda, making it simplicity itself for Fetch to have jumped down onto its roof and from thence to the ground.

"A bit thick, wouldn't you say, Woodcock, for the little beggar to repay all Lady Felicity's kindness to him by bunking off at the first opportunity?" Dickie heaved a sigh. "But then again it's undoubtedly for the best. We would never have known what he would be up to next. One of these days we could have found ourselves charged as accessories before or after the fact when the police came banging on the door looking for the 'goods.' "

"There is that, sir."

"Yes, well, I'd better go down and break the news to the poor old bean. She wasn't particularly worried. Thought, like I did, that he'd gone back to our room. I wouldn't be surprised if she has an attack of the weeps when I spill the beans. That we are back to being a dogless couple after a day and a half of marriage."

Having geared himself up to break the news that would break his bride's heart, Dickie entered the sitting room with its seaweed colored chairs to find himself temporarily unable to get Foof's attention. She was being talked at by a middle-aged woman with bleached ash-blond hair and protruding eyes seated across from her. Miss Hastings was also present and, but for the black sock she was darning, faded conveniently into the beige wallpaper.

"My husband—Mr. Samuels"—the woman's voice declared her to be from the midlands—"is a commercial traveler for Hartwoods' Hairbrushes. Their top seller. Of course it means he's gone from home a lot. And he's been complaining lately that he's not as young as he used to be. Says he's been getting some bad headaches. But as I keep telling him he only has to keep going for another fifteen years. After that he can sit back and enjoy the results of what we've accomplished during our very happy marriage." Mrs. Samuels paused just long enough for Foof to open her mouth, then was back in full flood. "And as I sometimes have to remind him, I've done my share in building us a nice little nest egg. Right from day one I've always handled the money. Paid all the bills. Bought his clothes, from suits to hand-kerchiefs. Decided what we could afford to spend on holiday. It means a lot being able to say—right down to the last safety pin—what's ours and what isn't."

Foof, catching sight of Dickie hovering in the doorway, was about to break in and introduce him, but Mrs. Samuels was off again, as relentless as a train that would not have attempted to stop had thirty people jumped on the line.

"But, as I like to say, there's a big difference between being careful and being mean. I've always seen that Mr. Samuels takes a packet of biscuits and a Thermos with him on his trips so that he doesn't have to bother about stopping in at some café where you don't know what the food's like. And I've always encouraged him to let my cousin Miss Hastings come on holiday with us each year to a nice place like this and help her out a bit with the price of the room. Isn't that right, Ethel?"

Mrs. Samuels finally drew a proper breath.

"What's that, Mavis?" Miss Hastings jerked forward in her chair, jabbing her finger with the darning needle.

"I was telling the young lady that we always take you on holiday with us."

"Not always." Miss Hastings dropped the darning bobbin and sock into the lap of her gray skirt and sucked at her injured fin-ger. "If you remember, dear, you went to Margate without me twice." Her eyes shied away from her cousin's suddenly accusing glance, "but I am grateful, of course I am, for everything you and Leonard have done for me over the years."

"As you've tried to demonstrate, in your own funny way!" Mrs. Samuels gave a barking laugh that reminded Dickie that he still had to break the news to Foof about Fetch's disappearance. But the awful woman had finally spotted him. "Ah, here comes your husband by the looks of him, Mrs. Ambleforth. Mine still isn't back from having to go up to the head office this morning. Like as not it'll be late when he shows up. But you can't keep a man on a string all the time, can you? And I hope that years from now you're as happy with your man as I've been with Mr.

Samuels. Not a morning gone by, including this one, that he doesn't say how he worships the ground I walk on."

"How lovely." Foof got to her feet, introduced Dickie to the two women (Miss Hastings displaying no sign of having seen him on the train), and after he had shaken their hands, she said that it looked as though her husband wanted a word with her. Following him out into the hall, she closed the door, tiptoed away from it, then put her arms around his neck and kissed him passionately. "Darling, promise you won't let me turn into that sort of wife. Wasn't she too ghastly for words? No wonder poor Miss Hastings looks like everyone's poor relation. I'm sure Mrs. Samuels only brings her on holiday so she can rub her nose in the fact that she doesn't have a husband who is a top-selling commercial traveler."

"And woe betide Miss Hastings if she doesn't act properly grateful." Dickie kissed Foof back. "But let's forget about them, old bean! There is something I have to tell you. A blot on the old honeymoon I'm afraid." Whilst speaking he produced an impeccable white handkerchief from his pocket and Foof made full use of it upon being gently informed that Fetch would seem to have disappeared from their lives as speedily as he had entered them.

"Oh, the poor darling! How we must have failed him!"

"Fudge!" Dickie placed a husbandly arm around her quivering shoulders. "That dog knew we expected him to turn his life around and he probably thought we would make him go to the sort of meetings that helped Woodcock's cousin Bert see the light."

"But I was sure he was growing fond of us." Foof sobbed harder.

"We'll get you another dog."

"There'll never be another Fetch."

"Chin up, old bean! Dickie returned the drenched handkerchief to his pocket. Let's go and find Mrs. Roscombe. You'll feel better after you've eaten, and then we'll go for a walk before it gets too dark for us to find our way back."

Unable to offer an alternative to this sensible scheme, Foof agreed with wifely submission. In the dining room at the back of the house they partook of cold beef, salad, thick bread and butter and cheeses. Afterwards Dickie went back to their room to fetch a coat for her. And they set out to walk along the cliffs under silky gray skies, upon which the moon appeared to be pinned like a crescent-shaped brooch. Now that Foof had rallied from the immediate shock of losing Fetch she became annoyed with herself and Dickie.

"We should have gone looking for him at once."

"What would have been the point? He would only have run off again at the first opportunity."

"Perhaps you didn't want to find him."

"That's not true." To his surprise Dickie realized he meant what he said. It was a rum go, but there it was. In a few meager hours he had developed a sneaking fondness for the little dog. Being a stuffy sort of fellow himself he couldn't help but admire Fetch's audacity. "You never know, he may still come back," he said, upon their walking back to the house.

Neither of them held out any real hope. And when they returned to their room there was no Fetch. Foof picked up her sponge bag from the dressing table where Woodcock had placed it, draped a towel and her dressing gown over her arm, and went along to the bathroom to wallow in a good cry and, mindful that she must not keep the other guests waiting, a quick soak. On her way back to her room she passed Miss Hastings, who was in her turn heading for the bathroom. Her face was puffy as if she too, had been crying. Another indication that the woman was in an agitated state of mind was that she had not properly closed the door to her room. Let alone lock it. But of course this wasn't London where people were inclined to be more cautious in safekeeping their property. Also, besides herself, Dickie, and Woodcock, the only other guests were Miss Hastings's cousin. And the husband who had possibly yet to return.

Telling herself that if she didn't watch out she would turn into a meddlesome matron, Foof entered her room to find Woodcock pouring Dickie a brandy from the bottle he had brought with him and listening to his employers detailed account of what Mrs. Samuels had been saying in the sitting room.

"A fiercely controling woman, sir, by the sound of it." The butler turned to inquire if her ladyship also desired a nightcap. He was interrupted when the door that Foof, like Miss Hastings, had left ajar was nudged open. Fetch came scurrying into the room with a mushroom-shaped object clamped between his teeth and a black sock dangling to the ground. Sitting back on his haunches, he dropped his loot at Foof's feet and uttering a prideful bark, cocked his head to one side, the better to view her appreciation.

"I say!" Dickie looked stricken. "He's well and truly gone back to his old tricks."

"It would appear so." Woodcock bent to pick up the darning bobbin and sock. "But one does find cause to wonder, sir, why—when the dog has been trained to snatch gentlemen's wallets, ladies' purses, and other commodities of value, he would present these homely items to her ladyship. And look so proud of himself."

"Perhaps he couldn't find Miss Hastings's purse," Foof felt compelled to say.

"I would think it doubtful she has any jewelry worth the taking lying around in her room," said Dickie. "And, potty as it sounds, I haven't a doubt in the world that Fetch knows the difference between the real article and paste."

"It is indeed a puzzle." Woodcock continued to stand with the bobbin and sock in his hands.

"Well, no real harm is done," Foof scooped Fetch into her arms. "Surely Miss Hastings won't make too much fuss when we return her property and explain that Fetch can be a little mischievous at times." She was prevented from continuing when a scream erupted from somewhere close-by. Such was its volume that the bed seemed to lift off the ground and Fetch wrapped his paws around Foof's neck, as she exclaimed, "Miss Hastings is going to make a fuss after all."

Woodcock put the bobbin and sock into his jacket pocket.

Then the four of them—Fetch being still attached to Foof like a fox stole—poured out into the hallway and found themselves moments later standing not in Miss Hastings's room, but that of her cousin, Mrs. Samuels. A man wearing a business suit lay on the bed. Facedown. And if he wasn't a corpse, he was doing a very good job of acting the part. Miss Hastings was cowering by the foot rail, whilst Mrs. Samuels stood in the middle of the room, her face as beached out as her ash-blond hair. Swaying like a tree in winter.

"Somebody get a doctor," she shouted as Mr. and Mrs. Roscombe arrived. "I think my husband's dead. I just walked in to find him like that. And I started screaming. It's such a shock. He was perfectly well this morning. But I suppose he must have felt ill, come back early, and lain down and had a heart attack."

"Yes, that must be it. Our poor, dear Leonard." Miss Hastings wept into her hands.

"You telephone for the doctor," Mrs. Roscombe told her husband, flapping him out of the room with her skirts. "And while we're waiting, how about I make a pot of tea? A cuppa will do you good, Mrs. Samuels, and you too, Miss Hastings."

"If I may be pardoned the liberty of making the suggestion." Woodock inclined his head toward Dickie. "I believe it advisable that the police also be summoned."

"Now why do you say that?" Mrs. Roscombe sounded all of a splutter.

"Because of the possibility that Mr. Samuels did not meet his death from natural causes."

"But what else could it have been?" His widow looked suitably bewildered. "I told you that it must have been his heart."

"Indeed, madam." Woodcock wore his most impassive face. "You voiced your view of the situation in a remarkably articulated manner for a woman in the full force of grief. I think we all received a clear picture of your husband returning to the premises and letting himself in through the unlocked front door. At an hour earlier than you had expected him. So that you were unaware until moments ago of his presence. But, for reasons that I would prefer not to discuss until the arrival of the police, I believe that something more sinister than a heart attack is afoot here."

"I'm sure I don't know what you can be getting at," said Mrs. Roscombe. "Poor Mrs. Samuels, as if you aren't going through enough as it is! Still, there's no choice is there? When there's talk of foul play—even if it's from someone that maybe just wants to make himself feel important." She gave Woodcock a doubtful look. "We've got to send for the police."

After hustling her husband through the door with a barrage of instructions on what to say when he got through to the station, Mrs. Roscombe went to stand alongside Mrs. Samuels. Not budging until some ten minutes later, when the door again opened and the doctor and a uniformed policeman crowded in upon them.

"Now, now! What's all this?" rumbled the constable.

"Some amateur trying to do my job for me?" The doctor cocked an irritated eyebrow.

"I am Mr. Richard Ambleforth and this is my wife, Lady Felicity." Dickie spoke out with the full force of a man who only travels in third-class train carriages by choice. "This is our butler," Dickie continued, clapping a hand on Woodcock's shoulder. "And I strongly urge you to listen to what he has to say because he is a man of vast mental resources."

"Is that so?" The doctor looked up from examining the body. "Go on, enlighten us. Explain how this man died."

"Very good, sir. It is possible I am grievously in error." Woodcock did not sound or look as though he thought this likely. "However, it is my supposition that Mr. Samuels has been stabbed. Most likely in the back."

"I don't see a carving knife sticking out of him." The constable was becoming more visibly annoyed by the second.

"Assuming I am correct in my suspicions, the murder weapon wasn't a knife. It was something much daintier. Most likely a hat pin. And it would have been removed from the body to be concealed here." Woodcock reached into his pocket and withdrew the darning bobbin.

"I don't understand." Foof clutched Fetch to her heart, which had begun to pound uncomfortably at the thought that the man Dickie most revered in the world was making an idiot of himself.

"You wouldn't, my lady," the butler spoke gently, "because you have never darned socks. But the majority of women have and, therefore, know that the handle unscrews." He proceeded to demonstrate. "It is hollow inside for the purpose of keeping the darning needles. And in this case"—looking down at the object he had shaken into his palm—"has been used as a receptacle for the weapon that was used to stab Mr. Samuels. It is either rusty, or still coated with his blood."

The widow screamed. "That's not just your darning bobbin, Ethel! The hat pin is yours, too. Why"—sagging into Mrs. Roscombe's arms—"would you take my husband's life, when we've both been so good to you?"

"Because she was in love with him," explained Woodcock at his most inexorable. "I venture to suggest that Mr. Samuels has been spending quite a few nights with her when you thought he was on the road. Her employer, Sir Isaac Gusterstone, is not often at his London residence, so they would have had the place to themselves."

"It's all true!" Miss Hastings wrung her hands.

"And then this evening Mrs. Samuels mentioned in your presence and that of my employers that her husband never left home without telling her how much she meant to him. Words which understandably would be a blow to your pride, along with your faith in Mr. Samuel's affections."

"Leonard told me his home life was wretched. And why wouldn't I believe him, Mavis, after seeing how you treated him. Always pushing him to work harder, never caring that he was already worn to the bone." Miss Hastings lifted her head even as tears continued to ooze down her cheeks. "At first he would only come to the flat for a bite to eat, that wouldn't take money out of Mavis's pocket, but little by little it all came out. His feelings for me. That they'd been there for years. Building up stronger every time we went on holiday, which was only so you could have me to lug the deck chairs down to the beach, but I'd try to see that Leonard got a little peace. And even some happiness."

"And when you found out he'd been filling your head with lies you crept up here and stabbed him." At that moment Mrs. Samuels's face was not one that most men would have loved. She looked ready to wrestle her way out of Mrs. Roscombe's arms and charge across the room at her cousin. Fetch gave a whimper, indicating he was not nearly as hardened a soul as might be believed, and burrowed his face into Foof's neck.

"I've located the puncture wound." The doctor straightened up.

"You haven't explained where you found the bobbin." The police constable scratched at his chin as he looked at Woodcock. "But it's lucky you did."

"Thank you." The butler inclined his head. "But it would have been introduced upon the scene without my participation. Am I not correct in that assumption, Mrs. Samuels?"

The room became very still.

"I don't know what you are talking about," she said at last.

"Ah, but I think you do." His voice rolled over her. "You used your cousin's hat pin to murder your husband and hid it in her darning bobbin, because not only did you want him dead, you wanted her to pay for the crime. Being a woman of enormous ego, I doubt you realized until tonight that the two of them were engaged in an affair. It was when you suddenly recognized the sock she was darning as his that you were assaulted with the truth. I imagine that you went up to your room shortly afterwards, possibly without addressing the issue with Miss Hastings, and found your husband lying facedown asleep on the bed. I had arranged for a taxi to be waiting when my employers arrived at the railway station. But we were informed by a porter that a gentleman had arrived on an earlier train from Nottingham. He told the taxi driver that he was feeling unwell and was given a lift in our place. And given the fact that Mr. Samuels had been in Nottingham today it would appear probable that he was the gentleman in question."

"He always had a headache," his widow ground out the words.

"A problem that will not afflict Mr. Samuels in future," responded Woodcock mildly. "It is even to be hoped that he died instantly after you went into your cousin's room while she was still downstairs and appropriated her hat pin, which conveniently for you was smallish in size, providing you the idea of hiding it in the bobbin."

The widow didn't have it in her to attempt a denial. "He deserved to die," she spoke in a monotone, "after all I did to make us a decent life together. And I'm glad you will have time to suffer, Ethel."

"I think I'd better go and phone the station," said the constable. "Detective Inspector Wilcox is going to be fascinated." Scratching at his chin as he looked at Woodcock. "To hear all the ins and outs of how you put all the pieces of evidence together."

"It wasn't difficult." The butler reached out to stroke Fetch between the ears. "I was fortunate, you see, in having the able assistance of someone who located the evidence and literally dropped it at our feet, isn't that so, Lady Felicity?"

"There's no other explanation, is there Dickie?"

"None at all," he said, repressing the faint smile that didn't seem quite the thing under the circumstance. And then, horror of horrors, he heard what sounded ominously like his mother's voice down in the hall. Even Woodcock paled, but Foof rose to the occasion in wifely fashion.

"Last one out the bathroom window buys the first round at the pub," she whispered, to which Fetch responded with a delighted woof before diving between the constable's legs and out the door.

Dorothy Cannell

Nottingham-born Dorothy Cannell has lived in Peoria, Illinois, for more than thirty years with her husband Julian Cannell. A teacher of English 110 at Illinois Central College encouraged the English-

woman to write for publication; seven years later she sold her first short story. In 1994, "The Family Jewels" won an Agatha mystery award for short story. Dorothy's novels blend murder most civil with a thoroughly wicked sense of humor. The Thin Woman, *her 1984 debut work featuring Ellie Haskell, has been a continual top-ten bestseller for mystery bookstores ever since. Out this year are* The Spring Cleaner *from Viking, and* Down the Garden Path *(Penguin). Dorothy's accomplishments not only include nine novels and numerous short stories, but four children, three grandsons, two dogs, and a cat.*

Sometimes a writer can't help memorializing a purrsonal moment. Prolific short story writer and mystery maven Jan Grape is in the throes of rearing kittens: a pair of black felines made for mischief and murder most feline. It seems they claim a kinship to a certain "uncle louie." (They are so wet behind the ears from Mama lickings that they have not even learned to Capitalize.) Still, they are chicklets off the old gumshoe. Seems there's a mystery in the neighborhood that needs the feline touch . . .

—M.L.

Kittens Take Detection 101

Jan Grape

SHE LIVED IN my neighborhood and looked a bit wrinkled, maybe slightly shopworn around the edges. Her dark hair was lightly streaked with gray. You couldn't tell her age but you never doubted for a minute someone might call her "Grandmother." Most people probably wouldn't look at her twice. Her grandson once said she had been born mildly retarded but I think her mental processes worked fine except for a minor slowing. Delilah Miller was her name, and I wished I'd been a better neighbor.

After my husband, Tommy, had been killed, I had leased out our house and lived in an apartment, but apartment rents in Austin kept skyrocketing so this past summer I decided I wanted back in my house. With the help of friends I renovated and redecorated until nothing remained as it had been. I had fallen in love with the house when Tommy and I had bought it all those years ago and I enjoyed living in it once again. The older neighborhood with large trees, flowers, and plush lawns reflected a settled and friendly place. And friendly it has become for me.

I had noticed my neighbor who lived on the corner almost every morning for several weeks as I power-walked around my neighborhood and always waved to her. Sometimes I stopped, especially when she offered fresh vegetables from her garden. I didn't stop often, however, because she liked to tell you about her grandson who was a master chef at some fancy hotel restaurant in Houston and it was the same story every time. She obviously forgot she'd already told you before. And it was difficult to get away once you stopped.

Recent cool rainy days, not exactly normal for autumn in central Texas but no doubt brought on by El Niño, had shortened my walks or even halted them. I didn't see Delilah during that time but didn't think much about it because of the weather. But when the rain ended and sunny fall weather came back and I still didn't see her, I wondered. She stayed on the edges of my mind, yet it was another three days before I stopped to ask.

The grandson had yelled out that he wasn't buying when I rang the doorbell. After I explained who I was and what I wanted, he peeked out, then opened the door only a little wider, but kept his foot against it as if to keep me from shoving my way past him.

"She went to visit her sister in Oklahoma City," he said. He looked as if he'd never eaten a fattening meal in his life. His skin was pasty white and his blue eyes were pale and listless. "She's even thinking of moving up there. Says she wants to be close to someone her own age."

"Probably a good idea," I said. "I was just worried she might be sick."

"I appreciate your asking," he said, then abruptly closed the front door and left me standing there, wondering if I should ring the bell again.

Maybe it was my imagination, but as I stood looking at that closed door all the short hairs on the back of my neck rose up. He was lying through his teeth, but I had no idea why I knew that.

Of course I admit to being nosy, but what gave him the right to be rude? My nosy nature stood me well in both of my life's careers.

My first career had been as a radiological technologist, a high-falutin name for a diagnostic X-ray tech. There my curiosity had centered on how the body worked and what went where. My second career, as a private investigator, was much more intriguing and being nosy was a definite plus.

I left my neighbor's porch and briskly walked home. When I got inside, Nick and Nora greeted me like I'd been gone for a week instead of the forty-five minutes it had taken to walk my four miles. "Hey, guys. Did you miss me?" They both miaowed how they thought I'd deserted them and how could I be so cruel?

When I moved from my apartment I left Sam Spade with my neighbor, Glenda Knipstein, who had found him originally. He knew and liked her and it didn't seem fair to move him from where he'd lived all his five years. Older cats don't accept change very well. Spade had fathered a litter in the spring and I couldn't imagine a home without a cat. The little ones were ready to be weaned shortly before I moved and I wound up with two kittens, one male and one female. Two would keep each other company, I thought. Little did I know two also meant double trouble. Because their father had been named Sam Spade (I'd called him Spade for short), I decided Nick and Nora would be appropriate names for the babies. They weren't any specific breed, but had the look of the chocolate Burmese.

The black balls of fur beat me to the bedroom where I stripped off my sweats and turned on the hot water in the shower. I closed the kittens out of the bathroom—they like to lick the water from my legs when I get out and their sandpaper tongues could tickle.

"does she really think we miss her?" nick said as the kittens settled down outside the door. nora put a paw underneath and pulled, hoping the door would open. nick just sat as if trying to figure out how the door worked—somehow it managed to baffle him.

"of course not, that's just the way she talks. haven't you got used to it yet?"

"well, I have better things to do with my time." he strolled to the bedroom trash basket, stood with his paws on the top edge, and looked inside. "hey, here's one of those popping things . . . oh yeah, she called it a rubber band. these are great fun to play with." he pulled the band out and began batting it around. "see, i told you i was too busy to miss mamma jenny." (the human female brought them here when they were nine weeks old and they knew she wasn't their mother, but they hadn't known anything else to call her except mamma jenny.)

nora kept thinking about how mamma jenny's face looked. "something is bothering her."

"what do you mean? she looks the same to me."

nora hopped up on the bed. "no. she's got that frown between her eyes. i've seen her look that way before and when it's there she's worried about something."

nick jumped on the bed, grabbed nora around the neck and began licking her ear. "you're always so observant. but who cares if she's worried? she is human and that's something i've noticed they do a lot."

"i care. she's a nice human companion and i want to stay here with her," nora said, pushing him away. she hopped off the bed. "besides, i want to learn to be a private investigator like her and uncle louie. if she's worried about a case maybe I can help."

"that's about the dumbest idea you've ever had." nick jumped up on the dresser and looked inside a little velvet box. he found a pair of shiny ball objects with wires on one end and some dangle gewgaws on the other. he knocked one of them to the floor.

both kittens pounced on the object and began batting and chasing it around the room. nick's favorite game was "keep away."

"why is that dumb?"

"because you're a cat."

"i know i'm a cat, brother, and that's why i'd be really good at this. i'm curious, i'm resourceful, i'm intelligent. uncle louie is an ace detective and i want to be just like him. i've read stories about his cases." midnight louie was a direct uncle on their father's side.

nick swished a doubtful tail in her direction.

"if you think cats can't read you're sadly mistaken," nora said. "uncle louie says we don't read words line by line but we absorb the whole pages by sitting on them or under them or around them. i've already learned and i'm sure you will soon too."

"you're nuts," nick said. he started chasing nora, but since he was twice her size, she was too quick for him. she ran down the hall and into the kitchen, hiding in the shadows of the dining table. in a while he gave up and sauntered back into the bedroom and hopped up on the bed, wetting his paw and washing his ear. to heck with them both, he thought. when his ears felt clean enough, he curled up in a ball and went to sleep. nora returned to the bedroom in a few minutes, saw her brother was asleep and sat down to wait for mamma jenny.

after mamma jenny got out of the shower and dressed, nora kept watching and wondering why her human mom was worried.

maybe if I get in her lap she'll talk to me and i'll find out what the problem is, she thought. nora jumped up on the dresser, walked over, and looked deep into the human's eyes. she knew sometimes she and the female person almost made a mental connection.

"Hey, little one," said Jenny. "What are you up to?" She picked up the earring Nick had sent skittering across the floor earlier. "Nick really likes shiny things, doesn't he?" She turned, dropped the earring back into its box, and put the lid on tight. She then looked around for Nick. "Oh. I see. Your brother is asleep and you want some company. Come up here and I'll pet you."

Jenny placed the kitten over her left forearm, all four of

Nora's legs dangling on either side of her arm. She headed for her favorite overstuffed chair in the family room, taking the morning newspaper along.

Minutes later the phone rang. The noise startled Nora, but Jenny kept petting the kitten as she answered. "Hello? Oh, hi, C.J." Jenny listened for a moment.

"Things are slow here. Boring. Now tell me what a great time you're having in Hawaii." She listened and giggled. "He didn't! He danced the hula to a whole song up onstage?" She laughed heartily this time. "I'd like to have seen that."

Jenny's partner, C.J., had gone to Hawaii for a Private Eye convention.

boring right now, too, thought nora, and dropped back off to sleep.

"No need for you to hurry back. Nothing exciting's happening. Stay another week if you want to.... No way. I wouldn't get mad. Nope. C.J., I'm serious. Take all the time you like. But next time I get to go and you stay home and work. Just hope it's someplace that's fun."

They exchanged more small talk and some business talk. Then Jenny said, "I'm a little distracted. My neighbor—you remember Mrs. Miller? I missed seeing her for a few days and when I stopped to ask about her this morning her grandson nearly bit my head off."

nora woke up and listened. so that's what's been on her mind! nick and i need to find a way outside and go to mrs. miller's house. i've seen a big gray-and-white cat near there. maybe he knows something. nora listened long enough to be sure she wasn't missing more important information, then went back to sleep.

That night I didn't sleep well. I kept dreaming about Delilah Miller and the dreams were not good. By morning I convinced myself to dig a bit deeper into the situation.

An old fault line known as the Balcones Fault runs along Austin's western edge. The eastern side of the city slopes into gentle rolling hills while the western side shifts into canyons and limestone bluffs. If that's not unusual enough, the Texas Colorado River (not the same one found in the Grand Canyon) meanders through the town. Most of the commercial part of downtown lies on the north bank of the river. The river has been dammed many times from the hill country on its way to the Gulf of Mexico. A chain of nine lakes formed from the dams make the Highland Lakes area famous as a recreation and living area.

We're close enough to the Gulf Coast to be subject to warm, moist tropical air sweeping north, which then collides with the cold invading Canadian air. So we're often hampered with heavy patches of fog. The fog today left misty crud on my windshield and gave all lights an almost surreal hazy ring. The gray day matched my mood as I drove the few blocks to work.

Our fourth-floor office in the LaGrange building always seems dark and empty without C.J. Besides being my partner she's also my best friend. I pushed open the door with its discreet sign reading G & G INVESTIGATIONS, closed it, and called our answering service. No messages.

I'll never be good at operating computers. I flunked mechanical ability in kindergarten and never recovered, but C.J. did teach me a few tricks. Like looking up addresses on the Internet. I remembered Delilah mentioning that her sister had never married and their maiden name was Bayliss. I found a Marilee Bayliss in Oklahoma City on Drakestone Avenue with a phone number listed.

There was no answer when I called, but an answering machine asked me to leave a message so I did. About an hour later, the telephone rang and a low alto voice asked for Jenny Gordon.

"This is she," I said.

"I'm Marilee Bayliss. My sister isn't here, whatever gave you the idea that she was?"

"The young man in her house ... a grandson, isn't he? He told me Mrs. Miller left a few days ago to visit you."

"Oh, my. Grady said that? I wonder why that boy lied? Well,

I guess that's not too unusual. He always did tell more lies than not—even when he was a teensy tyke. I haven't seen or heard from Delilah in a good week. Let me think a minute now. Okay, I went to choir practice last Tuesday night, I sing in the choir at Second Baptist, and I spoke with her just before I left here. In fact, I've been getting a little worried since I haven't been able to reach her by telephone. I called last Sunday. We nearly always talk on Sundays because the rates are cheaper." She paused a moment to breathe and continued. "I don't know what Grady's doing in her house anyway. He should be at that fancy hotel restaurant job of his, working, I would think. Unless he's taking vacation time or something. But for him to say Delilah is up here with me is an out-and-out lie."

"Do you know any place else Mrs. Miller might go, Miss Bayliss?"

She asked me to call her Marilee. "Goodness no. No place that I can think of. And now you've got *me* worried. Do you think I should report her missing to the police, Jenny?"

"Let me make some inquiries first. Maybe she got sick and had to go to the hospital."

"But surely Delilah would call. Or the hospital would. I'm listed as her next of kin for emergencies." She took another breath and her voice got higher. "Oh, my, oh, my. I'm scared something bad has happened to her. But why hasn't Grady called to tell me? Maybe I'll call and ask him what's going on. No. Maybe I'd better come down there and see to things myself."

"Miss Bayliss, uh . . . Marilee, try to be calm. I can think of several reasons for Mrs. Miller to be gone. Grady could be house-sitting for her. He probably only told me she was at your place just to get rid of a nosy neighbor." I didn't really think so, but didn't want to worry Miss Bayliss anymore than she already was. "Let me check around, Marilee. I'll call you back later today."

"What would you charge to investigate?"

"There's no charge. Mrs. Miller's a neighbor and friend. Besides, I'll only make a few phone calls."

I spent the rest of the morning calling area hospitals, including the bedroom communities of Round Rock, Georgetown,

New Braunfels, and San Marcos. I even called Scott & White, a large medical facility about an hour north of Austin where many people around the state go. To be on the safe side, I called the medical examiner's office to see if they had a Jane Doe fitting Delilah Miller's description. My final call was to the Austin Police Department's Missing Persons section. Each response was negative. By now my suspicions were increasing that this grandson of Delilah's had done something with his grandmother, and it wasn't a pleasant thought.

My late husband was a police officer before he resigned to open a private detective office and I have a few friends still at headquarters from those days. I persuaded a pal, Linda Cooper from narcotics, to pull the rap sheet on one Gradon Lee Miller aka Grady Miller.

"I'll call you back tomorrow morning," Linda said.

"I'll buy you a steak tonight at The Outback if you can have some information for me by then."

"Is seven too early?" she wanted to know.

"Perfect. See you then."

Without C.J. around I sure didn't want to stay in this lonesome office until it got dark, so I left a little after the noon hour. I stopped for cat food and a huge sack of litter before heading home.

Nick and Nora heard the garage door open and met me at the door leading to the kitchen. "Hey, guys! What's happening? Look, I got a new big sack of yummy kitten chow for you.

"And, I saved the best part till last. Ta-da." I held out the litter sack. "Fresh odor-free scoopable stuff for your box."

They both yawned and stretched and strolled over to their food dishes.

"well, la-di-dah," said nick.

"boy, are you going to be grumpy all day?" nora asked. "you're always the first one to complain. but when things are top-notch, do you ever act appreciative?"

"don't i let her pet me? don't i sleep curled up at the foot of her bed every night? okay. sorry. remember i'm in my teenage years and am prone to being moody and ill-tempered."

"that's no excuse. you must think whining or complaining is cute or something. believe me, it's not."

"okay, i said i'm sorry." nick bounded away, thinking, she's just jealous because I hid my new toy and she can't find it. usually she finds everything i hide but i have a new place she hasn't located yet and she can't stand it. he hummed little noises as he hurried into the family room and looked inside the flower pot. yep. it's still there.

nora sat quietly, pretending to eat but watching her brother the whole time. of course, he gives everything away by those little noises he makes, she thought. he nosed around the flower pot and then sauntered off nonchalantly. so that's where his new hidey-hole is. good. in a few minutes when he's forgotten all about it, i'll go get the bauble with the black strings and hide it where he'll never find it.

nick had found the little shiny toy when they were outside exploring. mamma jenny wasn't too keen on them being outside—afraid they'd get lost or run over or something. they had gone through the cat door leading out to the garage and nora once again found the box that opened the garage door, an old box, small and rather plain, but magical.

the box lay up on a shelf near the top of the garage. mamma jenny probably thought they couldn't jump up that high, but nora had found she could jump up on the big washer box and then it was only a short leap to the top shelf. when she put her foot in just the right place on the little box the garage door opened. if she waited a moment and put her foot on the same spot the door stopped again, leaving an opening just large enough for them to slink under, yet it would stay open so they could get back into the garage. of course since nick was getting so big she'd had to leave a bigger opening.

after mamma jenny left for work, and after both kittens had taken a nap, they had gone outside looking for the gray-and-white cat who lived near the corner house.

"hi," nora said when she found him snoozing under a tomato plant in the garden. "i'm nora and my brother's name is nick. we live over there." she pointed her nose toward their house. "do you live here?"

naturally he and nick had to smell each other first, then hiss a little before finally deciding their age difference was sufficient to let them be friends rather than enemies.

"no. i live next door. my name is bing clawsby."

"hi, bing. do you know that lady who lives here?"

"sure. mrs. miller. but i haven't seen her in several days." bing had a nice melodious purr and voice. "i wonder if she's on vacation or something. that man-child who's there now is mean. he keeps chasing me out of the garden but it's a wonderful place to nap. the dirt is soft and cool under these plants. mrs. miller never cared if i slept here." he walked to another plant and began scratching. "someone was digging in this dirt not long ago and it's very easy to hollow out a nice spot for napping."

"yes. i can see how nice it is," said nick. he kept walking around, found a spot that smelled quite pungent to him, and began scratching the dirt and pushing it aside. that's when he found the shiny bauble with black strings hanging from it.

"hey, don't use my sleeping places for a bathroom!" said bing. he didn't notice what nick was playing with.

"aw, come on," said nick. "i have better manners. we use a litter box indoors anyway."

"sorry, guess i'm not used to youngsters anymore. you guys still are kittens, aren't you?"

"sure are," said nora as she checked to see what nick was doing. she couldn't tell for sure but it looked as if he had something in his mouth. "mamma jenny told some friend on the telephone the other day, we won't be a year old for three more months." she saw nick pick up his treasure and turn to head home. "i guess we'll go," she told bing. "we aren't supposed to be outside and we'd better get back."

"probably a good idea," agreed bing. he obviously still wasn't too sure that nick hadn't messed up his napping spots.

nora didn't have a chance to retrieve the toy from nick's hiding place because mamma jenny came home earlier than expected.

As usual in central Texas, the sun burned off the fog and the day had shaped up quite nicely. I'd had no luck locating Mrs. Miller either as a patient or a corpse. Which was a relief in a way. Except what was I going to tell Marilee Bayliss? She'd probably want to come down and maybe that was best. Maybe Grady Miller would be obliged then to say where her sister had gone.

After a late lunch and changing clothes, I decided to move some plants to the patio to catch a few rays. Soon it would be too cold and they'd have to stay indoors for days on end. I knew I was putting off calling Marilee, but promised myself I'd telephone her when I had the plants situated.

But when I picked up the small ficus plant I saw a shiny gold-colored object half-buried in the dirt. "What's this?" I asked Nick and Nora, who pretended not to hear and didn't even look in my direction.

"Damn Sam," I mumbled. "It's a watch." Amazingly, this watch looked exactly like the watch Delilah Miller had worn. An old-fashioned one with black bands made of elastic cord.

"damn sam," echoed nora. "she found your treasure."

"i saw," said nick. "what should we do?"

"do? nothing. we'll just have to take our punishment."

"punishment? for what? we didn't do nothing."

"Okay, guys," I said. "Where did you get this watch?"

The kittens blinked innocent eyes and did nothing.

"Look, I know this watch wasn't here last night because I

checked the soil to see if it needed water." The kittens yawned and stretched and played dumb.

"Nora, what worries me is the lady who owns this watch is missing. And I'm very worried about her."

I sat down to look more closely at the watch, noticing the mud caked around the watch-stem. "Well, maybe it was in the flower pot all night," I told Nora. "It must have been there when I watered it this morning and that's how it got muddy. Also I can't imagine how you got Mrs. Miller's watch or even how you got out of the house."

Nora jumped into my lap and looked me square in the eyes. I'd swear that she could talk if she could only figure the proper sequence, but I didn't know exactly what she might say.

As I petted Nora, Nick strolled into the kitchen to his food bowl. I could hear him munching, and the little noises he made sounded as if he wanted to talk to me, too.

The telephone rang and startled both kittens, who ran like greased lightning to the bedroom. "Is this Jenny Gordon?" a familiar female voice asked.

"Yes. Marilee?"

"Yes. I'm at the Austin airport—would it be too inconvenient if you came after me?"

This wasn't a total surprise. Marilee had been quite worried about her sister and the natural thing was to come to Austin and see about things herself. "Of course not. I'll be right out."

when mamma jenny had gone, nora said, "we need to go back over to the house on the corner."

"nora, i'm not sure i want to. we got into trouble by going over there earlier and . . ."

"nick, i'm going whether you go or not. if you want to be a chicken, that's fine with me. but i just know uncle louie wouldn't sit and bat toys around. he'd get out there and make things happen." she headed out the kitty door and jumped up to push on the little magic box that made the garage door open.

"what can we do?" nick followed, just as she knew he would.

"i haven't the foggiest, but we have to try something."

when they got back to mrs. miller's house, friendly mr. bing clawsby was nowhere to be seen.

"bing must have gone back home," nora said.

"smart guy. won't catch him out nosing around trying to be a detective. trying out some human occupation. cats are supposed to spend their time sunning, sleeping, eating, playing . . ."

nora headed back to the garden and the tomato plant where nick had found the watch. "i told you if you wanted to stay home that was fine with me. you didn't have to come along." she began raking the dirt.

"why should you have all the fun? and, besides, i should be here to protect you if you get into trouble," nick said.

"you protect me? what a laugh." nora dug up an earring made of little white beads and dangle wires. "here's another treasure." she picked it up to show it to him.

"What are you animals doing?" The loud male voice startled the kittens.

Nora turned and streaked by the man, but Nick was slower and the man caught him. "Flipping cats. I don't want you digging in my garden." Grady followed after Nora, but she was much too quick. She scampered around the corner of her house and slithered under the garage door.

Grady took Nick and locked him in the tool shed.

nora was so scared she ran and hid under the bed. she entirely forgot she hadn't closed the garage door. she didn't even realize she still had the beaded bauble in her mouth. in fact, when she finally could think again her only worry was what the giant would do to her brother. oh boy, are we in big trouble. mamma jenny, please come home!

When I pulled into the driveway I noticed the garage door was not closed all the way. "That's strange."

Marilee said, "What?"

"My garage door is partially open. I'm sure I closed it when I left." The kittens were such scaredy-cats that I never worried they might dash out when the door opened. I pushed on the remote button and the door rose up slowly. "Well, it wasn't open enough for a person to get inside." I pulled the car inside, put the door down, and went into the house.

Marilee had been one surprise after another when I met her at the airport. Younger and prettier than Delilah, she had a nice sense of humor. She was slender with dark eyes, but her hair had been streaked or frosted or whatever women called it these days. When I asked her why she'd never married she said, "I saw what a hard life Delilah had—waiting on Ray hand and foot. I didn't want to be a slave for anyone."

"Can't blame you for that one."

"After Ray died Delilah still had to worry about Grady. His parents being killed in that car wreck when he was three was tragic."

"That is sad." I could relate. I'd lost my mother to cancer when I was twelve. My grandmother had helped my father raise me. I knew what it was like to lose a parent and to rely on an older person. My grandmother indulged me, and I had a feeling Delilah had done the same for Grady.

Marilee told me that she had telephoned her sister's house and that Grady had answered. "He sounded so strange and swore he didn't know where his grandmother might be. Said he hadn't seen her since last Thursday right after he arrived there."

Weird, I thought.

"That's why I thought I should come to Austin."

On the drive to my house we decided to proceed with caution. Marilee would come to my house instead of going to Delilah's. I persuaded her my guest room would be better than staying in a motel.

"Wonder where the kittens are?" I looked around inside, then went out to the garage and didn't find them out there either.

"They nearly always come to meet me," I said. I got my flashlight and headed for the bedroom. Sometimes they get scared and hide under the bed.

Sure enough, when I flashed the light under the bed, one pair of golden eyes flashed back green. "Nora, is that you?" The kitten made a small sound—not a meow—not even exactly cat-like. "Where's Nick?"

Nora acted like she wasn't interested in coming out, but I went to the back side of the bed, caught her front leg and tugged. She came out and I could feel her quivering.

"What's wrong, little one?" I looked her over carefully and could find no injury. Then I noticed something in her mouth and took it from her.

"A pearl earring. It's got mud caked in the little crevices too."

"It belongs to Delilah!" said Marilee. "She wore them almost all the time. Her husband, Ray, gave them to her on their twenty-fifth anniversary. They aren't real pearls, but she was so proud of them."

"There's no way this could have been in the flower pot like the watch. How did Nora get it, I wonder?" I kept petting her until she acted calmer. "And what's happened to Nick?" I searched the house more thoroughly, but I couldn't find him.

"I think it's time I made a phone call to a friend of mine at APD. The Austin Police Department," I explained to Marilee. "Lieutenant Larry Hayes, who previously worked with my late husband, is now in homicide."

That statement startled Marilee Bayliss, but she composed herself as best she could.

Larry wasn't at the office, but I reached him at home. He and my husband were partners for ten years. Since Tommy's murder, Larry likes to look out for me, much like a big brother. It works fine except when he thinks I'm out of line. Today he merely thought I might be losing it completely.

"I know it's a thin stretch, Larry, but I feel it in my gut."

"Okay, say I go along with you. We have no reason to search the house or grounds. No judge would give me a search warrant on gut feelings."

"I know you're right, but what if Marilee just knocks on the door, suitcase in hand, and demands to stay there in her sister's house? Maybe she can say that if Delilah has gone off, she would want her to take care of things." I could see Marilee nodding.

"Maybe that would work," Larry agreed.

"And, beside that, I'm searching for my cat. No reason I can't go in the backyard while Marilee's at the front door."

When I hung up Marilee said, "I think I have a back-door key to Delilah's house." She rummaged through her purse and came up with the key. "We traded keys years ago in case we ever needed to go inside each other's house."

"Okay, then we'll just go over and you can demand to be let in. If he refuses you can use your key."

Marilee went to my guest room to get her suitcase.

I sat down, still holding Nora, and spoke softly to her, stroking her and reassuring her that everything would be fine and that we'd find Nick. "Okay, sweetie. Maybe you can help me. Since you can't talk my language and I can't talk yours, maybe you can show me what happened."

Nora looked deep into my eyes before hopping down and heading into the garage. She jumped up on the washer and then up to the top shelf. In a moment the garage door opened—but only a small amount.

"How did you . . .?" I reached up and found a second remote control. "Oh, I see. That explains it. Okay. You both probably went outside and then you must have gone to Delilah Miller's house, right?"

I put the kitten down. She looked around as if to say "follow me" and took off, scampering down the street till she reached the corner house, then high-tailed it to the backyard.

Marilee followed me and we followed Nora.

Grady Miller was in the backyard, digging a hole at one end of the garden.

"Flipping cats," he was muttering. "I'll fix you. I'll move her where you'll never find her. Why can't you just leave well enough alone? All that scratching around here—digging her up. Smart-alecky flipping cats."

"Grady?" Marilee asked. "What on earth are you doing?"

"Aunt Mari, did you know grandmother is buried out here? I don't understand why those black cats just won't leave her grave alone. She was perfectly fine out here in the garden."

The strange look in his eyes told us more than we wanted to know. Grady Miller had gone mad. Something had snapped inside him and there was no one at home inside his head anymore.

Marilee stood rooted as if growing in the garden. She began to cry. The next few hours would be a sad ordeal for her.

Larry walked up from the front yard just in time to see Grady hand Marilee Bayliss the shovel he'd been using. Larry led the passive young man to his unmarked car out front and helped him into the backseat.

I didn't see any more because I'd just noticed Nora by the door to the shed. I couldn't hear Nick but I felt sure he was inside. Grady had probably killed my kitten with that shovel. And if he had I didn't know what I'd do to him—crazy man or not.

The door was locked, but Grady gave Larry the key when he asked for it.

I was so scared my hands were shaking and I had trouble opening the door. Finally I got the door open and immediately saw Nick lying on his side. His eyes were closed. Nora had rushed in with me. She began washing Nick's face. In another moment he opened his eyes and meowed pitifully.

"took you long enough to get here," nick told nora as he stood up. he was a bit wobbly but couldn't understand why.

"it's not easy getting humans to do what you want," she told him as mamma jenny picked him up. "and I had to have her help. it would have taken me forever to figure out how to get inside that shed."

Marilee was still crying, but I persuaded her to carry Nora while I carried Nick home.

Larry called the necessary medical personnel and police crime scene unit, then left to take Grady to Seton Hospital for an evaluation.

I found a lump on Nick's head where Grady had konked him. After calling my vet, he said the kitten probably had a concussion. "If there are no cuts or abrasions, just watch him for a few hours. If he shows any sign of stress call me and I'll meet you at my office."

Larry called later and filled me in on what he knew to this point. And I did my best to explain things to Marilee. "Of course the investigation is still going on, but Larry says Grady admits poisoning Delilah with some mushrooms. He got angry because she wouldn't give him the money to open his own restaurant. He said he only wanted what was due him. What he would inherit anyway."

"He was such a strange little boy I guess I'm not really surprised," Marilee said. "After his parents were killed in that car accident and my sister took over the responsibility for him he began acting even stranger."

"I guess when Delilah wouldn't give him any money he just snapped."

"There wasn't any money to give. Every penny she had went toward raising him."

"Wasn't there any money from his parents' deaths?"

"No. They didn't have any insurance and were heavily in debt. Delilah and her husband, Ray, paid off those debts. When Ray died, the little insurance money he had was what she used to put Grady through school."

"That's really sad, then. He killed her for nothing."

"I wonder if he went crazy and killed her or if killing her sent him off the deep end?"

"Guess we'll never know." I looked around for my kittens. "I'm just glad these little guys are okay. But I'm going to have to make sure they don't get outside again. It's too dangerous out there."

later that evening, nick and nora were curled up beside mamma jenny on the sofa. "did we do good, sister?" nick asked.

"we did just fine. but we'll need to talk to uncle louie.

learn his tricks for picking locks and whatnot and how he convinced his human to let him roam outside." nora cleaned her brother's face once again. "hmm," she said. "wonder if there's a junior PI badge or something we can get?"

I looked at my kittens, "You guys did such a great job I'll have to declare you officially cat detectives and put you on the payroll. Wonder how much shrimp and fish to pay you each week?"

"what's a shrimp and fish?" asked nora.
    "who knows?" said nick. "but i'm quite sure you'll find out."

Jan Grape

When Jan's not taking care of Nick and Nora (their real names), who turned one last spring, she's working on a short story [sixteen published including the Anthony- and Shamus-nominated story "A Front Row Seat" in Vengeance Is Hers (Signet, 1997) and four due out in 1998.] or promoting Deadly Women, the Edgar-nominated nonfiction book about women mystery writers she coedited with Dean James and the late Ellen Nehr. Jan also writes for Mystery Scene, writes the Private Eye Writers' newsletter, "Reflections in a Private Eye," and occasionally helps her husband, Elmer, with their bookstore, Mysteries and More in Austin, Texas. Nick and Nora made sure their story was told correctly by spending time on Jan's lap as she typed, especially Nora, who even supervised the final printout by sitting next to the printer.

Mr. Bill Crider will try just about anything in the fiction world, and has gone pretty far with his cat characters, for which he was rewarded with an Anthony Award nomination. So I guess he is a pretty cool cat, even when he has chosen to write about a dog. Or is it a dog? The critter in this story is a film star, that is for sure, and Mr. Bill Crider's affection for those thrilling days of yesteryear when real men acted opposite dogs and horses instead of the opposite sex is evident. 'Course, that could sometimes make for a passel of trouble, pardner. (And why were we cats never considered suitable mascots in cowboy movies? We get along very well with horses. Maybe we were just too much competition for the hero.)

—M.L.

El Lobo Rides Alone
Bill Crider

ONE OF THE first things they tell you in Hollywood is to never work with kids or animals. That's fine advice if you can afford to take it, which I can't. Lately I've found myself dealing with a parrot, a cockatoo, some cats, and, God help me, even the Easter Bunny. So far, however, things have turned out okay.

Even at that, I wasn't so sure I wanted to tangle with a wolf.

"Goddamn it, Ferrel," Mr. Gober said. He has a voice like a camel with a cold, and the telephone receiver vibrated in my hand. "How many times do I have to tell you. It's not really a wolf. It's a dog that's playing the part of a wolf. The dog's name is Drifter."

Mr. Gober is the head of Gober Studios, not one of the majors exactly, but in the years right after the war he was doing just fine financially and otherwise.

Now and then, however, there would be a little bump in the road, something that might affect the flow of money into his bank account. Like the time Brett Morris (real name: Willy Benarski), star of a number of tough-guy detective flicks (*Kiss Me and Die* being the most recent), was photographed wearing a flimsy nightie and a feather boa, not to mention the lipstick and earrings. When something like that happens, I'm the guy Gober calls to get the photos and negatives back and to get the studio off the hook.

Gober pays me pretty well for my work, so I don't complain that he never seems to get my first name right. It's Bill, not Goddamn it.

"It looks like a wolf to me," I said.

"That's what everyone says, but it's just makeup and acting. How many dogs do you think could play a wolf so well that you believe it? Drifter deserves an Oscar if anyone ever did. This damned town can really break your heart."

I started to mention that only people who had hearts could get them broken, but Mr. Gober isn't noted for his sense of humor.

"Okay," I said. "So it's a dog. And you say that someone's trying to kill it?"

"I said that someone's trying to *poison* it. And I want you to find out who it is."

"Why not call the cops?" I asked.

It wasn't that I didn't need the money. I just wasn't sure that I wanted to have anything to do with the wolf, even if it was a dog.

"You know better than that," Gober yelled. Well, he didn't actually yell. It just sounded that way. "This has to be kept quiet. No publicity, no cops. The crew's out there at the Stilson Ranch making the movie, so whoever's trying to poison the wolf is one of ours."

"I thought you said it was a dog."

"That's what I meant. Now get out there and take care of things."

I sighed and hung up the phone. I had a long drive ahead of me.

Santiago Canyon, where the Stilson Ranch was located, was only about forty miles from my office as the crow flies. Unfortunately I wasn't traveling by crow. I was driving my 1940 Chevy, which wasn't exactly built for speed. That was fine. Some of the roads I had to take at the end of the trip weren't built for speed, either.

As I drove, I thought about the wolf (or the dog) and what it meant to Gober Studios. It all had to do with a series of Westerns that had started out as low-budget fillers for the bottom half of double features. The first one had been called *El Lobo Rides!* and it had generated a lot of fan mail both for its star, William Berry, and for the wolf. Or the dog, whose name in the picture wasn't El Lobo at all. It was Fiero, which was supposed to mean something like the "wild one." I don't know much Spanish, so I have no idea if the translation is accurate.

The title role was Berry's. He played Don Jaime Cortez, the foppish young landowner who at night (under cover of darkness) became El Lobo, the fierce defender of the downtrodden residents of Old California. El Lobo rode a black horse, wore a black outfit and black mask, and carried a black bullwhip. His sword was silver, but it had a black handle.

He was accompanied on all his missions by his trusted critter companion, Fiero, who ran along beside him and, when El Lobo was occupied with dealing out rough justice with his whip and sword, was likely to give the bad guys a quick nip in the backside or chomp on their ankles.

If any of that sounds familiar, don't let it bother you. Gober's lawyers were on the ball, and there were no copyright infringements, or at least none that anybody was going to take to court. Zorro doesn't have a wolf. Or a dog.

El Lobo Rides! not only did a nice job of filling out its double bill but became so popular that it flipped over and became the number one feature at a lot of houses in the Southwest.

Gober was nobody's fool, and he knew he had something, so the second feature got the top of the bill. It was called—you guessed it—*El Lobo Rides Again!* Say what you will, the guys who come up with titles for Gober's pictures are geniuses.

But, be that as it may, *El Lobo Rides Again!* pulled them into theaters all over the country, and the third flick in the series, *Revenge of El Lobo!,* was released as a stand-alone feature. It did twice the business of the other two put together, and Gober was feeling finer than frog hair.

William Berry found himself number ten in the list of top box-office attractions, and Fiero, the wolf (or the dog) was everyone's favorite canine. Little kids all over the country were nailing pieces of rope to sticks to make El Lobo whips and then chasing their younger brothers and sisters all over the house. Half the puppies in the United States were being named Fiero, and the other half were being named Drifter. Gober Studios was riding high.

And that's when Mr. Gober got the idea of making the next El Lobo Western, *Son of El Lobo,* a big-budget picture, in full color, no less. He hired Donnie Powell, the hottest kid actor in town for the role of the orphan boy, Raul, who discovers El Lobo's secret identity and who is then adopted by Don Jaime. And who gets kidnapped by the evil Alcalde, who suspects El Lobo's true identity.

Naturally it would be a tragedy if Drifter were poisoned. It wasn't that he couldn't be replaced, though maybe the quality of the acting would suffer. But it would set the picture behind schedule, and Drifter's recent illnesses had already caused more delays than Gober liked.

Training a new dog to play the wolf would take even longer, and you never knew how well the new "wolf" would work with the human stars. If he didn't like them, things could really get sticky.

A gleaming black postwar Buick Roadmaster passed me just before I turned off to head for the ranch. I wondered if I'd ever be able to afford a car like that. Not at the wages Gober was paying me, that was for sure, but the little Chevy was running fine. It could go a few more years.

I drove to the location on a rutted, dusty road and pulled over to where the other cars and trucks and trailers were parked just outside a small western town, the same town that appeared in all Gober's Westerns, and those of a couple of other studios. They just changed the signs on the false fronts for each new picture. Sometimes they didn't even bother to change the signs, but as far as I knew, no member of the paying public had ever complained.

When I got out of my car, Harry Gallun rushed up to meet me. Harry was the producer, and we knew each other from a couple of jobs I'd done for Gober in the past. Gallun's last name rhymed with "saloon," but not many people knew it. They thought it was pronounced like a form of liquid measure. Gallun never corrected them.

"You're just in time, Ferrel," he said. "It's happened again."

Gober must have warned him that I was on the way. Gallun was a nervous little guy with a bad toupee and a worse mustache, one of those thin little jobs that looks a lot like it's been drawn on with an eyebrow pencil. And maybe it had.

"What's happened?" I asked him.

"Drifter's sick. It's really bad. I think maybe he's a goner."

Harry looked and sounded distraught, but I couldn't really tell anything from that. Producers are that way a lot, even when things are going pretty well.

It was hot, it was dusty, and I was already beginning to sweat. I took off my fedora and combed the top of my head with my handkerchief. The truth is, there wasn't much there to comb, but at least I wasn't wearing a bad toupee.

I stuck my hankie back in my pocket and said, "Let's go see the wolf."

"Drifter's not a wolf," Harry reminded me. "He's a dog."

"Right. I keep forgetting that."

I could tell Drifter was a star: he had his own trailer. He was lying stretched out on the floor, panting and looking a lot like a wolf, although a very sick wolf. He was nearly six feet from nose to tail, and mostly grayish black. I figured there was a lot of German shepherd in him, but there was a mixture of something else, and some of his shaggy hair didn't belong to him. I wasn't good at guessing weight, but I figured him for over a hundred pounds. He was a big dog. Or wolf.

There was an unpleasant smell in the trailer's air, and being a skilled detective, I deduced that it was coming from Drifter, or from the nasty-looking liquid that was dripping from his jaws.

There were several people standing over the big dog. One was William Berry, who looked about as much like a Spanish Don as Monte Hale or Johnny Mack Brown or any of a dozen other B-Western stars did, but he was smooth and handsome, and he was making the most of his big chance. He'd spent years playing second bad guy to Roy Barcroft before working his way up to better roles and finally getting a break in *El Lobo Rides!*

Another onlooker was Terence James, the director, known mainly for his efficiency. William "One-Shot" Beaudine worked faster than James, but not a whole lot faster.

Donnie Powell was there too, standing beside a knockout blonde I didn't recognize.

And of course Ray Olan was there. He was Drifter's trainer, and he was kneeling beside the dog, stroking his neck and wiping his mouth with a damp cloth.

Olan was the one who asked who I was and what the hell I was doing there.

"He's a private dick that Mr. Gober uses now and then," Harry said. "He's here to find out what's going on."

I wasn't overly fond of being called a dick, but I'd been called worse. So I didn't say anything.

"He'd damn well better find out quick, then," Olan said. "I'm pulling Drifter off the set if nothing's done by tomorrow. That's if he lives through this."

Olan was short, with bristly red hair and freckles that covered about half his face. I don't think he liked me much, even though we'd just been introduced. I didn't mind. I have that effect on a lot of people.

But not on the blonde, who introduced herself to me as Evelyn Powell, Donnie's mother. She was short, not much taller than Donnie, and almost painfully thin but with curves in all the right places. She didn't look old enough to be the mother of a twelve-year-old.

When I told her that, she smiled and gave me a look that fried my toenails. Olan glared at me even harder, but the blonde didn't notice him. Or if she did, she didn't seem to.

She looked in my eyes and said, "Donnie's only eleven and a half. He plays older."

Donnie looked fifteen, if you asked me, and I would have bet you twenty bucks that he was sneaking smokes behind the trailers, but I was willing to believe anything those eyes told me. And Donnie was polite, certainly. I have to give him that. He shook hands like a grown-up and called me "Mr. Ferrel."

Terence James didn't. "What do you think, Ferrel?" he asked.

"I just got here. I haven't had time to think a lot. Have you called in a vet?"

"We did that two days ago," Olan said. "He couldn't tell us anything. He just said these spells might have been caused by something Drifter ate."

"So who feeds him?"

"I do," Olan said. "And there's no way I'd feed my own dog poison. He's my meal ticket."

It's always touching to talk to someone who really loves animals. Maybe not everyone would feel that way, but I'm just a sentimental kind of guy. I looked down at Drifter, who was still panting but who didn't look in any real danger of dying now that he'd stopped vomiting.

"Has there been any other trouble on the set?" I asked.

"Hell, no," Terence James said. "I run a tight ship. But we're already two days behind schedule. You either help us out of this, or I'm getting a new wolf."

"He's not a wolf!" Olan said.

"I don't give a damn if he's a pedigreed polar bear," James said. "I'm going to bring this picture in on schedule. Just keep that in mind. The animal—whatever he is—had better be ready this afternoon."

We all watched as he stalked out of the trailer. I said, "Is the dog going to die, or not?"

Olan looked up at me and said, "I can't tell for sure. He's been like this twice before. He got all right both times, but we've got to find out what's making him sick. That's your job, right?"

It was, but I wasn't going to be able to do it standing there. I told Gallun that I wanted to talk to him outside, and we stepped out into the sun. I could see the little town in the distance, with its saloon and livery stable and water troughs. Even though I knew it was mostly a fake, it looked as real and solid as the cars that were parked nearby.

I'd always wanted to sit around an Old West saloon, so I asked Gallun if we could talk in private there.

"I don't see why not," he said. "I think Terence is going to shoot a couple of scenes at the Alcalde's house this afternoon, so we won't be in the way."

We walked down the dusty street, and I could smell the horses tied to the hitch rails, not to mention the soft little piles of dung the horses had dropped in the dust. I could hear the flies buzzing around the dung and around the horses, too. They'd crawl on the dung and then crawl on the horses. It was no picnic, being a horse.

Gallun and I stepped around the dung and up onto the wooden sidewalk that fronted the saloon. We pushed through the batwing doors just like William S. Hart. The inside of the saloon looked the way it does in the movies: a lot of round tables scattered over the floor, the long bar to the left, the stairway leading up to the second floor, the cheap chandelier, the door in the back that leads to the office of the crooked saloon owner.

There was no one around but us. I took off my hat and laid it on one of the tables, then removed my jacket and hung it on a chair back. Gallun and I sat down, and I tilted my chair back on two legs, feeling a little like Bob Steele.

"So the vet didn't have any idea what was wrong with Drifter?" I said.

Gallun shook his head. "No. He said it wasn't some disease, though, or at least no disease he'd ever seen."

"Which leads us to the idea of poison."

"That's right. What else could it be?"

I didn't have the answer to that one. Whatever it was, that wolf was sicker than a dog. Or vice-versa.

"And you haven't had any other trouble on the set?"

Gallun looked around as if someone might be spying on us, which was when I knew that Terence James hadn't been exactly truthful with me. But then who ever expects directors to be truthful?

"Some of us did have a little trouble," Gallun said when he was satisfied that no one was around.

"What kind?" I asked.

"The kind Drifter's having."

"You were poisoned?"

"That's right."

Gober hadn't mentioned that little point, but then no one expects studio heads to be even as truthful as directors.

"Tell me about it," I said.

"Well, it wasn't exactly the same," Gallun said. "We know who did it. It was the caterer."

"The caterer tried to poison you?"

"I don't think he did it on purpose. You know, on some sets you get pretty good food. It's not always that way on one of Mr. Gober's movies. At least not on one like this."

He didn't have to say that Gober was widely known as a tightwad. Gober's idea of a big spread for the crew was sandwiches with peanut butter and jelly—the kind that came in glasses you could wash out and use when the jelly was gone. On a big budget shoot, with big stars, he might do better, but he wasn't ready to take a chance on *Son of El Lobo,* which wasn't a proven property, though it seemed pretty much of a sure thing, given the way the other features had performed.

I said, "So you were poisoned by peanut butter?"

"No. Not peanut butter. It was tuna fish. Or maybe chicken salad. I can never tell the difference."

I could, but that was because I didn't like either one of them. I asked Gallun what had happened.

"The sandwiches were delivered while Terence was shooting a scene, and the caterer just left them out on a table. They got a little ripe."

In this heat, I could believe it. "But you ate them anyway?"

Gallun smiled sheepishly. "We were hungry, and we didn't think about the possibility of food poisoning."

"But nobody died. Nobody got carried to the hospital."

"No. We're prepared for emergencies. We have a medical man."

"A doctor?"

"Not exactly. We have a gaffer who went to med school for a year or two. He knows what he's doing."

"I guess I'd better talk to him," I said.

Herb Ward was the gaffer. He was tall and skinny, with hair that was too long and he had dirt under his fingernails. He didn't look like he'd been to grade school, much less med school. But looks can fool you, especially in Hollywood.

Gallun brought him to the saloon, and we sat at the table. I thought it would be great if we could have a beer, but there wasn't any. They don't use real beer in those mugs you see up there on the screen. I'm not sure what it is, and I don't want to find out. I'm afraid it might have something to do with the horses.

Ward was happy to talk about the food poisoning.

"I saved their asses," he told me. "I should get a bonus."

We both had a laugh about that. Gober gave up bonuses like Bob Feller gave up bases on balls.

"So how did you save them?" I asked when we were through with the jollity.

"Emetic," he said. "Syrup of ipecac."

I knew about ipecac. It was a damned dangerous plant derivative and if you didn't take it in the diluted syrup form, you were as good as dead. But when you needed to get something out of your stomach, fast, it was just the right thing.

"I thought gauging the proper dose for something like that was pretty tricky," I said.

Ward shrugged. "I have some experience. Dosage is based on weight. It worked just fine."

"I wonder if it would work on a dog."

"I wouldn't know," Ward said. "I went to med school, not vet school. But you'd better not give the dog much." He thought that over, and then said, "Are you accusing me of something?"

"I don't know. Maybe. Where do you keep the ipecac?" He started to tell me but I interrupted him. "Show me. It'll be better that way."

We had to go outside, so I put my hat and jacket back on. It was even hotter than it had been earlier, but I'm a professional tough guy. I could take the heat.

As we walked through the dust, Ward said, "I don't have any reason to poison that dog. You know that, don't you?"

"I guess I do. And while we're on the subject, who do you think might have a motive?"

"You should know the answer to that one. You're the detective."

He had a point. And I had a suspect. But I wasn't going to tell Ward that.

He took me to a little trailer that wasn't exactly clean and showed me an old Crosley refrigerator. It had been white once, but it was a sort of dingy yellow now, with rust spots on it here and there. Someone had attached an iron band around it so that it could be padlocked right under the handle.

"Before you ask, yes, I'm the only one who has a key," he said, unfastening the lock.

He opened the door and showed me the ipecac. "There it is. But hell, you can buy the stuff at any drugstore. You don't even need a prescription."

"You have to sign for it, though."

"Yeah. But there are a lot of drugstores in Southern California."

"No doubt about that," I said.

I didn't really think Ward had anything to do with Drifter's mysterious illness. He had nothing to gain from it. I'd just wanted to check and make sure the medicine was where it was supposed to be.

It was, and it didn't seem to me that anyone would have easy access to it. So someone had a private supply. And it didn't have to be ipecac. It could be something else. It could even be something worse.

The logical suspect was William Berry. Rumors had been going around ever since the first feature that he thought the dog (or the wolf) was getting too much screen time. And most weeks the dog's fan mail outweighed Berry's. Berry knew that the El Lobo role was most likely his only shot at becoming a big-name star, and he most likely didn't want a dog to screw it up for him.

And then there was the not-so-well-known fact that Berry just didn't like animals in general. If you've seen him on the screen, you might think that he's a wonderful horseman, galloping across the plains while the "Song of El Lobo" plays in the background.

But that's not Berry doing the galloping. That's his stunt double. It helps to be playing a role that requires a mask. For the close-ups, Berry straddles a barrel with a saddle on it. The barrel's hung between a couple of poles by a rope, and some stagehands bounce Berry around to give the appearance that he's riding. You might have noticed that you never actually see his face and the horse at the same time.

So all I had to do was figure out how Berry got an emetic or some kind of poison into the dog's food. If Olan did the feeding, then Olan controlled the food supply. It was time to talk to him about that.

I went back to Drifter's trailer. The dog (or wolf) was sitting up now, looking around and seeming to feel a lot better than the last time I saw him. He growled when I walked into the trailer, and Olan, who was sitting nearby, laughed.

"I don't think Drifter likes you," he said.

It was clear that Olan didn't like me either, and he liked me less after I asked my first question: "Where do you keep Drifter's food?"

"Where nobody can get at it except me," he said. "No one gets near it, and I don't trust you any more than I trust the other people on this location. I'm not going to tell you where the food is."

"Sure you are. Think about it."

He thought about it, and I could tell by the look on his face that it wasn't easy for him. Either that, or he was having severe gastric distress.

Finally he said, "You'd squeal to Gober, wouldn't you?"

"All part of the job. So, where do you keep the food?"

He led me to the back of the trailer, where he had a refrigerator a lot like the one Wade had showed me earlier, except that it wasn't rigged with a lock.

"Not exactly Fort Knox," I said.

He looked offended. "Nobody knows it's here. It's as good as a safe."

I didn't think so. "Open it up."

He did. There were a lot of packages wrapped in white butcher paper and secured with white paper tape.

"Ground round," Olan said. "Nothing but the best for Drifter."

"And nobody knows this is here?"

"That's what I said."

He had to be wrong. Anybody with more than five active brain cells could have found the food supply in about a minute and a half.

"Okay," I said. "That's all I wanted to know. I'll see you on the set."

"Not if I see you first," he said.

What a wit. Next thing I knew he'd be taking over for Milton Berle.

I hung around the set the rest of the afternoon and got to watch Terence James shoot one scene, which involved Raul, El Lobo, and the Alcalde, who was played by Donald Sandstrom, a first-rate villain in a couple of swashbucklers I'd seen a few years before the war. He'd lost a little hair since then, but so had I. He was still good at being slimy.

The scene also involved Drifter, and that was what worried James.

"Can he do it?" he asked Olan.

Olan was standing off to one side, away from cameras and cables and crew members. Drifter (or Fiero) was sitting beside him, still looking more than a little bedraggled. Evelyn Powell was standing nearby. She didn't look bedraggled in the least.

"He can do it," Olan said.

I doubted he could do it, whatever it was, and I could tell that James had similar doubts, but he called for everyone to take their places. When things were arranged to suit him, he called out "Lock 'em and roll 'em."

I heard the clapper, and then James said, "Action!"

It was a nice scene, I had to admit. The Alcalde had Raul in a headlock, with a pistol pressed to his temple.

"If you take a single step," the Alcalde said, "I will kill the boy."

The Alcalde seemed to have the upper hand, all right. El Lobo stood frozen, his whip drooping. He could see that he had no chance of using it to snatch the pistol from the Alcalde's hand without the Alcalde getting off a shot.

Sandstrom, playing the evil Alcalde to the hilt, gave a sinister laugh, one of the things that he did about as well as anyone in Hollywood.

"And now, señor," he said, "I will ask you to remove your mask!"

El Lobo sighed and started to comply, but what the Alcalde didn't know was that Fiero was creeping up behind him.

As Berry raised his hand to his mask, he yelled, "Now, Fiero!"

The dog (or wolf) made a good try. He came up off his

haunches and went for the Alcalde's gun hand. He was probably supposed to grab the gun in his mouth, but he missed by about a foot or so, bounced off Sandstrom's thigh, and fell heavily back to the ground.

The Alcalde's pistol went off, Donnie Powell screamed, and Terence James yelled, "Cut! Cut!"

Donnie was running around the set with his hand pressed to his ears. His mother chased him, but she couldn't catch him. He screamed that he was deaf, which I doubted, and he took off toward the trailers.

Olan was kneeling down by Drifter, who looked as if he couldn't quite figure out what was going on.

William Berry walked over to Sandstrom and started talking about the scene.

"I don't see how you could miss at such close range," he said.

"I wasn't shooting at the kid," Sandstrom said. "You know that. When the dog hit me, the gun went off."

Berry nodded. "Yeah, that's what I figured. But the way that kid's been complaining, I'd just as soon guess you'd shot him."

"You know the pistol wasn't really loaded," Sandstrom said. "Just a blank."

Berry shrugged. "Too bad."

I wanted to listen to more of their conversation, but Terence James was yelling at Olan.

"I want that dog off my set!" he said. "I'll get another one to-morrow!"

It wasn't going to be that easy, as I'm sure James knew. There just weren't many dogs around that looked enough like a wolf, no matter how much fake fur was used. Besides, I was pretty sure they'd already shot some scenes with Drifter. They'd have to find his twin if they wanted another dog.

Olan pointed all that out to James, who wasn't mollified, but it was getting late, so the director gave up. Temporarily.

"If the son of a bitch isn't ready tomorrow," he said, "he's gone. I mean it."

I was the only one who laughed at the "son of a bitch" remark. I guess I'm the only one who thought maybe James meant it literally.

Olan led Drifter off the set without saying anything. He was probably saving all his snappy comebacks for me. I followed him. There was one more question I wanted to ask him.

"Hey, Olan," I said. "Wait up."

He turned, not looking especially eager for my company.

"If you don't find out who's poisoning my dog," he said, "I'm going to be out of work. And so is the dog. I don't think Mr. Gober is going to be happy about that."

He was right, but it didn't make him any more pleasant to deal with.

"When you feed the dog, do you always watch him eat?" I asked.

"Of course I do. You think I'm stupid?"

I didn't think it would be a good idea to answer that, so I just told him thanks and went on my way.

That evening I went into Corona to have dinner. It was no coincidence that I happened to wind up in the same little restaurant where Olan, Evelyn and Donnie Powell, William Berry, and Donald Sandstrom were eating.

Evelyn asked me to join them, which I did, even though Olan was scowling like a wolf. Or a dog. Sandstrom and Berry didn't seem to mind, however, and Donnie was polite, as usual, though he whined about his ears a lot. We all had Mexican food, and everyone but Donnie had a bottle of beer.

After we were finished, Evelyn Powell excused herself, and I asked Olan who was looking after Drifter.

"He's fine. He's in the trailer. It's all locked up, and I'll be back there in an hour or less. James has someone standing guard too, so there's no danger."

Not unless someone had already taken care of the food supply. I suggested that Olan lay in a fresh bunch of ground round.

"Hey, that stuff costs money, and Gober isn't paying for it. I am. It's all just fine. The packages haven't been opened since I got them."

I wasn't so sure about that, but there was no need to argue. I asked if everyone was having a great time on the shoot, aside from the problems with Drifter.

"Damn dog," Berry said. "I wish we could just dump him, write him out. We don't need a dog."

Olan shoved his chair back from the table. "The hell you say. Drifter's carrying your damn pictures!"

"Oh, stuff it," Berry said. "You know as well as I do that I'm the main attraction. People don't pay money to see a dog doing stupid tricks."

"Oh, yeah? What about Rin Tin Tin? Huh? What about Lassie? Huh? Huh?"

I was wrong about Olan. He had been saving some of his snappy comebacks for Berry.

Donnie was watching the argument with wide eyes. I was about to say something to stop it, but then Evelyn came back, looking a lot different from when she'd left. She had splashed water on her face and washed off her makeup. She'd gotten water on her hair, too, and combed it somewhat differently.

When Olan saw her, he jumped up, forgetting completely about Berry.

"Are you okay?" he asked.

"Of course," Evelyn said. "I'm fine. I just ate too much. It's probably time that Donnie and I got some sleep."

I told her I thought that was a good idea. She and Donnie left with Olan, while Berry, Sandstrom, and I ordered another round of beer.

"So what's going on between Olan and Mrs. Powell?" I asked.

"They like each other," Berry said with a smirk.

"A lot," Sandstrom added. He could smirk even better than Berry. Better than nearly any other actor in Hollywood, as a matter of fact.

"Define *a lot,*" I said.

The waitress brought the beer, still in the bottles. That's the way I like it.

Sandstrom took a pull and said, "Let's just say that I think they find each other more entertaining than they find the movie."

"They entertain each other, all right," Berry said. "I've seen the trailer rocking."

I thought about that and decided I believed it. He didn't have any reason to lie.

"You don't like the wolf much, do you," I said.

"It's a dog, and I don't like it. I'm the star, not that mongrel."

Sandstrom laughed. "Star? I wouldn't get that big-headed yet, if I were you. Wait until the movie's a hit, at least."

"I've had hits. And Gober knows it. I'm not doing another movie with that damned dog. Never. El Lobo rides alone." His face lit up. "El Lobo rides alone! I like it! What a title! It's a natural."

He was right. I was surprised that Gober's geniuses hadn't thought of it already.

"What are you going to do about the kid?" Sandstrom asked. "Not to mention the dog."

Berry rolled his beer bottle between his palms. "That damned kid. He's tried to steal every scene he's been in. He's worse than the dog."

"You're stuck with him," Sandstrom said. "He's El Lobo's son."

Berry took a long swallow of beer. "We'll see about that," he said.

We finished our beers and talked a little more. When we left the café, I had a pretty good hunch about what had been done, and how. All I had to do was prove it.

The next morning, Terence James was ready to go bright and early, and so was everyone else. I'd taken a room at the little motel in Corona, so I was there with the rest of them.

James had relented a bit, and he wasn't going to reshoot the scene with Drifter until later in the day, adding a little to the recovery time. Instead, he was going for an action bit, in which Donnie Powell, as Raul, was being pursued across the plains by the Alcalde's men. El Lobo, of course, would ride to the rescue. Or his stunt double would.

Donnie Powell, unlike Berry, was an excellent horseman, so he was going to do his own riding in the scene. There was nothing tricky about it. He was just going to gallop straight down a path familiar to anyone who'd ever seen any Gober Western: the same trees, the same rocks, the same mountains in the background.

The wranglers were getting the horses ready when I struck up a conversation with Olan, who was watching the setup with Drifter lying at his feet.

"How's the wolf today?" I asked.

Olan gave Drifter a glance. "He's a dog, and he's doing fine. We're filming his scene this afternoon, and he'll be great. You'll see."

I hoped I wouldn't be around for it. I was ready to get back into the city. All that sun and sky were making me nervous.

"You haven't been telling me the truth about everything, Olan," I said.

He balled his fists. "I don't know what you mean."

He knew, all right, but I told him anyway. "You've been having a nooner with Mrs. Powell every so often."

He took a swing at me, but I just stepped aside and it went wide. I'm short and a little overweight, but I'm very light on my feet.

"Don't try that again," I said. "I might have to shoot you."

Drifter growled and showed his teeth, but he didn't move.

"I'll shoot the dog, too," I added.

I didn't have a pistol, but Olan didn't know that. He probably got all his ideas about private eyes from Bogart pictures. He let his hands drop to his sides.

"What business is it of yours what Evelyn and I do? We're both grown-ups."

"Sure. And I don't care what you're up to with her. But it proves that you aren't with Drifter all the time like you said you were."

"What if I'm not? No one gets in that trailer."

"Anyone could get in. Especially if they knew what was going on. Besides, I think you were lying about something else."

"Damn you, I wasn't lying."

"Okay. But if I find out you haven't been feeding the dog, I'll know better. I think I'll ask Donnie about it."

Olan's face was so red that I could hardly see his freckles. "All right. All right. The kid feeds the dog sometimes. Evelyn and I need some time alone, so we can get rid of the kid by sending him to feed Drifter."

"That's what I thought. And if you keep it up, the kid's going to get rid of the dog."

"You think Donnie's doing that to Drifter? That's ridiculous! Donnie's a good kid. He wouldn't do anything to Drifter. They're pals."

"No, they're not. Evelyn has a little problem with retaining her girlish figure, and I think she's taking an emetic after meals."

I'd seen that kind of thing before, and it explained the way she'd looked after the previous evening's meal. I figured that Donnie knew about his mother's little problem, and so he probably knew where to get his hands on an emetic.

I told Olan, "Donnie's a scene-stealer, and he knows as well as Berry that the dog is taking screen time that could go to someone else. Hell, maybe Evelyn's in on it. Maybe she's encouraging the kid to feed something to the dog, and she's distracting you on purpose."

He took another swing at me then, but his heart wasn't in it. He knew I was right, or he strongly suspected it. I grabbed his arm and twisted it up behind his back. He hardly even struggled. Drifter watched with interest but didn't bother to growl. He might have been glad to see Olan getting pushed around for all I knew.

"Okay, okay, maybe you've got a point," Olan said. "What're you gonna do about it?"

"Talk to the kid," I said.

Donnie was watching Berry, who was talking to his stunt double, explaining how heroic the double should look when riding to the rescue.

"You have to make me look good," Berry said. "I want the audience to know what a great rider I am."

Donnie's face was dark with contempt, but he didn't say anything.

"Hi, Donnie," I said, walking up beside him. "I want to ask you something."

"Fine, sir," he said, polite as always.

"It's about what you've been putting in Drifter's food," I told him.

I have to give the kid credit. He didn't deny a thing. He just stomped down on my instep as hard as he could, and while I was yelling and hopping around, he jumped on a horse and took off. Fast.

Everyone else stood there watching, just as if they didn't know what was going on, which, come to think of it, they didn't.

That meant it was up to me to stop the kid. I hadn't been on a horse in so many years I couldn't count them, but I figured that riding one must be like riding a bicycle: once you know how, you never forget.

So I pushed Berry and the stunt double aside and mounted up. At first the horse wouldn't move, but then I popped the reins, and off we went. I felt the wind in my face, and when my hat blew off I felt for about one second like El Lobo himself, riding wild and free beneath the open sky.

After that second, I felt a lot of other things, none of them pleasant. I bounced in the saddle like I had a rubber butt. The muscles in my thighs cramped. The reins burned my hands. There was no way on earth I was ever going to catch up with Donnie Powell.

But someone else was. A gray blur passed me on the right, loping along with that characteristic wolfish gait. That Drifter was quite an actor, all right. Fiero the wolf was on the case, looking as if he'd never been ill.

I watched it all unfold just like a scene in a movie. Donnie didn't even know Fiero was after him. He headed past a low knoll, and Fiero ran up the side of it, jumped just as he got to the top, and flew low and flat and level straight at Donnie Powell.

He hit Donnie in the midsection, and the two of them hit the ground rolling. Donnie didn't stand a chance. By the time I rode up, Fiero was sitting on his chest, staring down into his eyes, and drooling into his face.

Donnie didn't even try to wipe off the drool. He just lay there, terrified.

I managed to stop the horse, which was a lot easier than getting off him proved to be, considering the pain I was in. Now I know why cowboys are bow-legged.

"That's fine, Fiero," I said. "I'll take it from here."

Fiero didn't move. He probably wasn't sure I was capable of handling things. I didn't blame him.

It took a few minutes for everyone to arrive on the scene. The first one was Olan, who coaxed his animal away from Donnie, who sat up and looked around for his mother. She was the next one to get there, and he jumped up and ran into her arms.

"Is there anything you'd like to tell me about that dog?" I asked Olan.

He looked around, saw that no one was listening, and said, "He's actually about half timber wolf."

"That's what I thought," I said.

"Goddamn it, Ferrel," Gober said when I reported it all to him, "you don't deserve any bonus. You have a lot of nerve asking for one."

I was standing in his office, up to my ankles in carpet. I couldn't sit down, not yet. Maybe in a few days. Not that Gober cared.

"After all," he went on, "it wasn't you who saved the picture. You scared Donnie, and he might have been killed, running away like that. It was Drifter who saved the picture. He knew all along who the guilty party was. He's a better detective than you are. If he could've talked, he would've told us."

"Right," I said, and he was. Fiero, or Drifter, had known who was making him sick maybe as far back as when he'd jumped for the Alcalde's pistol and missed. So I agreed with Gober. Up to a point. "If the dog could talk, you wouldn't need me. But he can't, so you do. Besides, I deserve combat pay for what I went through."

I couldn't see why Gober was being so difficult. The picture was saved, one way or the other. I'd been right about Evelyn Powell's taking an emetic. The food poisoning that had affected the crew gave Donnie the idea of trying a little food poisoning of his own. He thought that if he could get Drifter out of the way, he'd get more time on-screen. I was glad he didn't know that Berry was hoping to get rid of him. There was no telling what he might have done.

Gober pretended to think things over. "Well, all right," he said finally. "I guess we could add a little extra to your retainer this time. But don't expect me to make it a habit. You won't have that dog to save your bacon the next time."

"He's not a dog. He's at least half wolf."

Gober stared hard at me. "He's just a good actor. Having a wolf on the set would be dangerous."

"You're right. It would be dangerous. That dog's a hell of an actor, though."

"And a damned good detective, too," Gober said. "If you ever need an assistant . . ."

Kids and animals, I thought. Never again. But there was no need to tell Gober that.

"I'll keep him in mind," I said.

Bill Crider

An instructor of English at Alvin Community College by day, by night Bill Crider moonlights enough for quintuplets. Besides writing three Texas-set mystery series, featuring Sheriff Dan Rhodes, Carl Burns, and Truman Smith PI, he has written Western and horror fiction as well as many cat stories, including his Anthony Award nominee, "How I Found a Cat, Lost True Love and Broke the Bank at Monte Carlo." His novel, Too Late to Die, *won an Anthony Award and he was nominated for a Shamus Award for best first private-eye novel. But Bill can't help writing about these critter-crime cases, this time without the usual cat. He lives with his wife, Judy, in bucolic Alvin, Texas, with three basic domestic house cats, Speedo, Geraldine, and Sam.*

There is not much that Miss Esther M. Friesner and her not-insignificant other, Mr. Walter J. Stutzman, will not try. She is of a highly imaginative sort, despite a doctorate in higher education, and apparently he is, too. I am with Mr. Oscar Wilde: Ignorance is like a delicate exotic fruit; touch it and the bloom is gone. Only I consider education more like a long-stemmed cactus; touch it and your bloomers are gone, and you quickly learn not to touch it. Miss Esther M. Friesner and Mr. Walter J. Stutzman take us into the genteel atmosphere of an English country estate, where a jewel of a solution lies in the paws of a small rodent. I have no particular hankering to go back in time, but it does seem that small rodents were much more plentiful then, if not as resourceful as Miss Esther M. Friesner's and Mr. Walter J. Stutzman's variety of same.

—M.L.

A Hamster of No Importance

Esther M. Friesner and Walter J. Stutzman

"A JEWEL THIEF is a fellow who knows the price of everything and the value of everything, too," said Algy. And having said this, he looked hopefully around the table to see whether his mot had scored him a social triumph among the smart set who patronized this little corner of the Café Royal.

It had not. The five other young men there foregathered favored poor Algy with frowns so alike in conformation and condemnation that they might as well have been the product of a single face.

"I only meant—," Algy began, his voice faltering.

"—to make an ass of yourself?" Bertie concluded. He was the scion of an upper-middle-class family, with a father who had made his fortune in trade as a manufacturer of ladies' boots, yet in this place he stood on an equal footing with the sons of England's peerage, and heaven help the soul who forgot it!

Algy was himself the heir to a minor baronetcy, but the rules of the group applied to him as well and he didn't dare crush Bertie's sarcasm with his birthright. Apart from being possessed of a sharper tongue than Algy, young Bertram was also the handsomer of the pair. His looks tended toward that golden, Greek, gracious ideal of lineaments and coloring, the paragon to which Algy aspired in vain. Although Algy asserted that his own hair was strawberry blond, to be honest it hewed to the gingery end of the spectrum. As for his profile, from forehead to nose it was passable, but at the lips it hesitated, took fright, and presented a chin that was not so much in retreat as in utter rout, a flaw which he clumsily sought to cover by cultivating a beard and sidewhiskers. Unfortunately for Algy, his facial hair was far more humorous than any of his verbal sallies.

Thus was a baronetcy devalued in favor of bright badinage and manly beauty. At this table a democracy of wit reigned, coupled with an oligarchy of appearances. So it had been decreed by the uncontested master of the revels and so it must be.

"You're just lucky *he's* not here yet," Bertie remarked. He leaned back in his chair, victor of the field, and studied his well-buffed nails languidly. "If *he'd* heard you make such a half-baked attempt at repartee—and stealing from one of his own quips to do so!—he'd rule you off the turf for life."

"Would I?" A deep, mellifluous voice with more than a hint of good humor in it rose up from behind Bertie's chair so abruptly that it startled the tradesman's beautiful son almost out of his seat. Every face at the table turned from scowling censure of poor Algy to slavish adoration of the imposing gentleman who had finally come to join them.

"Oscar!" young Monty cried. He was one of those buds of those highest branches of the British nobility where the sap runs thinnest, a proud specimen of that same breeding program that renders pedigreed dogs too flimsy-skulled for any service save moronic barking at goldfish, and thoroughbred horses so fine-boned that they break their legs under a hard look. In young Monty's case, the stout Saxon rootstock that once upon a long-gone time had produced blue-eyed, gold-haired warriors had dwindled to propagating pale, aimless aesthetes who nonetheless owned a sort of elfin beauty to die for. It was all in the cheek-bones.

Beauty was something that Oscar understood. Beauty, according to Oscar, was all that made life worth living. (Although if pressed to the point, he might amend this to beauty and a reliable tailor.) He paused for a moment to pat young Monty on the head with a nursemaid's fondness for her most fragile charge, then seated himself in the midst of his admirers. "I have just come from the theater," he announced. "As I expected, the rehearsal of my play is going brilliantly. The actors are almost worthy of their lines."

"I can hardly wait to attend the performance," Clarence spoke up eagerly. Of the six juvenile toffs there assembled, his raven hair struck a jarring note in what was otherwise by and large a symphony in the key of blond.

"Oh, I say, neither can I," Algy blurted. "I wish you all the best of luck with this one, dear Oscar."

A hush such as might have honored the better class of funeral fell upon the table.

Geoffrey was the one to break it. "You idiot, Algy," he growled. "One never wishes 'good luck' in the theater. That's *bad* luck of the blackest stripe!"

"Oh. Oh, dear." Algy's fine pink hands fidgeted over the outsides of the small, curiously pierced wooden box which he'd brought with him to the Café Royal that day. "I *do* apologize, Oscar. I didn't know."

"Nonsense," Wilde said in his rich baritone. "I wouldn't have expected you to be familiar with theatrical beliefs; you haven't troubled *me*. Superstitions are like bad reviews: They only apply to others. The sole faux pas of which you are guilty is implying that my work requires *luck* to succeed when it possesses *art.*"

"I—That is—I didn't—"

"Oh, hush, Algy. No one cares," said Philip cheerfully. He was the group's *true* strawberry blond, a lad who owned such a degree of bumptious good health as to be quite unfashionable outside of huntin', shootin', and fishin' circles. He was forgiven this flaw by Oscar and the rest on account of his having a plethora of wealthy relations willing to entertain his friends as lavishly and as frequently as they liked. "Drop it and get back to your surprise."

"Surprise?" For an instant, Oscar's beefy face betrayed a child's avid curiosity. "Algy is seldom the vehicle of surprises."

"Vehicle or victim," said Geoffrey, smoothing back his dark gold hair. "Who's to say? He *claims* he's got something astonishing in that box of his. Clarence suggested that it might be the Ormond pearl."

"The one that vanished two weeks ago from Lord Reddingworth's town house?" Oscar's brows rose ever so slightly. "Algy, you naughty boy!"

Algy blushed until his cheeks threatened to match his sidewhiskers. "I'm afraid it—it's not— I mean, I'm not *afraid* it's not the Ormond pearl, but—but it isn't. That is, I would never—"

"Good Lord, Algy, no one's accusing you of thievery," Bertie snapped. "That would require imagination."

"Imagination to an astounding degree, given that the thief took only the pearl and left behind the rest of the Reddingworth jewels," said Philip. "Worth a pretty penny too, and all in plain sight of anyone who'd filch the pearl, but ignored regardless. The police don't know what to make of it."

"The Reddingworth jewels are mostly large rubies, cut and set in such a manner as to suggest the hiring of Barbary apes by certain London jewelers," Oscar commented. "I have seen them adorning the bosom of the dowager Lady Reddingworth. I could not possibly tell you which was in poorer taste."

"You'd adore this jewel thief, Oscar," said Clarence. "You and he seem to be of one mind on the paramountcy of aesthetic refinement."

"Indeed?" Oscar looked only mildly interested. "Jewel thieves and such are quite beyond my ken. I am generally less than *au courant* with those items in the daily press intended to thrill and astonish the common readership. I always find more satisfactory sensationalism in my diary."

"Well, there's been a series of thefts," Algy began.

"*Jewel* thefts," Monty cut in.

"But not the usual sort." Algy was determined to reclaim the conversational spotlight, and with it, Oscar's attention.

"And what is the 'usual sort' of jewel theft, dear boy?" Oscar inquired lightly. "I confess myself less than adequately educated in such matters."

"Er, *you* know." Algy was invariably thrown for a loop when tossed an unexpected question, even in jest. "The sort where the thief steals *everything.* All the jewels, I mean."

"Yes, whereas *this* felon appears to be discriminating," Geoffrey provided. "The Ormond pearl is merely the latest in his series of . . . selections. I believe he's also got the Sforza emerald from Lady Gregory's town house, the Hadrian tourmaline from Sir Hilary Brougham's place, the Milk-of-Kali moonstone from the Grimshaw collection, and Lord Ffellowes's sapphire—the one they call the Peacock Blue—to his tally."

Oscar frowned briefly. "He's welcome to the Sforza emerald, I'm sure. Whatever possessed Lady Gregory to have a stone of that quality set in a brooch of such baroque monstrosity—"

"Oh, the thief doesn't take the *settings,*" Monty chirruped. "Just the stones. Pries them loose first, he does."

"Ah?" Oscar's heavy, sensual lips curled up slightly at the corners. "Then I think I am in agreement with you as to this fellow's faultless aesthetic compass. Clearly his pilferings are not swayed by mere monetary concerns. All of the jewels you've mentioned are famous for their beauty—I have myself been privileged to see the Milk-of-Kali and it caused me to break out in sonnets—yet a single one of Lady Reddingworth's repulsive ruby necklaces would be worth a score of moonstones on the open market."

"Yes, but the Peacock Blue's also worth about twice the entire Reddingworth jewels," Algy put in. "And it's always easier to sell loose stones."

"Aren't *you* the knowledgeable one," Bertie said nastily. "I've heard that your father was a bit near in matters of pocket money. So is *that* how you've been supplementing your allowance? A dash of burglary?"

"How *dare* you!" Algy exclaimed, rising from his seat.

To his chagrin, the others—including Oscar—merely laughed at his indignation. "Dear boy, it was only a joke," Oscar said, easing him firmly back down into his chair with one hand on his shoulder. Although the playwright cultivated a fashionable air of world-weariness, he was still a big man and possessed surprising physical strength. When he wanted a person to sit, that person *sat.* "No one is accusing you of the thefts, although I do wonder where you picked up that tidbit of information concerning the marketability of stolen goods."

Algy dropped his eyes, seeking to avoid the issue, but Monty readily piped up, "Oh, from all those detective stories he's been reading! That must be it. It *is* it, isn't it, Algy? When we were all staying with the Grimshaws and everyone else was off punting on the Isis, I came into the library and saw you reading . . . now what *was* the title?"

"Nothing, it was nothing," Algy muttered. "A trifle, not worth remembering—"

"The Bloodstained Beryl of the Borgia Brood!" Monty snapped his fingers, delighted at having dredged up the memory. "You loaned it to me after you were done with it, remember, Algy?"

"No." Algy groaned, squirming miserably. His weak denials availed him naught. He was fairly taken in his secret vice and all the table knew it, except for Monty who, as usual, didn't have an inkling as to the social damage his innocent words had done.

"The Bloodstained Beryl?" Bertie repeated. "Sounds like it's about jewel theft. Research, Algy?" he teased.

"And he *was* at the Grimshaws," Clarence contributed, getting into the spirit of the game. "I believe that's what the police refer to as opportunity."

"Well, for that matter, so were you!" Algy snapped.

"True, but *my* father's not famous for his niggardliness like yours," Clarence shot back.

"Tsk. You're forgetting that mere money's not the object of these crimes," Geoffrey pointed out. "We all know how fond Algy is of Oscar's work. There was a time when you couldn't find him without his nose sunk in a copy of *The Picture of Dorian Grey*. Dorian was also a collector of exquisite gems, and they do say that imitation is the sincerest form of flattery."

"Now see here—!" Algy spluttered, his cheeks a bright crimson against the ginger of his sidewhiskers. It was a disturbing contrast of shades, and one that offended Oscar's sensibilities.

"This has gone far enough," Oscar said, stepping in to make peace. "If you mean to argue evidence, you must confess that every one of us—myself included—have shared Algy's so-called opportunity. We have *all* enjoyed the hospitality of each of the thief's victims, singly or as a group, at one time or another. Indeed, I am still tempted to remember the Gregorys' chef in my will, in appreciation of his lyric treatment of roast spring lamb."

Bertie was having too good a time tormenting Algy to let the matter drop. "What about motive, then?"

"Which one?" Oscar asked mildly. "Money or art?"

"Oh, both would do for Algy." Bertie tossed the answer off with a little flip of his hand.

"Whereas you would only need to do it for the sake of art," Oscar remarked. "No, no, Bertie, I am afraid that in matters of motive we are all once more constrained to share Algy's purported guilt."

The young men at the table exchanged furtive, uneasy looks. Oscar's words rang true: There wasn't one among them who couldn't use either the cash from the sale of the stolen jewels or the cachet from possession of such sublime exemplars of lapidary beauty.

Monty did not care for such feelings of inner turmoil. Bewilderment made his head hurt. In pure self-defense he opted to blunt the conversational dagger: "Well, at least Algy's innocent as far as the Ormond pearl goes. He's got the perfect alibi, as those dreadful Scotland Yard people would say. He wasn't even in England two weeks ago."

"Might I remind you that two weeks ago was merely the time when the theft was *detected*?" Clarence said. His tone was somewhat chill.

"Hmm. Lord Reddingworth is some connection of yours, is he not?" Oscar inquired.

"He is my uncle."

"Are you then his heir?"

Clarence bridled. "I am first my *father's* heir. My future security requires neither my uncle's fortune nor his jewels."

"What a young man requires and what he desires are seldom one and the same thing. That is the foundation of some of our better society marriages." Oscar gestured for the waiter's attention and pretended disinterest in the coo and flutter of appreciation his remark produced among the young men. Even Geoffrey laughed, which caused not a few curious glances in his direction.

The object of this scrutiny was not unaware of his observers. In a breath his expression winked from easy good humor to fleeting irritation. "Oh, for heaven's sake, Monty, don't look at me like that. It's been over a year!"

"Er, yes, but—" Monty writhed in his seat.

"I'm fine. All is forgiven, as the saying goes. Uncle Simon invited me to dine with him Thursday next. That ought to prove *he's* gotten over the whole teacup-sized tempest. I wish you would."

"Er, yes, Monty, do," Algy said a trifle quickly. "A dinner invitation's got to be proof positive that the whole silly thing's blown over."

Monty frowned, then realized he was wrinkling his brow. Nimbly he resumed his usual look of bland amiability and said, "Oh, piffle. I'm sick to death of these endless uncles. I'd much rather know Algy's secret, even if it's not the Ormond pearl. Do tell, Algy!"

With a small, self-deprecating smile, Algy placed his hands on the lid of the little wooden box. "It's not such a great surprise," he explained. "It's more of a rarity. You see, my uncle Ludovic—"

Monty uttered a short, muffled squeal of dismay at the "U" word.

"Control yourself, Monty," Oscar said out of his own boundless smug serenity. "Algy cannot help having an uncle, although I would like to think he might have done something to prevent having one named Ludovic."

"Uh, well, at least Uncle Ludovic spends lots of time out of the country," Algy offered. "He is an amateur archaeologist."

"If he's so in love with digging up old ruins, he ought to spend more time in the House of Lords," Geoffrey quipped, and was rewarded with an approving smile from Oscar.

Algy blinked rapidly. "Um, yes," he said. "Anyway, that's where I've been these past weeks, visiting Uncle Ludovic in the Holy Land. And that's where I got . . . this."

The lid came off the box. The assembled company leaned forward as one to peer inside. As the unspoken code of their group demanded the worship of all things beautiful, they were likely under the impression that Algy's surprise was some antique article of adornment, a jewel such as might have rested in the bosom of a pharaoh's daughter. They were not at all prepared for what actually resided in the box.

This time Monty's shriek was neither short nor subdued. The waiter fetching Oscar's drink almost dropped his tray at the shrill exclamation, "It's a *rat*!"

Algy hunched himself protectively over the open box. "It is *not* a rat," he said rather hotly. "If you'd take the trouble to look, you'd see that it doesn't have a tail."

"It's a *tail-less* rat!" Monty maintained. "That's *much* worse. I've heard they're venomous."

"Twaddle!" Algy made a face. "You've barely heard of the Battle of Hastings, Monty. A venomous, tail-less rat, what next? Look at the shape of the head, you idiot! It may be a rodent, but it's no rat."

"Then what is it?" Bertie demanded. "Apart from vermin, I mean."

"It's—" Algy hesitated. "Well, we're not exactly sure. No one's ever seen such a creature before. Uncle Ludovic found it in the bazaar at Damascus. The creatures may be common as house-flies in that part of the world, but the rogue who sold Uncle this one had discovered that the sahibs bought them only as oddities. He meant to keep it so; wouldn't even give it a name."

"Probably had 'em stocked by the crateful in some dismal, opium-soaked hovel," Monty volunteered. Now that he knew the small, furry creature was not a rat, he was ready to be charmed by its appearance. "Pretty little thing. Fine coat, good color, clear eye, nice conformation—"

"Lord, Monty, are you thinking of petting it or using it to hunt foxes?" Clarence snapped.

"You must call it *something,* Algy," Philip said, amiably. "A chap can't very well go around saying 'Look at this dear little not-a-rat I've got here' now, can he?"

Algy stroked the diminutive ball of golden fur in the box ten-derly. "There was a German chap staying in our hotel. He'd also purchased one of these creatures and remarked upon the animal's habit of hoarding food in its cheek pouches. 'Quite the little miser,' he said, and named his pet accordingly, in his native tongue."

"What was that?" Monty asked.

"*German,* you—!"

"Faugh, Algy, I'm not *that* thick. I meant what was the name he gave it?"

"Oh." Abashed, Algy muttered, *"Hamster."*

"Hamster..." Oscar pronounced the word carefully, savoring it the way a wine-lover might roll a mouthful of burgundy over the tongue. He shook his head. "The word lacks beauty, which scarcely surprises me. The Germans create exquisite music, but apart from that, they tend to make things large, awkward, and heavy, including their words, their *wursts,* and their women. *Hamster* reminds one of *ham,* which in turn makes one think of pigs. That may be marginally better than thinking of rats, but hardly a great improvement. I fear, Algy, that with such a name your pet will never be popular in this country."

"Particularly since Algy's is the only one of its kind," Geoffrey pointed out. "Aesthetics aside, simple biology dictates that—"

Oscar gave him a cool glance. "I should not be too ready to spurn aesthetics. May I remind you, aesthetics has produced Michelangelo's *David,* Botticelli's *Venus,* and DaVinci's *Mona Lisa.* Biology, on the other hand, has produced your uncle."

"*Uncles* again!" Monty groaned while Geoffrey subsided into a gloomy pout.

"There, there, Monty." Philip patted his companion chummily on the back. "For this weekend at least, we shall be free of all avuncular influences. We are to be the guests of my aunt, Lady Barbara Delapye, and she has the good taste to be a widow."

"A widow," Algy repeated. "A widow is one who knows the value of marriage and the price of—of—" He abruptly became aware of the weight of six extremely critical stares and floundered about in an excess of splutters and stammers until at last concluding, "Er . . . What do you think I should pack?"

I have seen them, the ones of whom the Giver-of-All-Good-Things spoke before transporting my palace hither, after the fashion of the *jinni* in the old tales. He begged me not to bite them, should they try to touch my fur. I did not. They did not impress me sufficiently to merit any attention, including the righteous chastisement of my teeth. I will go back to sleep and await the bounty of the Giver-of-All-Good-Things.

"You *didn't,* Algy." Monty stood in the doorway of Algy's room, gazing with tremble-lipped horror at the object reposing atop the chest of drawers. "Tell me you didn't pack *that.*"

"I didn't *pack* him . . . exactly." Algy hurried over to check on the wooden box that housed his exotic pet. "One doesn't *pack* animals."

"Don't try to confuse me. You *brought* him, that's all that's material. Lady Delapye will have a fit."

"She will not." Algy's negligible chin rose sharply in defiance. "She's already seen Oscar and pronounced him charming."

Monty's eyebrows rose. " 'Oscar'?"

Algy fell into a coughing spasm. "Ye—ye—yes," he said at last. "That's what I've named the little fellow."

Monty's laugh had often been compared to the sound a filly might make were an incautious groom to back her into a chilled pitchfork. "Oh, my dear, that *is* rich! 'Oscar,' no less." With a whoop he was off, his shrill cries of "I say, fellows, wait until you hear *this*!" echoing through the stately halls of Bishop's Ashlar.

Crestfallen, Algy checked on the tenant of the small wooden box. "Well, *that* was a mistake," he told the drowsing animal. "When will I ever learn to keep my mouth shut? I only open it to humiliate myself or ruin someone else's life. Still, I suppose that of the two, humiliating myself's the better choice." He lightly caressed the hamster's downy fur with the tip of one finger. "There was the time I enraged Bertie when I couldn't seem to say two words together without one of them having to do with footwear. If anyone ever doubted his aversion to being reminded of his father's trade, *that* settled the question. Then there was the time at the Café Royal when I asked Philip how he'd liked riding with the Quorn hunt, because I'd been up that way visiting Aunt Wilhemina and I could have sworn I recognized him when the hunt went by. You'd have thought I'd placed him at the scene of the Massacre of the Holy Innocents from the way he denied it. No wonder: We all know the scorn Oscar feels for foxhunting, only . . . I forgot. Monty says that I'm the reason Geoffrey's marriage to Lady Mary Bythorn came a cropper, but that's impossible. I'm certain that there was a perfectly simple explanation for what he was doing with that strange dark-haired man in the study at Lord Pengarde's place during the croquet matches. All I did was ask Lady Mary if *she* knew the fellow; I thought he looked familiar, somehow. She went to investigate, and ended the engagement the next day. Geoffrey himself says his uncle was irate at first—he had *so* wanted the match—but now he quite mollified, understands the situation, no hard feelings, women will change their minds about marriage over the silliest things. *Tchah,* Monty will talk just to hear his teeth click. On the other hand, that was the same weekend I suggested to Lady Mary's mother that a nice stained-glass window might be the perfect memorial for her late husband. She came within an inch of slapping my face over the blancmange. Of course I'd read his obituary, so I knew that he'd died from defenestration, but . . . Good Lord, how was *I* supposed to know it meant *that*?"

In the box, curled up on a bed of cotton wool, the hamster yawned prodigiously, revealing incisors whose length and sharpness were the stuff of wonder. This impressive dentition seemed an impossibility, the teeth appearing to be too large to fit within the outwardly dainty mouth. Algy smiled affectionately at his pet.

His attention was distracted by a knock at the door. He turned to behold Clarence's valet, a youth called Thompson, attending him. Rumor said that Clarence had engaged Thompson for his looks more than for his skills as a gentleman's gentleman. Indeed, with the proper wardrobe, the valet might have passed easily for one of the beautiful young men who frequented Oscar's preferred table at the Café Royal. Like all of them save his own master he was golden-haired, a dark gold shading off into exquisite bronze.

Then he opened his mouth and the dream of beauty was shattered.

"Oi, sir, moi master sez as 'ow 'e'd loik a word with you doirectly, if it's quoit convenient."

"Er, yes," said Algy. "Where might I find him?"

" 'E's in t' loibr'y, sir. Know the way, do you, or want as Oi should bring you?"

"No thank you, Thompson; I am quite familiar with the house."

"Roight, then, sir. Oi'll just be goin' abaot me business then." With a flash of perfect white teeth that *almost* erased all memory of his execrable accent, Thompson was gone.

Algy saw to replacing the lid of little Oscar's box before taking himself off to the library. In so doing, he noticed that the hamster had once more rearranged the soft cotton bedding provided for him, shoving great wads of it against the sides of the box and effectively plugging up more than half of the air holes.

"*Tsk.* This won't do at all," Algy muttered, but to put the box to rights would take time, and because he disliked disturbing his sleeping pet, he decided to set the lid atop the box more loosely than usual, a temporary measure to prevent little Oscar's demise by suffocation. "I'll only be gone a minute," he said, though whether this was for the benefit of little Oscar or his own conscience he could not say.

Well have I named him, my beloved Giver-of-All-Good-Things, for lo! now he offers me my freedom. It is but the work of a moment to bestir myself and push against the roof of my palace. I cannot deny the fiery spirit of exploration within me. My kind burrow where we will.

Another push, another, and—ah! The roof is off. I clamber over the wall and am free. What place is this? The smells are all strange. There are too many flowery scents here, on this plateau. My nose has ever been a more reliable guide than my eyes, yet I can perceive many large, sparkling objects here, like the glittering turrets of some legendary city. I think they are flasks or bottles, such as the storytellers of the bazaar teach may contain *jinni.*

I am not about to worry off the stoppers to see if this proves true, certainly not now for—one comes! I hear an approaching tread too heavy to be the well-known footsteps of the Giver-of-All-Good-Things. I must conceal myself, but—where?

Aha! A space between two bottles! Small, but never too small for me. Here will I wait and watch and—

Merciful powers! What is the dark one doing to my palace?

Algy found Clarence, as per Thompson's words, in the library. The raven-haired young man was immersed in one of the London dailies. "You wanted to see me?"

Clarence folded the paper and set it aside. "See here, Algy," he said by way of greeting. "We've just had word that Oscar's to join us after all."

"Oh, good!" Algy exclaimed. "They must have cleared up that little problem with the rehearsals, then."

Clarence assumed the frown of a nanny confronted with an especially backward child. "I would not call the—the *defection* of the second leading man as a 'little' problem."

"But his grandmother was taken ill," Algy protested. "Oscar told us so when he tendered his regrets. The man is her sole living relative and—"

"And for *that* trifle he disappointed Oscar when he might have hired some good woman or another to look after the old dame? Algy, you surprise me."

"Not half so much as you surprise me," Algy muttered sotto voce. Aloud he said, "So the grandmother's better now?"

"No, she's dead. Her grandson's sent word to the manager that he's too torn up to return to the production, the silly twit. An *actor* with such highly attuned family sentiments? *Hunh!* A fine career *he'll* have. But that doesn't signify. Oscar decided to place the production in abeyance until such time as he might find a suitable replacement for the part. He'll be coming up on the three o'clock train."

"The three o'clock train . . ." Algy tapped his temple absentmindedly. "Now why does that sound—?"

"—familiar?" Clarence finished for him. "Allow me to jog your memory: It is also the train by which Lady Mary is arriving. You promised Lady Delapye that you'd motor down to meet the girl."

"Lady . . . Mary?" Algy colored violently. "Not Lady Mary Bythorn?"

"Of course Lady Mary Bythorn!" Clarence snapped. "You know she's a connection of Philip's. Why this shock?"

"When Lady Delapye requested the services of my motor, she didn't name the young woman I was to meet. Now I see why. Oh, dear. Does Geoffrey know?"

"Perhaps. Why should it matter? You heard him: All is forgiven."

"But still, a broken engagement, and I—"

"You give yourself far too much credit as a *provocateur* of domestic havoc, Algy." Clarence consulted the cathedral clock on

the library mantelpiece. "Look at the time: You really ought
to go."

"Certainly," said Algy, and turning smartly on his heel, he
caught the toe of his shoe just under one of the silk scatter rugs
bedecking the room and pitched headfirst into the doorjamb,
rendering himself unconscious.

How *dare* he! I did not seek this. It does not belong here.
It is the symbol of rank trespass, an abomination to my
very soul! It must go, and go quickly.
    It will be a perilous thing I undertake, far to climb, the
chance of a fatal fall, but I will do it. No risk shall be too
great if I may requite this offense. Ah, the knave!

Algy came back to his senses sometime later, nicely tucked up in
his bed with a cold compress on his brow. Disjointed scraps of
conversation assailed his ears, making his head ache.

"—saw anything to equal it. Quite incredible."

"That's our Algy. Bertie, do you recall the weekend we were
visiting Sir Hilary?"

"Hard to forget the embarrassment. He couldn't walk across
a clear floor without tripping over his own feet. He stumbled
into me, and I had the bad luck to knock up against that priceless
Ming vase."

"Oh, Sir Hilary put a price to it smartly enough, once you'd
broken it."

"Don't remind me. I had the devil's own time explaining the
bill to Father. He kept my funds on the short leash for a month
after."

Someone chuckled. "Good thing Sir Hilary didn't try sending
you the bill for the Hadrian tourmaline as well. It did turn up
missing about a fortnight after your visit."

"Your visit as well, Philip. *And* Algy's." There was nothing
friendly in Bertie's voice.

"Speaking of Algy, has Lady Delapye sent someone else to
the station?"

"I doubt it. She's been out of the house since breakfast: One of her cotters' wives has fallen ill."

"Oh, dear. That will mean calf's foot jelly or I don't know Aunt Barbara. It's her answer to every ailment from pleurisy to the plague. Looks like Algy's had a change of luck, her being gone, else he'd find himself facing whole tureens of the stuff."

"Oh, *bother* Algy. We were counting on his motor. Now Oscar's going to be left stranded at the station! Hasn't anyone taken—?"

"—Algy's automobile? Geoffrey did, I think."

"Since when does Geoffrey know how to—?"

"—learned it from *him,* I'd venture to say."

"What, Thompson? My valet knows his station, which is *not* to give driving lessons to—"

"—gave him *some* sort of lessons, at any rate."

"Bertie, you *wicked* boy. Get the smirk off your face this instant!"

"—livid, absolutely livid. No wonder the girl jilted him. No one knows the details, but—"

"—should've kept his mouth shut like a gentleman, no matter what he saw at Lord Pengarde's. Algy never was one to learn discretion."

"Well, it's not like he was one who ran tattling to Geoffrey's uncle. *That* was Lady Mary."

"Can you blame the girl? They say it was the vice that daren't speak its name."

"If it daren't speak its name, how do they call it anything?"

"Oh, shut up, Monty."

It was at this point that Algy decided it would be better for all concerned were he to remain mum as to the return of his consciousness. He did so fine a job of acting as one still sunk in oblivion that he in fact fell into a deep sleep.

He was roused from this by the sound of a great commotion in the house. The room was dark, except for the dim glow of a nightcandle on his bedside table. Clearly he had slept for hours. He was a bit dizzy when he first stood up, but quickly regained command of his limbs (as much command as he ever had) and lurched for the hallway.

"I say, what's all—? Oh! I *beg* your pardon!"

True to the evil fairy that had cursed him in the cradle, Algy's first step out of his room had sent him blundering into the sweetly made person of Lady Mary Bythorn. Lady Mary gasped with surprise, but was otherwise unharmed.

Algy did not see it so, and began to apologize at an enormous rate until Lady Mary made so bold as to silence his chattering lips with a touch of her fingers. "Please, I'm fine. *You're* the one who's been injured. Poor man, I heard what happened."

"Oh, you did?" Algy blushed, then managed a feeble chuckle. "Clumsy me, eh what?"

"*I've* never thought you clumsy." Lady Mary's smile lit up her whole face. "A spot of hard luck could befall anyone. Only consider what's happened to poor Lady Delapye!"

"Er?" Algy inquired.

"Her ruby. The rather large one that Lord Delapye sent her from India. She had it set in a ring in his memory, after that horrid business with the maharajah's pet tiger. It's gone, you know. The ruby itself, not the ring. Certainly not the tiger. Quite, quite gone."

"Good Lord! When did this happen?"

"She thinks it must have been taken sometime between three and five this afternoon."

"Oh, I say, good."

"Algy! How could you—?"

"What I mean, Mary, is that at least here's *one* thing no one will be able to blame on *me.*"

" 'E done it," said Thompson, pointing.

All eyes turned with one accord to stare at Algy. The whole of the weekend houseparty had gathered in the gold parlor of Bishop's Ashlar at their hostess's imperative request, along with the full complement of abovestairs servants. At first there had been great speculation as to the reason for this call to assembly. Lady Delapye swiftly settled all wagers by announcing that thanks to the splendid character of a good and faithful employee—albeit not one of her own—she hoped to settle the whole ugly affair of the purloined ruby discreetly and instantly, without recourse to the police. She then ceded the floor to Thompson, who most emphatically took it.

"*Oi* sawr 'im. Oi was in me master's room, tendin' to me duties with the door owpen a moite. First Oi thinks nothing of it, seein' one o' 'er loidyship's guests go boi in the 'all, but there was something furtive-loik abaot 'im wot draw me oy. Kept lookin' over 'is shaolder every few steps. Dark doin's was afoot an' no mistyke."

"Dark doings," Oscar repeated from his place in a rose chintz-covered chair. "Do you enjoy quoting the shilling shockers, Thompson? Or are you an aficionado of melodrama?"

Clarence's valet lifted his chin. "Oi'm only doin' me duty. Oi follered after 'im and sawr 'im sneak into Lydy Dellerpoy's rooms."

"So you assumed he'd gone there to steal the ruby."

Thompson lowered his beautiful brown eyes. "Oi'd rawther not sy *wot* it were Oi assumed just then, sir." Monty tittered and Lady Delapye coughed in a reproving manner. "That's woi Oi didn't mention wot Oi seen roight off. It was only lyter, when Oi found out 'er lydyship wasn't in the 'ouse at all, an' when the ruby'd gone missin' that I knew it was moi duty to speak."

"You did well, Thompson," Lady Delapye said. She turned to Algy and added, "Young man, return my jewel at once and we shall say no more of this."

"I don't have it!" Algy protested. "I *couldn't* have it! I've been bedridden since half after two."

"Bedridden?" Clarence laughed nastily. "Come on, Algy, you had a nasty knock on the head, but it didn't cripple you. You make it sound as if you'd left both your legs in the Crimea!"

"Well, I *was* in my bed from half after two until just now," Algy maintained stubbornly. "And the rest of you are my witnesses. I awoke long enough to hear you there, talking about me. Would you care to have me repeat what you were saying?" He gave them all a meaningful glare.

"Why, you little sneak, playing dead on us like that!" Bertie exclaimed. "I'm glad I didn't waste too long at *your* bedside."

"Can't say any of us did," Monty confessed sheepishly.

"Gracious, what *were* you chaps saying about good old Algy?" Geoffrey drawled. "It sounds as if it was rich. I'm sorry I missed it, but I was at the station until past four. There was a bit of a problem on the London line—cow on the tracks or something—and the train was late. We didn't get back to Bishop's Ashlar until shortly after five."

"More nearly half after five," Lady Mary put in. "We stopped in the village."

"My fault entirely," Oscar admitted graciously. "I wanted to obtain some cigarettes. Speaking of time—" He returned his attentions to Thompson. "When, approximately, did you spy poor old Algy playing the footpad?"

"Four o'clock, it was."

"You sound astonishingly certain of the hour."

"Well, sir, the master'd gone off with the other lads about two, and Oi know *that* 'cos 'e come to me with 'is evenin' dress an' said, 'It's two o'clock, Thompson. We're just going down to the village tobacconist to surprise Mr. Wilde with some of those violet-scented cigarettes he likes.' "

"Ah! No wonder the poor clerk gaped so at my own request," Oscar interrupted. "And here I thought that he was merely in awe of my genius."

"Indeed, sir." Thompson nodded once, then resumed his narrative. "My master went on to say, 'We might pop by the Bear and Bush afterwards, but we ought to be back well in time for tea, so just see whether you can't brush these off before then.' The 'owl 'house was that quoiet with the young gentlemen gone, which is woi Oi s'powse Oi 'eard '*im* treadin' abaot loik Oi said."

"*Heard* me? You said you took up your ugly little spying because you *saw* me pass by Clarence's door." Algy challenged.

"Oi *sawr* you go boi after Oi *'eard* a sound in the 'all, rawther loik someone trippin' over 'is own feet. That's woi Oi looked up from me work in the first plyce."

"Tripping over—?" Monty sighed. "I'm afraid he's got you to the life, Algy."

By this time, Algy was livid, which did no favors to his complexion. "I did *not* do it!" he bellowed. "And I refuse to say I did on the basis of this—this former guttersnipe's testimony!"

"I will not have you impugn the character of my manservant," Clarence said stiffly. "Thompson may not be well spoken, but his duties do not include oratory."

"What *do* they include?" Bertie murmured.

"Character?" Algy repeated bitterly. "Before we canonize the fellow, perhaps we ought to search his belongings. Yes, and those of the other servants as well!"

Here an indignant muttering arose from the gathered above-stairs staff of Bishop's Ashlar, liberally salted with the phrase "I shall give notice." Lady Delapye hastily smoothed the ruffled plumage of her domestics and assured them that no needless searches would be made.

When next she addressed Algy, her voice bore an Arctic breath: "Since you are so keen on investigating Thompson's belongings, sir, you might volunteer to put your own effects to the test as well, purely as a gesture of good faith."

"But I never—!" Algy's objection was swallowed whole by Oscar's soft yet forceful voice.

"I agree with her ladyship," he said. "From what I gather, at the time the ruby vanished, the only people left in the house were yourself, Thompson, and the other servants. If the perpetrator were indeed a servant, I doubt that the theft of a single gem would have satisfied him. *Were* any other of your jewels missing, Lady Delapye?"

"None." Her ladyship spoke with conviction. "I spent most of the afternoon paying a sick call. I returned to Bishop's Ashlar just in time to greet your own arrival, Mr. Wilde."

"So you did, and we all enjoyed a delightful teatime."

"It was after tea that I discovered my loss."

"You are certain that the ruby was in its place this morning? It was not, perhaps, stolen at some earlier date and only today missed?"

Lady Delapye drew back her shoulders. "That ruby was my dear husband's last gift to me. I wear it daily. I only removed it from my finger because I felt it inappropriate to wear to a sick-call."

"I see." Oscar sighed and rolled his eyes in Algy's direction. "I am afraid that under the circumstances, dear boy, you really must permit a search of your room."

He comes again, the Giver-of-All-Good-Things, and lo, a hubbub follows in his wake! So many pairs of feet, and I here, beneath the bed, trapped by my own good offices, unable to reach the refuge of my palace. What do they here, so many of the great clumsy ones? My beloved Giver-of-All-Good-Things sits apart on the window seat, dejected, while they violate the sanctity of his belongings.

But see! One of their number, a blossom of beauty sweeter-scented than the Persian rose, remains aloof from this untoward rampage. She sits beside him, offers him kind words. How gentle she seems! I am fond of my dear Giver-of-All-Good-Things but—alas!—I admit that he is not one of surpassing grace. I wish to return to my palace, yet were I now to prostrate my unworthy self at his feet he might leap up in surprise and land—!

It bears not thinking on. Ah, behold! One of their number even now dares to fumble his oafish hands within the very precincts of my palace! There is no more time to lose. I *will* return, and then let them only *try* to stick their thick fingers where they do not belong.

I will go to the female. She will help me.

"Aha!" cried Clarence, one hand frisking the cotton wool bedding in the hamster's box. "There's something here!"

"It's probably Oscar," Monty said.

"I beg your pardon?" the original possessor of that name inquired.

"Shut up, Monty," Algy hissed. In a louder voice he called across the room to Clarence, "Of course there's something in there: My *hamster* is in there, and he doesn't like being disturbed. Get your hand out before he bites your finger off."

"Oh, I don't think this is a hamster," Clarence countered, a malicious glint in his eye. "Rubies seldom bite." With that, he thrust his find victoriously into Lady Delapye's hands.

Her ladyship plucked off the wisps of cotton wool and studied Clarence's offering. "Rubies seldom smell of bay rum either," she remarked, handing him back the cut-glass stopper belonging to one of the scent bottles on top of the chest of drawers.

"How did *that* get in there?" Clarence goggled at the object, dumbfounded.

"More to the point, how ever did you manage to muck about in that box without getting bitten?" Algy demanded. "Unless . . ." A frightening thought crossed his mind. He sprang from his place and dashed for the chest of drawers.

"—what I get for listening to you," Clarence muttered to the rest of the young toffs as Algy shouldered past. "Next time you've got a bright idea about where to search, do it your—"

"He's gone!" Algy cry of distress overwhelmed all other sounds. "Oscar's gone!"

"You *did* say 'Oscar,' dear boy?" the playwright queried.

"Eeek!" Lady Mary screamed from the window seat.

"My dear Lady Mary, you mustn't take on so," Oscar said with a low chuckle. "If Algy's chosen to name his pet after me, I certainly don't—"

"There's a rat in my lap!"

"A tail-less rat!" cried Monty. "Watch out, they're venomous!"

"Oscar!" Algy exclaimed with relief.

"Get him off me! Get him off!" Lady Mary was frozen with fear. "He's—*ugh!*—he's being *sick* on me!"

At this point, the furry dumpling in Lady Mary's lap gave a

mighty heave, opened his mouth wide, and deposited something round and shining on her skirt.

Oscar leaned nigh to see what the hamster had wrought. "It appears your pet and I have more in common than a name. Pearls of great price come out of his mouth, too."

"Let me see that!" Geoffrey commanded, striding forward.

"Don't! You'll scare him!" Algy's warning came too late: The hamster leaped from Lady Mary's lap and shot between the many milling pairs of feet, out the door.

I have erred. I equated the female's kindness with a stalwart character, but she is timorous and given to hysterics. Perhaps it is just as well. It is not enough that I have thwarted the interloper's scheme; I must reveal him utterly!

"I can*not* believe we're spending an evening in one of the finest old homes in England chasing a rat through the lumber room," said Bertie.

"I'll thank you not to refer to my namesake as a rat," Oscar rejoined before Algy could stand up for the honor of his pet. "Besides, I haven't had this much fun at a houseparty in years. What would you prefer we do to pass the time, Bertie? Play hunt-the-slipper?"

At the pointed reference to his father's trade, Bertie subsided. In an attempt to divert the group's attention from his discomfiture, he called out, "Any sign of him yet, Algy?"

"Maybe," Algy replied. His voice came somewhat muffled. He was on hands and knees amid a miniature Stonehenge composed entirely of luggage. "I think he may have sought out my valises—familiar scents and all that. That German chap in the Holy Land told me that these hamsters have quite an astonishing sense of smell. There's a scrabbling sound coming from inside my— No, wait a moment, that's not *my* valise. . . . Oh dear, not only is it not mine, but I'm afraid that little Oscar's gnawed himself rather a substantial hole in one corner." Algy's head popped up from among the trunks and portmanteaus like a surfacing mole. "The tag says its yours, Geoffrey. I'm frightfully sorry, I'll buy you a replacement directly we return to London."

"Don't trouble yourself, Algy, please," Geoffrey replied with some urgency, weaving his way between the tumuli of luggage. "Here, let me have it; I'll get the jolly little fellow out for you. Step back, do step back and allow me to—"

"No need, old chap." Algy picked up the valise before Geoffrey could reach him and agitated it gently, no more than a handspan from the floor. "I'll just shake him out easy as one—" True to his word, he gave the valise a shake. "—Two—" and another "—thr . . . Oh, I say!"

Three soft plops sounded. Three luminous gems—a tourmaline, a moonstone, and a sapphire of extraordinary size, color, and fire—rolled over the lumber room floor. Algy gaped, still holding the marvel-yielding valise aloft. The sound of tiny claws scrabbling still came from the depths, until the gnawed-out hole in the corner yielded at last the bright-eyed countenance of the hamster, one side of its face bulging unnaturally. The little beast dropped almost casually to the ground and waddled straight up to Lady Delapye. Using its nimble pink paws, it pushed at the swelling in its cheek until it spat out the missing ruby at her feet. Lady Delapye's feelings at this juncture were not to be gauged by ordinary standards.

There were, however, others in the group whose reactions were more vivid. As if motivated by one and the same will, Geoffrey and Thompson attempted to bolt from the lumber room, only to find their egress firmly blocked by Mr. Wilde. Thompson made the mistake of trying to fight his way through only to find himself sitting on the floor nursing what promised to be a black eye of spectacular brilliance.

"Egad, where did you learn to fight, sir?" he demanded.

"Surely at a better school than the one where you studied that atrocious Bow Bells accent you've been affecting," Oscar countered. "You know, Thompson, a good actor remains in character. Earlier, when you were repeating for us your master's instructions concerning his evening dress, you dropped it entirely in favor of his manner of speech. However, the lapse was so brief that at the time I thought I'd imagined it."

"An *actor*?" Clarence gawked at his manservant, scandalized. "I've been being dressed by an *actor*?"

"Better than being undressed by one," Monty whinnied.

"I wasn't an actor when you hired me, sir," Thompson said, facing his master resolutely. "True, I long nourished a passion for the theater, but I was unable to see my way clear to a career behind the footlights. The accent which Mr. Wilde supposes I affected was mine from birth; it had no place upon the London stage. My dream remained just that, until—" He raised his melting eyes to Geoffrey.

"Well, the game's up, isn't it?" Geoffrey made a gesture of resignation and sighed. "Just as well; I'm tired of living a lie. I, too, adore the theater. My birth forbade me to come any nearer the stage than a box seat, yet there was nothing to bar me from practicing my beloved craft in secret. It is perhaps fitting that it all ends here, where it all began. One summer's day three years ago, during a lawn party at Bishop's Ashlar, I stole away from the rest of you and was declaiming the soliloquoy from *Richard III* when Thompson surprised me in the pergola."

"He swore me to secrecy," Thompson said. "I agreed, for a price: that he school my voice, refine my speech, and generally help me prepare for the now gloriously attainable life of a thespian."

"Secrecy," Geoffrey repeated bitterly. "A secrecy shattered— and my life with it—when *he* walked in on us." For the second time that evening, Algy found himself looking down the length of an accusatory finger.

"That—that was you?" Algy regarded Thompson quizzically. "But the fellow with whom I caught Geoffrey was dark-haired."

"A wig," said Thompson. "The same one I used earlier today, to confuse any accidental witnesses who might have spied me when I planted the ruby in your room, in that creature's box." He glared daggers at the hamster, who sat unconcernedly grooming himself in the middle of the lumber room floor.

"If you planted a ruby, how did the box come to yield a cut-glass stopper?" Lady Mary asked. "And then, how did he happen to, er, present me with that pearl?"

"Sod me if I know, your ladyship," said Thompson, momentarily regressing to his roots.

"The Ormond pearl," Geoffrey clarified. "I hoped to sell it to the same buyer I found for the Sforza emerald. Your readings were correct, Algy," he said with a wobbly grin. "It *is* easier to sell loose stones. Easier to steal them only one at a time, too. If I'd lifted whole lashings of jewels at a go, the hue and cry of the infuriated gentry would have brought me to earth in short order. But steal only one gem from the nabobs and they're almost grateful; gives them something to talk about over dinner besides politics and gout."

"Why did you do it, old man?" Philip asked, putting one arm around Geoffrey's sagging shoulders.

"Why? Why, for the money, naturally."

"I thought that your uncle provided for your needs."

"*Did* provide." Geoffrey's pathetic gaze now turned to Lady Mary. "He did *so* want us to marry. I tried telling him that I didn't love you, but he threatened me with disinheritance if I failed to secure your hand, so I complied. It was my greatest triumph as an actor to date."

"Oh! Geoffrey, how *could* you?" Lady Mary burst into tears. Algy took her into his arms and comforted her.

"Sir, you are a cad!" Lady Delapye declaimed.

"If so, my lady, he is an unsuccessful one," Oscar interposed. "Had Algy here not discovered Geoffrey and Thompson doing— doing—" For the first time in his life, Oscar was at a loss and was forced to inquire: "What *were* the two of you doing?"

"*Volpone*," Thompson replied.

"*That's* the vice that daren't speak its name?" Monty cheeped. "*Acting?*" Everyone shushed him so that Oscar might go on.

"So, had not Algy's discovery reached Lady Mary and had she not broken off the engagement, Geoffrey would have drawn her into a loveless marriage and then, my lady, *then* you might name him cad with impunity."

Monty sidled up to Geoffrey. "Disinherited after all, were you? When the wedding fizzled?" Geoffrey nodded. "Carrying a grudge against poor old Algy over it all this time?" Another nod. "Got the idea for laying the crime to his account when we were all teasing him about the jewel thefts, back at the Café Royal? Had Thompson plant the ruby in his room while you were out meeting the train? Perfect alibi, all that sort of thing?" A third nod caused Monty to reach the edifying conclusion: "Oh, I say, Geoffrey, *bad show!*"

"Hmm, perhaps not so bad as all that, young Monty." Oscar tapped his lips thoughtfully with steepled forefingers. "Our Geoffrey's chief offense is to have loved his Muse not wisely, but too well, thereby losing much. Shall he now lose liberty besides? Lady Delapye, I appeal to your sense of charity: You have your ruby back again and I myself will pay to have it reset. Will you insist on pressing charges against this poor boy?"

Lady Delapye frowned ominously, but ended by saying, "I have better things to do than give testimony in criminal court. I will not prosecute."

"As for the other gems, I will see to it that they are all restored to their rightful owners."

"What about the Sforza emerald?" Bertie asked.

"I hope that Geoffrey will introduce me to the purchaser so that I may persuade him to sell it back to me. It will likely cost the earth, but still, we must set things right. Which is more than Lady Gregory will do with that poor, helpless emerald."

"Whatever the cost, I would like to advance it to you in a good cause," Algy said, his arms still cradling Lady Mary. "I don't want to see poor Geoffrey suffer any more."

"You would do that for me after what I—?" Geoffrey looked to be on the verge of tears.

"No real harm done." Algy smiled down at Lady Mary's russet head. "And who knows? Perhaps some unlooked-for good."

Fairly trembling with apprehension, Geoffrey raised his eyes to Oscar's and said, "When you do return the stones, you—you won't say a word about Thompson and me?"

"Assuredly not. That would defeat my whole purpose, which is to see my latest play staged as originally scheduled, now that I have found my new second lead"—he threw one arm around Geoffrey—"and his understudy." Thompson, too, was embraced. "Two sterling thespians," Oscar went on, "whose singleminded efforts toward the success of my play will be second only to the pains they shall take to repay their several benefactors out of their salaries."

While most of the assemblage gathered 'round to applaud Oscar's clever resolution of the situation, Algy reluctantly released Lady Mary and knelt to offer his hand to the hamster still sitting at Lady Delapye's feet. The little creature jumped eagerly onto his palm. He stood up, stroking its silky head, and said, half-joking, "I believe we are forgetting the true hero of the hour."

"*Tsk,*" said Lady Delapye. "You ascribe entirely too much volition to a dumb beast. That creature merely obeyed its instincts. When Thompson placed the ruby in its cage, perhaps it took a liking to the smell of the thing and determined to discover the source. This it accomplished when it found the rest of the stolen gems, all of which were doubtless well imbued with the scent of their purloiners. It carried the ruby with it on its quest for much the same reason that a squirrel will carry one mouthful of leaves to another, hoping to amass enough for a nest."

"Then the hamster has a taste for living in the midst of luxury?" Oscar smiled and patted his namesake delicately. "We *do* have a lot in common. Algy, might you write your unhappily named Uncle Ludovic to see if he might obtain another hamster as a worthy companion for *me*?"

"Oh, and one for me, too!" Monty chirped, ever ready to vault aboard any fashion trend Oscar sanctified. He was not alone.

"One for me as well," said Philip.

"And me," Bertie chimed in.

"I don't know ..." Having been so recently made aware of his valet's deceit, Clarence was no longer as impulsive as his friends. "To import the creatures all the way from the Holy Land won't be cheap. Your little Oscar is an intriguing pet, Algy, and he has willy-nilly solved a mystery, but still, the cost—!"

I am content. I have served well my dear Giver-of-All-Good-Things. The older female seeks to discredit me, overlooking the fact that not only did I remove the ruby from my palace and use its scent to discover the treasure-cave itself, but I also brought back a *different* gem as evidence of my discovery! Fool.

The other great clumsy ones throng about me with praises. These I deserve. Moreover they make inquiry as to the chance of bringing hither more of my kin. This I approve, in the hopes of a female of my kind finding her way into my palace of unbridled sensual delight. And yet there is among them one who questions whether the cost in mere money would be worth the supreme pleasure of intimacy with my kind! *Faugh*, humans . . .

Verily a human is one who knows the price of everything and the value of nothing.

Esther M. Friesner and Walter J. Stutzman

Esther M. Friesner and Walter J. Stutzman share living space, two teenagers, a couple of science fiction writing credits, and a marriage license. They also jointly cater to the whims of two large cats, Oliver James and Nero, and the househamster, Bertie. Bertie is the latest in a line of noble househamsters whose members have included Lady Morgana, Boris, Woody, and the original Huey the Oracular Hamster.

Esther's publishing credits are mostly in the science fiction/fantasy field: twenty-five novels (or so), over one hundred short stories and assorted poetry and articles. She has won the Science Fiction and Fantasy Writers of America Nebula Award twice, and was once a finalist for the field's populist Hugo Award.

You may have gathered that Midnight Louie is no slouch when it comes to keeping up with trends; I pride myself on my up-to-the-minute savvy. So I am especially proud to present an example of contemporary "true-crime" writing, nonfiction by J. A. Jance, who covers the Pacific Northwest in her J.P. Beaumont mysteries, and the Southwest in her best-selling Joanna Brady series.

This piece relates more to the Beaumont books. It is remarkable for showing that the human species has a knack for deduction even when the only witness able to testify to the crime in question is pretty much mute. The piece also demonstrates how real-life incidents move authors to import animals into their books and stories.

Authors, do not thank us with other than an extra pat or tidbit in our bowls! We are humbly happy to serve as inspirations, and friends.

—M.L.

Mandy: "Free to Good Home"

J. A. Jance

MANDY CAME TO us as a refugee from the classified ads—a ten-year-old golden retriever who, according to the woman I talked to on the phone, lived in a family where the children had grown up and left home and where the parents were moving into a no-dogs-allowed condo.

With four kids still at home, two goldens of our own, and a yard with no fence, the last thing we needed was another dog, but

Bill, my soft-hearted husband, sensed that a sad story lurked behind the unvarnished classified-advertising words. That afternoon we loaded up cars with kids and dogs and went to meet Mandy.

When I saw her limping stiff-legged down the steps of the house, my heart sank. What a frail, silver-haired old lady of a dog she was. Surely our loud, boisterous family with our two fat and sassy five-year-old dogs was no place for such an elderly girl. The well-dressed woman who had placed the ad seemed to agree with that assessment.

"We should probably try to find a place where she'll still be an only dog," the woman said. "But if nobody else takes her . . ." I leaned down to pet Mandy. My hand came up gray and grimy. "She needs a bath," the woman told me. "I just haven't had time."

That day we left without Mandy. After a week or two with no call, Bill and I assumed we were safe. Certainly we didn't need another dog, but a month later, the phone rang. Nobody had taken Mandy. Did we still want her? That very afternoon, kids, dogs, and cars again trooped over to her house, this time to bring her home.

The woman led Mandy out to the car on a leash. At home, our dogs don't go anywhere, including upstairs, without picking up their stuffed toy animals or a ball or two and carrying them along. Mandy came to us with nothing familiar—no dish, no blanket, no toys—only a leash she obviously wasn't used to and a collar that was far too tight.

After owning the dog for ten years, I expected leave-taking would be a painful process for the woman. At the last moment, however, a telephone rang inside the house, and the woman rushed away, handing the leash over to me without so much as a backward glance. We had told the woman that we'd try taking Mandy for a few days to see how it worked out, but after witnessing that little episode, Bill and I agreed on the way home that no matter what, Mandy wouldn't return to her previous owners.

Bringing a stranger—human or animal—into your home is always a risky proposition. We knew almost nothing about

Mandy, other than the fact that she was ten years old and suffered from arthritis. Bill, both big-hearted and scientific, immediately prescribed a regimen of buffered aspirin that we administered coated with peanut butter. The pain medication did seem to offer Mandy some relief. Her movements appeared to be less hobbled.

It seems reasonable that someone trying to give a dog away would bathe her and polish her up some, but weeks after we'd first met her, Mandy *still* needed a bath. She reeked. The insides of her ears were crusted with greasy wax. A mat of tangles three inches thick ran up and down the backs of both hind legs. Worried about how she would respond to strangers working on her, Bill and my daughter helped hold her down while I clipped off the painful clumps of tangles. Bill gave her a bath, which she seemed to enjoy, but the first few times we tried to brush her, she shied away and hid under a table.

Once Mandy was clean, she obviously liked it. She was fastidious about grooming the parts of herself she could reach, but those stiff old hindquarters were beyond her. Now that the distressing snarls of hair were gone from her legs, she let us brush her regularly. She was shiny and clean except for a funny dusty smell that wasn't at all like that of our other dogs.

We'd been told that Mandy wouldn't eat dry dog food, but dry was all we had. It didn't take long for sibling rivalry to work its magic. With two other dogs peering hungrily over her shoulder, Mandy ate her dry dog food and cleaned her dish with relish.

Walking her—a job which has long been my traditional task—proved to be the toughest challenge. Allowed out on her own, Mandy hadn't been trained to do her job on a leash the way our other two dogs did. Without a fence around our yard, this became an important issue. After several disheartening attempts, including a few indoor accidents, I finally decided to risk the possibility of her running away. Leashless, but armed with a tiny bagel bribe, I led Mandy out to the designated walking area where we achieved instant results. She made absolutely no effort to run away. Mandy knew where home was now, and she wasn't leaving.

With Mandy setting the example, our other two dogs learned to follow her leashless lead, which created a new maxim in our family which says: Old dogs can teach new people new tricks.

Those first few weeks weren't easy on us or on Mandy, either. For one thing, she had to suffer through the process of being given a new name. We live in a family headed by an electronics engineer. Our other dogs, Nikki and Tesla, are named after the electronics pioneer, Nikolai Tesla. Consequently, Mandy, too, had to have a scientific handle. She became Mandelbrot for long, named after the inventor of fractal geometry.

For days Mandy lay in whatever room we were in, not sleeping but warily watching our every move. Whenever anyone walked near her, despite her terribly stiff hindquarters, she would scramble desperately out of the way. Our other dogs, spoiled brats that they are, knew we would step over or around them. Mandy had no such faith, at least not in the beginning.

Her leaping out of the way combined with her abject panic when someone entered the room carrying a broom told us more about her previous life than we wanted to know. We were all happy that this gentle, sweet-tempered old dog was spending her retirement time with us.

No one had taught Mandy to fetch. Our other dogs' silly game of returning countless tennis balls she regarded with arch disdain. She had never met a rawhide chew bone until she came to live with us, and she seemed mystified the first time we gave her one. Eventually she not only learned to like them, she also learned that possession is nine-tenths of the law and that boss dog, Tesla, wouldn't be allowed to steal a rawhide Mandy was working on.

That old dog was a fly stalker *par excellence*. I think when she was dirty, pesky flies must have made Mandy's life miserable. She would lie perfectly still, watching them circling in the middle of a room. Suddenly, stiff and crippled as she was, she would leap up and snag one out of midair. She was quick about it, and she caught far more than she missed.

Months passed. Mandy made it clear that she liked being part of our family. She thrived on the petting and on the constant attention. Wherever someone was sitting, she was there, too, huffing noisily at them or touching people with her paw, reminding them to pet her.

The other dogs, littermates and lifelong companions, stayed with each other, but Mandy stayed with me. If I went downstairs to write, tough as it was, she hobbled downstairs to join me, lying with her head next to my feet while I worked away at my computer. If I was upstairs reading the newspaper, folding clothes, or making dinner, that's where Mandy was as well.

For several months, she trudged all the way up to the top floor of our three-story house and slept in the bedroom with Bill and me, but one night, in late August, she simply refused to climb the stairs. No amount of coaxing changed her mind. She took to sleeping on the cool tiles in the front entryway, flopping down gratefully onto them with weary but contented sighs.

Then, in early September, her limp was suddenly much worse. Aspirin no longer seemed to have any effect. Bill and I loaded Mandy into the car and took her to our neighborhood vet. She was terrified, and we were helpless to comfort her. She lay in the backseat, trembling like a leaf. Her terror brought tears to our eyes and lumps to our throats. The vet, a kindly man, also responded to her fear. He brought a shot of cortisone to Mandy on the floor of the waiting room without making her sit on the scary metal examining table. Afterward, we took her to the local Burger King on the way home and treated Mandy to her very own hamburger. She loved it.

The next week she seemed better. One morning when I let her outside, two crows were strutting unconcernedly across the front yard. With a puppylike growl Mandy leaped off the porch after them. I don't know who was more surprised—Mandy or the crows—but the next morning, when she stepped off the front porch again, she seemed to slip and fall, dropping all the way to her stomach. When she came back inside, she was no longer putting any weight at all on that one hind leg.

We returned to the vet. He gave her another shot and Mandy had her second Burger King treat, but this time the medication didn't seem to help at all. Oh, she still hobbled up and down the stairs to the basement to be with us when we went there, but it was a painful struggle for her—a gift of companionship that was heartbreaking in its generosity.

Once more we returned to the vet. This time he put her under anesthetic, took X rays, and did an extensive blood work-up. He was puzzled when he gave us the results. He could find no sign of arthritis. He suspected a torn ligament in her knee. His suggestion was either to leave her as a three-legged dog or to take her to a canine orthopedic specialist who might be able to do reconstructive surgery. Over Mandy's third Burger King hamburger, we decided that although the "free pet" price was rapidly escalating, we both wanted to give the specialist a try.

Armed with X rays and test results, I took Mandy to see the new vet. As we sat in the waiting room, she lay primly where she was told. A lady with a gangly ill-behaved puppy pointed out Mandy's behavior as being exemplary. In the small treatment room, waiting for the vet, time and again she put her paw on mine, reminding me not to forget to pet her.

Bill came from work and met us there. This vet, too, wanted to administer anesthetic and take more X rays, so with one last pat on the head, we turned Mandy over to him and left. That afternoon he called us with the awful news—bone cancer with nothing to be done. The vet told us gently that she'd obviously had the tumor since long before we had owned her and that the best thing to do would be to let her go. "Don't even take her home," he advised. "She's already here. She isn't scared right now. Seeing you upset will only upset her."

I knew he was right.

So we let Mandy go that afternoon—free to another good home. She had lived with us for only six months, but none of us were tough enough to let her go without a tear.

By the time she left, the ridge around her neck from the too-tight collar was almost gone. Her silvery white coat was silky smooth and shiny. She still smelled dusty, but there were no tangles in the curly fuzz on her hind legs, and the insides of her ears were pink and clean.

We loved Mandy, and we missed her. Bill went back to reading the free pet columns. Three months later, our college-aged son came home for Thanksgiving vacation bringing with him a seven-pound starveling of a puppy he had rescued from the Pullman, Washington, pound. There was no way we could say that strays weren't welcome in our home, so a dog we call The Bone came to live with us.

In the last year Bony has grown to be one hundred thirty pounds of primarily Irish wolfhound, at least that's what the vet who did his $178 root canal told us. He's a long-legged ragamuffin of a dog who snags balls out of the air by jumping five feet straight up. He has an amazing appetite and a propensity for eating anything that isn't nailed down, from prescription sunglasses to coffee-table bouquets. Taking in a brand-new puppy was another can of worms entirely from adopting a dignified old lady dog, but Mandy had taught us that there's always room for one more.

The Bone never met Mandy, but he owes her, and so do we.

P.S. The above was written a number of years ago, since Bony is now a relatively dignified seven while Nikki and Tess are fast becoming white-faced old ladies in their turn. But Mandy lives on. Through the miracle of fiction, she's still alive and well and growing old gracefully along with J. P. Beaumont's grandmother, Beverly Piedmont. Whenever the fictional Mandy steps daintily across the pages of another book, I'm always delighted to see her.
—JAJ, 1998

J. A. Jance

Best-selling author J. A. Jance has been writing murder mysteries for fifteen years, winning an American Mystery Award for Best Novel in the process. A graduate of the University of Arizona, this married mother of five has spent two years teaching high school English, five years as a K–12 librarian on an Arizona Indian reservation, and ten years selling life insurance.

Life insurance won't help the victims in her two popular mys-

tery series, but her protagonists will. Crusty but lovable homicide detective J. P. Beaumont makes Seattle his beat. Female sleuth Joanna Brady features in psychological thrillers employing the rich Native American lore of the Southwest. Judy's most recent books, all from Avon, are Rattlesnake Crossing *and the* New York Times *best-selling* Skeleton Canyon. *In January 1999, J. P. Beaumont comes to the fore again in* Breach of Duty.

Can you imagine a big, tough cop worrying about being called a fuzz-lovin' sort of guy? Well, it happens, especially when the "fuzz" love-object in question is animate and four-legged. I do not understand why macho types feel they must deny their softer, critter-caring sides. I am as hard-boiled as a nineties guy can be without getting pilloried in *Ms* magazine, and *I* have no trouble snuggling up publicly to needy fur-bearing creatures. Of course most of them happen to be highly female. But I am open-minded. I even snuggle up publicly to two-legged, *skin*-wearing females and never fret for a second that I might be taken for a sissy. So to you human guys so worried that real men don't pet puddytats, I have but three little words: get over it. Or I'll bite you.

—M.L.

On the Take
Carolyn Wheat

TEN—COUNT 'EM—ten. He'd never meant to have ten. Who the hell did?

But there they were, all ten of them, meowing and swirling around him, rubbing up against his legs, getting their fur all over his blue uniform pants, and you know what, it was kinda nice having living creatures glad to see him when he opened the door. Happy that he was home instead of bitching that he was late again and what did he mean stopping off at Hanratty's for a coupla beers with the guys, and was he sure that bimbo Shawna Taylor hadn't come on to him again?

Ten cats beat the hell out of one wife. Especially a wife who'd started out as a cop groupie herself, so she knew from personal experience how the girls at Hanratty's went after the married guys.

But ten. You could live down one or two, maybe. Three—not so easy, but you could pass off three as halfway normal. Ten was way the hell out of range. Dooley down at the stationhouse—oh, he could hear Dooley now. "Ten freakin' cats in a freakin' studio apartment, what the hell's that all about? That the only pussy you're gettin' these days, Perkie?"

You couldn't even say "Don't call me Perkie." Ten cats, you couldn't say nothin'.

Fernandez would start in, too. Where Dooley led, Fernando followed. Evil twins, separated at birth, even if Dooley was a big black linebacker and Fernando a little Puerto Rican with more mouth than muscle.

He sighed at the injustice of it all, then reached down and patted the head of the animal nearest his leg. He'd named them all, but it took a minute to recall that the orange one with the amber eyes was Linda. He'd named them after old girlfriends, and the sad thing was that he had maybe two names left. Three more cats and he'd have more of them in his apartment right now than he'd ever had women in his whole life.

Linda arched her back and leaned into his hand, purring loudly. She swished her tail flirtatiously and turned around, coming back toward him for more.

If only the human Linda had behaved the same way instead of brushing off his roving hands, pushing him away when all he wanted was a little loving.

The cats never pushed him away. They loved the feel of his strong hands on their silky fur.

He had to get rid of them. Well, six of them, anyway. Four wouldn't be completely out of line. He could maybe keep four and survive the stationhouse.

But where could they go? It wasn't like there were a lot of farms around here, ready to take in a couple more barn cats. There were farms Upstate, but Upstate was a big green world of

Unknown as far as he was concerned. Born and bred in Brooklyn, he'd just about barely been ten miles from Greenpoint, and he didn't know any farmers.

His mother? Would she take in a cat or two? Old ladies liked cats, didn't they?

Ha. In books, maybe. But Anthea Rose McKechnie Perkins wasn't an old lady in a book, she was a beer-drinking, bingo-playing baseball fanatic who'd screw up her face and say, "You bring them dirty moggies over 'ere, I'll give you such a clip on the ear'ole." Fifty years Anthea Rose had been out of Liverpool, but her tongue remembered the old country all too well. And so did the hand that had clipped him on the earhole so many times he still had a ringing on the left side of his head.

So Mum was out. Where else could he take his pets, the ones he couldn't keep?

Not the shelter. He looked into the sad green eyes of Betsy, the first one he'd brought home, and thought of them putting her into a little cage and then a little oven and suffocating the life out of her sinuous little black body, and it made him feel as if he was the one about to die from lack of oxygen.

No, not Betsy. No matter what, Betsy had to stay.

But the others had to go.

If only he knew where.

"Hey, kid," Dooley called out as the rookie entered the station-house, two cardboard containers of coffee in his hands, "You bringin' Perkie coffee now? You gonna clean up his desk for him, too? Make him breakfast like a good little wife?"

The kid was very young and very fair, which was why Dooley loved riding him. His blush started at the nape of his neck and climbed, inch by visible inch, up to his forehead. Even his scalp under short blond hair glowed red when he was embarrassed—which was pretty much most of the time.

Fernandez made a salacious remark about other things good wives did for their husbands, and the kid's blush deepened to a near-purple.

"You seen my partner?" The kid turned to Olivetti, the oldest guy in the squad, and the only one besides Perkins who treated him with a modicum of respect.

"In the can," Olivetti said, shifting his cigar from one side of his mouth to the other.

The kid set the coffees down and opened one up. It was so light it looked like hot milk; he opened four sugar packets at once and emptied them, then stirred the sweet mess with a red plastic stick.

"Hey, thanks, Randy." Perkins stepped to the desk, picked up his coffee, popped a little hole in the plastic top, then drank it straight. The kid wondered whether maybe you started out drinking it milky and sweet and as you got older, more experienced, you gradually cut down the sugar and milk and you finally drank the black, oily-looking mess that looked as if it belonged in your car instead of your stomach.

He wondered if he'd ever grow the hell up.

Their first stop was a bodega on Seventh Avenue. Nice little place, open practically all night, and Perkins knew they had a little book going in the back room, which was why he and Randy were there. Every four months or so you had to write up a place like that. You'd never shut it down, and maybe you didn't really want to, truth be told, but you had to write them up, give them a fine to pay.

The idea hit him as soon as he crossed the threshold. Stores had cats in them all the time. Well-fed, friendly cats who sidled up to the customers or sat on bags of rice, sunning themselves in the windows.

Just what Linda and Heather and Tiffi needed: good jobs in the neighborhood. They'd be well cared for, and the best thing was, he could still see them when he wanted to, still reach his hand down to their level and feel the soft welcome of their furry bodies against his rough skin.

But how to get the idea across without the kid hearing? He liked Randy, even if he was the wettest-behind-the-ears rookie he'd ever seen, but you had to admit, the kid's baby face gave away everything. If he found out about the cats, it would take a Manhattan minute for Dooley and Fernandez to catch on, and from that moment on, his life would be a living hell.

So he put his hand on the store owner's arm and gently eased him into the back room, saying he had to talk to him alone. He asked Randy to stay outside and wait for bettors to come in with their betting slips.

Hector Rosario didn't like the idea. "No *gatos*" about summed it up. "I don't like no *gatos* in here. This is a clean place."

"Yeah, but it could be cleaner if you didn't have mice. Cats can help with that," Perkins said in his most persuasive tone.

"I don't got no mice," the bodega owner protested, his mustache quivering with indignation. "I don't got no mice, and I don't got no cats. No *animalitos* nohow."

"Yeah, but you could have cats. I mean, one or two cats in here, make the place homey. Make the customers feel at—"

"Two? Whaddaya mean two?"

"One it is," Perkins cut in before the man could change his mind. "I can have her here by eight tonight."

The little man's eyes narrowed shrewdly. "And what do I get in return for taking this cat off your hands?"

Perkins sighed. He'd known this was coming, although why, he had a hard time fathoming. Surely giving a home to his beloved Linda ought to be reward enough in itself. But it was a hard world, and you had to give in order to get.

"Well, you're lucky this time, Mr. Rosario. I don't see any evidence of gambling this time around. But I'll be back in another four months, and I'd better not find any betting slips in your till."

Rosario smiled, his gold tooth flashing, as he hefted a huge bag of kitty litter from the shelf.

The kid couldn't believe it. Oh, he'd learned all about it at the Police Academy; he wasn't stupid. He knew there were cops on the take in the old days, but he'd thought those days were long past.

But here was his partner, his own partner, a guy who hardly even cursed on the job, he was so squeaky-clean, taking a bribe to look the other way.

That bodega was dirty. Randy knew it and Perkins knew it, and yet they'd walked out of there without writing the guy up. No search of the cash register for betting slips, no arrest, and Perkins taking the guy off into the back room for a private chat.

It added up to just one thing: corruption.

And he, Randy Piasecki, was in it up to the bright-red tips of his ears.

The same scenario, more or less, played itself out four more times. Two of the store owners actually seemed to like the idea of acquiring feline employees, which made Perkins feel good, but at least the others said yes in the long run.

"For you, Officer Perkins, I could maybe take in a cat," Leventhal the butcher said. "A tiny little *katz,* not a big fat *mamzer* eats so much it never wants to catch the mice."

Greek Tony the shoemaker growled a little about the price of milk, but when the fire code violation in back of the store was mentioned, he gave a gruff assent to letting Andrea move in with him. The pizza guys agreed to take two, which really made his day, and made him glad he'd thought of pretending he'd seen a mouse run from their rest room to the storeroom in the rear of the pizzeria. Heather and Jeri would feast on mozzarella and anchovies, and he could stop by and pet them when he picked up his pie every Thursday, which he did like clockwork.

The one place he didn't ask was the Chinese restaurant.

But all in all, it had been a good day. Five cats placed. One to go. And the kid none the wiser, which meant he'd kept his secret from Dooley and Fernando.

When a good cop goes bad, he goes real bad. That was the wisdom Randy had been taught at the Academy. It might start with a free cup of coffee, but corruption was a slippery slope, and pretty soon you had cops with summer houses in the mountains and fancy cars and boats, even.

They'd stopped at a lot of little businesses, and in each and every one, Perkins had taken the owner for a private consultation where Randy couldn't hear, and they'd left each and every store without writing up any tickets even though violations were jumping right out at them from every corner, and after they'd left Perkie had a smile as big as the Bronx on his homely but pleasant face.

It was exciting in a horrible sort of way.

Horrible because Perkie was a good guy and a good partner and you didn't rat out your partner no matter what he did, and besides, Perkie never made him blush. At least not on purpose.

Exciting because he felt like Serpico. The fate of the entire NYPD rested on him, an untried rookie. He could go along with the corruption, ask for a cut of the take, and become a grizzled old veteran with cynicism oozing from every pore.

Or he could be a hero. Blow the whistle. Turn his partner in and let the world know that he wasn't cut from the same dirty cloth.

He didn't yet know which road he would take, but the very fact of knowing there was a road and that his next steps would determine not only his personal future but affect a lot of other people thrilled him to the core.

Dooley and Fernandez wouldn't mess with him if he was Serpico. They'd scorn him as a man who turned on his partner, but they'd be scared of him at the same time. Scared of what he might find out about them.

If only it was Dooley instead of Perkie who was on the take. It would be easy then; he could ruin Dooley's miserable life without a second's hesitation.

But Perkie was different. He liked Perkie. He didn't want Perkie to be a dirty cop.

But he was. Randy had seen it with his own eyes.

Five cats and one cat carrier.

First you had to chase the cat you wanted, and of course all the others ran, too, hiding under the bed or jumping onto the kitchen counter. Annie made it onto the top of the refrigerator even though he'd decided to keep her.

Finally he had the right cat inside the little suitcase with holes in the side. The captive howled in protest, sounding like a cross between a banshee and a little kid whining "Mommy, I don't want to go to camp." He'd march down the steps anyway, determined to follow up on his day's work by delivering his darlings to their new homes.

They were scared at first. All of them. Piteous meows and hiding in corners and Perkins felt like an executioner turning around and going back home for another one. But they'd get used to their new surroundings, and he'd made it very clear that the cats had better be looking healthy and happy the next time he stopped in for a visit.

Finally it was done. Five gone, five left at home. He was going to a West Indian roti stand tomorrow; that would be perfect for Tiffi, who had a taste for spicy food.

He'd been up all night. Tossing and turning in the bed, then padding to the fridge to finish that carton of Ben and Jerry's, then explaining to Ma why he wasn't sleeping so good and finally convincing her it wasn't because he'd seen a particularly grotesque murder the day before. Try as he might, Randy could never quite convince Ma that after a whole three months on the job, he wasn't Columbo and hadn't yet stumbled across his first dead body.

He didn't tell her about Perkie. He couldn't. He'd already convinced her that Officer Perkins practically walked on water, and he couldn't shatter her illusions. It was, after all, a man's job to shelter his women from the harsher side of life, so he sighed and carried the increasingly heavy burden of his suspicion all by himself.

What should he do?

The options were clear in his mind. There was no ambiguity. He just didn't want to do any one of them. He didn't want to go upstairs and talk to the sergeant, who would call Internal Affairs and wire him for sound so he could bring down his best friend on the force and resign himself to nineteen years and nine months of isolation from his fellow cops, none of whom would ever talk to a snitch ever again. All he'd ever wanted to be was a cop, and ratting on his partner would kill that dream dead.

But if he went along with it, if he closed a blind eye—what then? Someday, sometime, someone else would start to suspect. It might start small, but after a while, after Perkie started driving a new car and talking about vacations in the mountains and when he finally announced that he had a boat—well, everyone knew what that meant. You had a boat, you were going down. No two ways about it.

And since he, Randy Piasecki, was Perkie's partner, he'd go down too, even if he never so much as spent a minute on that boat.

It wasn't fair.

How could Perkie do a thing like that to him?

So, okay, with a heavy heart and all that, he'd go to the sarge and tell what he'd seen. And the sarge would pick up the phone and—

Or would he? What, after all, had Randy seen? Trips to back rooms, that's all. No money changing hands, no deals being made. Just private conversations and no tickets written.

It wasn't enough.

But it was suspicious.

The answer hit him as he buttoned his blue uniform pants. He had his own little tiny tape recorder, a present from his uncle Julius last Christmas. Why Jule thought a cop needed a pocket tape recorder was anyone's guess, but it turned out he was right, because that was just what Randy needed today. He'd wire himself, get the evidence on tape, and then decide what to do with his information.

If he had it on tape, the sarge would have to listen. And if, by some miracle, he was wrong about Perkie, he could destroy the tape and go back to business as usual.

He sighed with relief as he slipped the recorder into the inside pocket of his blue uniform jacket.

One more to go. One more cat placed and he could relax. Four was okay. A little over the line, maybe, but he'd promised Annie the night before and he couldn't disappoint her. She was a feisty little thing with emerald eyes and a snarling hiss that scared felines twice her size into backing down.

He smiled as he remembered her staring down at him from the top of the refrigerator.

One more. Tiffi, short for Tiffani, and although he liked the cat well enough, the real-life Tiffi had skipped out of the Valentine's dance at P.S. 211 with Ricky Mogelescu, leaving him to wander disconsolately through the crowd like a total loser. So Tiffi was the one he had to place today; the Jamaican roti guys were pretty laid-back and he didn't foresee any problems.

Until he parked his car on Nineteenth Street, behind a white van. He put his cop placard in the window and locked up, then walked along the street toward the bodega on the corner, prepared to stop in and see how Linda was doing in her new home.

But out of the alleyway between the brownstone and the brick apartment house, there came a little mewing sound. A tiny, tiny sound that cracked his heart wide open, because he knew at once what it was and that it was up to him to do something about it.

The kittens were about a week old. Four of them. Cute as bugs, splattered with orange and gray and white as if a painter had shaken his brushes at them. One had a little smudge on her nose and another had a bright orange tail and—

He was in love.

Purely and simply in love.

All the other cats he'd found in the neighborhood had been grown, or nearly grown. They'd been dirty and hungry, so thin you could feel their ribs when you petted them. Scared of people, and for good reason. He'd had to coax them, leave food for days at a time, then bring the cat carrier and make his capture.

But the kittens tumbled toward him without fear, their tiny pink tongues exploring his hand, their needle claws digging into his skin but so delicately that he felt nothing. Their little noses enchanted him, and their huge eyes sucked him right into their world.

He had to have them. And Mama Cat, too, if she wanted to come. She was either dead or out hunting breakfast.

"I'll be back," he promised them. "I'll get the carrier and come back for you. Just wait here until I'm off duty."

Four and four make eight. If Mama showed, nine.

He was almost back to square one.

Randy hated the hot roti shop. Not the music, which was a nice bouncy reggae, or the guys with their giant knitted hats. It was the smell, which was bad because it was goat and now he knew it was goat. The smell hadn't, in truth, bothered him before he knew, but now that he knew, he pictured a little goat with little horns on its head, turning on a spit. Which wasn't what you saw because roti was sort of ground up, but still.

Goat.

The place wasn't open yet, so only the cook was there. Perkie motioned him into the back room, telling Randy to stand watch outside.

But Randy didn't. He edged toward the beaded curtain that separated the two rooms and slipped his hand into his pocket, fumbling for the buttons on his recorder. Finally, realizing he couldn't be seen, he took the thing out and turned it on, then held it up so that the microphone faced the doorway.

What he heard chilled him to the bone.

"You've got to help me out here," Perkie said. "I'm a desperate man. I need you to take at least two, maybe three."

Take?

Take what?

Wasn't it supposed to be the other way around? Wasn't the roti man supposed to give something to Perkie? Something like money?

Unless—

Oh, no. Not that. Not drugs. Not Perkins the squeaky-clean using the storefronts to push dope. Making semi-honest businessmen peddle crack or heroin or—

Why else would the roti man take something?

Why else would Perkins be so desperate? Some big drug dealer had Perkie by the shorts and now Perkins had to strongarm the shopowners into pushing the product?

This was big. Big and dirty and disgusting and pretty exciting, too. Because he, Randall James Piasecki Junior, had it all on tape.

He'd be on the news. HERO COP BUSTS DRUG RING.

He was blushing already.

Hero cop.

The beaded curtain swung open and the roti man came back into the front part of the shop. Randy nearly dropped the recorder, and was fumbling with his jacket pocket when his partner stepped in front of him.

"You won't be needing that," Perkie said, and Randy nearly wet himself. Had Perkins seen the recorder? Was this the part where the honest cop got wasted by the drug dealers?

But Perkie added, "We're not writing any tickets here. I didn't find any *ganja* in there. For once." The roti shop was well known in the neighborhood as the best place to score a fat joint.

So unless Perkie was being incredibly cagey, he really thought Randy was trying to get his ticket book out instead of trying to put his tape recorder in.

Outside, on the street, Randy considered his next move. Should he try to get a little more on tape? Get Perkie to admit he was dirty? He slipped his hand into his pocket and pushed the record button.

"Y'know, I kinda heard a little bit of what you were saying back there," he began in a tentative tone.

"Oh, jeez, man, you don't know what a relief that is." Perkins let out a long sigh; some of the tightly wound tension in his shoulders relaxed. "I mean, at first I didn't want you to know, but now, I need your help, partner. I need it bad."

"Help?" Try as he might to control his voice, it squeaked into the adolescent register Fernandez loved to mimic. "You want me to help you shake down the businesses on our beat?"

"Well, shake down is kinda strong," Perkie objected. "I'm only asking them to do something that will be good for them in the long run."

"Good for them? I mean, like I hear what you're saying, but is money everything? Sure, they'll make money in the short run, but in the long run, they could wind up dead. And so could you. I don't want any part of this."

"Dead? Money?" Perkins stopped dead in the street, earning a glare from a nanny wheeling a stroller. "What are you talking about?"

Oh, no. Perkins knew. He understood that he was being taped, and now he was getting cagey. Randy considered how to say what he had to say without actually using the words. If he said it flat out, Perkie would continue to stonewall, but if he hinted, maybe he could slide an admission out of his partner.

"I mean, people like going into a store and seeing a cat in the window. They like stopping to pet it, hearing it purr." Perkie smiled as he warmed to his subject. "You sit in that pizza place, eating alone, it's nice a cat comes over and rubs your leg, maybe even jumps into your lap. You can feed it some cheese—but not pepperoni. Too spicy."

Randy's face went beet red and he sputtered as he said, "Don't pull this crazy act on me. Don't treat me like a kid. I know what I know and I heard what I heard. You forced that guy back there to take two, and he didn't even want to take any. You're making these guys sell dope for you and I don't want any part of it. Got that?"

"He's taking cats," Perkie said with a bewildered air. "My cats. I—well, the truth is, I got these cats. A lot of cats." He hung his head and now the blush crept into his face, even if he was old enough to drink black coffee and like it.

"I picked them up in the neighborhood," he explained. "They looked so sad, so hungry. I never meant to keep them, just feed them and maybe find them a home, but that's not easy, you know."

"Cats."

"Cats. I had ten yesterday." Perkie's blue eyes pleaded with Randy. "You know what Dooley and Fernando would have to say about ten cats?"

"Oh, yeah. I got that picture clear. Ten?"

"Ten. So I got five placed, and today I was gonna hit up the roti guys and it would all be over, but then I found these kittens in the alley, and now I'm back to nine, only the roti guy said he'd take two, so that makes it eight, but that is definitely four too many, you know what I mean?"

"Kittens."

"I'll show you."

And he did, and when Randy Piasecki saw the four little guys with their big sparkling eyes and cute little button noses and whip tails and baby claws, he was in love too, because any guy who hated to think about a goat turning on a spit was bound to fall for kittens, so it turned out all right in the end. He took two and Perkie took two, and they managed to place three others with the pharmacy and the deli and the bakery.

But not the Chinese restaurant.

Carolyn Wheat

Brooklyn lawyer Cass Jameson debuted in Carolyn Wheat's Edgar-nominated novel, Dead Man's Thoughts. Mean Streak, *the series' fourth entry, also garnered a 1996 Edgar nomination from the Mystery Writers of America. The Cass Jameson mysteries now number six, and Carolyn won the Agatha, the Anthony, and the Macavity Short Story Awards in 1997. She has taught mystery writing at the New School for Social Research in New York City, and was Artist in Residence at Oklahoma Central State University. Though she once kept four cats in a one-bedroom Brooklyn apartment, she now lives in California without benefit of furry companionship. Her Brooklyn cats, known as the Gang of Four, are featured in "The Black Hawthorne"* (Cat Crimes in D.C.). *"Cat Lady" appears in* Cat Crimes II. *She is currently working on a story about a cadaver dog, mainly because there aren't any cadaver cats (with the notable exception of Midnight Louie, of course).*

Harbinger

Jean Hager

THE MORNING RAIN had become a fine October mist when Marisa Markham knelt and laid six long-stemmed yellow roses on the grave.

"I'll miss you, Tiana," she whispered.

Three weeks ago, she'd come back to Cherokee County for one day to attend Tiana's funeral in the little Indian Baptist Church, but had not joined the caravan going to the cemetery. Nor had she gone by Tiana's grandmother's house. Partly because she was pressed for time but also because, when Tiana's grandmother squeezed her hand and whispered an urgent,

"Come see me," something in Emma's black eyes had made Marisa recoil.

The funeral wreaths had been removed and now the grave was bare except for the yellow roses, Tiana's favorite flowers. Marisa ran her fingers over the sculpted vine that bordered the simple brass grave marker and read the inscription through a film of tears.

TIANA FOURKILLER
1972–1998

Shivering, Marisa got to her feet. She felt the damp in her hair, the wetness on her face. The haze of her breath hung in the air.

"Good-bye, Tiana," she murmured.

Burying her hands in her jacket pockets against the cold, she crossed the cemetery, hurrying past her grandparents' graves where, earlier, she had placed half of the dozen roses she'd bought that morning in Tahlequah. Exposed to the sodden chill, the roses already looked bedraggled and infinitely sad.

Reaching her car, she got in and drove back down the graveled road toward her grandparents' house—her house now. She passed the white clapboard Methodist Church, the little post office, her Uncle Howard's gas station–convenience store, all familiar to her still.

Throughout her school years, her parents had spent summers making research trips for her father's many articles and books on ancient cultures, sending Marisa to her grandparents in Park Hill, a few miles south of Tahlequah, in the heart of the Cherokee Nation of Oklahoma. While she had looked forward to seeing her grandparents each year, after a couple of weeks with only the older couple for company, she'd grown bored and restless. The remainder of the summer had been a blur of hot, turgid days and long nights so still you could hear a twig snap as it fell from a tree half a block away. She had felt stuck in some endless, dreamlike dimension.

All of that changed the summer of her tenth year when Tiana and her mother came to live with Tiana's grandmother, Emma

Cornsilk. Thereafter, summers flew by as she and Tiana, and often Tiana's cousin Johnny, wandered over the countryside around Park Hill, fishing, swimming, gathering wild blackberries, visiting Tiana's Cherokee relatives, and exploring the woods for secret hideouts.

Many of their evenings were spent sitting on Emma Cornsilk's front porch, drinking fresh lemonade and listening to Emma's stories about the Little People who lived in caves and spent all their time feasting and dancing, and the ancient monster, the Ut'ken, who was slain by the brave Cherokee hunter, and the Thunder Boys who made thunder when they wrestled. Most of Emma's stories were enchanting, and the youngsters begged to hear them again and again.

But on occasion, Emma's mood turned dark. Then she talked about fearful Night Walkers and Ravenmockers, Cherokee witches. At those times, Emma seemed a different woman, brooding and frightening.

During her college years, Marisa had still managed to get back to Park Hill for two or three weeks each summer, and she and Tiana, an art student at the university in Tahlequah, always took up their friendship as if they had never been apart.

After her college graduation, Marisa's visits to Park Hill had been less frequent as she focused on making her mark in a Chicago advertising agency. Tiana had stayed on with her grandmother, after her mother's passing, determined to pursue a career as a painter. Finally, Tiana's dedication had begun to pay off. She was becoming known as a rising star in a new generation of Indian artists. But Marisa had not seen her old friend in almost two years when Emma called to tell her that Marisa was dead.

The cruel irony of it made Marisa's throat tighten as she turned down a narrow black-topped lane to park beside the old house that was her legacy from her grandparents. Now, she thought, the value of Tiana's paintings would skyrocket as news of the young artist's untimely death got around and collectors realized that the work of Tiana Fourkiller would remain forever fixed at the current number of paintings.

Marisa entered the house by the back way, through the

kitchen. She shrugged off her jacket, put the kettle on the old propane stove to heat, and emptied and replaced the two aluminum pots she'd set on the floor of the porch-turned-utility room when it started raining to catch the water leaking through the roof. The last family who'd rented the house had, according to a neighbor, moved out several weeks ago. They'd left without notice and owing three months' back rent. When she'd come back for Tiana's funeral, Marisa had been dismayed at the house's state of disrepair, and had decided to take her vacation and make whatever repairs she could with her scant savings. Being an absentee landlord wasn't working out, and she had decided to put the house on the market. But repairs to the roof and a general sprucing up would have to be done first.

Tomorrow would be soon enough to think about that. First, she told herself as she made tea and opened a can of soup from the groceries she'd brought with her, she had to say hello to her Uncle Howard—and visit Emma, which she dreaded. Even now, she wished she could postpone the duty call yet again. But Emma would have seen her car at the house, and she couldn't delay any longer.

As Marisa drove up, Howard Walters was picking up litter around his gas station–convenience store, the only place in Park Hill where you could buy gas or grocery staples. She honked and Howard grinned and came to meet her.

She and her uncle had spoken briefly at Tiana's funeral but, other than that, their contact in recent years had dwindled to an exchange of Christmas cards. Howard was a widower and his only son, who was retarded, lived in a group home in Tulsa. His clear pleasure at seeing her now made Marisa wish she hadn't been so neglectful.

Howard gave her a big bear hug. "Gawd Almighty, you turned into a full-grown woman when I wasn't lookin', Marisa!"

"It's so good to see you, Uncle Howard!" She returned his hug and stepped back for a better look at him. In his late fifties,

Howard had developed a paunch and all that was left of his hair was a gray fringe over his ears and around the back of his head.

Marisa eyed his stomach. "Looks like you've grown a little yourself."

He laughed and slapped his leg. "You always did have a mouth on you, Marisa. What're you doing back here so soon after the funeral?"

"I'm getting the house ready to sell. I've discovered that the rental business isn't for me."

He nodded sympathetically. "Yeah, that last bunch was a band of no-accounts. Never did mow the lawn. Did they wreck the house?"

She shook her head. "They just let it go. The worst part is they moved out owing three months' back rent."

He patted her shoulder. "Well, come on in and have a Coke."

"Okay, but I can't stay long. I'm on my way to see Emma Cornsilk."

She followed him into the store. There were no customers, but as soon as school was out, the kids would begin to straggle in. At the back of Howard's store, four small booths, a pool table, and a couple of video game machines provided a gathering place for the community's children. As kids, when Marisa and Tiana weren't roaming the countryside, they'd hung out in the back of the store.

They sat in one of the booths and drank Cokes out of frosty cans.

"Emma's taking Tiana's death awful hard," Howard said.

"What happened, Uncle Howard? All Emma said was that the medical examiner had ruled Tiana's death an accident."

"She fell off that cliff east of here. It was getting dark, and I guess she got closer to the edge than she realized. Fell wrong, broke her neck." He stared at the scarred tabletop and shook his head. "What a waste."

Marisa remembered the cliff well. When they were twelve, she and Tiana had built a clubhouse above the cliff by nailing together old lumber, using trees as the four cornerposts. Marisa knew every inch of that place. How could Tiana have misjudged her location so badly that she fell off the cliff, even in the dark?

"Was she drinking?" It was the only explanation Marisa could think of.

It was a moment before he lifted his gaze to hers. "Not that I heard, but Tiana had changed. She could've started drinking or using drugs. I just don't know."

"She wouldn't use drugs," Marisa said. "Not after all of Johnny's problems." The last time Marisa saw Tiana, she'd told her that her cousin was using heavily. He'd been arrested twice for possession and couldn't hold a job. She'd been desperately worried about him.

"Now there's another waste," Howard said. "Johnny's about run Emma crazy, and now with Tiana's death—" He heaved a sigh. "Ben's back, living with her, too. I don't know how much more that woman can take."

Ben Cornsilk was Emma's only son, a quiet, dour man who'd been a brawler when he was young. Ben had been married and divorced twice that Marisa knew of. He'd taken little notice of Marisa during those childhood summers in Park Hill, except occasionally to rake her with his dark eyes, as if he were trying to work out where she'd come from. His mere presence had always made her nervous.

"I thought Ben was working in Kansas City."

"He was," Howard said. "He got into a knife fight, punctured his lung. I guess they let him go." He sighed. "We got enough problems around here without adding Ben Cornsilk to the mix."

"I always thought of Park Hill as a safe haven from all the drugs and violence going on everywhere else."

"It's not the same as it was when you were a youngster, Marisa. Too many kids around here start smoking pot before they're in their teens. I'd guess Johnny did too, but nobody realized what was going on till he started getting into trouble. By then, he was into the hard stuff."

"Where do the kids get the drugs?"

He stared at his hands, which clenched his Coke can tightly.

"I wish I knew. The kids still come here, but they won't talk to me about drugs, or who the pushers are."

They sat in silence for a few moments. Marisa finished her drink and slid out of the booth. "I need to get on over to Emma's. I'll come by for a longer talk in a day or two."

"You'd better." He walked out to her car with her.

A battered old Chevrolet and a nearly new Cadillac were parked in Emma Cornsilk's driveway. When Emma opened the door to Marisa, her face was still cratered by grief. "I've been waiting for you, child," she said without preamble. "Come in."

Tiana's cousin Johnny got up off the couch as Marisa entered the living room. His handsome face broke into a grin. "Hey, Marisa. How you doin'?"

"I'm doing just fine, Johnny. How are you?"

"Better than I've been in a long time. I just got out of rehab a couple of days ago. Got a job in Tahlequah. I start next week. Grandma's letting me bunk here till I get on my feet."

His eyes were clear, his jeans and cotton shirt freshly laundered. He was like the old Johnny, the one she remembered from her childhood. "That's wonderful. Tiana would be pleased."

At the mention of his cousin, Johnny's smile faded quickly. "She'd been after me to get some help. I wish I'd done it before, but I guess it took her death to wake me up."

"Somehow," Marisa said, "I think she knows."

Johnny gave her a grateful look and turned to Emma. "Grandma, I'm going to gas up my car. You need anything from the store?"

"No." Worry flickered in Emma's eyes. "Will you be gone long?"

"No, Grandma."

Emma watched him leave. Marisa suspected she was wondering if he would really stay off drugs this time. Marisa glanced out the window and saw Johnny get into the old Chevrolet and roar away. Emma didn't drive, so the Cadillac must belong to

Ben. So he was around somewhere. Marisa hoped he stayed out of sight until she was gone. She'd never known how to talk to him.

Emma said, "Tiana left something for you. Wait here. It's in Ben's bedroom. He's asleep. He's working the night shift this month."

Emma came back carrying a framed canvas. "One of the last things Tiana said to me was to make sure you got this if anything happened to her." Grief pulled at her face, made her mouth tremble. "It was almost like she knew she was going to die."

The painting was a landscape, showing a corner of a wildflower-strewn meadow next to a shadowed woods. It could have been any of several places Marisa remembered from her childhood ramblings. The sweet sadness of nostalgia almost overcame her.

"It's beautiful," she said and blinked back tears. "I'll treasure it forever."

They sat in Emma's living room, talking. Emma soon turned the conversation to her niece, voicing thoughts that must fill her mind, day and night, since Tiana's death.

"She said she was going out there to paint," Emma said. "She should've come back when it started getting dark." Her fingers made little pleats in the skirt of her cotton dress. "I don't believe she got disoriented and fell off that cliff, Marisa."

Marisa didn't know how to respond. "If she was carrying an easel and her paints, she could have stumbled . . ."

Emma gazed out the window. "There was a screech owl in that tree in the front yard for three nights before she died."

A shiver reminiscent of childhood fear slithered through Marisa. The screech owl was a favorite disguise of evil Cherokee witches. In Cherokee lore, a screech owl in the same place three nights in a row was a harbinger of death. Emma was in one of her dark moods, probably had been in it since Tiana's death.

Marisa reached out and covered Emma's age-worn hand with her own. "I'm so sorry, Emma. I loved Tiana too, and I'll miss her terribly."

Emma stared at Tiana's hand as she squeezed it, and a tear trickled down her lined cheek.

As soon as she politely could, Marisa excused herself and left. As she got into her car, she glanced back at the house and saw a face at a back window. Ben Cornsilk watched her with those secretive eyes, just as he'd watched her when she was a child.

The next morning, Marisa contacted a roofer who promised to come by and give her an estimate for repairs that afternoon. She drove to Tahlequah and bought a paint roller, brushes, and enough antique white paint to cover the inside of the house. Fortunately she wouldn't have to do anything to the outside since her grandparents had installed vinyl siding a couple of years before their deaths. And she thought the gray carpet would be fine after a good cleaning, which she could do herself with a rented steam cleaner from the grocery store.

Back at the house she followed an impulse and phoned Johnny at Emma's house. "Would you like to come by for dinner this evening? Nothing fancy. Just spaghetti and a salad." She wanted to learn more about Tiana's death, but she didn't want to burden Emma with her questions.

He was clearly surprised, but pleased by the invitation. "Sure. I'd like that. Is six o'clock okay?"

"Perfect. See you then."

Marisa painted until four o'clock when the roofer arrived. He climbed around on the roof, went out to his truck and did some figuring, then knocked on the back door.

"All the roof over the utility room needs to be replaced, and you got some damage over the main part of the house too. I could do it for somewhere between two-fifty and three hundred, depends on what I get into once I start tearing off shingles."

It could have been worse. He could have told her she needed a whole new roof. "When can you do the work?"

"Couldn't start till Friday or Saturday. I've got another job to finish first."

"That's fine." She signed the agreement he handed her.

"Tiana wasn't drinking when she fell off the cliff," Johnny said that evening at dinner, in answer to Marisa's question. "She never touched the stuff. She was a regular crusader on the subject of drugs and alcohol. Preached to me about it all the time. She even tried to get me to tell her who my dealer was, so she could go after him."

"Did you?"

He shook his head. "No way. Around here, snitches can get seriously hurt."

For some reason, Marisa thought of Ben Cornsilk. What did Johnny mean by "around here?" Did the dealer live in Park Hill, or was Johnny referring to the general area?

Marisa tried another tack. "Where is your Uncle Ben working?"

"At a factory in Muskogee."

"They must pay well. That's an expensive car he's driving."

He gazed at her for a long moment, as if trying to penetrate her mind, before his dark eyes flashed away. "He gets some overtime, and living with Grandma saves on rent."

He obviously didn't want to talk about his uncle, so Marisa dropped it. "Emma doesn't think Tiana fell off that cliff by accident."

"Aw, you know Grandma. She's superstitious. She heard a screech owl before Tiana died, so she's convinced something evil—a witch or something—caused Marisa to fall."

"So you never thought it was anything but an accident?"

He looked at her intently. "She sure didn't jump. What else could it be?"

Murder, Marisa thought, but she didn't say the word because it sounded so farfetched. Who could have wanted to kill Tiana?

After Johnny left, Marisa took Tiana's painting into the bedroom and propped it on the dresser. The more she looked at it, the more familiar it seemed to her. She backed away to study it and, for the first time, noticed something hanging from a tree trunk. Going closer, she saw that it was a piece of weathered gray board.

All at once, she knew what she was looking at. Tiana had

painted the place where they'd built their clubhouse when they were twelve. That board must be all that was left of it. She picked up the painting and held it next to the lamp. The detail was incredible, so meticulously done that the scene appeared to be three-dimensional. Every blade of grass, every leaf was clearly defined. As she studied the painting, even the lines in the gnarled trunks of the trees seemed to jump out at her. Then, on the trunk where the rotting board dangled, she suddenly saw the outline of a bird. It reminded her of one of those drawings in which children were instructed to find the hidden pictures.

Marisa looked more closely at all the tree trunks, but the only identifiable figure she could see was the bird at the base of the tree in the foreground. Belatedly, she realized that it was a screech owl.

Frowning, she started to return the painting to the dresser and almost dropped it. She caught it facedown and, for the first time, noticed something written in tiny letters on the back of the frame. Bending closer, she made out the words: *Tree of Death.*

A spider of apprehension crawled up Marisa's neck. Tiana had instructed Emma to make sure she got the painting. Was Tiana trying to tell her something with the screech owl and the title? If so, Marisa wasn't getting the message. All she was getting was a vague feeling of foreboding.

The feeling did not leave her as she tried to watch a sitcom on her grandparents' ancient television set. Even with an antenna on the roof, the picture was fuzzy.

Before retiring, she rechecked the doors and windows to make sure they were securely locked. She didn't sleep for what seemed hours. When, at last, she did, she dreamed of running through a dark wood pursued by a flock of screech owls.

The next day, Marisa painted until mid-afternoon. She'd finished the living room, kitchen, and hallway and decided to wait until the following day to tackle the bedrooms. After cleaning her brush and roller, she stripped off her paint-spattered old shirt and jeans and took a hot bath. Feeling refreshed, she dressed in clean jeans and a sweatshirt, pulled on a denim jacket, grabbed an apple, and went for a walk.

With no particular route in mind, she soon realized that she was headed for the place in Tiana's painting, the spot where they'd built their clubhouse above the steep cliff. Her subconscious had known, even before her conscious mind, that she had to see it again before she could accept that Tiana's death was accidental, as the medical examiner had concluded.

The October air was crisp, perfect weather for walking. The scenery was perfect, too. Cherokee County was prettiest in autumn after the leaves had turned. Fortunately, she'd come back when the foliage was at the peak of its glory.

She entered the dense woods, where occasional rays of sunlight penetrated the leaves, dappling the ground like pools of gold. The temperature seemed to drop several degrees. Pulling her jacket together in front, she finished the apple and paused to toss the core on the ground for the birds.

She thought she heard a noise behind her. Turning, she peered into the trees all around. The noise didn't come again, and she told herself that she'd probably heard a branch fall or a squirrel rattling leaves. The woods were full of small animals and birds.

She continued walking until she'd reached the spot depicted in Tiana's painting. It looked exactly as Tiana had painted it. The four trees that had served as the cornerposts of their clubhouse were still there, the trunks gnarled with age. And there was the piece of board hanging from the tree nearest the cliff. She walked in between the trees and sat down on a fallen log.

Closing her eyes, she inhaled the scent of the woods. For a moment, she was thrown back to her twelfth year when she and Tiana had worked for weeks to construct the clubhouse. They'd confiscated a couple of old glasses and plates and forks from Emma's house and hidden them there to use when they brought food and a Thermos of Emma's lemonade with them.

Marisa opened her eyes and studied her surroundings more closely. Nothing remained of the clubhouse but the piece of board hanging from the tree and a couple of rotting two-by-fours which were barely visible beneath the weeds that had grown up in the intervening years.

She drew in a deep breath and stood. She could no longer avoid looking at the place where Tiana had died. She walked the hundred yards to the cliff, an outcropping of limestone. Standing a couple of feet from the edge, she could look down at the ground some forty feet below where Tiana had fallen. She had forgotten that big slab of limestone which protruded from the earth at the base of the cliff. If Tiana had hit her head on that, she would have died instantly.

"She looked like a broken doll when we found her," said a voice behind Marisa.

Her heart lurched. Adrenaline spurted through her and she felt the hair at the back of her neck stand up as she backed away from the edge. Ben Cornsilk stood among the trees, watching her. She knew instinctively that it was Ben she'd heard earlier. He'd followed her there.

Still edging away, she demanded, "What are you doing here?"

"Same as you, I guess," he said. "Remembering Tiana."

His dark, brooding eyes fixed on her like lasers seeking a target, filling her with the impulse to flee. But she couldn't let him know how frightened she was. If he'd wanted to push her off the cliff, he could have done so before she knew he was there. Good Lord, her imagination was running away with her. Why would he want to push her off? She was no threat to him.

He looked lean and fit, punctured lung or not, and she remembered that he'd been a runner in school. He appeared to have fully recovered from his knife wound.

All at once, Marisa recalled a scene from her childhood. She and Tiana had come to the clubhouse, and Marisa had gone out to look over the cliff. Tiana had followed, but she'd stayed back, standing in the trees about where Ben Cornsilk now stood. *Don't get too close,* she'd said, her tone anxious. *Come back, Marisa, please.*

"Tiana was afraid of heights," Marisa said.

He gazed at her for a long moment. Marisa felt exposed and

vulnerable. If she ran, she was sure he could catch her. "I know," he said at length.

She edged a few steps closer to the path she'd taken through the woods, her escape route. "Uncle Howard said you were injured in Kansas City."

He studied her some more. "What else did Uncle Howard say?"

"About you? Just that you were back, living with Emma."

"Living off Emma, don't you mean?"

A tremor ran through her. "No. Your living arrangements are none of my business. Or Uncle Howard's, either." He still hadn't moved. The adrenaline rush that had galvanized her was easing and her heart rate had slowed down. If he meant to hurt her, wouldn't he have made his move by now? "I have to get back to the house," she said. Then she turned and strode briskly into the trees, feeling his eyes on her back.

His voice followed her. "Watch your back, Marisa." It sounded like a threat. She started to run, slapping branches out of her way, and didn't stop until she'd reached the edge of the woods, expecting every second to feel the clap of his hand on her shoulder.

Once she'd cleared the woods, she paused to look back the way she'd come. She heard nothing except her own labored breathing. He hadn't followed her.

Sweat poured off her, more from fear than exertion. She took off her jacket and walked the rest of the way, looking over her shoulder every few steps. She didn't see Ben Cornsilk again.

But she couldn't get the meeting out of her mind. She told her Uncle Howard about it the next day when she visited his store. "Stay away from that cliff, Marisa," he warned. "And stay away from Ben Cornsilk."

"When did he come back?" she asked.

"Five or six months ago."

"He was here several months before Tiana died, then." In fact, he must have joined the search party because he'd said she'd looked like a broken doll when they found her. "Could he have pushed her off the cliff?"

He shook his head. "Nobody knows what Ben Cornsilk will do, especially when he's mad. He's unpredictable. You stay out of his way, you hear?"

"I will, Uncle Howard." It would be an easy promise to keep. She changed the subject. "Do you ever think about retiring?"

His heavy brows shot up. "And do what? I'd go nuts if I didn't have this place to come to every day."

"I'm surprised you can make a living here."

He shrugged. "I do okay. Make enough to cover my expenses and keep Kevin in that place in Tulsa. He's better off there than with me."

Kevin had stayed at home as long as his mother was alive, but after that, he'd been a problem. He had balked at staying at the store with Howard all day, and Howard hadn't liked leaving him home alone. After Kevin had wandered away and gotten lost several times, Howard had found a place where he'd be supervised.

Looking at her uncle now, Marisa was aware of how much he'd aged in the last few years. It must be so lonely, living in his house by himself. And no doubt he worried about what would happen to Kevin when he was gone. No wonder he couldn't think of retiring. He was probably trying to accumulate a trust fund for his son.

"You're a good man, Uncle Howard," Marisa said.

She left when the bus stopped outside and deposited a load of schoolkids. Most of them would come into the store for a snack before walking home.

That night, as she sat in bed, trying to read, her gaze kept straying to the painting propped on the dresser. Why had Tiana titled the painting *Tree of Death*? No death had ever occurred there that Marisa knew of, except for Tiana's, but obviously that was after she'd finished the painting. Could she have had a premonition that she would die there? Even so, it was the tree Tiana had singled out in the title, not the cliff, which did not even appear in the painting.

She was sure Ben Cornsilk had followed her out there today. Why? Was he afraid she'd find something there, some clue to how Tiana had died? Had Ben Cornsilk killed Tiana? The man had depths to him that could hide anything. But why would he want to kill his niece? Marisa could think of no possible reason.

Laying her book aside, Marisa sat on the edge of the bed and stared at the painting. Once she'd noticed the outline of the screech owl on the tree trunk, it was the first thing she saw whenever she looked at the painting. The position of the owl on the tree trunk made it appear to be perched on a big rock at the base of the tree. The rock could be the same one that had marked the spot where she and Tiana had hidden their glasses, plates, and forks, along with small treasures they found—unique stones and leaves mostly. They'd borrowed Emma's shovel and dug out a hole big enough to accommodate everything they might want to stash there. Marisa wondered if their hoard was still there. How curious it would feel to handle those things from her childhood. She wished she'd thought to look under the rock while she was there.

She would go back, she decided, when she was sure Ben Cornsilk wouldn't follow. Maybe she'd find whatever it was that Ben was afraid she might see.

The opportunity came on Saturday. Marisa was buying milk and bread at her uncle's store when Ben Cornsilk came in. She returned his muttered hello with a nod and lingered beside the bread rack while Ben chose a sandwich from the refrigerator, added chips and a candy bar, then went to the counter to pay.

"I'm working a twelve-hour shift today," he said to Howard. "Noon to midnight. So I'm taking a sack lunch."

"You like what you're doing over at that factory?" Howard asked, making conversation.

"It's a job," Ben said.

Howard sacked the items Ben had laid on the counter. Ben paid him and left without another glance in Marisa's direction.

"I'd just as soon he didn't come in here," Howard said.

Returning to the house, Marisa checked on the roofer, who said he'd finish the job that afternoon. She put the final touches on the bathroom, and the painting was done. The white paint had transformed the house. It now looked bright and clean. Monday she'd rent a carpet cleaner, and find a realtor to handle the sale.

It was after five when the roofer knocked on the door to say he was leaving. She'd been feeling restless, waiting for him to finish. If she was going to the cliff, she wanted to be back home before dark. Hurriedly she wrote out the check for the roofer. Then she got her jacket and keys, locked the house, and started for the woods at a brisk pace.

Once she'd reached the site of the clubhouse, she flopped down on the fallen log to rest for a minute before trying to move that big rock at the base of the tree. Years ago, it had taken both she and Tiana to budge it. While she caught her breath, she scanned her surroundings carefully. She had no idea what she was looking for, but she could not lose the notion that Ben Cornsilk feared she might find a clue to Tiana's death there. She found none, however.

Giving up on that, she bent over the rock and tried to lift it. It seemed to weigh a ton. But she and Tiana had moved it when they were twelve, so she just had to get a good grip. She dropped to her knees, wrapped her arms around the rock, and jerked it toward her, moving it several inches. Another couple of jerks, and she'd uncovered the hole.

It was dim in the woods. She bent to peer into the hole. Something was in there, all right. She reached in, expecting to pull out a plate or a glass. Instead, her hand closed on something cool and slick, but not hard. Pulling it out, she stared at a plastic bag filled with—what? She bent closer and caught the sweet scent of marijuana. Heart pounding, she reached in and pulled out another bag, and another and another, until she'd pulled out about two dozen bags, half of them filled with marijuana. The other half contained a white powder, cocaine or heroin. She'd never seen either, so she wasn't sure which it was.

As she knelt there, staring at the plastic bags piled on the ground outside the hole, everything fell into place. Ben Cornsilk was dealing drugs. In all likelihood, he'd supplied his own nephew, Johnny, before Johnny went into rehab. He had probably followed her there that other afternoon, fearing she'd uncover his hiding place.

Tiana must have found out and threatened to expose him. So he'd killed her.

Marisa gazed at the drugs, frozen, until the sound of rustling leaves made her heart leap. Scanning the tree branches overhead, she finally saw what had made the noise. A screech owl was perched on a limb, staring down at her with big, unblinking eyes.

Suddenly, she wanted out of there, wanted to be back, safely locked inside her grandparents' house. Should she take the drugs with her? No, she'd put it all back and report what she'd found to the county sheriff. With both hands, she pushed the plastic bags into the hole. She had reached for the rock, to tug it back over the opening, when she heard someone coming through the woods by the same route that Marisa had followed. Ben Cornsilk! He must have left work early.

Panicked, she jumped up and ran. Not the way she'd come, for that way she'd run right into Ben. She ran the other direction, toward the cliff. From there, she could find another way out of the woods.

Behind her, a spine-tingling shriek split the air. Emma Cornsilk's frightening stories of screech owls who were harbingers of death came back to Marisa. Nothing but superstition, she thought in an effort to calm herself. But she'd always heard that screech owls didn't screech in the daytime. What did it mean?

She ran faster, but she didn't hear the owl again. When she was well out of sight, she paused to listen and heard a different sound—heavy footsteps tromped through dead leaves, then stopped abruptly. She pictured Ben, standing beside his hiding place, seeing that someone had moved the rock, someone had found the drugs. Then he'd wonder if that person was still around.

Marisa heard the footsteps resume, hurried this time. He was running toward her. Marisa sprinted toward the cliff, praying that she wouldn't misjudge where the edge was in the growing dusk. With relief, she found she could still see it well enough. She ran along the edge, looking for the path that had been there when she was a child. She couldn't see it, so she picked a spot and ran toward it, thinking that perhaps Emma was right, after all. Had the screech owl been warning her of her own impending death?

At the edge of the woods, her foot caught in the brush, and she fell, facedown. The fall momentarily knocked the breath out of her. Forcing herself to her hands and knees, she finally managed to draw in a gulp of air and struggled to her feet. But she'd delayed just long enough for her pursuer to burst out of the woods and see her.

"Who's there?"

She had started to run before she recognized the voice. She halted and turned back. "Uncle Howard?"

"Marisa! I told you to stay away from here. You okay?" He was coming toward her. Something about his manner alerted her, the way he held his arms out, the wariness in his tone. What was going on?

She backed away. "Wait!"

He paused. "What?"

"Don't come any closer!"

"Marisa, what's wrong with you?"

"Those drugs . . . they're yours!" There was no other reason for him to be in the woods. Howard didn't walk anywhere unless he had to.

He had moved to within a few feet of her. "Now, Marisa, we can work this out. It's not as bad as it looks."

"Tiana found them, didn't she? She was going to turn you in."

At last Marisa understood. Tiana had moved the rock, perhaps looking for childhood treasures, as Marisa had been. She'd found the drugs, but she hadn't known who'd put them there. So she'd painted the scene, leaving the clues for Marisa to find, if Tiana wasn't around. Then, Marisa supposed, Tiana had staked out the tree, waiting to see who would come for the drugs.

Had she been as shocked as Marisa to see that it was Howard? Had she, in anger, shown herself, threatened to go to the sheriff?

Suddenly fury flooded through Marisa. "How *could* you get involved in such a dirty business?" Her voice shook. She moved sideways away from him as she spoke, looking for an opening in the trees that she could spring through.

"Listen, Marisa! If it wasn't me, it would be somebody else. I can't make a decent living in the store. Do you have any idea how expensive it is to keep Kevin in that home? I was desperate, Marisa." He was actually trying to justify what he'd done.

She saw her opening, and ran. But he was right behind her, fueled by fear of exposure. And she'd only gone a few steps when he caught up with her. He grabbed her arm, his fingers like steel bars, pressing into her flesh.

"Let me go!"

"I can't do that, Marisa. I'm sorry. I wish it hadn't come to this." He was pulling her back toward the cliff.

She fought him with all her strength, tried to dig her heels into the ground, but she was no match for Howard. She'd never imagined he was so strong. The owl was right, she was going to die.

They cleared the trees. "You can't get away with pushing me off the cliff, like Tiana," she cried. "Nobody will believe there were two accidents."

"Maybe not," he panted, "but they'll never suspect me." He got behind her, grasped both her arms, and with his body began shoving her toward the edge of the cliff.

Frantic, Marisa tried to think of a way out. Within seconds, it would be too late. A few more steps, and he could push her over. Sobbing, she struggled and tried to kick him, all the while being pushed closer to the edge.

Then, from behind them, a shout rang out. "Stop! Don't move another inch, Howard!"

Howard's grip loosened on Marisa's arms, as he turned to look, and Marisa wrenched free. She stumbled away from the cliff. Ben Cornsilk stood at the edge of the woods with a gun pointed at Howard. He held it straight out in both hands, just like on TV. "One move toward her, and I'll kill you," he said, his voice as steady as a rock.

But Howard didn't move toward Marisa. Instead, he lunged for the edge of the cliff and threw himself over.

Three days later, Marisa carried her suitcase to her car, preparing to leave. A few minutes earlier, she'd seen the screech owl perched in a tree at the edge of the yard. Somehow she knew it was the same one she'd seen in the woods. It was almost as if he was watching her.

There was a "for sale" sign in the front yard, and the realtor had already shown the house twice. She'd assured Marisa the house would sell within two or three months. A lot of people wanted to move their kids out of cities and into rural areas where they'd be safe. Marisa had managed not to laugh at that.

Johnny's old Chevrolet rattled down the road, turned in, and came to a stop beside Marisa's car.

"Leaving already?" he asked as he climbed out.

"It's time," she said. "I'll probably drive only halfway today, and get home tomorrow."

He cocked his head, looking down at her. "Are you really going to be all right?"

"I'm fine."

"Heard your uncle's still in a coma. They don't expect him to make it."

She nodded. She'd gone to Howard's house to search for the phone number of the group home. She'd found it, along with papers establishing a trust for Kevin. Marisa had called the trust company and Kevin's housemother to inform them of Howard's condition. She'd assured the housemother that Kevin's room and board would now be paid by the trust company. No point in mentioning that the money was probably drug money. Then she'd gone by Emma's house one last time to thank Ben Cornsilk for saving her life.

"Speaking of uncles," she said, "I understand Ben was on the police force in Kansas City."

"Yeah, he worked undercover as a narc. Got pensioned off after a dealer nearly killed him with a knife. Came home, got a job as a security guard at that Muskogee factory. Yesterday I learned Tiana told him she was trying to find out who was dealing drugs to the kids around here, and after she died, he went to the sheriff and volunteered to work undercover for him without pay. It was all he could do for Tiana, I guess. He didn't want Grandma and me to know about his undercover work. Ben said he didn't want us to be involved. But it all came out when he caught Howard."

Marisa sighed. "You knew it was Uncle Howard all along, didn't you?"

He ducked his head and nodded sheepishly. "He used to supply me. When I came home from rehab, he said if I didn't want to do business with him anymore, that was okay, but I'd better keep my mouth shut or he'd hurt Grandma. I knew he'd do it, too."

Marisa shuddered at the possibility of Howard hurting Emma. She'd thought she knew her uncle so well, and she hadn't known him at all. "I was sure Ben was the drug dealer. I never ever suspected Uncle Howard, though I guess I should have. His store is the gathering place for all the kids around. It's an ideal situation for somebody who wants to deal drugs."

"I'm sorry, Marisa," Johnny said. "I know you were real fond of Howard."

"He was a different person out there on the cliff. You said once that Emma thought something evil had killed Tiana. It turns out Emma was right. That's what I saw in Howard's eyes and heard in his voice when he was trying to kill me. Pure evil."

"Ben found the drug stash by studying Tiana's painting, the same as you. He even suspected Howard, but he couldn't prove it. I wondered why lately Ben was never at the house, except to sleep. Now I know he was spending that time watching that drug stash, waiting for the dealer to show up."

"So he never even went to work that Saturday?"

Johnny shook his head. "No, he just told Howard he was going, then went out to the woods and waited."

"Well—it's over now," Marisa said. A lot of things were over, including the last vestiges of her childhood. "I better get on the road." On an impulse, she embraced him. His arms tightened around her convulsively.

"I'm proud of you, Johnny. Hang in there."

"I will. Uncle Ben will make my life hell if I don't stay straight." He stepped back. "I wish you were going to be around. Come back to see us."

She watched him drive off, then checked the house one more time and put Tiana's painting in the trunk of her car. Then she walked over to the tree where the owl was perched. "Take care of things around here," she said, and then felt a little silly, talking to an owl, who merely gazed back at her with big, wise eyes.

She drove away without a backward glance. She and Johnny both knew that she would never be back.

Jean Hager

Oklahoman Jean Hager is the author of more than fifty novels, including fourteen mysteries in three series: the Mitch Bushyhead and Molly Bearpaw Cherokee series published by Mysterious Press/Warner and the Iris House Bed and Breakfast series published by Avon. Twice an Agatha Award finalist, she has had several stories in anthologies, has been inducted into the Oklahoma Writers Hall of Fame, and was named Writer of the Year by the University of Oklahoma. No mystery that she lives in Tulsa with her husband, Ken, and "the queen of the household," a miniature schnauzer named Missy, who often travels with the couple.

A t last. A cat tale that has no tail. Lisa Lepovetsky is a prolific short-fiction writer who has the good taste to cast a cat
in a central role. A manx cat yet. This is a breed that lost its tail
from the git-go, by act of nature, not accident or man. Should I
add that this lissome, tail-less specimen is female? That goes a
long way toward stirring my interest, but being of the dainty
gender does not mean that she is not a deadly hunter when it
comes to discovering clues that lead to nailing a murderer. So is
Miss Lisa Lepovetsky.

—M.L.

Final Reunion

Lisa Lepovetsky

I USUALLY GOT along pretty well with my mother's older sister Agatha Windom—maybe because I never really cared
whether or not I inherit. I'm comfortable enough with the in-
come from my bed-and-breakfast; I didn't need to wheedle anything out of her.

If I wasn't interested in the money, why did I bother with
Aunt Agatha's miserable reunions? Why would I join a bunch of
bloodthirsty relatives each year, not the least of whom was
Agatha herself?

To be honest, it was because I'd made a promise to my dying
mother about staying connected to my "roots." Attending Aunt
Agatha's annual reunion relieved my sense of guilt for not visiting my relatives more. It also reminded me why I avoided them

the other fifty-one weekends each year. And Aunt Agatha's one saving grace was that she didn't complain that I brought Lady Lucy with me.

Lady Lucy is my tail-less striped manx; she travels everywhere with me. I found her at my backdoor one bitterly cold morning in January five years ago, and she waltzed right into the house and made herself comfortable on the seat of my easy chair. I didn't question her for a moment; she obviously belonged in my eighteenth-century stone cottage. We both knew immediately that we were made for each other. She was pitifully thin and rather nervous—she still runs under the bed whenever strangers come to the house—and had obviously been through some terrible trauma. That's why I named her Lady Lucy Duff Gordon, after one of the survivors of the *Titanic* disaster.

Through some bizarre feline reasoning, Lady Lucy seemed to actually like Aunt Agatha, which is another reason I forced myself to attend her reunions. Aunt Agatha always planned her yearly reunion for early October, which was a blessing because it's usually cooler in northern Pennsylvania then, lower temperatures helping to lower tempers as well. Although the truth is, I suspect she secretly enjoyed it when the relations were all at one another's throats.

But this past October was the exception that proves the rule; the mercury hadn't dropped below seventy-eight in a week, and when Lucy and I arrived on Friday afternoon, it felt as though Aunt Agatha had moved to the Amazon.

My cousin Melba opened the door before I had a chance to ring the bell. Melba still lived in the family mansion with Aunt Agatha then. Except for one thing, Melba is the stereotypical middle-aged spinster: graying hair cut serviceably short, conservative skirts and pants that were both practical and comfortable, wire-rimmed glasses—and a tongue that can cut like a razor blade.

The exception to type is Melba's passion for golf. She treats her golf clubs as if they were made of gold, carefully cleaning them with a chamois cloth after each game and storing them in a genuine Moroccan leather bag she must have paid a small fortune for. I often marvel that Melba can bring herself to actually hit a golf ball with one of her precious clubs.

Despite her often dour appearance, I've always rather liked Melba. She has a quick, biting wit, and a wry insight and honesty. Melba wiped her brow that hot day with a linen hanky as she shut the door behind me.

"My God, Essie, you look like a limp rag," she said, dragging me into the gloomy foyer. "This heat's incredible for October. They don't expect it to break for another week. And the humidity!"

Melba glanced at the carrying case in my hand and smiled. "I see you've brought Lady Lucy. It'll be interesting to see how she gets along with Adrienne's new ball-and-chain." She bent down and stuck a couple of fingers through the door of the case, and the Lady rubbed her chin against them and purred loudly. "How about an iced tea? I steeped it with lemon mint."

I nodded. The air conditioner in the cab hadn't worked, and I felt rather prickly—both physically and emotionally. "That sounds wonderful," I said. "I'll take my things upstairs. The rose room, as usual?"

Before Melba could answer, a little shriek sounded at the top of the stairs, and Adrienne Windom-Bosworth bounded down the steps toward me. I cringed. Sometimes it's nearly impossible to believe she and Melba came from the same womb. Adrienne and Melba are day and night, sun and moon, vacuum and solid rock. Adrienne's bleached curls bounced against her elegant shoulders as she kissed the air near my cheek. Her cool powdery skin and perfect pink chiffon sundress made me feel even more tired and grimy.

"Hello, Adrienne," I managed, then turned to Melba. "Maybe I'll take a rain check on that tea and just jump into the shower. Then I might begin to feel almost human."

"Essie, you always look marvelous," Adrienne lied. "We have so much catching up to do. I can't wait for you to meet my Wilson. We were so sorry you couldn't make it to the wedding last February, but of course the weather was dreadful. You're going

to adore him; everybody does. He should be back any minute—
never misses his two-mile run."

Melba smiled grimly. "I'll take your bag up, Essie." She
grabbed my suitcase and headed upstairs, her gray dress and hair
blending in with the dusky stair carpeting until she almost
seemed to disappear.

Adrienne glanced at Lady Lucy's case and wrinkled her
pretty nose. "I see you've brought that . . . animal again." I nodded and gritted my teeth, determined to avoid an argument so
early in the weekend. I noticed the Lady's purring had stopped.
"I hope it doesn't bother Wilson," Adrienne continued. "He's
rather allergic to furry things."

"I'll try to keep her out of his way."

Adrienne seemed to accept this and chattered on for a few
more minutes until I sneaked in a question as she stopped to
catch her breath.

"So, who else is expected this year?"

"As far as I know," Adrienne mused, "we're it. Well, and
Philip Wolfe, Mother's doctor. Melba insisted on inviting him to
dinner, since he's been coming out here nearly every day to check
on Mother, since her fall." She leaned toward me conspiratorially
and I thought I heard a soft hiss from the carrying case. "But you
and I know why she *really* invited him." She straightened up
again. "That's about it, I guess. Of course, there aren't many others left who could—or would—come."

"Speaking of Dr. Wolfe," I said, "how is Aunt Agatha's leg?"

"Actually, it's her hip. The good doctor said it'll be fine, but
she is eighty-two; can't even stand up these days without Father's
old silver-headed cane. She's locked in the drawing room right
now, working on some papers or other from the safe—not to be
disturbed. You know how she is."

"Didn't she hire some help this year?"

Adrienne shook her head. "Can you believe it—she was outside in the garden all morning, cutting asters for the table and
more mint for juleps later. She could hardly walk when she came
back in. But she'd never admit how bad it is—still fancies herself

the *grand dame,* you know. Won't let anybody except Melba lift
a finger to help cook dinner."

"She's afraid the rest of us would poison her for the family
jewels," a male voice intruded from behind me.

I turned to see a blond man in white shorts and a Princeton
University T-shirt enter the front door. He quickly tucked a pair
of miniature binoculars into his shorts pocket and dabbed un-
necessarily at his face with a small towel.

"Oh, Wilson, meet my cousin Essie Booker from Philadel-
phia. She owns a bar down there."

As he held a hand out for me to shake, I gritted my teeth. "It's
not exactly a bar, Adrienne. It's an English-style pub—the Hart
and Dragon."

I was immediately sorry I'd bothered correcting her, as they
both looked blankly at me for a moment. I would get nowhere
this way, I could see. Then Lady Lucy meowed softly, distracting
us, and I excused myself to shower and change.

Dinner was the usual dismal affair: overdressed guests, over-
cooked roast beef and vegetables, underdone potatoes. Aunt
Agatha obviously hadn't learned to cook in the year since I'd
last seen her. Melba had made an excellent English trifle, but nobody ate much, since we were all sweltering in the evening dress
Aunt Agatha demanded. Even the collar of Wilson's silk shirt
was soaked under his suit by the time he finished picking at his
dessert. Adrienne was dressed in a scarlet floor-length gauze
dress from which only the toes of her gold sandals peeked when
she walked. She, of course, still looked cool and fresh.

Philip Wolfe had arrived just before dinner, greeting Aunt
Agatha pleasantly; she didn't seem to return his hand-grasp quite
as warmly. I tried to make up for her coolness with some inane
chatter, but he simply smiled shyly and looked uncomfortable. I
hoped his bedside manner was somewhat better. Tall and
straight, he sat awkwardly across the table from Melba, looking
more like a butler unexpectedly invited to eat with his employ-

ers than a guest. He ate little and said less, though I noticed he and Melba exchanged a couple of brief glances during the meal.

I'd let Lady Lucy out of her carrying case as soon as we'd reached my room, and when I'd come down for dinner she'd followed me and immediately curled up in Aunt Agatha's satin-covered lap while we ate. I even noticed that the old lady slipped her a tidbit or two during dinner. Nobody else realized Lucy was there, and Wilson seemed no worse for the wear, despite the terrible allergies Adrienne had claimed for him.

"Well, Melba," Adrienne began, leaning forward predatorially after I helped clear the table and serve coffee. "Tell us the truth—what's really going on between you and the good Dr. Wolfe? Do I hear the distant peal of wedding bells?"

I felt, rather than heard, Aunt Agatha gasp at the end of the table. From the corner of my eye I saw her small body tremble slightly in its black satin, a few white hairs vibrating above the braids pinned to the top of her head. She gently placed Lady Lucy on the floor, then rose slowly and majestically, clutching her cane for support, and without a word hobbled into the foyer and up the dark stairs. With a silent sigh, Lady Lucy padded over and curled up beneath my chair.

Philip followed her with narrowed eyes, his lips pressed tightly together. Then he took a large gulp of his wine.

"How could you?" Melba glared at Adrienne when Aunt Agatha had gone. "You know how Mother feels about our relationship."

Philip continued to say nothing, but I saw a muscle twitch in his jaw. Despite what Adrienne had implied in the foyer earlier, this was the first I'd heard of Melba showing interest in any man. I was pleased for her, but decided silence was the better part of valor for the moment.

"You can't let her run your life forever, Melba," Adrienne sighed, picking an invisible piece of lint from her dress. "Why don't you just marry him and get it over with?"

Melba stood and I could almost see her weave the strands of her anger together. She and Philip locked eyes for a moment, and then she spoke. "For the same reason you keep coming back here once a year, sister dear," she hissed. "Because of the money."

Melba glanced at me. "I'm sorry, Essie, but it's true. I'd have put Mother in a retirement home and married Philip years ago, but she'd disinherit me in a heartbeat. She's terrified of losing control of Adrienne and me, and being left alone in her dotage. So she keeps that golden carrot dangling in front of us. And I for one am not about to walk away from a fortune."

"So you hang around this mausoleum waiting for her to die." Adrienne scowled. "Look at you. When was the last time you bought some new clothes?" Adrienne was a master of uplifting herself on everyone else's ashes.

Philip tensed and opened his mouth to say something, but Melba shot him a dark look and he just shook his head and said nothing.

"And you should speak for yourself about the inheritance," Adrienne continued. "Wilson and I come here because we love Mother, don't we darling? And she adores Wilson."

I glanced at Wilson. He sipped his water and grinned, watching the sisters spar as though he were enjoying a tennis match.

Melba wiped at her damp forehead. "I'll bet she does, the way he fawns over her. It's revolting. At least I'm honest. And I know Philip is worth waiting for." Her eyes flickered to Wilson, who frowned as she said, "I won't be stuck with a phony gold-digger and two last names."

"Come on, Essie," she said, grasping my arm before Adrienne could respond. "Let's get you some air." She propelled me out onto the back veranda. "You sit out here and wait for me. I'll see Philip to his car, and then you and I will have a nice long chat." Lady Lucy jumped up with an annoyed yowl and dashed ahead of us.

Melba reappeared briefly a while later, but only to say she was taking a walk in the gardens, explaining apologetically that she was simply too upset for idle chitchat. So the Lady and I sat for an hour or so in one of the rattan rockers on the veranda, listening to the last hardy crickets argue about when the weather would return to normal.

Entering the house later, I recalled that Aunt Agatha kept a decanter of brandy on the drawing room table, and decided to have a nightcap. As I slid the heavy pocket doors of the dining room apart, Lady Lucy squeezed between them ahead of me. I entered the dark room, trying to remember where the light switch was. I moved my hand along the flocked wallpaper, nearly tripping on something just inside the door: Aunt Agatha's cane. I bent down to pick it up. The carpet beneath it felt damp—maybe Aunt Agatha had spilled some brandy trying to carry a glass and hold the cane simultaneously. I sniffed my fingers. There was no odor—the moisture was water, apparently. I called to Aunt Agatha, but got no answer. Lady Lucy was back at my side, twisting nervously between my ankles and mewling.

Finally, I found a button on the wall, and the room flooded with light. I soon saw why Lucy was so upset: Aunt Agatha lay on the floor across the large room, a puddle of blood oozing around her head. A golf club lay near her feet, its long metal shaft and leather grip coated with blood.

Carefully approaching the body, I checked for a pulse and heartbeat, but found neither. The windows were open, though the room remained hot and stuffy, and the drapes were fastened back with their tasseled ties. A painting on the wall across from the window had been swung aside, revealing an open wall safe. I left to find the others.

Melba was in the kitchen, setting out breakfast things on the sideboard. She'd changed into a white chenille housecoat. When I told her about her mother, she sank into a chair and sighed.

"Are you sure she's dead?" she asked calmly. Melba never reacted the way you expected.

"Yes," I said. "Someone must have broken in and killed her with your golf club."

"My golf club?" Melba was on her feet now, showing some real emotion. She ran out of the room toward the drawing room.

Adrienne and Wilson were on their way down the stairs, still in their dinner clothes, though Wilson had removed his coat and tie.

"I saw the lights on," Wilson said. "What's up?"

I explained, and Adrienne screamed and nearly swooned. When we entered the drawing room, Melba was next to Aunt Agatha, holding the golf club, inspecting its shiny wooden head—for cracks, I suspected.

"Melba!" Adrienne screamed. "What have you done?" Lady Lucy spat and hissed, peering at them from behind my feet.

"Me?" Melba turned, holding the club higher, and for a moment I thought she might use it on her sister or Wilson. I stepped between them.

"You'd better leave this where it was," I said. "Where do you keep your clubs?"

She took me through the kitchen into a small storeroom, where her polished leather golf bag lay on its side on the floor. She gasped and picked it up, hanging it gently on a large padded hook on the wall. I noticed Lady Lucy sniffing at a pink streak of liquid on the yellow linoleum and bent to examine it.

"Blood?" Melba asked, wrinkling her nose in dismay.

"No, I don't think so. Water, apparently."

"And some of it's gotten on my bag," she muttered, wiping a drop off the bag with her fingertip.

"Nobody touches those clubs but you," Adrienne said imperiously from the doorway. Wilson had followed her and stood behind her, frowning suspiciously at his sister-in-law. Lady Lucy peered at them with narrowed, suspicious eyes; her ears were flat against her head.

"The front door is still locked," Adrienne continued. "I just checked. So nobody got in. You're the one who wanted her dead, Melba. You're the one who hated her. Oh, my God, you've killed our mother, just so you can marry Philip Wolfe." She leaned into Wilson's shoulder, and did a fine job of looking frail.

Wilson glanced around. "Where is Dr. Wolfe?" he asked.

Melba merely glared at him, pushing them aside as she walked back to the drawing room. After putting a piece of plastic wrap over the wet streak on the linoleum and warning Adrienne and Wilson not to touch anything, I followed. Melba was standing in the center of the room, staring glumly at her mother's body.

"I suppose we'll have to call the police," she said quietly. "It doesn't look good for me, I guess."

"I'm not so sure," I said as Adrienne and Wilson entered.

"How can you suggest otherwise, Essie?" Adrienne asked as they entered the room. "She certainly had motive—the money and freedom to marry Philip. She obviously had the means; it was her club that killed the poor woman. As for opportunity— have you both been together since dinner?"

"No," I admitted, "but I haven't been with you two, either."

"And she's changed her clothes," Adrienne added, ignoring my last statement. "Where's your dinner dress, Melba?"

"I put it in the wash," Melba said. "I spilled some gravy on the skirt, and didn't want the stain to set."

"How convenient," sneered Adrienne. "I didn't see you spill anything." I hadn't either, but didn't say so.

Wilson crossed to the sideboard and picked up the phone. "I'll call the police," he said smugly. Melba didn't try to stop him.

As he dialed, Lady Lucy curled herself around Adrienne's ankles. I was surprised, since the Lady didn't usually seem to care much for Adrienne. But, typical of cats, she often seemed to relish contact with people who'd rather avoid her. I watched her, listening vaguely to Wilson's voice droning into the telephone. Adrienne was barefoot, and her pale ankles showed starkly beneath the puckered red hem of her dress. She grimaced and firmly pushed Lady Lucy away with one delicate foot.

After Wilson hung up, he said, "They'll have someone here in a few minutes. Of course, Essie, you'll tell them everything you know about what happened tonight."

"I intend to," I answered. "I'll even tell them who I believe killed Aunt Agatha."

"Of course." Wilson nearly smiled when he answered; I wanted to slap him. He turned to Adrienne, but he was obviously still talking for my benefit. "As I mentioned a few minutes ago,

I'm not so sure it was Melba, darling," he said. "I'm inclined to suspect Dr. Wolfe, myself."

Melba made a growling, hissing sound that reminded me of the noise Lady Lucy makes when the neighbor's dog sniffs around our porch, but I held out a hand to silence her.

"I don't think Philip had anything to do with this," I said.

"But he must have known where Melba keeps her clubs," Wilson said, his brows furrowing with sincerity. "He's here all the time; he knows the house almost as well as we do. And considering his relationship with Melba, he certainly had a motive for killing Agatha."

"Possibly," I conceded. "But as her physician, he had much better, subtler methods at his disposal than bludgeoning her to death. No, I think I'll tell them first that you tried to hide a small set of binoculars when you came in this afternoon from your 'run.' I wondered then why you weren't out of breath and sweaty. When I saw the safe behind the painting this evening, I realized you must have been outside the window earlier, watching as Aunt Agatha opened her safe, trying to learn the combination."

"What . . . Me? Are you crazy?" Wilson sputtered, but I was just warming up.

"And I wondered why the handle of the golf club had more blood on it than the head, until I remembered the water under Aunt Agatha's cane. She wasn't bludgeoned with the golf club at all, but with her own cane, which the killer then washed off, maybe at one of the outside taps on the front porch. You probably thought the water would dry quickly, Adrienne, but in this humidity—" I paused to catch my breath.

"That's ridiculous," Adrienne pronounced.

"Is it? Well, the police have tests to find out whether there's ever been blood on the cane. Also, those wet streaks on the floor of the storeroom are the kind of marks a red water-soaked gauze dress might make. And your dress . . ."

"What about my dress?" Adrienne's voice was cold, angry.

"Gauze is so delicate isn't it?" I asked. "When it's exposed to sudden changes in temperature, it shrinks right up. You must have tried to dry your dress with your hair-dryer; that's why it's so much shorter now than it was at dinner. I probably wouldn't have noticed it, except when you pushed Lady Lucy away, so much ankle showed."

"How could you think I'd kill my own mother?" Adrienne's chin puckered and she forced a tear from her eye.

"Actually, I don't," I continued. "I think Wilson did. That's why he hid his jacket and tie—when they're recovered, they'll most likely show traces of blood. He was probably opening the safe when Aunt Agatha surprised him. Maybe she attacked him with her cane, or maybe it was just convenient. Anyway, he beat her to death with it.

"I don't know whether you were in on the planning stages with him, Adrienne, but you washed the cane off for him, replacing it with the golf club, not bothering to hang the bag back up, which Melba would definitely have done. In fact, she'd never have dirtied one of her clubs that way.

"Then you put the wet cane back in the room, leaving a trace of water under it. But the cane was too far from Aunt Agatha for her to have simply dropped it as she died; she couldn't have walked that far without it. So someone else must have used it— to kill her, obviously."

Melba sank onto one of the armchairs, crying. I was moved, until I heard her say, "I can't believe they used one of my poor golf clubs." Sirens began wailing in the distance.

I looked around for Lady Lucy, and there she was, curled up purring at Aunt Agatha's feet. It seemed she was the only one who'd really miss the old woman.

Lisa Lepovetsky

A marathon runner in the art of short-form fiction, Lisa Lepovetsky has more than two hundred fifty pieces of fiction, nonfiction, and poetry in magazines (Ellery Queen's Mystery Magazine, Grue, Space and Time, *etc.*) *and anthologies* (Death in Dixie,

Dark Destiny I and II, 100 Wicked Little Witches, *etc.*). *No wonder she teaches writing/literature/communications classes for the University of Pittsburgh. For diversion, she also writes and hosts mystery theaters and dinner theaters for organizations, restaurants, and cruises. An active member of Mystery Writers of America, Sisters in Crime, and Horror Writers' Association, she serves as Author Advocacy Chair for Pennwriters. Lisa has raised a variety of birds, dogs, rodents, and reptiles throughout her life, and owned her own pet grooming business for seven years. She has two grown daughters and lives in St. Marys, Pennsylvania, with her husband, Howard, and a tank of tropical fish.*

I find it hard to believe Miss Barbara Paul was a respected university lecturer before turning to mystery writing. Her fiction shows a downright dark and fiendish bent that one would like to think only the uneducated might appreciate. Her animal of choice is exactly that: a real *animal*! Meet Dev, the Tasmanian devil. Dev is about to meet some very bad customers of the human variety. Don't waste any time worrying about Dev!

—M.L.

Go to the Devil
Barbara Paul

THE NURSE PUT a clamp on the bandage around Lew's upper arm and told him he'd have some seepage. "Come back right before closing time and I'll change the dressing. Do you want something for pain?"

"I could use something," he admitted.

She gave him two white tablets and a paper cup full of water. "What you really need examined is your head. What were you thinking of, going after the worst-tempered animal in the park with no gloves?"

"I was wearing gloves!" Lew protested. "They just didn't come up far enough."

"Wear longer ones."

He gritted his teeth and said, "They don't make them any longer, and thank you for your sympathy."

The nurse laughed and said, "Go on, you'll live."

Outside the First-Aid Station, Becky was waiting in the Jeep. "Still hurts, huh?"

"I took some pain pills." He climbed into the passenger side. "Dev's learning. He knew not to waste any effort trying to bite through the gloves—he went straight for the nearest soft spot."

"Oh, he's smart. Smart and mean." Becky started the engine. "Next time, I'll go in with you. I don't have any exposed arm for him to sink his teeth into." The heavy gloves they used for handling animals reached all the way up to Becky's armpits, but they barely covered Lew's elbows.

He sighed. "At least I got that guy's watch back for him."

"Did he even say thank you? I'll bet he's long gone."

But he wasn't. A father with two small children in tow (who had finally stopped crying), the man was waiting worriedly where they'd left him. They hadn't even gotten out of the Jeep before he started his litany of apology and self-justification. "I can't tell you how sorry I am—are you all right? You scared the daylights out of us, you know—but you must have been scared, too, weren't you? I really am sorry. I had no idea you'd just go in there like that—I thought you'd shoot him with a tranquilizer gun or something."

"That would kill him," Lew said. He walked up to the fencing and scanned the enclosed area; Dev was nowhere in sight. "Tranquilizer darts are for lions and bears and the like. There's no dosage for small animals that's effective without being harmful. They have to be tranked the old-fashioned way, up close and with a needle."

The man shook his head. "He surprised me. He came right up to the fence and snatched my watch before I knew what was happening."

"You're lucky he didn't leave claw marks on you," Becky pointed out. "The sign says stand behind the yellow line. That's five feet back from the fencing."

"I know, but I, I kind of forgot about that when I couldn't get a clear view. I've never seen a Tasmanian devil before, and I wanted a good look. All those trees and overhangs blocking the sun—it's dark in there!"

"The devil's a nocturnal animal," she replied. "He needs to adjust gradually to coming out during the day. He's probably in one of his burrows."

"Look, I really am sorry about this trouble, but I didn't know he'd just come up to me like that . . ."

The animal attendants tuned him out. Eventually the man decided he'd apologized enough; he took his children and left.

The moment he was gone, the Tasmanian devil emerged, not from one of his burrows but from his cave; he sat on a rock, staring ferociously at the two watching him. Black fur with white markings on his chest, full grown at nineteen pounds, big head and jaws, looked like a misshapen dog.

"Proud of yourself, Dev?" Lew asked. "This has been a really fun day for you, hasn't it?"

Becky said, "We're going to have to put a ditch along this stretch of fencing. That guy could have lost a hand." The devil started nattering at them. "Now what's he complaining about?"

"Who knows." Lew raised his voice. "Oh, Dev—surprise coming for you this afternoon. We've got you a playmate. Uh-huh, that's right. No creature should be the only one of his species in an animal park—not even a nasty-dispositioned S.O.B. like you." He paused while the devil snarled and growled at him. "We tried to get you a female, but there just aren't any available right now. But the male we got is too young to be a threat. You can teach him to be as foul-tempered as you are."

"If Dev doesn't eat him for breakfast first," Becky said.

nabble nabble nabble don't they ever stop the noise, sometimes NABBLE NABBLE NABBLE or screeeech or har-har-har cough, stupid look on he face, she voice hurts ears, wrong fish again, want *that* fish not *this* fish, where's ocean full of tasties, where's my pretty, stupid he took my pretty, lay your hands on me again stupid he and I take another hunk out of you, want my pretty back it's mine mine MINE, night/not-night this place, stupid little stream of water with wrong fish, no juicy things in shells, no dead birds or cows, now Two-Legs everywhere, watch-

ing pointing going nabble nabble, stupid he and she don't
know wrong fish from right fish, just go away bring dead
cow GO AWAY

Martinelli slapped a new clip into the Beretta and made sure
one bullet was in the chamber. If Joey tried anything cute, he'd
blow a hole in him you could see daylight through. Martinelli
halfway hoped he would try something; the damned kid was
more trouble than he was worth.

"Ready?" Damone growled.

"Yeah, I'm ready. Sal, why don't we just blow this kid away?"

"He has a gift. We need him."

"So find somebody else with the same gift," Martinelli said.
"You know the guy can't be trusted."

"Because he had a drink with one of Polo's soldiers?" Damone led the way out of the house to the Lamborghini parked in
the driveway. "Hey, they went to school together. They're from
the old neighborhood."

"You and Polo went to school together."

"Yeah, well, that's different. Me and Polo—we always hated
each other." Damone got into the car. "Polo was crowdin' my
territory even in school."

Martinelli slid in behind the wheel. "It's a bad idea, Sal. You
send Joey after Polo, he sells you out."

Damone laughed. "You're just worried 'cause you know the
kid wants your job. No, Joey won't sell me out to Polo." The laugh
faded. "He wouldn't dare."

"It's a mistake," Martinelli repeated stubbornly.

"Tell you what. You find me another piece of talent can set a
bomb as clean as the kid's, and I'll dump Joey. A bomb that leaves
no trace of itself. You know anybody else can build a bomb like
that?"

"Not offhand," Martinelli admitted.

"Then we stick with Joey. We just watch him real careful,
that's all."

"Okay." Martinelli still wasn't satisfied, but he knew when to
stop pushing.

They drove in silence another ten minutes until they reached one of the parking lots adjoining the animal park. "There's a place," Damone said.

Martinelli pulled into the vacant slot. "Where we meetin'?"

"By the Tasmanian devil's pen."

"Tasmanian devil?" Martinelli was surprised. "That's a cartoon."

"It's also a real animal," Damone said testily as he got out of the car. "Christ, Martinelli, don't you know nothin'? Not many zoos have a Tasmanian devil, especially here in this country. Big attraction, lots of people around. Get the picture?"

Martinelli grinned. "Then you *don't* trust him!"

"I don't trust nobody, don't you know that by now? Come on, let's go."

"Dev hates him," Becky said.

"Dev hates everything," Lew replied. "Give them some time."

The park photographer had recorded the arrival of their new addition and left. The new young male they'd brought into the pen had spent his first few minutes whimpering and looking around at this bewildering new place where he found himself. He weighed about a third of what Dev weighed and had the same oversized head and black fur, but his white markings were on his rump instead of his chest. Then he'd spotted Dev and trotted over on his short legs to greet one of his own kind only to be met with a kick from Dev's hind leg and a thorough cussing-out in Tasmanian devilese.

"Uh-oh," said Becky. "Look at his ears." The normally pink interiors of Dev's big ears had turned purple, always a sure sign that a Tasmanian devil was agitated. The younger animal read some signs of his own and slunk away.

Lew and Becky were inside the pen, gloved and padded but keeping their distance from the two sharp-toothed inhabitants. Devils led solitary lives but would share space in the wild; the two animal handlers were hoping for a similar development here. The sex of the animals sharing space didn't seem to matter; devils had a brief, intense mating period each March and that was it for the year.

Lew decided formal introductions were in order. "Dev, this is your new pen-mate. His name is Taz." He glanced at Becky, who rolled her eyes. "Taz is someone for you to quarrel with, when he gets a little older. Won't that be fun? Just give him a chance to grow up first, will you?"

Taz had stopped whimpering and was exploring his new surroundings, already growling and complaining about what he found. Becky said, "Okay, let's see what happens when we put out a double portion of meat. Ten bucks says Dev won't let the little guy have any."

"No bet." They left the pen; the devils would get their meal through a trough that was manipulated from the outside. Lew opened the meat locker that was filled, today, with double portions of beef. "Dev's favorite. Oh, hell, they forgot the bones—no, here they are. Okay, ready?"

They each grabbed one side of the aluminum feeder and slid it into the trough. Becky pulled the handle that rolled the feeder to the inside end of the trough and lifted the gate there. Dev was already waiting, but it took Taz a moment to trot over once he'd caught the scent.

Feeding was the one true social interaction devils shared; the presence of sufficient food gave them the chance to show off, to try to outdo each other in displays of savagery. It was a noisy affair; Dev and Taz bumped and jostled each other, prompting snarls and growls and much baring of teeth. Young Taz's soft barks and snorts played in counterpoint to Dev's continuous monotone growling—which suddenly escalated into the bloodcurdling scream that invariably struck fear into even the largest of carnivores.

"Geez, what a noise!" Lew said. Becky was covering her ears.

It scared Taz, too. He backed away from the meat. "Afraid of that," Becky said.

Lew took out a flashlight and shined the beam straight into Dev's eyes; Dev didn't abandon his meal, but he did look away from the light long enough for Taz to steal a piece of beef. "Maybe we should try feeding them separately," Lew said.

"And deprive them of the fun of fighting over it? That would be cruel, Lew."

"Yeah, you're right. Dumb suggestion."

dead cow good, more dead cow than insides hold, eat anyway, keep from Other, MY dead cow, Other eat wrong fish, dead cow mine, stupid he and she bring Other, still nabble nabble never stop, want my pretty back WANT MY PRETTY nabble nabble, take dead cow to burrow stay under, Other go away GO AWAY

The parking lot was right across the road from the Tasmanian devil pen; they paid their entrance fees and went in. Martinelli spotted Joey first, the kid's thick wavy hair lifting in the breeze, shirt unbuttoned almost to his navel, one perfect gold chain around his neck. *A gold chain,* yet . . . doing the retro thing. "There he is," he said to Damone.

The kid was talking to two of the zoo attendants. "I can't see anything. You sure there's a Tasmanian devil in there?"

"Two," the male attendant said. "But they've just been fed so they're sleeping now. But please, sir, step back behind the yellow line."

Joey took his time but stepped back. "Why? Can the buggers climb the fence?"

"One of them can climb a little way," the female attendant said. "Tasmanian devils can climb trees. This one can get about five feet up the fence before he falls—and he can thrust his nozzle through the openings. He's attracted by shiny things—he could go for that gold chain you're wearing."

Joey looked startled. "Oh, go on!"

The man said, "It's the truth. He snagged a watch just this morning." He pointed to the bandage on his arm. "And did this to me when I went in after it. So stay behind the yellow line, please."

The woman was looking at his arm. "Lew, you've got a lot of seepage there. You'd better go get that bandage changed."

"We have to feed the rest of the marsupials."

"I'll start—you catch up when you can."

He looked at the bandage. "Yeah, maybe I'd better. Keys to the Jeep?"

"Want me to drive you?"

"Naw, I can manage." She handed him a set of keys and the two of them headed off in opposite directions.

"So, Joey, you givin' the zookeepers a hard time?"

The young man wearing the gold chain turned. "Oh, Mr. Damone—I didn't hear you come up. I was just trying to get a look at this here Tasmanian devil, but he's holed up somewhere asleep." A family of four strolled up, saw there was nothing to see, and strolled away again.

"So, you been havin' any more drinks with Polo's soldier?"

Joey laughed easily. "Naw, just that one. Hadn't seen the guy in years."

"So what did you talk about?"

"Mutual friends, the old days, everything but today. He didn't mention Polo and I didn't mention you. It was the only way to keep it friendly, see." Martinelli snorted. "You got a problem with that, Martinelli?"

"Yeah, I got a problem with that. How do we know you didn't make a little deal while you were having your friendly drink?"

The younger man whirled toward Martinelli's boss. "Mr. Damone, I don't deserve that," he said heatedly. "I've proved myself to you, haven't I? I've done good work for you. The warehouse job, Alfio's restaurant—they couldn't be traced back to you, could they? So why do I have to stand here and take this lip from Martinelli?"

"Martinelli's just lookin' out for my interests," Damone said, unruffled. "It's what he's paid to do. But you—you're still an unknown factor, kid. You came through for me twice ... but will you come through a third time?"

"Just tell me what you want," Joey said earnestly.

Damone looked around. The crowds he'd expected at the pen

weren't there, since the Tasmanian devils were keeping themselves out of sight for the time being. Two boys crossed the yellow line and peered through the fencing, but they gave up quickly and left. No one in earshot. "I want you to take out Polo. And I want you to do it Sunday night."

"Polo, huh? You got it." Joey started dancing back and forth from one foot to the other. "Why Sunday?"

"Don't ask questions, kid," Martinelli said, "just do what you're told." There was a meeting of crime bosses Sunday, and Damone wanted to send a message about what happens to a boss who encroaches on another boss's territory—but Joey didn't need to know that.

"It doesn't have to be a big bomb," Damone was saying. "But it does have to be precise. Polo's the only one I want."

"Well, that makes it harder," Joey said, still dancing. "Big bombs are easy—just take out everybody and you're sure to get the guy you want. More chance of getting the wrong guy with a small bomb."

Damone thought that over. "That's gonna be a problem. Maybe before Sunday—"

"Hey, sorry, but I can't hold it any longer—I gotta go pee." He pointed. "Men's room right over there. I'll be back in five minutes."

"Oh, fer cryin' out loud," Martinelli said in disgust.

"Five minutes," Joey promised and took off running.

"Didja see that?" Martinelli asked rhetorically. "Right in the middle of talkin' business, he has to go pee!"

Damone was none too pleased either. "This kid is too full of himself. He needs a lesson."

"Glad you see that, Sal."

What neither of them did see was the package sitting on the meat locker by the devils' pen. And when Joey pushed the button on his remote control, neither of them ever saw anything again.

BIG thunder, ears hurt, ground move, dirt in eyes, burrow falling dig dig dig, hard to breathe dig dig dig, hole in dirt

sky BREATHE, climb out shake off dirt, breathe and
cough, smoke in air, Two-Legs everywhere running running NABBLE NABBLE NABBLE ears hurt, much
noise, HOLE big hole in hard fence go GO hide, hide
from Two-Legs hide and watch, hide, quieter now, strange
things, pretty things, new pretty on Two-Legs, want pretty,
MY pretty, follow Two-Legs, hurry hurry, thing on wheels,
jump in back, hide from Two-Legs hide

The harried-looking cop introduced himself as Detective Sebert.
"You say you've got an escaped animal here?"

"A Tasmanian devil," Becky said. "They're rare and expensive
and we had to wait a long time to get this one. He was under-
ground in his burrow at the time of the explosion and that protected him from the blast. Our other devil was inside a small rock
cave and we have him in a cage now. But the one that escaped—
we want to make sure the police don't shoot him."

"Why would we shoot him?" Sebert asked. "Is he dangerous?
An attack animal?"

"He can be dangerous, but devils generally avoid human beings. He won't attack a human unless he's provoked, but . . ."

"But what?"

"He's very easily provoked," she finished lamely.

Sebert said, "Look, I've got two corpses here, I can't go running around looking for your animal. If he's dangerous, I'll put
out an all-points on him—"

"No!" Becky cried. "That's just what we *don't* want you to do!"

Lew came trotting up to them. "I can't find him. We're going
to need an organized search."

Becky introduced Sebert and Lew. "Detective, he can't have
gone far," she said. "Devils can't run fast—they have this
rocking-horse gait that keeps them from being effective hunters.
They're scavengers. In the wild they live off dead things they find
because they can't catch even a rat. They just can't move fast."

"They're meat-eaters?" Sebert asked, beginning to get
worried.

Lew said, "Their fancy name is *Sarcophilus harrisii. Sarcophilus* means 'flesh-lover.' If they have plenty to eat and you don't bother them, they're not dangerous. But a Tasmanian devil on the lam—huh, Lord knows what could happen. They're extremely volatile. We've got to find him *now,* before somebody takes a shotgun to him."

Sebert thought a moment. "You say he can't have gone far? I can't do much until the bodies are identified—"

He was interrupted by a uniformed cop. "Detective, young couple over there noticed something—might be important, might not. Young guy standing there watching, real calm like, little smile on his face. Everybody else was running around, screaming, but he just stood there watching."

"Description?"

"About nineteen or twenty, thick black hair, gold chain around his neck."

"We talked to that guy," Lew said quickly. "Right before the explosion."

"What about?"

"Just told him to stand behind the yellow line."

"Could you ID him?"

"Sure."

Sebert turned back to the uniformed cop. "What else?"

"Nothing, really," the cop said. "This young couple, they watched him cross the road to the parking lot. He got into a black van—went in through the back doors and his dog jumped in after him—"

"His dog?" Sebert turned back to Lew and Becky. "Does your Tasmanian devil look like a dog?"

"In a way," Becky said. "Head's too big for a dog."

Lew shrugged. "More like a dog than any other animal."

"Then what?" Sebert asked the cop.

"Then nothing. He drove away."

Becky asked, "And our devil was in that van?"

"Sure sounds like it," Sebert said. "You two are coming downtown with me. I want you to look at some pictures."

bump bump roll start stop, bad smell sick sick, noise
NOISE, fall can't walk, know this, bump bumped before,
roll start stop, new place, stupid Two-Legs making bump
bump, stop, STOPPED no bump no roll, wait, wait, Two-
Legs back, DEAD COW smell DEAD COW, start again
bump bump roll DEAD COW

"That's him," said Becky, staring at the picture. Lew confirmed
her identification of the young man with the gold chain.

Detective Sebert gave a grunt of satisfaction. "Thought it
might be. Wait here—I'll be back in a minute."

Lew and Becky waited, fidgeting but not talking. Sebert's
minute had stretched to twenty before he returned.

"The guy you identified is Joey Bufano," the detective said,
sitting down opposite them, "and we've been after him since he
turned eighteen. Kid's got a natural talent for handling explosives. His bombs don't leave anything traceable behind—nothing
at all." Sebert paused. "I think Joey Bufano is one of those people who're born without any conscience at all. There's something
missing in Joey. He never gives a thought to the people he kills
or to all the property he wipes out—he just likes to see things
blow up. So somebody gets hurt, so what?" Sebert threw his arms
out. "*Ka-boom!* That's where he gets his kicks."

"Oh, my," Becky said faintly. Lew swallowed.

The detective went on, "Joey's only loyalty is to his own
whim. He was in and out of juvie half a dozen times as a kid and
he didn't learn nothing. We got nineteen unsolved explosions on
the books and we know Joey was behind every single damned
one of them—but we can't prove it. We've never even been able
to place him at the scene . . . until now."

"So what are we waiting for?" Lew asked. "Let's go get him—
he has our devil!"

Sebert sighed. "It's not that easy. Joey Bufano doesn't have a
fixed address—he moves around a lot. He keeps all his gear in
that van of his, even sleeps in it sometimes. He'll stop with a
friend or rent a room when he's handling a volatile substance,
stay a week or two, and then move on."

"So where is he right now?"

"We have no idea. You see the problem?"

"License plate," Becky said.

"He keeps changing 'em. I think he buys counterfeit plates from out of state. That young couple at the animal park who saw him get into the van—they didn't think to check the plate. But he's wily, our Joey is. And about as stable as the explosives he handles."

Lew and Becky exchanged a look. "So what do we do?" Becky asked. "Just look for the van?"

Sebert shook his head. "Do you have any idea how many black vans there are in this burg? Forget the van. What we do is look for Joey. I just now put out an APB on him and every cop in the city will have his picture within minutes—we fax it right to the patrol cars. Joey may be wily, but he ain't invisible. Sooner or later, someone is going to spot him and call it in. They have orders not to approach."

"What if it's later instead of sooner?" Lew asked. "This Joey kills people without thinking twice about it—what's he going to do the first time the devil growls at him?"

Nobody had an answer to that.

"*Sheesh!*" Joey yelled, startled. "Where the hell did you come from?"

The animal in the back of the van snarled at him and started a low growl.

Joey reached from the driver's seat and turned on the overhead light to get a better look at what was in the back of his van. "Hoo. You are without a doubt the *ugliest* dog I've ever seen! What happened? Your owner get sick of looking at you and kick you out? When did you get into my van, hmm?"

Dev growled and took a couple of steps toward the Two-Legs.

Joey followed the devil's eyes. "My cheeseburger? That's what you want? Here, take it—I got a sack full." He tossed the burger to the floor of the van and laughed out loud when he saw the devil take the whole thing in one bite, paper and all. "Man,

now *that's* what I call an appetite! Here, have another." Dev
chomped it down and snarled a demand for another. Joey laughed.
"Hey, don't be shy! If you want one, just ask for it."

By the time the sack was empty, Dev had eaten five burgers
and Joey one. But the animal seemed to want more.

"That's all there is. Now I know why your owner kicked you
out. You eat too much." The animal had been amusing for a
while, but now Joey was bored with the game. "Okay, dog, time
to go." He got out of the van and went around to open the rear
doors. "Come on, now. Out."

Dev snarled at him but didn't budge.

"I said *out.* Damn it, don't make me come in there after you!
Get out here!" His raised voice brought a similar response from
Dev, whose growls and snarls took on a higher pitch. "*Sheesh—*
what's with your ears? They're purple!" Cursing, Joey climbed
into the back of the van. "I . . . want . . . you . . . *out* of here!
C'mere, you stupid mutt." He reached for Dev's ruff . . .

. . . And screamed with pain as the devil's sharp teeth sank into
his hand. Instinctively he kicked out toward the animal and felt
those same teeth in the calf of his leg; he screamed again and sat
down, hard. Dev backed away, muttering and snarling and growling. Joey had always scorned carrying a gun as something only
thugs had to do, but he would have given twenty years of his life
for a gun right then.

He tried inching his way toward the rear doors—and Dev
sank his teeth into the man's other leg. Joey was gritting his teeth
against the pain; both his legs and one hand were useless. He
tried using his good hand to drag himself forward toward the
driver's seat; but when Dev moved to intercept him, he stopped.

For the first time since he was a small child, Joey Bufano felt
real fear. This animal from hell that had appeared so mysteri-
ously out of nowhere now had him pinned against one wall of the
van, and there was no doubt in Joey's mind that the beast wanted
to kill him. Joey lay very still, very quiet.

The beast began an angry, scolding, screeching, growling, ver-
bose, snarling tirade that made Joey's hair stand on end. Then
as abruptly as he'd begun, the animal stopped vocalizing and

opened his mouth as wide as he could—a hundred and twenty degrees. Letting the man get a good look at *all* the sharp teeth he had to work with. "What *are* you?" Joey whispered in dread.

There wasn't much maneuvering room among all the gear stowed in the van, so Dev's next move took him close to Joey's face. But by watching the beast's eyes, the man saw it wasn't his face the creature was interested in. With a scream Joey threw up his arms to protect his throat just as the devil lunged.

"Somewhere along in here," Detective Sebert said as he peered through the windshield. "The cops who spotted him in the Burger King followed him down Avonleigh as far as Hawk Street before they lost him. Lots of little twisty streets in this area."

Seated next to him, Becky was looking out the side window. "It's so dark. How can you find a black van in the dark?"

"He won't leave it on the street. He'll have a garage or shed or something. No warehouses in this district. Maybe a vacant house with a place to park in the rear."

Lew was in the backseat, crowded up against a large portable kennel and a duffel bag of gear they'd brought. "So what do we do," he asked, "break into every possible hiding place we see?"

"If we have to. What we do is look for *likely* places. We're not the only ones looking, you know—there are patrol cars all through this area."

"So what's likely?"

"That is." Sebert stopped the car. What had caught his eye was an old garage next to a house that had a "For Rent" sign in the front lawn. The garage had a row of glass panes at about eye level in the sliding door. "You wait," Sebert told the other two. With a gun in one hand and a huge flashlight in the other, he approached the garage door quietly. He stood at one end of the row of glass panes and in one quick movement shined a light inside. Then he shook his head and walked back to the car. "Nothing but old oil stains on the cement."

But before he could get back in the car, the night quiet was ripped apart by a scream so loud and so bloodcurdling that Sebert could feel the gooseflesh rising on his arms and back. "What the hell was *that*?"

The other two were hurriedly pulling their gear out of the backseat. "That was our devil," Becky told him. "He's alive!"

"God, that was eerie!" Sebert had never heard a sound like that before, and it rattled him. "Hold on, you two—we're not going anywhere until I call for backup." He used the car radio to tell the patrolling police cars where to find them. "Silent approach. And I mean really silent. I don't even want to hear your engines running."

"Becky, take the duffel," Lew said and picked up the kennel. They headed down a short street that ended in a cul-de-sac.

"Are you sure that scream came from this street?" Sebert asked. "It sounded all around us to me."

"It came from here," Lew assured him. "We've heard it a few times." He put down the kennel and looked around. "But which house?"

There were eleven houses, six on one side of the street and five on the other. The streetlights showed a once-fashionable street that had long since grown shabby. All eleven buildings were huge old houses that had been divided into apartments; there could be a couple hundred people living there now. But however many there were, they were all inside or not at home; the street was empty except for Sebert and the two animal handlers.

It didn't stay empty long. Uniformed police began arriving in pairs, moving in quietly on foot, their patrol cars parked several blocks away. Sebert set them to checking out the street, to look for some indication of which of the eleven houses concealed Joey Bufano.

"Come on, Dev," Lew said, "tell us where you are."

The devil made them wait another ten minutes before he obliged, and this time the scream made every cop in the street jump. "Jesus," said Sebert, "it's even worse the second time!"

The scream had come from an old carriage house, its six cubicles presumably now sheltering the cars of the inhabitants who lived in the apartments above. The cops circled in as Lew and

Becky put their ears to one garage door, then another. Becky waved an arm: *This one.*

Sebert pressed his ear against the old wooden door. "Someone talking," he said in a low voice.

"That's the devil," Lew said, almost whispering. "He's very vocal. They're in here."

Whatever was going on in there, it had started before Joey Bufano had gotten out of the van and locked the garage doors. Two of the cops pulled the doors open, wincing when the hinges squeaked. But they abandoned all attempt at silence when they saw what was inside.

The back doors of the lighted van were wide open. Joey was cowering against one side of the van, his hands raised as if to ward off an attack. His shirt sleeves were in shreds and his forearms were bloody. Facing him, growling and chattering and baring his teeth, was the Tasmanian devil, who clearly had the situation well in hand. "Get him away from me!" Joey screamed. "Get him away!"

"I think you'd better let us handle this part, Detective," Lew said.

Sebert listened to the sounds the devil was making and looked at the sharp teeth he was displaying and said, "I think you're right."

Lew brought in the kennel and set it down not on its bottom but on one end, the door open and ready to receive one extremely angry animal. Becky opened the duffel and took out two pairs of long heavy gloves covered with scratch marks and a case containing a hypodermic needle. "Tranquilizer," she told Sebert. "I hope we don't have to use it."

"Will it hurt him?"

"He'll hurt us when we give it to him." The last thing she took out of the duffel was a net, which she handed to Lew. "Your reach is longer than mine."

"Okay," he said. "You go in the front way, I'll take the back."

Lew shook out the net and waited until Becky had eased into the passenger seat. Lew got into the rear of the van on his knees, holding the net close to his chest with his gloved hands.

"Get him out!" Joey cried. "He keeps going for my throat! He's trying to kill me!"

"It's not your throat he wants," Lew said, "it's your chain."

"What?"

"Your gold chain. Give it to him. Easy, now. No sudden moves."

With shaking hands Joey undid the gold chain and looked at Lew.

"Drop it on the floor of the van where he can see it. Right in front of him."

Hesitantly Joey reached out toward the devil and dropped the chain. Dev immediately pounced on it; he took the chain in his mouth and moved a few feet away, already forgetting about the man he'd been terrorizing. He had what he wanted.

"That's it?" Joey screeched. "He wanted my Goddamn *chain*?"

"Keep your voice down," Becky said quickly. "And *don't move.*"

Lew was opening the net now, preparing for the toss. He maneuvered past Joey's gear as close to Dev as he dared and let fly. The weighted ends sailed over the devil's head and the net landed softly on top of him.

The second Dev felt the net settling about him, he let out a scream that put the first two to shame. Joey screamed with him. The more Dev fought the net, the more entangled he became— all the time cussing and roaring and snarling and bawling out the world and in general putting on such a display that the cops crowded around the rear of the van to watch.

"I have seen some class-A temper tantrums in my time," Sebert said wonderingly, "but that one surely is king."

Becky squeezed between the two front seats to pick up the weighted end of the net and give it a twist. Lew did the same at the other end and pulled the net taut. Now the devil was not only caught in the net, he was also suspended in midair—and he had plenty to say about that. The two handlers carefully made their way out through the rear, the cops backing away to give them room. Inside, Joey was sobbing with relief.

"Bring 'im out," Sebert ordered.

Dev gave it his all, but the two handlers proved to be too

much for him. Devil and net went into the kennel together. Two cops dragged Joey out of the van.

"Well, Joey," Sebert said. "You ready to tell us about that blowup in the animal park today? Or do we lock you up with the Tasmanian devil a little longer?"

Joey looked around vaguely. "That was a Tasmanian devil?" he asked, and fainted.

While the two cops carried Joey out to a patrol car, Sebert turned to the animal handlers. "Say, you wouldn't think of renting that critter out, would you? I want to thank you both. Your devil led us straight to Joey. You were a big help."

"Our pleasure, Detective," Lew said with a big grin. "All's well, and all that."

"Hope your devil's little adventure wasn't too traumatic for him."

Lew laughed. "It'll probably be one of his fondest memories. The devil is a tough little animal, Detective, in case you didn't notice."

Sebert was nodding his head. "I noticed," he said. "Believe me—I noticed."

dead bird, no dead cow, Other sassing talking back, stupid he and she just watch, no nabble nabble, Other make more nabble nabble than Two-Legs, hole in fence gone, way out gone, need practice, practice climbing, over top way out, climbing out, stupid he and she watching, go away need practice GO AWAY

Barbara Paul

Barbara Paul has a Ph.D. in theater history and criticism and taught at the University of Pittsburgh, but became a full-time writer of science fiction and mystery in the late seventies. Her most recent book is Full Frontal Murder, *a new entry in her Marian Larch series from Scribner.*

Her "other" occupation, she says, is holding doors and open-

ing cans. From this clue, the intuitive mystery reader will deduce the presence of several cats in her life. First came Godfrey and Daniel, two elegant, white abandoned cats. Word quickly spread where the neighborhood patsy lived, and soon a young tabby named Slick invited himself in for keeps. Then, during a blizzard, two small orphans of the storm showed up on the snowy doorstep, so Mimi and Pest joined the household. Now a "No Vacancy" sign guards the back door.

A Baker Street Irregular

Carole Nelson Douglas

THERE I AM in my usual position, with my back to the wall.

Only this wall is made of sooty, solid brick, without so much as an occasional windowsill that a bloke can sink his nails into for a fast climb upward.

That is behind me. In front of me stands another wall, a ragged, rank-smelling living wall of the worst guttersnipes I have ever laid eyeballs on. They have chased me into this cul-de-sac with a hail of sticks and stones (and other less sharp if more odiferous offerings of the London streets), and even now are debating whether to cut off my tail or my head.

I catch the glint of steel amid the rust, and the odd glimmer-

ing tooth behind the smoke-smudged grins. I recognize this un-
happy gang of street Arabs as the worst enemy of my kind and
prepare for a mad but likely fruitless dash through their closed
ranks. I expect to leave some part of my hide behind, perhaps
even my life.

" 'Ere now. Wot's this cat done to you?"

The speaker is the same species as my tormenters: human
boy, but he is taller and wears a better grade of rag. I recognize
a certain street-sent authority in his tones.

They mumble, of course, and cannot come up with a clear
case against me, other than that I am black of coat and alone.

"No sense doin' away wi' a cat that can catch rats and mice.
I'll take 'im."

More grumbles, but the filthy ranks part as the taller boy
comes near. "Come on, puss. Ole Wiggins'll find a nice piece of
work for you, all right."

I do not fancy putting myself into the custody of one of these
young ruffians, but this Wiggins seems to have some place among
them and there are times when it is best for my kind to appear
meek and mild.

I allow him to pick up my panting form.

"Oof! A big-um. You must be good at your game, old fellow.
Off we go now."

And Wiggins walks between my would-be murderers as they
part like a thatch of greasy hair before a flea-comb.

This Wiggins is not a strapping lad, and soon he is puffing
from carrying me about. Luckily, the journey is short and soon he
is ringing the bell of a door far too respectable for either of us.

At length a bustling, motherly sort of lady opens it, lifting
her sparse eyebrows to meet the lace edging the cap on her
snowy head.

"What's this, young Wiggins? You don't mean to say that
Himself has ordered a cat for some reason?"

"No, ma'am, Missus Hudson. But I thought that per'aps 'im
and the doctor would like a crayture around the place. 'Tis too
quietlike upstairs, and some boys were settin' to kill it."

"Oh, the poor thing!"

The door swings wide. There is nothing like being a potential victim for stirring sympathy in the female breast, a fact the wily Wiggins seems to know as well as myself.

"But I doubt *he* will have anything to do with that creature," Mrs. Hudson calls after us as Wiggins hauls me up a long and dim stairway.

At the top is a closed door, on which Wiggins knocks.

Moments later the door is opened by a City-lookin' chap, very smart and well-fed in his appearance.

"Well, Master Wiggins. Has he sent for you then?"

"No, sir, Doctor Watson. I came on me own. Found this cat about to lose 'is 'ead to an ugly mob and I figgered you and Mr. 'Olmes might like some company. 'E's heavy enough to be a champion mouser, an' that's the truth."

"Hmm." Dr. Watson frowns as I am dumped on the floor like a hod of coal. "I wouldn't mind a nice, gentle cat, but I doubt that *he* fancies the breed, though he is as fastidious as one. I've never heard him mention one, as a matter of fact."

This glaring omission is about to be corrected, I predict, for a tall, thin bloke comes from an adjoining room. He is in the process of thrusting his angular arms into a jacket.

"What's this, Watson? Wiggins? Has someone left a curiosity on the doorstep?"

" 'E's curious, all right, Mr. 'Olmes," Wiggins says, stepping aside along with Dr. Watson to reveal my not-so-humble self.

"A cat?" Mr. Olmes says, wrinkling his upper lip in the same fashion I do when presented with a particularly rank supper. "An unreliable and womanlike creature, with none of the dog's supreme sense of smell and need to make itself useful around the house."

" 'E's a tom, sir, and he will eat vermin."

"So will a boa constrictor, but I do not keep one about the premises. Speaking of which, Watson, I am expecting a rather . . . er, celebrated client at any moment. I hope you will stay, Watson, to . . . translate, as it were. And Wiggins, tote that animal elsewhere. Perhaps Mrs. Hudson has a yen for a sneak-thief about the kitchen."

The chastened Wiggins complies by hoisting me like an unneeded sail and heading down the stairs, up which drifts a sublime scent of mincemeat scones blended with an exotic attar of gardenia, sandalwood, and cinnamon. So much for looking down one's long, persnickety nose at a cat's sense of smell.

I instantly deduce that the celebrated client is entering the door below and wiggle until I escape Wiggins's too-careless grasp.

" 'Ere now, you rascal—get back 'ere or I'll 'ave your whiskers!"

I have been more obscenely admonished by those bigger and uglier than the likes of Wiggins and pay no heed, not when I smell a rat.

The rat turns out to be an exotic variety, perhaps a vicuna. It is also dead and meekly decorating the hem and collar of a cut-velvet coat.

"Sock-rah Blue!" cries the lady who wears the coat. "Is this a new sort of butler Eeenglish?" She pauses and frowns at the looming stair. "And am I expected to scale these stairs like an *alpiniste*? *Mon Dew!* But the Eeenglish like their exercise."

With that she lifts her ratty hem and sweeps upstairs.

I scamper after, ignoring Wiggins's outraged orders to return.

At the top, she does not ring the bell, but raps smartly with the silver head of the parasol she carries, which is tall enough to serve as a cane.

The now-familiar form of Dr. Watson opens the door and I reenter the rooms on a wave of perfume and foaming skirt folds, virtually invisible when I insinuate myself beneath the flouncing fur.

"Meestair Olmes?" she inquires.

"N-No . . . Madame." Dr. Watson proceeds to blush, a most awkward human propensity that I am happy to avoid by virtue of my furry coat. "I had no idea that he was expecting . . ."

"Madame Sarah Bernhardt," comes the tall man's thin, high voice.

He is standing by the chimneypiece, which is cluttered with a pungent array of knickknacks arranged for the seeming sole purpose of being knocked down by a clever cat. The art nouveau purists may complain about overstuffed Victorian domiciles, but I find them admirable for my principal avocations: napping, claw-sharpening, and eternally rearranging the accessories.

A nearby tabletop glints with vials and decanters that will shatter into many pretty shards when overturned, a veritable millionaire's playroom to a lowly street waif like myself.

But Madame Sarah Bernhardt is not interested in the toys. "The appointment was made for the Marquess de Ligne," she says haughtily.

"A bit of wishful thinking on your part, no, Madame?" Mr. Olmes removes a catniplike pinch of loose herbs from the toe of a Persian slipper and stuffs it into a pipe bowl.

Madame Sarah bridles, as they say, though I do not see reins anywhere near her person. "You will not smoke that disgusting pipe in my presence."

"Forgive me. A nervous habit. I was merely toying with the things." Mr. Olmes steps away from the fireplace to indicate a seat.

Madame Sarah regards it as I might contemplate a dog carcass, then impales her parasol tip in the carpet and launches her voluminously swathed form at the spot, seating herself as if she were an empress, which she has impersonated on occasion. For there is no disguising her face and figure, which I have seen on certain theatrical posters around old Londontown.

I also see, despite the richness of her flowing garb and the softly frizzled cloud of hair surmounting her small, sharp face like a scarlet fleece, that she is a frail bird of sorts, small and bony and often cold, no doubt, because of that. Such a person is in vital need of an enterprising pet and protector, like myself.

I arrange myself under the folds of her train, enjoying the shelter of such a rich tent, but peeping out from the rat-fur hem.

"I should be able to solve the matter of your missing diamonds," Mr. Olmes says thoughtfully, "but I cannot speak to their continuing safety if you persist in displaying them to the public."

"There was no word in the papers of the loss! Your deductive powers are as phenomenal as they say."

"No, Madame, but there was much word in the papers of their presence, and one fact leads to the other conclusion as a rainbow follows rain. A child could deduce as much."

Mr. Olmes gives a chilly little bow. In his own way he is as skillful a performer as herself. I can feel her robes shift as she straightens her small form to give him closer attention. Despite the heaviness of her attire, she is a creature of fog and phantasm, an airy, artful female, like more than one feline *fatale* I have known.

"You must think me a child, Meestair Olmes, for risking my pretty baubles, but it is as Mr. Barnum does in America: good advertisement."

"I would be bold enough to say, Madame, that you require no more advertisement than yourself and your achievements upon the stage. Jewels are best kept discreet if they are to be kept at all."

"But I am *not* discreet, Meestair Olmes. It is one of my most admired qualities, do you not think so?"

His already thin voice goes a bit higher when he replies. "I am not an advertising consultant. I would appreciate a succinct report of the jewels, their lodging when not on display, and your household."

"What is this 'suc-sinct'? Such a word! So ugly, like much of Eeenglish."

"Brief, Madame Bernhardt," the good doctor puts in. *"Bref."*

"Ah." She seems to relish the assignment, sitting even more regally erect and loosening a crisp torrent of French-laced English. The rise and fall of her melodious voice, reminiscent of a cello, is sufficiently bespelling that I am able to creep from under her hem and find room to spread out under Dr. Watson's chair.

The story is simple. To attract public attention to her current London tour, she displays her jewels in the lobby of her hotel each day. "I did theez during my American tour as well."

"And did that not result in an attempt to steal the jewels?"

Mr. Olmes asks quickly. He had settled in another chair, leaning back to watch her as if she were performing, his eyes half-closed. It is in just such a position that I myself am most alert.

Madame Sarah casts down her dark and lustrous eyes.

"You are right. It was most exciting. My private railroad car was to be stormed, they thought, so the men brought out pistols, Wild West pistols. I took one myself. I have it with me at my hotel. Had I seen the thief I would have—" She lifts the parasol like a rifle barrel and sights along its ruffled length at Mr. Olmes's heart.

From my spy-spot beneath Dr. Watson's chair I see a smile touch his thin lips, though his eyes still seem closed.

"You would be a virtual Annie Oakley, no doubt."

"I would be bet-air than Anne Oaklee."

"But the thief of your jewels here allowed you no such opportunity."

"*Non.* They were gone one morning. Like that." She snaps her fingers sharply as if trying to rouse Mr. Olmes. His faint smile increases; he knows that by appearing to ignore her he only increases her efforts to capture his attention. I, too, have practiced this aloof art, the better to lead my prey into my paws.

Truly, this Mr. Olmes and I have much in common. How unfortunate that he also has a senseless prejudice against my kind.

Madame Sarah answers his abrupt string of questions. The jewels were kept in a lapis lazuli case she had been given on one of her tours. No, it was not especially strong, but it was pretty. It was kept in her bedchamber.

That causes those sleepy eyelids to flicker. And how many persons had access to her bedchamber?

"Mistair Olmes, you are a so-naughty gentleman to ask!" She proceeds to tick off a formidable list: her maid, her butler, her pageboy, her theatrical manager, her visitors. . . . Her bedchamber, in fact, serves as her dressing room, her office, her home away from Paris. Many of its furnishings travel with her.

Mr. Olmes sighs. "And no one else?" he asks tartly after she has supplied a list of a dozen-some people.

"Well . . . my new admirers, of course. The American Charles
and that charming Eeeenglish Duke. Also the Prince of Wales.
And," she adds airily, "Otto, Absinthe, and Malice; Melange, Fifi,
and Guillotine."

Further incisive questioning reveals that the latter individuals
are all of an animal nature. Absinthe and Malice are "lovely little
green snakes, you say, *non*?" Otto is a boa constrictor and Guillotine a *panthère noire*. Melange and Fifi are apparently dogs.

My ears perk up. I decide that the homely delights of Mrs.
Hudson's kitchen are no competition for the *exotique* atmosphere of Madame Sarah's entourage, of which I intend to make
myself a vital and pampered member at the earliest opportunity.
I have always yearned for foreign travel, and it strikes me that I
can do that by visiting her fabled bedchamber alone. So what if
I have to share it with a few snakes of the scaled and human variety? I like to play with snakes . . . before I eat them. Otto, however, is big enough to eat me.

"It is as I feared," Mr. Olmes says, sighing. "I will have to visit
the premises."

Madame Sarah raises her eyebrows and so do I. (I have long,
supple eyebrow whiskers, so I am even better at it than the famed
thespian, if I may say so.) Mr. Olmes is showing reluctance to do
what most mortal men trip all over their gaiters rushing toward.
Who *is* this bloke, anyway?

Dr. Watson, however, is on his feet, stuttering and strutting
and showing Madame Sarah out, promising to accompany Mr.
Olmes to her hotel two hours hence.

I had become so absorbed in the lady's dilemma and drama
that I regret to say I had forgotten that I was supposed to be forgotten.

"What is that?" Mr. Olmes asks, pointing at me as if his finger is a truncated parasol.

"Ah." Madame Sarah's rustling, shimmering exit stops in an
instant. "*Ma ami, la chat noir. Ma petit Guillotine.* Shall I call him,
what? *Minuit.*"

"Midnight," Dr. Watson translates, glancing cautiously at Mr.
Olmes.

"Meed-night," Madame Sarah repeats, well pleased. "I will take heeem with me. A souvenir of Eeeengland."

And so I leave Baker Street for a far better address in Piccadilly.

First Madame Sarah's pageboy, a far, far better dressed and anointed individual than the sturdy Wiggins, is called to fetch me to the carriage.

Mr. Olmes observes my removal like a night watchman overseeing the rats chased into the Thames.

"A most unfortunate animal, Watson. Surreptitious and unreliable, as I said."

"I do not know," the good doctor suggests as I am borne away in the arms of luxury. "I am reminded of the cat that may look at a queen. Midnight has found far better circumstances than he had."

"*Chez* Sarah. A circus!" Mr. Olmes snorts, heading for the battered slipper on the chimneypiece. "And finding the jewel thief will be a search among clowns."

Then I am carried through the door and away from Mr. Olmes and Dr. Watson and away from Baker Street forever, as it turns out.

"Then you," Dr. Watson ventures as the door closes upon me, "must be the ringmaster and restore order."

Pardonnez moi. I will be the ringmaster. *Minuit. Monsieur Minuit.* Mr. Midnight. It has a ring to it.

But first I must play ringmaster, as Dr. Watson so aptly put it.

Madame Sarah's hotel rooms are a pussycat's paradise, filled with draperies to climb, peacock feathers to slay, and scent bottles to overturn. I barely have time to get the lay of the landscape before the Baker Street Brigade are on my tail.

I figure that if I identify the jewel thief I will be in good odor around here for eternity. But there is a lot of odor around here, I discover. Otto, the boa constrictor, is an obese ophidian bloke trying for the world weight record. Fortunately, he is fed by the pageboy and spends much of his time digesting.

Once home, Madame Sarah strips off her cocoon of a coat, dons a silken dressing gown fluttering with marabou feathers at wrist and neck (smack-smack) and takes a pair of slim green serpents from a box. They accommodatingly entwine her wrists, occasionally lifting their sleek heads to sniff the air with darting tongues.

Well, every Eden has a snake in the grass or two, but the one I am looking for undoubtably has two legs.

Guillotine is another matter. He is big, *Mon Dew,* he is big. And black as the anvil of Hephaestis. (I have slipped into a theater or two in my time to gobble up mice and mythology.) But his teeth and claws are filed and he has become soft with a life of lounging on pillows. He greets me with a friendly cuff, I spit back my name, rank, and antecedents, and we achieve a state of truce.

Melange and Fifi require a bit of nose tattooing, but after whimpering their apologies for challenging my presence, they show talent as now and future body servants. That leaves only two unsubdued creatures. One is the vampire bat that spreads its fanged jaws and wide wings on Madame Sarah's elaborate headboard; the other is a large rat-tailed creature that nests at the foot of her traveling coffin.

All right. Madame Sarah is a bit eccentric. You had not noticed yet? But she is not totally *fou,* as in mad. The vampire bat turns out to be stuffed (after I sink my claws into its throat and encounter cotton batting) and the sleeper in the coffin, which she calls "Pocahontas" (do not ask me why), turns out to be a perpetual inhabitant of the arms of Morpheus. (More mythology gleaned from the stage plays.)

So I have the place under my paw before you can say Mr. Olmes and Watson, who shortly thereafter turn up, both natty in City top hats, although Mr. Olmes wears his usual air of martyrdom when confronted with Madame Sarah.

After a tour of the premises (he blanches at the bedroom and the vampire bat, coffin and Pocahontas; sniffs when he encounters me sprawled on a leopard-skin pillow licking my feet; and coughs discreetly into a linen handkerchief throughout his tour of the aromatic scene), he makes a pronouncement.

This time, he carries a cane, and with it he lifts certain draperies as if hunting a concealed villain.

"I require a dramatis personae," he tells the actress, who has attempted to twine around him like Otto, to no avail. Madame Sarah is beginning to lose her temper.

"Unnatural man!" She stamps her slipper-clad foot, causing Absinthe and Malice to hiss on her wrists. "I have told you all that I know. Facts, you care only for facts. Names and places, and who was where when. And all in this maddening Eeeenglish, which I must master somewhat. Soon you will be accusing my *adoree Minuit,* my latest love, of the crime."

"Your manager has been with you for three years," Mr. Olmes says again. "Your pageboy for two. What about this American?"

"Char-lee Olsen. An employee of Mr. Barnum I met on my most recent American tour. A . . . press agent. How can I explain? You Eeenglish do not understand drama! You Eeenglish do not understand commerce! You Eeenglish do not understand Woman! Or Cat! Ah. You must have feeeling to see. *Femme. Chat.*"

Mr. Olmes blinks. Perhaps he needs spectacles. "And the jewels were returned to your bedchamber each night? From there they vanished. I must be indelicate, Madame. I must inquire into the motives of your . . . admirers."

"I! I am the motive of my admirers! You dare to say someone might *use* the Divine Sarah?"

"Someone. Some man." Again the smile.

"Yes. It is true. I love as I act. With passion. I do not expect you to know this word. It is French. That is why you are good at what you do, Meestair Olmes, and why I am good at what I do. Sometimes I think . . . only sometimes, that the opposite is all. I see you care to catch my jewel thief as much as I care to catch your so-difficult attention. I would be grateful if you recover my jewels. That is all. Is it not enough?"

Mr. Olmes laughs. "You rule the stage, Madame; do not seek to rule raw intellect. Now tell me of your lovers."

She confesses, within my hearing and none other than his. Dr. Watson has been drawn into the menagerie outside. Her lovers are many. They are of her choosing. They often fail her, and she can blame no one but herself. But she is free.

Mr. Olmes washes his face in his hands when she is through.

"You challenge my facility. Anyone you know is capable of betrayal. You court such perfidy. Yet you master it."

"Ah! I think, with the proper encouragement, you might become French."

"I am French. Thanks to my grandmother."

She nods. "One night. The jewels were there. The next morning they were not. You would blame a lover. You would blame me. You may be right. I hope that you can find a way not to be. Is that too much to ask?"

"It is indeed." His eyes narrow. "But the solution you suggest is too obvious. There must be another."

Madame Sarah sighs, which does nothing for her bosom, for she has none to speak of.

"I count upon you, Mr. Olmes. Is that not the expression?"

He does not answer.

Of course, no one counts upon me, but me.

I have one advantage over the human investigator. My four-footed (and footless) friends.

Otto had seen nothing, having been absorbed in absorbing.

Absinthe and Malice had occupied their arboreal boxes on the night in question. The stuffed bat was not talking. Guillotine had been sleeping. Fifi and Melange had been banned from the bedroom for barking when Madame Sarah . . . well, when Madame Sarah had received visitors.

Her visitors included the English duke and her manager, but not the American, Charlie Olsen.

The bat was still not talking.

As for the creature at the coffin bottom named Pocahontas, it proves to be a New World marsupial. Do not ask me what a "marsupial" is—something you have for supper on Thursday? (*Mardi* is Thursday in the French.) What a dimwit! Pink nose, pink paws, pink tail like a rat. Bigger than a rat, with piggy-pink eyes.

But they are nocturnal, a fancy way of saying they have insomnia, which is a fancy way of saying they cannot sleep at night.

"What did you see?" I ask.

"Not much. I am very nearsighted," Pocahontas says.

"Did anyone enter the bedchamber?"

"*Sock-rah Blue*," Pocahontas says. "There are more people in Madame Sarah's bedchamber than could tree a 'possum."

"What is this 'possum?" I ask.

"*L'opossum, c'est moi!* I see all by night."

"Then you must have seen the thief."

"*Non.* No thief. I see only the men come and go."

"One must have taken the jewels."

"What are jewels?"

"Bright, blinking things."

Pocahontas licks her pink lips. Her nearsighted eyes blink in the lamplight. "I know nothing of jewels. I know only the joy of my babies, hanging from my tail, weighing down my pouch. He took my babies from me."

"That is terrible? Who did?"

"My captor. Then he brought me here, with so many strange creatures. I sleep during the day, dreaming of my babies; I awake at night, mourning my lost babies."

"This is terrible! I have chosen to reside with Madame Sarah, although she does not know it. It is only fitting that she be a dupe. But you . . . you are a prisoner. And the others?"

"The others accept their captivity. They have no babies to mourn. Find my babies, Mister Midnight, and I will be forever grateful."

I leave Pocahontas, shaken. I thought us all willing prisoners of the charming Madame Sarah, but now I see differently.

Now I see a system behind the seeming circus.

"The method is madness," Mr. Olmes says to Dr. Watson in Madame Sarah's hotel parlor the next morning while they wait for the mistress to present herself, "but it is very clever nevertheless."

"And how have you discovered it?" Dr. Watson asks.

Mr. Olmes hoists something small from the watch pocket in his vest.

"A cameo locket?"

"Precisely."

"Taken from Madame Sarah's premises? I protest."

"Do not bother. It was . . . deposited in my custody by one of her menagerie. The creatures have been crawling over me since I arrived."

"An animal committed the crime?"

"A clever creature, one with very adept . . . paws. A creature that has been trained to act beyond its perceived intelligence."

"A dog, you believe?"

"Oh, much more intelligent than the average dog, Watson. An independent sort of thing, far more apt than we think."

"A cat? The black panther?"

"No, although cats can be nocturnal, and this jewel theft was committed at night."

"Then what? Surely the boa constrictor did not swallow the evidence? You will not have to perform an autopsy—?"

"Madame Sarah, animal-lover that she is, would have forbidden dissection. Luckily, it is not necessary."

"Then tell me."

He holds up a bit of fuzz.

"Rat-hair?"

"Not necessarily. Theatrical crape hair. False hair used in beards. Mixed with . . . other hair."

"Madame Sarah has played trouser roles."

"Indeed! Madame Sarah has played everything. The hair in this case is dark hair. Undercoat."

"The panther's, then?"

"Possibly. I found some snagged on the prongs that hold the missing jewels."

"Which are missing no longer, thanks to you."

"Admirable, Watson. Which are 'missing' no longer, but have been left in their hiding place."

"Where on earth did you find them?"

Olmes shrugged. "In the coffin."

"In a kind of pouch under the satin upholstery!"

"*Above* the satin upholstery. In another kind of pocket, a living, breathing one. The opossum is a marsupial, Watson."

"This sounds like a biology lecture. I know my biology, dear fellow: a marsupial bears its young at a very early stage, when they are are teaspoon-size, then nourishes them in a pouch. The kangaroo—"

"Is not the world's sole marsupial."

"No, there is the duck-billed platypus, also of Australia . . ."

"And the New World opossum."

"Of North America. It has a pouch?"

"It has a pouch and prehensile toes as well as night vision and intelligence on the order of a pig, a good step up from that of the dog. One and its young were recently exhibited around London as a curiosity. Surely there is only one adult opossum in London. The thief took it from its young, Watson, then deposited the opossum here as a gift. When Madame Sarah's jewels were transferred each night from the lobby display he managed to wrap the jewels in a veil of crape hair mixed with shed opossum hair and waited. Night. The maternal instinct. The jewels."

"In the opossum's pouch! How did you know?"

"Cat hair."

"Cat hair?"

"They shed, you know, Watson. Quite continually. Even that cat who visited Baker Street so briefly. I found its damnable hair in my watch pocket! Yes. Remember how it approached me not long after we arrived here and tried to toy with my watch fob? I soon checked the time—who would blame me when confronted with the idiosyncrasies of Madame Sarah?—and found a wad of black cat hair in my pocket! Along with this . . . cameo. Naturally I began contemplating pockets and animal hairs and small treasures. From there it was but a rational step to the opossum that had recently been introduced into Madame Sarah's menagerie."

"Brilliantly, done! Once again you have shown the superiority of the British intellect."

"Well, the superiority of my own intellect."

And mine. That is all I could do, after all. Line Mr. Olmes's pockets with some of my precious bodily outcroppings to get him looking in the right direction.

As for Pocahontas, her evil master, Charlie Olson, soon after was apprehended trying to extract the lost booty from her pouch. The jewels had been under everybody's noses all the time. Madame Sarah, sympathetic to her pet's suffering, thereafter salts her own clothing pockets with marabou feathers and trinkets for Pocahontas to gather.

Pokey, as I call her, understands this ploy, and dutifully gathers the planted objects, explaining to me that her maternal pickpocketing tricks make Madame Sarah feel better.

As for her lost litter, she confesses that she now prefers the pampered single life, especially the sleeping privileges in Madame Sarah's coffin.

Madame Sarah pouts for a while because she is unable to lure Mr. Olmes into her boudoir, but soon forgets one imperious Eeenglishman in the face of so many.

And *moi?* I am given a ribbon-collar in the French tricolor of red, white, and blue, which dangles a golden coin as a medal of valor. I do not wear costumes, so the novelty of *Chez* Sarah soon feels stifling, and I hit the cobblestones again.

Soon after I am snagging tidbits and dodging street Arabs with the rest of the alley cats, especially now that I bear the dog-collar of Madame Sarah.

One day I dodge into the skirts of a pair of perambulating ladies.

"Oh, the poor, hunted, starving thing," cries one, a sure sign of a forthcoming tidbit.

I stop to intertwine their skirts with purrs.

The other bends to pick me up. "Not so starving, Nell," she says in skeptical American tones, poking me in the stomach.

"Oh, Irene, I should so like a nice, comfortable cat that would sleep on my feet at night to keep them warm."

"I suppose Saffron Hill could use another mouser," the second lady concedes, "and he was someone's pet. Look at this odd collar. No wonder the street Arabs were chasing him."

"I shall call him 'Midnight,' " Miss Nell rhapsodizes, tickling my chin.

"Most original," Miss Irene says in a tone that means the opposite. "At least this gold *Louie d'or* on his collar should help out mightily with household expenses."

"Gold Louie?"

"An old French coin worth many pretty pennies. Now where, and with whom, has this fellow been?"

"What does it matter? Midnight ... Midnight *Louie,* since he must be French, poor thing, is going home with us."

And so I do, though I find the housecat life tame on Saffron Hill. Madame Sarah's international entourage has given me an itch to see more of the world, so I soon bid Miss Penelope Huxleigh and Miss Irene Adler a fond *adieu* to go on to better and bigger things.

In America.

But that is another story.

Carole Nelson Douglas

The real-life Midnight Louie was a feature article subject when Carole was a journalist in Minnesota. When the big black alley cat's fictional form stalked into her career as a multi-genre novelist, she became indentured to a feline Sam Spade with hairballs who writes his own chapters. Besides starring in his own award-winning cozy-noir mystery series (Cat in a Golden Garland, Cat on a Hyacinth Hunt *etc.*), *Midnight Louie has a newsletter, T-shirt, and Webpage: http://www.catwriter.com/cdouglas. Carole also authors the acclaimed Irene Adler historical mystery series about the only woman to outwit Sherlock Holmes, and escaped Louie's clutches long enough to edit a short fiction anthology,* Marilyn: Shades of Blonde. *She and husband, Sam Douglas, share their*

Fort Worth home with a rescued menagerie: the seven cats are alley boys Longfellow, Panache, and Midnight Louie Jr., and the Persian girls Summer and Smoke, Victoria and her daughter, Secret. Xanadu, an abandoned chow-mix dog, has learned to get in touch with her inner feline.

Now there is a critter in the wild that is often referred to as catlike, and I supposed that is because it has clever mitts and can get into mischief faster than the average human can claim a door prize. Mr. Bruce Holland Rogers, who has often written flatteringly and successfully about my particular species, takes a walk on the wild side with this story. I have never made the personal acquaintance of one of these creatures, but they show native talent for scavenging and getting themselves into Other Critters' Business as well as trouble, a high recommendation in my book. Sometimes, they can even show the way to a crime against nature, if not against human nature. And sometimes I think human nature *is* the crime.

—M.L.

Masked Marauders of the Mossbelt
Bruce Holland Rogers

A YEAR AGO, when I was still in L.A., Claire had called me from Oregon and said, "How's business?"

"The same," I told her. "Being a starving investigator is a lot like being a starving screenwriter, but without the glamour."

She laughed. "You ought to move up here, Maddie. Eugene has crime too, but the air is cleaner."

"Small towns are what I moved away from."

"Eugene isn't a small town. It's a small city."

"A small city. Great. I can have boredom *and* anonymity."

"You'll eat better. I can get fresh greens every day."

"Be still my heart."

"Think about it, Maddie. I miss you."

That was a sweet thing to say, though sweet hardly ever gets to me unless you're talking actual chocolate. So I didn't think seriously about moving north until my landlord boosted my rent by half. Then I started a line of thought that ended at this table in the Café Zenon, where Claire was spearing a bit of salad and saying, "Springfield! Maddie, I can't believe I got you to move up here only to see you living in *Springfield*! It's so shabby!"

A lot of people in Eugene have this attitude about the town on their eastern flank. And the truth is, Springfield and Eugene *are* worlds apart. "Springfield I understand," I told her. "Fundamentalists, loggers, pulp-mill workers, K-Mart. It's an old style extraction town where everything is drawn in straight, unimaginative lines. Eugene is ..."

I looked out the rain-spattered window of the Zenon, searching for words to describe the town. It was a crazy mix. The buildings on the mall were new, or old with expensive face-lifts. This end of the mall was all about bank buildings, development money. A few blocks away, there was a public square with its Saturday market for organic produce, tarot readings, tie-dyed merchandise smelling faintly of marijuana. Blocks from there was the hangout of the mall rats, body-pierced goth types. Most were throwaway kids whose parents didn't want them; others were middle-class teens who thought life on the street was romantic in a dirt-and-leather sort of way. Then a transition back to money: a software company and the parking garage that the city built for it in some sort of sweetheart deal, or so some of the locals said. Eugene was also a college town with its share of political correctness and troglodyte fraternities.

"I haven't figured out how things work here," I told Claire. "It makes me edgy."

"What do you mean?" She balanced a hazelnut on her fork. "Things work here the same as everywhere. People are people."

"Towns aren't the same. Think about L.A. Los Angeles is all about being discovered. I mean, that's what you and I were doing there, right?" I opened my purse, tapped a True out of the pack.

"What's the deal with this town? Do the tree huggers and old hippies own the town's soul? Or is it the bankers?"

"We don't have tree huggers," Claire said. "We have tree *sitters*. And the bankers are all from California." Lowering her voice, she said, "You might not want to go around telling people that *you're* from California."

"I'm not. You know that. And where I am from is nobody's business."

"You've changed your license plate already, right?"

"All my contacts are in L.A., Claire. I'll probably be driving down for work every so often. For a while, I'm a resident of both states."

"Maddie, change your license plate!"

"What, you're telling me that wandering gangs of Oregon natives go around vandalizing cars with California plates?"

"It happens."

"Oh, come on."

She looked at my unlit cigarette. "You can't smoke in here. This is a Breathing Only restaurant."

"You chose it to torture me." I looked wistfully at the sidewalk tables where one lone smoker sat. His coffee steamed. One hand clutched his coat lapels to keep the wind out, and in his other hand he held a cigarette. A soldier of nicotine braving the elements. Good man.

I said, "So what's a tree sitter?"

"There are protesters who rope themselves to trees to keep them from being logged."

"In the forests, you mean?" I pictured vast landscapes of fir trees bearing protesters like tie-dyed fruit. It seemed unlikely.

"Yeah, sometimes, I think," Claire said. "But I'm talking about protesters in the city. Back when the parking garage was being built, we had tree sitters right here, downtown, trying to save the trees on that lot. The police pepper-sprayed them and used tear gas on bystanders. It was a mess. The cops still have black eyes."

"Moorish beef," the waitress said, setting my entrée before me. Actually, what I'd asked for was steak, plain and simple. This

was as close as the Zenon could come. Angus top sirloin on a
skewer, served with mutabbal. I didn't know what mutabbal was,
but I could tell it was vegetables. I offered it to Claire.

She said, "It's the only edible thing on your plate."

"And it's all yours." I sliced into the meat. It glistened red.
Usually I have to cook a steak myself to get it this rare.

"Animal fat is going to kill you, Maddie."

"Nonsense. Genghis Khan ate nothing but milk and blood,
and he conquered half the world."

"But look at him now," Claire countered. "He's *dead*!"

"You know I always celebrate with steak when I land a case."

"A case? You've got work already? How?"

"A prospective case, anyway. I took out an ad in the *Weekly*."

"So what's it about?"

"Claire, I haven't had a full interview with the client yet, and
I couldn't tell you anyway. There's a reason for calling myself a
private investigator."

She pouted. "I thought we were friends."

"We are friends. You can even have a bite of my steak."

"Yuck."

I lowered my voice. "The case has to do with raccoons," I said.

"Raccoons?"

"Shh. That's all I can say. Keep it to yourself."

"Oh, come on! You've got to tell me more than that."

"Sorry, Claire." I smiled. If she was going to torture me with
a nonsmoking restaurant, I had my ways of getting even.

The client's name was Elizabeth Foulkes. She owned an art
gallery downtown and lived on the slope beneath Hendricks
Park. The house featured high hedges, iron gates, gables, a little
tower, and *two* weathervanes. In Beverly Hills it would have
qualified as a cottage, but in Eugene, this was a palace. A rain-
glazed lemon-colored Mercedes convertible sat in the driveway.
The license plate said FLKS2.

She was at the door before I could ring, a woman, late forties,
in a dark red suit that I guessed was a size eight. Red was a

good color for her. Like Claire, she had the kind of complexion where she'd have to be careful with color. Her hair, black with silver streaks, was pulled back behind her head. She said, "Ms. Hughes?"

"Call me Maddie, if you don't mind."

"Then call me Elizabeth."

A black standard poodle stood behind her, watching me, trembling with excitement, but not charging up to crowd the doorway as dogs often do. "You don't object to dogs, do you?"

In fact, I do. I've never particularly liked being slobbered on, and my seal-point Siamese would eye me suspiciously if I came home smelling like the enemy. I kept my comment to, "He seems well trained."

She laughed. "So you don't like dogs. But she *is* well trained. I can guarantee that Cassatt won't jump up or lick you. Good enough, or shall I lock her away?"

"Good enough. Let's not jail the innocent."

"Won't you come in, then? I'll make us some tea."

I followed Elizabeth, and Cassatt followed me, sniffing but not actually planting her wet nose on me. The living room featured some interesting sculptures: here a shouting man whose skin erupted with spines, there an abstract sort of tree. The art hanging in the hallway included two acrylic paintings, a collage, and two color photographs of empty, wetly luminescent streets. When we got to the kitchen—a space bigger and better lit than my living room—the dog stopped where the carpet did. She stood at the threshold of the tile floor and whined. "Now you stop that," Elizabeth scolded. "Hush! Sit!"

The dog sat.

"She's not allowed in the kitchen?"

"A dog in the kitchen is a nuisance." A low flame had already been warming the tea kettle. Elizabeth turned up the heat. Laid out on the table were cups and saucers, a sugar bowl, silver spoons. I got the impression that Elizabeth Foulkes did nothing without a plan. There was a stack of eight-by-tens facedown by the sugar bowl, and a big manila envelope, too.

"So tell me about the burglary. Nothing was taken but some

photographic negatives? Seems to me you'd have things of more interest to burglars."

"I must have given you the wrong impression over the phone," she said. "The burglary wasn't here. It was at Josh's warehouse. His home, actually. It's not zoned for residential use, but he has a bedroom upstairs, just off of his darkroom. That's where the burglary happened."

"Who's Josh?"

"Josh Bunch. There are two of his photographs in the hallway. He's one of my favorites, and he hasn't done too badly for the business, either."

A first tendril of steam drifted from the nozzle of the tea kettle. It reminded me of cigarette smoke. I hadn't noticed any ashtrays, so I didn't even ask.

"What was on the negatives?"

"A variety of images. Pictures of me, that's how I got tangled up in this. Portraits. Josh doesn't usually do portraiture, but I had commissioned this work. Josh came here to the house, made a few dozen exposures, and then days later he brought the contact sheets by. Some of the exposures were missing, though. I called to see what was going on, why he hadn't given me the full set, but no one answered. Sometimes he doesn't answer his phone. Actually, his phone could be lying unplugged someplace for days and Josh wouldn't notice. You'll see what I mean when you get to his place. You will need to go there, yes?"

"If he doesn't mind."

"Oh, he won't mind. He wants the negatives back. They're his bread and butter."

The kettle whistled. Elizabeth warmed the pot, then started the tea steeping. Then she opened her dishwasher and took out an ashtray. She said, "Mind if I smoke?"

I was digging inside my purse almost before she finished her sentence. "I'll have one myself if it makes you feel better," I said.

Elizabeth smiled, then said, "When Josh didn't answer his phone, I drove to the warehouse myself. I found the door ajar. I didn't notice that the lock had been broken. It was dark."

"What time was this?"

"Seven-ten."

"You sound pretty sure of that."

"I live to a tight schedule. I have to know what time it is. When I knocked, no answer. So I went in . . ."

"That's not such a good idea."

"I didn't know the place had been broken into. Besides, I was thinking about those missing contact sheets. I thought the pictures of me in the kitchen might be his best images, and I didn't have them." She gave me the contact sheets.

"The missing negatives would be this size, too?"

"Some of them would be two and a quarter like these. Mostly, though, Josh uses a view camera."

"Bigger format, then?"

"Yes."

Some of the pictures were circled with a white grease pencil, others with a red one, a few with both. "What are these marks?"

"Josh is such a primitive. I mean, he just goes out and *shoots*. That's even the word he uses. I've been trying to train his eye. It needs training. His finer images are often a matter of chance, I think. Until I started working with him, he was printing exposures he never should have bothered with. We have a routine now. He makes contact sheets, then circles the images he likes in white. I go back and circle the ones that are *good* in red. The red ones he prints, and I sell the best of those in the galleries."

"Galleries? You own more than one?"

"I started in L.A., and that is still where I do my best business. Most of the artists I show here are from Los Angeles as well."

"Better keep that secret, from what I hear."

Elizabeth rolled her eyes, blew a stream of blue smoke. "God save me from these 'Californication' politics. A few local artists used to take me to task for featuring so many Californians. But I'd tell them I wasn't selling handicrafts. I was selling *art*."

"Calmed them right down, I bet."

"Oh, they love me all right." Then she said, "So you're not from around here."

I should have been more circumspect. "Kansas by way of Hollywood," I confessed.

"Good," she said. "You've lived in the real world."

I laughed, then flipped through the contact sheets. "Living room, living room . . . Where was this one taken?"

"My office upstairs."

"Can I have a look at the room?"

"I don't see what the point would be. I mean, the burglary was of Josh's place."

"You never know. I like having the whole story. But go ahead. Tell me what you found at Josh's."

"He wasn't home. I started up the stairs, and halfway up I heard noises in the darkroom, things hitting the floor."

"And it didn't occur to you that you might be walking in on something?"

"I wasn't thinking about anything but those proofs. Josh is a little . . . unreliable. Dealing with him can be exasperating, and when I want something and can't have it, I become focused. Franklin would say *obsessed*."

"Franklin?"

"My husband. Not that he isn't that way himself. Anyway, it turned out to be the raccoons. Josh always kept them out of the bedroom and the darkroom, but whoever had broken in had left the door open. Do you take sugar?" She poured. I took one polite sip. Tea is coffee's weak sister. It does nothing for me.

"What does your husband do?"

"He's a real estate developer. That makes him about as popular around here as us Californians, even though he was born in Eugene."

"Tell me about the raccoons."

"They're Josh's pets, in a way. He found the four of them as orphaned kits. He bottlefed them, then installed a dog door for them. They're wild. They forage on their own. But they also wear flea collars and will let Josh pick them up. He leaves them snacks. They have the run of his warehouse—the downstairs part. Josh catches them and hauls them to the veterinarian once a year."

"Is it legal, keeping wild animals like that?"

"Josh wouldn't know, and he wouldn't care. Anyway, when I turned on the lights, one of them looked at me but the other two kept examining the chemical shelves. There were several bottles on the floor, a couple of them broken."

"I thought there were four raccoons."

"There are four, but I saw only three that night. The place was a mess, and that's part of the problem, you see. It was hard to tell what the burglar had done and what was the work of the raccoons. Not that the particulars of the crime scene mattered to the police. They just wanted to know what was missing."

We discussed my fees. Then I said, "Are the negatives really worth that much to you?"

"Josh's best work goes for seven hundred dollars a print. A lot of what he photographs is ephemeral, parts of buildings that are about to be torn down, window displays of stores that have gone out of business. Eugene is changing. Some of the buyers for Josh's work want it for the nostalgia. Images like those streets hanging in my hallway, those Josh could capture again if he were patient and waited for the right weather and the right time of day. But many of the stolen negatives are irreplaceable." She lifted the manila envelope. "And then there is this matter."

I opened the envelope. Inside were negatives the same size as the contact sheet exposures.

"When I saw the mess in Josh's room, I was upset," Elizabeth said. "And I was thinking about the missing contact sheets. These negatives were the right format. I didn't look at them. I put them in my purse moments before Josh showed up and we called the police."

"Wait a minute. You took the negatives that you want me to recover?"

"No. I took the negatives that I thought were mine, that I had commissioned. That's how I felt at the time. The physical negatives belong to the artist, of course. And in any case, I took the wrong ones. The ones I wanted *were* stolen."

I held one of the negatives up to the light. I have a hard time looking at a negative and imagining a print, but I could tell these were pictures of buildings.

"So why haven't you just given these back to the photographer?"

"While he was on hold with the police, Josh asked if I had disturbed anything. We both assumed that a detective would come over and look for evidence. Now, if I'd been thinking, I could have said that I took these negatives to protect them from the raccoons. But what I said was, no, I hadn't touched a thing. And once I'd said that, I couldn't easily change my story, could I? Not without some embarrassment. Not without having Josh think God-knows-what about me. As it turns out, the police don't take burglary reports in person. They mail you a form to fill out."

"So you're hiring me to recover the negatives that are really missing, and to 'recover' the ones you just gave me. Either way, Josh continues to see you as a patron of the arts, rather than a woman who dresses well but has sticky fingers."

Her laugh sounded nervous. "That's it exactly."

I took the contract out of my purse, had her sign both copies, and gave one to her. For my advance, she gave me a check written on the gallery's account.

"You don't mind showing me the rest of the house? Everywhere that Josh took pictures?"

I didn't know what I was looking for. Cassatt followed us, sniffing at me again, but at a polite distance. There were small sculptures in every room, prints or paintings or photographs on every wall. Elizabeth's office was tidy, well lit.

When we were almost done with the upstairs, I put my hand on the doorknob of the last room.

"Not there," Elizabeth said. "That's Franklin's study."

"Is he home?"

"No. It's just that we're both very particular about a few things. That room is Franklin's *sanctum sanctorum*. I don't go in there. I don't even open the door."

"Would Josh have gone in?"

"No. Absolutely not."

"Then I don't need to see it, I guess." We went back down the carpeted stairs. "I don't know what the chances are for recovering the missing negatives," I said. "Maybe I'll have a better idea after I've seen the crime scene and talked to Josh. I don't want to spend a lot of your money looking for something that can't be found."

"Do give it some time," Elizabeth said. "Even if it's hopeless, give it some time."

Josh Bunch's warehouse-cum-apartment was in the Whiteaker neighborhood, the more interesting part of town. Whiteaker was low rent. Artists live there, sprinkled among the students, the Mexicans, old hippies, and drug addicts young and old. There were good restaurants, a teahouse favored by the spike-haired punks and their goth cousins, and working-class taverns. According to Claire, the neighborhood had the best organic grocery in town. Claire also told me, scandalized, that she had seen prostitutes in Whiteaker, as if she thought she could leave all that behind in Hollywood.

The warehouse stood in the shadow of Skinner's Butte. A row of shabby apartment buildings climbed partway up the Butte's slope, but most of the Butte was undeveloped, a forest island in the middle of the city. I could see why raccoons would like it. The businesses nearby were a welding shop, a store for used bicycles, and something called Salad Supply. I had no idea what a Salad Supply business would be. Claire would know. Claire would care.

What I cared about was that none of these places had bars on their windows. Whiteaker might be Eugene's toughest neighborhood, but East L.A. it was not.

I knocked on Josh's door, then knocked again. At last a window opened above me and someone called out, "You the private dick?"

I looked up to see a bearded face, salt and pepper. I said, "Try to imagine why that term has never appealed to me."

"I'll be down. Hang on."

"I'm paid by the hour. I can wait."

When he finally appeared at the door, he ushered me into about twelve thousand square feet of dusty chaos. There were boxes full of junk stacked on shelves or piled onto other boxes. I saw one complete manikin and the arm of another, a stack of ancient photography magazines, an electric train set with some twisted three-rail track. Old Lionel track like my dad's set, worth some money if it were in better shape. And scattered everywhere I saw the remains of old buildings. Weathered wooden balls, cracked capstones, iron finials, railings, and what must have once been a garden gate. And dust.

"Pardon my asking, Mr. Bunch, but you've got a darkroom upstairs from *this*?"

"Well, yeah. I do. See, that's where I got ripped off."

"With this dust?"

"Jesus. Elizabeth told me she was sending a lady dick. She didn't mention you were a housekeeping critic."

"Okay, hold it. I'm here to help you out, right? You cool it with the lady dick stuff, I won't say another word about your housekeeping. It's not like I care."

"As a matter of fact," he said, "the dirt *is* a problem, but so is cleaning. The darkroom, I do keep the darkroom clean. But this stuff down here is all part of what I do. Can't get rid of it. Don't have time to keep it tidy."

"You take pictures of these things?"

"Sometimes. But a lot of it is sort of research."

"Research?"

"Yeah, research." He shrugged. If I didn't get it, then I just didn't get it.

On one of the shelves I spotted a little wicker basket, the sort of thing that cats like to curl up in. Inside was a ball of gray fur with a striped tail curled around it. "Your raccoons have names?"

"That's Pillsbury. She's the homebody. Twinkie and Iris are probably up on the Butte somewhere. I haven't seen Marco Polo for months."

"True to his name."

"Yeah." Josh grinned. We were doing better now. "He's the male. Got a territory to cover."

"So show me around." Raccoons were a safe subject, so I stayed with them. "How do your masked friends get in and out?"

He took me around back to show me the dog door. Along that rear wall was a row of mismatched cabinets and hutches. Each cabinet door had three locks on it: an eyehook latch, a slide bolt, and a little padlock. The padlock keys dangled from strings. I was slow. It took me a moment to figure out the story.

"What's inside the cabinets?"

"Little stuff. Toys, tools. Things I'd lose track of. And some food."

"Things that the raccoons like to get into, right?"

"They like to get into *anything.*"

"But you tried to keep them out with a succession of locks."

"They kept figuring them out. You know those child-protector latches, the plastic ones people put in their kitchens to keep toddlers out of the pots and pans? That was the last thing I tried before the padlocks. The raccoons were stumped for a month. Then one of them figured it out. Iris, probably. But not even Iris is going to figure out a lock that works with a key." He laughed. "At least I hope not."

"What's the upstairs like?"

He led the way. At the top of the stairs, the door was closed. This door had a slide bolt too, one too high for the raccoons to reach. "They had figured out the doorknob," Josh told me, "but this bolt always kept them out."

The bedroom wasn't tidy, exactly. A hot plate sat in one corner next to a pot that was crusted with something brown. A cabinet that served as a pantry, door open to reveal cans and packages of Ramen noodles, stood between two ancient refrigerators. Dirty clothes formed a pile that seemed to be crawling from underneath the unmade bed. But the room wasn't dusty.

The photographs tacked to the wall showed buildings, parts of buildings, inanimate objects, streets. Some were color, most black and white. "I like this one," I said, indicating a building facade.

"That's one of the ones I'd like to have back. That old hardware store was torn down a month ago."

"And the negative is gone."

"It's gone."

I considered the other photos. "People aren't your favorite subject."

Josh pointed to a refrigerator door, at the one image that wasn't an original photograph. It was a page from a photography magazine, an image of headless manikins wearing white suits in a shop window. The caption said "Shop Window, Paris, by Eugène-Auguste Atget, *ca.* 1914."

"Atget is my hero," Josh said. "The people are in that photo. They just aren't *in* the photo."

"But you were doing a portrait for Elizabeth Foulkes."

"Within reason, I'll give Elizabeth what she wants. She's done a lot for me, and it's not like she has an easy life."

"Looks pretty plush to me."

"Have you met her husband?"

"No."

"Then you don't know what I'm talking about. Anyway, I'll make some allowances for Elizabeth. It's not like she's trying to change what I do."

"But she is. Isn't that what the red and white grease pencils are all about?"

"She's showing me what sells. That's not going to change what I shoot, or even what I print. It changes what I bring to her. I take the pictures for my own reasons."

"Where were the negatives?"

"In the darkroom, on the shelf. In binders."

"Binders?"

He opened the refrigerator door I'd just been looking at, and I realized that it was, in fact, an upright freezer. There were binders stacked inside, dates on their spines. Josh pulled one out and flipped it open to show me. The negatives were inside plastic sleeves.

"You keep them in the freezer?"

"The ones that I'm not actually working with, yes. Negatives deteriorate."

"So what, exactly, did the thief take?"

"Two binders. My most recent work. And some loose negatives that were lying there on the table."

"Pictures of . . . ?"

"The usual. Shots around town."

"Can I see the darkroom?"

He showed me. There were three enlargers, a shelf holding an assortment of cameras, and rows of bottles.

"I'd think that any of this would be more interesting to a thief."

"You'd think so. When I told the cop on the phone what had been taken, he said, 'So who were you blackmailing?' "

"I was wondering that myself."

He shrugged. "It seems weird to me. What are the negatives worth to anybody? A junkie would take a camera. You know a camera is ready cash."

"So this happened the same night that you gave Elizabeth the contact sheets of your portrait session with her."

"Yeah. Well, I didn't give them to Elizabeth, actually. Her husband took them. He was drunk. He holes up in that study of his and guzzles Scotch. Elizabeth was at the gallery. She doesn't close until five on Sundays."

"Elizabeth said that you hadn't given her a full set of proofs."

"I printed them all. I reviewed them all. I gave them all to Franklin." He shrugged. "Doesn't matter which ones she liked if I don't have the negatives."

When we came back out of the darkroom, Pillsbury was in the bedroom, sniffing at the crusted pot next to the hot plate. Josh said, "I forgot the door." He clapped his hands. "Out, you!" He ran at her. Pillsbury blinked her black eyes, stood her ground until the last moment, then turned to amble back down the stairs.

"I thought raccoons were nocturnal."

"They're awake whenever they think there's an opportunity to eat. And they're smart. I'm sure she heard us go up the stairs and *didn't* hear the door close. She knew what that meant."

Josh closed the door. On the back of the door he had tacked up his phone bill, utilities bill, and what I guessed were letters that needed answering. There was also a court document. It was partly folded over, and someone had scribbled a date and time on the blank side, along with "Don't forget!"

"A summons?" I said.

"This rent-a-cop caught me on a fire escape. I was trying to get an early-morning shot of High Street from above. I had the shot set up, and he told me to put my equipment away and get the hell out. I said okay. But I was working with a view camera on a tripod. It had taken me half an hour to get everything set up. I finished the shot, but decided I wasn't happy with the angles. I moved the tripod and set up for the next exposure. He didn't like that. He had the cops on the scene by the time I had packed up my equipment, and now I've got to fight a criminal trespass charge."

"That's a serious charge, you know."

He shrugged. "Not like it's the first time. I see a picture, I go there. Listen, if you can track down my negatives, great. But don't spend a lot of Elizabeth's money if you think the chances are slim. The gallery has to make it on its own. Franklin won't bail her out again. That son of a bitch just gets meaner all the time."

"He hits her?"

"Nothing like that. He brings in the *real* money, though. He doesn't let her forget it."

"Thanks," I said. "I'll be in touch."

I was pretty sure I knew who had the negatives, though the motive for the crime was fuzzy. I did some more checking. At the county court, I found that Josh had been charged with trespass or criminal trespass twice before. No convictions so far, but he clearly wasn't learning to take private property seriously.

I made calls about Franklin Foulkes and his business, Foulkes & Hatton. The company had its fingers in a lot of development pies all around the county and as far away as Corvallis. Most were strictly private projects. There was one joint venture with the city of Florence. In other projects, Foulkes & Hatton was a minority partner. There were opportunities for shenanigans, I was sure. There always are in business. Nothing, however, was particularly suspicious.

Back in Josh's neighborhood, I visited some of his neighbors. One of them remembered the lemon-yellow Mercedes, but had seen it outside of the warehouse a little before five. He was sure of the time. The sun hadn't set yet. No, he didn't remember the license plate.

Then I went home, took a bath, and did some thinking. There's nothing like a hot bath and a cigarette for joining up thoughts, for making patterns clear. Mostly, I thought about raccoons and the locks in Josh's place—a series of small locks downstairs, one big lock upstairs. Josh didn't lock the upstairs pantry or cupboards. He didn't need to, as long as he locked the one big lock. And I thought about Elizabeth's poodle who knew enough to stay out of the kitchen.

I called Josh, told him that I knew he'd been in Franklin Foulkes's study.

"Yeah. Elizabeth took a phone call and I had a peek."

"You took a picture, actually. Of what?"

"Of the window. Of the light coming in."

"Franklin has a car just like Elizabeth's, right?"

"He picked them out. I know because Elizabeth complains about it. Yellow isn't her color."

"I know. I bet it makes her look sick." Claire had the same problem.

Elizabeth wasn't too keen on having me go into Franklin's study when he wasn't home, but I insisted. "It's central to solving this case," I said. "You want the negatives, you have to let me in there."

"You don't think that Franklin . . ."

"Let me into his study and I'll show you what I think."

The study's furniture was all leather and dark wood. A regular boar's den complete with a globe the color of parchment. Elizabeth and her dog stood in the doorway watching me, unwilling to step inside.

There were a rolltop desk, some oak file cabinets, and a small conference table. At the end of the table stood a tripod holding a whiteboard.

"Franklin has business meetings here?"

"Rarely," Elizabeth said. "Don't disturb anything. The sort of arrangement Franklin and I have is delicate."

I stopped in front of the liquor cabinet. Lagavulin. Talisker. Oban. "I like his tastes."

"Maddie . . ."

"The file cabinets don't have locks, I see." I opened one. It was crammed with file folders, tax records. "What do you want to bet that after today he gets some locks put in?"

"Ms. Hughes, mine is already a difficult marriage. If all you're doing is *fishing* . . ."

"The negatives are in here, Elizabeth." I opened the next drawer. No luck. "Somewhere. Not long ago, your husband might have even left them sitting on top of the desk, knowing you wouldn't so much as open the door. You and Cassatt are well trained. But you let the raccoon man into your house and his manners aren't so good." I opened the bottom drawer. More files.

"I don't understand."

"People are often like their pets, Elizabeth. You and Cassatt can be relied upon not to go places where you aren't supposed to go. That's why your husband never worried about anything in his office being seen by the wrong person. But Josh Bunch and his raccoons will go anywhere that they aren't physically barred from going." There was a file-size drawer in the rolltop desk. I opened it, and there, with recent dates written on the spine in Josh's hand, were two binders. I took them out.

"Franklin stole them?" Elizabeth stepped into the room and didn't seem to notice that Cassatt followed her. "Franklin is the burglar?"

I opened the first binder, and there were the missing contact sheets. Centered on the first one was an image of this office, circled in white grease pencil. The window was a soft glow to one side. On the other side was the whiteboard. "You had a phone call. Josh took this picture while you were busy, and for some reason it gave your husband a scare. Do you have a magnifying glass?"

"There's one with the dictionary." She brought it, then peered over my shoulder. "It's not a very interesting image."

A contact print is usually pretty sharp. This one magnified so well that I could tell I was looking at a site drawing, a big piece of paper taped onto the whiteboard. Shaded circles represented trees. They were connected by red arrows that spiraled from tree to tree toward the center of the site. Also in red was a date—a date still three weeks in the future. The trees closest to the center were circled in black, and in black next to the date was the word "Permit?" The streets around the site were labeled, too. We were looking at the plans for a whole block.

There was a heavy black rectangle taking up most of the site, but a few trees along one side were outside of this boundary.

"I understand that the politics of tree cutting in Eugene are tricky," I said, "but I still don't get this. Your husband thought Josh was going to blackmail him. Or maybe he just thought that Josh would make this print and lots of people would see it. But I don't see how it's incriminating. I don't see why he bothered to break in and snatch it." I looked at the liquor cabinet. "Josh did say Franklin had been drinking."

"Listen," Elizabeth said. "We are going to put those back. We are going to close the drawer. We are going to leave this room exactly as we found it."

"Elizabeth, don't you want to get to the bottom of this?"

"No. Franklin hasn't destroyed the negatives. That's a sign that he understands their value. Maybe he's just looking for a way to get them back to Josh, minus the one Franklin doesn't want seen."

"Your husband committed a felony."

"No one was hurt. Franklin *must* have been drunk. It does make him impulsive."

"These belong to Josh Bunch."

"And one way or another, Josh will be compensated. Maddie, I don't want a confrontation with Franklin. I like the way we have things arranged. I like how we stay out of each other's way. It's bad enough that Josh barged into Franklin's office, but if my husband knew that I had been in here, it would bring to a head a lot of things that I don't want to deal with. I have the galleries. I have a home I'm very happy with."

"So if Franklin does get around to destroying these negatives, these irreplaceable works of art, well that's just tough luck for Josh?"

"I hired you, Ms. Hughes. I'm the client."

"And if I help you hide evidence, I'm guilty of obstructing justice."

"You have obligations to me."

"I have obligations to the state that just issued me a brand-new license, too. You find a way to get the negatives back to Josh. If you do, then as far as I'm concerned, there was no crime."

"I can't confront Franklin!"

"I don't care how you do it, but you find a way."

"All right!" she said, putting the negatives back in the drawer. "Josh will get them. Give me back the other negatives, and he'll get those, too. Now we're finished. Done."

Elizabeth's advance check cleared, which was nice. And when I made a follow-up call to Josh in a couple weeks, I found that his negatives had arrived in a parcel post-marked Corvallis.

"I'll be damned," I said.

But I wasn't finished with the case. I still didn't understand it. I dug up the records on the lot I'd seen the plan for. Foulkes & Hatton was a minor player in the plan with an itsy-bitsy stake. I drove by the site, a big wooded lot close to downtown. One of the last such lots. Ripe for development.

I called Claire. "What's the big deal with tree cutting in Eugene?"

"Maddie, I told you about the parking garage."

"So the city needed the lot and a few protesters were very rude about it. And maybe the police were rude, too."

"You're missing the big picture. There are supposed to be hearings for permits. There's a public review process. With the garage, the city hurried things up, scheduled the cut for the Sunday morning before a public hearing on Monday. By the time of the hearing, the trees were gone."

"The city broke the law?"

"Not technically. They played games."

"Claire, that's politics."

"Fascism is politics, too, Maddie."

"The city council does something you don't like and they're Fascists. Come on, Claire."

"Well they sure have their hands full now, after what they did. Activists have been showing up for every hearing. Public or private, tree felling permits are tighter. Even if you get a permit, you're liable to have tree sitters on your property when you go to cut."

"I still don't get it." Meaning I didn't see what advantage Foulkes had been angling for. Then I added, "This town still makes no sense to me."

"If your blood wasn't full of beef hormones," Claire said, "you'd think better. This town isn't all that hard to figure out." Then she added, "Whatever happened to that case you were taking? With the raccoons?"

"Nothing came of it. Wild goose chase."

"You're lying."

"Okay," I said. "No wild goose chase. It was a wild raccoon chase."

"You never tell me anything."

"Nothing to tell. Like I just said, this town is one big puzzle to me."

Not long after that, I got a call from an L.A. investigator who contracted out sometimes. He offered a job that took me out of Eugene for a few months. I told Claire I was going to take it.

She said, "You're not moving back down there, are you?"

"It'll be months before I'll have a Yellow Pages ad up here. I've got to take the work as it comes. But, no, I'm not going back to stay. I'm keeping the apartment in Springfield."

"Springfield," Claire said. "I still can't believe . . . *Springfield.*"

The job was a sit-and-watch. I kept an eye on a wandering wife and the guy she had moved in with. I took pictures. It was just the sort of work that I like least, but the money was good. When that job was done, another offer followed, and then another. My answering machine in Springfield wasn't taking any messages, so I stayed where the work was. It was three months before I was back in Oregon.

Claire took me to lunch to celebrate my return. On the way to the Café Zenon, she told me that now I really did have to change my license plate. It was imperative.

"Why?"

"I'll show you." She drove past the block that I'd seen on Franklin Foulkes's site map. The trees were gone, all except for a few small ones near the street. In their place was a gaping hole. The first pilings and walls for a foundation had been poured.

"There used to be trees on that lot," she said. "Thirty big ones. Black walnuts. Oak trees. Cherry trees. And they all came down because of a Californian."

"Claire," I said, "you are talking nonsense. That lot is owned by a local developer."

"It is now," she said. And she told me about the major partner in this development, a Californian, who had brought in a crew on a Sunday morning and cut down almost all the trees before anyone thought to call the cops and see if a permit had been issued.

The Californian held a press conference to apologize. Where he was from, no one had to ask permission to cut down trees on his own land.

The fine, said the city, is four thousand dollars a tree.

So this Californian, he pleaded for a compromise. What if he sold out his stake to a local developer, one more sensitive to local concerns?

"Wait," I said to Claire. "Don't tell me. He sold out to a company called Foulkes & Hatton." Then I laughed. "Now I get it."

"Get what?"

But I shook my head. There was that business about confidentiality.

Claire told me how the Californian got out with a modest profit, and without paying a fine. Franklin Foulkes had held public hearings about a building design that would save the trees on the perimeter. His company even tried to come up with some designs that would save the few trees that were left standing in the center of the lot when the police had stopped the cutting. But it was hopeless. You just couldn't put up an office building with those trees in the very middle. He got a permit to cut them.

"And were there protests?" I asked her as she parked in front of the Zenon. "Tree sitters?"

"A couple tree sitters. Their hearts weren't in it. The real damage had already been done."

"By a Californian."

"See why you ought to get your plate changed?"

"I'll change it." I wondered who had been in Franklin Foulkes's study with him, looking at his site map. The California partner, probably. Maybe a city councilman or two.

While Claire was feeding the parking meter, I noticed a yellow Mercedes convertible parked two cars ahead of us. The license plate was FLKS1. And even though I'd never seen Franklin Foulkes, it was easy to pick him out from the other diners as we entered the café. He was at a table with four other suits.

The Zenon was crowded. Claire and I had to join the little knot of customers waiting for tables. Claire studied the menu while I watched Foulkes. Toothy smile, easy laugh. Handsome, more or less. With his unfading smile, he looked a little too perfectly relaxed. A lot of practice goes into creating that sort of apparent ease. I'd seen a lot of out-of-work actors operate in the same mode.

Claire looked up from her menu. "That's him!"

I nodded. The Zenon is a noisy place, so I couldn't hear what joke it was that made Foulkes tip his head back and roar. I bet it wasn't that funny.

We were still waiting for our table when Foulkes and his companions headed for the door. As Foulkes brushed by, a man waiting behind us for a table said, "You're Franklin Foulkes, aren't you?" I turned. The speaker was middle-aged, wore a flannel shirt and a felt hat. "I just want to shake your hand," the man told Foulkes. "A lot of people in town really appreciate what you've done."

Foulkes shook the man's hand. "Just running a business," he said, "but thank you."

When we were finally seated, Claire looked out the window in the direction of the building site. "Twenty stories," she said. "We'll be able to see it from here. But like Foulkes said in the newspaper, dense development saves trees elsewhere."

"He's a real hero, that Franklin Foulkes," I said.

"Let's split some crostini," Claire said, and added, "He might run for city council."

"He'll win," I predicted.

"He just might get my vote," Claire said, "even if he is a developer."

I laughed. "Claire," I told her, "I'm finally getting a feel for this town."

Bruce Holland Rogers

A versatile writer of more than fifty short stories in a variety of genres, Bruce Holland Rogers has a master's degree in creative writing and has taught university writing workshops in Colorado and Illinois. Now a full-time writer, he lives in Eugene, Oregon, with his wife, Holly Arrow, and their three-legged cat, Osha. The tripodal Osha is a gray tortie whose tan blaze provides her other distinguishing mark: the Greek letter Lambda on her forehead.

"Enduring as Dust," a satire of Washington bureaucracies that features many cats named Dust, was inspired by an elusive female stray cat named Dust, who ran away from the home that Bruce had found for her. The story was nominated for the Mystery Writers of America Edgar Allan Poe Award and won the Cat Writers' Association (CWA) Johnny Cat Litter-ary Award. The first story about Maddie, the character in Bruce's tale here, "Hollywood Considered as a Seal Point in the Sun," won the CWA's Muse Medallion for short story. This time, though, his "smart and adaptable" urban racoon family take the limelight.

What happens when you take one natural-born cat-lover and mix in a propensity for telling tales of imagination and insight? You get Miss Elizabeth Ann Scarborough, an award-winning fantasy writer whose ruminations on justice in this world and the next result in the introduction of a "Brother Catfael" for the clawed and whiskered set. I am told that the protagonist is based on a feline of her very close acquaintance.

—M.L.

Final Vows

Elizabeth Ann Scarborough

*Dedicated to the memory of General Mustard—
more loved than he ever knew.*

AT FIRST HE thought the flame above his ears was the white light he'd been chasing, trying to get within pouncing range. But now, as he pried his encrusted eyes open, he saw it was just a candle.

He lay there dazed, among the waxy smoke of candles and the tinkle of wind chimes, a cool breeze rippling his matted, fever-soaked coat.

Hmm. He no longer felt too hot or too cold. Stiff, though. He could barely sit up, his muscles were so constricted. He took a long horizontal stretch, avoiding the candles and keeping his tail well out of the way, then stood on his hind paws and stretched upward, batting with his front paws at the curling candle smoke before dropping again to all fours.

Wherever this was, it wouldn't do to lose his self-respect, and he began setting in order his striped saffron coat, white paws and cravat with short, economical licks. He wrinkled his nose and lifted the outer edges of his mouth at his own smell. He had been to the vet. Dr. Tony and his wife, Jeannette, were lovely people and really knew how to pet a fellow, but their establishment reeked of antiseptic and medicine and Mustard did not like medicine.

When he looked up from cleansing the underside of his tail, another cat sat there, a female, surgically celibate, as he was, clad all in black from nose to tailtip, ear points to claws. "Finally awake, are you, lazybones? About time. Come along now. It is high time you met The Master."

"I do not have a master," Mustard said. "My personal attendant is female." He looked around him and considered the stone walls, the tiled floors without so much as a rug to warm the belly on, the ceiling so high birds tantalizingly flitted through the rafters, cheeping and leaving droppings on the floors and furniture. His home was a log cabin with his own private solarium, though his junior housemates had made free use of it as he couldn't always be bothered to run them off. (Besides, they were bigger than he was, all except the Kitten. She had been a rather sweet little thing who begged him for hunting stories and when he growled in annoyance, would flop purring beside him.) His house was set in a large yard with a strip of forest in the back where he caught many tasty adjuncts to the healthful but monotonous diet of low-ash kibbles his attendant provided. His last happy memory was of sitting at the picnic table being petted by his old friend Drew, who had stopped by to visit.

"Don't look now, but we're not in Kansas anymore, Red," the black-robed female told him.

"My name is not Red, it is Mustard," he said. "And I do not live in Kansas. I was born and raised in Fairbanks, Alaska, but for the past ten years have resided in the state of Washington. It is warmer there and I may go outside and it is altogether more congenial. Are we there still?"

"Your questions will be answered at length," she said. "When you've met The Master. And don't fret about a little nicknaming. You'll have to take a new one when you join the Order. I was formerly known as Jessie Jane Goodall but now am known simply as Sister Paka, which is in the Swahili tongue the name of our kind."

"Humph," Mustard said. "Affected. I've fallen into some cult, haven't I?"

She turned her new-moon dark tail to him and waved it for him to follow. Since he wanted answers and had nothing better to do, he graciously obliged.

He was not, however, prepared for how weary he would be or how long the corridors were—miles and miles of them, stone-walled or pillared, lined with trees and bushes; his favorites, roses. He was mortally shamed and self-disgusted to have to pause to rest from time to time on their journey, which felt more like a quest of many days' length from the way it taxed his strength. Normally he was light and spry, even though well advanced in years for one of his kind. He considered himself merely seasoned, toughened, tempered, but today he felt every second of every minute of every hour of every day of every week of every month of every year of his life.

He expected impatience and jeering from the so-called sister, but instead she simply squatted on her haunches, closed her eyes, and wrapped her tail around her front paws until he pronounced himself ready to carry on once more.

At last they padded up a long, long flight of stairs, high into the rafters, by which time even the flitting birds could not hold the exhausted orange cat's attention. The lady in black scratched at an enormous wooden door, partially open, and from within an unusually deep and sonorous voice, a voice like the rumbling growl of a big cat—the kind Mustard had once seen in a television movie—bade them enter. Mustard straightened his white cravat and remounted the three steps he had backed down upon first hearing that echoing tone.

Sister Paka pawed and pawed at the door but couldn't get it to swing farther open. Mustard meanwhile had regained his breath, and with a deep sigh walked to the door, inserted first his nose, then his head, shoulders, and upper body, and walked in. She entered grandly behind him, tail waving, as if she always sent her messengers to announce her entrance. She bumped into Mustard's behind immediately.

He could no longer go straight ahead, because a big hole took up most of the floor space, about an inch from his front paws. Hanging above the hole was a gigantic metal thing, a bell, which he recognized from the tinier versions he'd entertained himself with on various overly cute cat toys. That had to be why the so-called Master's voice sounded so deep and sonorous—it was bouncing off this humongous piece of hollow iron. Cheap trick. Mustard repressed the urge to growl. That hole was so deep it made the sound of his breath and heartbeat echo back up to him. And the edge was very, very close.

Sister Paka sat back on her haunches and swatted at his rump. "Kindly move forward, please. The Master must not be kept waiting. Do you think you're the only soul he must counsel today?"

"Who said I wanted counseling?" Mustard asked, but proceeded around the hole and the bell, hugging the wall as tightly as he could, since his exhaustion made him tremble. He was far less than his usual balletic self. Fine first impression he'd make. He could not help but hope the Master was a cat-loving human with kind hands and some nice tidbit and a bit of sympathy for a cat as ill-used as himself. He would love to feel warm fingers stroke his fur now. He didn't actually like cats, if the truth were known. He was a people sort of cat. He called his own person a personal attendant, just to keep it clear to others that he knew she was probably an inferior breed—especially since she had always had more time for his housemates than for his own excellent self, but he had loved her touch nonetheless.

He could see the other side of the bell hole now. A chair—a plain, straight-back chair with a bed pillow on the middle, was the only furnishing in the tower. On the pillow reposed another cat. This cat was a male—an old male, even more orange than Mustard himself. The old cat was absolutely rusty around the stripes, actually.

"Peace, my son," the old cat said.

Sister Paka put a paw on Mustard's neck to force his head down. He bit her hard on the right leg and she fell beside him. He could tell she wanted to hiss but instead she lay there, submissively, on her side, though he could have torn her throat out if he'd wished.

"Peace, I was saying," the old cat said again. "Paka, see that bit under his cravat? He missed a spot. Get it for him will you, my child?"

Sister Paka put the paw of her wounded leg onto his chest, and, carefully leaning forward, gave the spot a lick and a promise. "There now," she said. "Much better."

The Master purred. "Yes. And that is a nasty-looking bite you have there."

Mustard hurriedly gave it a lick, causing Sister Paka's fur to partially cover his fang marks.

"Much better," the Master said. "And so are you, my son. We had nearly despaired of seeing you on your pins again. The damage to you was great."

"Damage?" Mustard asked. "I don't remember."

"You no doubt slept through much of it, as our kind tend to do. But when Tony and Jeannette brought you here, it was after they had put you to sleep to spare you pain. They thought certainly you were dead, but as they were readying your earthly shell to return to ash, you stirred. Already you were beyond their knowledge and your lady had been told you were dead. They did not wish to raise her hopes only to have her lose you again, so they brought you to us."

"And you are?" Mustard asked, tapping his tail against the edge of the hole. He stopped that at once. It hurt.

"*I* am Mu Mao the Magnificent, spiritual leader of this order. Sister Paka you have met. The order is the Spiritual Order of Our Lady of the Egyptian Bandages. We are an interdenominational feline monastery and convent for the spiritual enlightenment and growth of our kind. While the noncelibate may study here, only the surgically celibate may take vows. Otherwise— well, we *are* all cats, after all." He twitched his ears in a humorous way. "Any vow taken by a more corporeally unenlightened cat would be meaningless in the face of our natural compulsions. But once altered, we may concentrate on higher matters."

"So, then you yourself are—?" Mustard asked.

"Yes. You see, in many of my former lives I was a human being, a priest, holy man, shaman, what have you until I finally was allowed to achieve my highest form in this incarnation and became a cat. But my corporeal urges interfered with my ability to concentrate, so I voluntarily left my littermates and my safe abode and as a tiny kitten walked to the veterinarian's to go under the knife so that I might help others."

"He's what's called a bodhisattva by Buddhists," Sister Paka said with awe.

Mustard was impressed. "I like Tony and Jeannette—my doctors—very much but I always complain when I have to go. It smells bad there, and I dislike needles and having patches of fur shaved. I would never have gone for the surgery myself except my attendant forced it upon me. I admit, life has been calmer since. I have time to study and read many subjects."

Mu Mao purred approval. "This is good. And although you are now emaciated, it is clear that you have kept sleek and active under normal circumstances."

"I am a fine hunter of vermin," Mustard said without false modesty. "And chase down even the fastest horoscope scrolls, however they may attempt to roll from my grasp."

"You are versed in astrology as well?" Sister Paka asked rather breathlessly.

"Oh, yes. From the time I was a tiny kitten such scrolls were toys my attendant obtained for me and me alone at the food-procuring place. None of my housemates were allowed to chase them. I alone was deemed worthy." His white cravat stuck out beyond his nose with pride, so even he could see a few pale hairs without taking his eyes from the cat on the chair.

Mu Mao did not sound as approving as Mustard might have hoped, but flicked the bushy rust-and-cream tail shielding his paws. "Did you not seek to share with your housemates the knowledge you acquired thus?"

"Of course not! They were *my* scrolls," he said, baring his teeth and then, seeing the old cat's eyes, added quickly, "Well, the Kitten asked about them once and I did try to explain a few of the rudiments to her but she was much too young to grasp much of it."

"But that is a good start," Mu Mao the Master said in a tone sage enough to reflect his apparently exalted status.

"A good start of what, please?"

"A good start on your new life."

"My new life?"

"Well, yes. You've passed through number one and are now heading into your second."

"Then I didn't—survive?" He looked down at himself, all around at himself, and began licking furiously to reassure himself that all parts were there and solid and working.

"It's amazing you survived intact long enough to be brought to us," Mu Mao said. "Your mouth and your entire digestive tract was ulcerated. Something caustic, Tony thought. Something sudden."

"Something," Sister Paka said, "poison."

"But how can that be? I always ate the same thing, and have not even hunted much in recent years."

"Apparently you ate something out of the ordinary. And that something may linger to kill your former housemates as it killed you. The young one would be in particular danger, I should think."

"The Kitten?" he asked, remembering the way the fur on her belly curled like a sheep's wool and how fluffy her tail was and how, though she was cute, she had the taste to be black so that it wasn't all that obvious—and she never tried to take Susan's attention away from him.

"Yes. And the others."

"I don't care—," he began to say with a spit, but catching the slight hiss from Sister Paka, stopped himself. Mu Mao gave him a warning look.

"Yes, well. I understand you have made that evident over the years. If you are to join us here, you must give up your greatest vice."

"I told you I've *been* neutered."

"A natural function is not a vice. You must abandon the baser instincts of our kind in search of enlightenment."

"I never said I wanted to be enlightened, though I like a sunny patch as much as the next cat. Why would I want to stay here? You're all cats. No human petting, and I've yet to see a food dish."

Mu Mao said, "Well, we shall see. You'll realize what this life is to be about soon enough. Sister Paka, you must take Mustard with you to the fish pond. A few more of those poor primitive spirits can be released from the bondage of their present lives in order to sustain his own, and then he may work in the garden while he regains his strength."

Sister Paka told him it was his duty to take the largest and fattest of the fish from the pond. "They've learned whatever lessons life as a fish can teach," she told him, "and are ready to move on."

He obligingly caught one and would have done more but she assured him they were always there for the catching and he didn't want to eat too much at first or it would make him spew. He felt sore inside and realized he wished to avoid that.

She then showed him his duties. "You will be the tender of the roses to begin with," she said.

"Oh, good. I *love* roses," he replied, and began nibbling at the petals of a fat red one.

"I'm told those that are a bit brown around the edges have the best flavor," she said casually. "Aged a bit. Not so green-tasting."

"Oh?" he tried a somewhat wilted one. It was good—had a slightly cheesy flavor. He tried another. Yes, she was right. Much better than the red one. And with the wilted ones gone, the bush looked nicer too.

"You may dig here." She indicated a spot where a new rose bush sat waiting to be pushed into place once a hole was prepared. "And here as well, though for other purposes." This time she showed him a spot in the garden where several humps of earth bore the scents of various brethren—this was the communal litterbox.

When he had pruned a few roses, he slept in the sun, but his dreams were troubled and his feet pedaled, running to or from something. It was a shame that his daytime naps were so unsatisfying, too, because as the sun set and the shadows grew long in the courtyards and the other cats disappeared from view, the night grew very cold.

He stood there shivering, looking about for some pile of still-warm grass, some bit of fabric to nest in, but there was nothing. Finally, a somewhat familiar face, a slightly softer golden-orange than his own, poked into the courtyard from around the pillar.

"There you are! We missed you. How good it is to see you again, my old—uh—companion," the golden cat said in a voice that Mustard now recognized.

"Peaches! Are you here too?" He had almost disliked Peaches when he was alive, because Susan had loved Peaches best. Even when she was petting Mustard he always knew she would rather be petting Peaches and when Peaches's name was mentioned or he walked into the room, Mustard would hiss at Susan that she wasn't fooling him and jump down from her lap, often leaving her with scratches to let her know just what he thought of her taste. Of course, when she was gone, Peaches wasn't such a bad fellow. And now Mustard was downright delighted to see him.

"Not Peaches this time around, you know. Peaches died and when I was reborn I was sent here. Because I was already on my eighth life when I was Peaches, and an old soul, I do remember that time, and you, my brother. But now I am here among our kind as Brother Paddy."

"Oh, you would pick a name like that!" Mustard said in disgust.

Peaches/Paddy backed away from him and sat on his haunches and washed his paw calmly. "The name was chosen for me."

"Sure, sure. Everyone always likes you best," Mustard said with his old bitterness then, remembering his more immediate and practical concern, asked, "You wouldn't know where there was an extra bit of fabric to curl up in for the night, would you? It's cold."

His old acquaintance said simply, "Follow me. It is time for Ves-purrs."

Whereupon they reentered the great building with the bell tower. To Mustard's amazement, it was now lit by candle glow and the floor was totally covered with cats, their paws curled underneath them, tails wrapped around their bodies, purring so loudly the very stones of the building seemed to be—er—purrmeated with the contented throb. "What's this?" Mustard murmured.

"We are giving thanks to the Maker for creating such a wonderful form for us, for giving us a pleasant place to be, and kind companions."

"There are an awful lot of kittens here," Mustard said, noticing the young ones who occupied two entire wings of the building.

"That is because so many unwanted are dumped or killed. They are innocents and come to us to learn how to prepare lives outside our walls, if that is their desire, or to take their vows."

Mustard was silent.

"I thought you would still be with Susan, until you died of your long years as I did," his companion ventured. "But I'm told you were poisoned. Susan must be beside herself with grief."

"Oh, you know Susan. She got a new kitten and another grown male besides the old girl and me."

"You must have been very distressed. I know you always wanted to be top cat."

"Well, yeah, but that didn't last for long. The old girl was bigger, you know, and she got bolder and started beating the living daylights out of me. I have to admit, I didn't like the Kitten at first, but she's a nice little thing and very respectful. And Susan didn't really bond with the male, but he kept the old girl in line." He cried suddenly. "How can you stay here? I miss Susan so much. And she always liked you best. Can't you go back?"

Brother Paddy nee Peaches licked Mustard's face. "I taught Susan what she needed to learn from me. Now it is time for other lessons for all of us. Come. Join us."

He didn't feel like it, of course, but the thrumming purr relaxed him and he found himself joining in until his own purr lulled him into sleep, his body curling among four others whose warmth and softness made a better bed than Susan's comforter.

But though his body was comfortable, he began recalling the pain, the betrayal. And he saw the Kitten, sniffing for him, calling for him, and at last trotting toward someone calling, holding out something attractive and deadly . . .

Mustard awakened and leaped from one small bit of floor to another, and bounded past the cats sleeping on the bell-tower steps till he reached the landing. He scratched on the door.

The sonorous voice called to him, "Enter."

"Won't be but a minute, Mu Mao," he said, declining to call the old fellow "Master." "Just want to look out of your tower here and see if I can find my way home."

"So you have decided to attempt to rejoin the world, my son?" the old cat asked, his upper whiskers twitching.

"Of course. Susan is mine. I'm going back to her."

"Very well." The old cat hopped nimbly upon a windowsill. Mustard leaped up beside him. The leap wasn't as easy as it would have been before he came to this place, but it would have been impossible earlier in the day. This sort of thing was fine for cats who only wanted to be with other *cats*, he decided.

For just a moment it seemed to him that all the world was spread out below him, like the globe in Susan's office. And then he saw that it was just the Sound and the Strait surrounding his own little town, and there he saw the propane tanks beside Tony's office and farther off, Susan's red roof he had so often napped upon and the wide green yard of his home.

"Ye—oowwwt," he said to Mu Mao.

"In good time, my son. Do you see there? Dr. Tony and Jeannette are getting into their van with that bundle Jeannette is carrying. I sense we will be seeing them soon. You may save your strength by riding with them as far as their clinic, at least."

"I am still very tired," Mustard admitted.

"Then rest here with us," Mu Mao said. "There is yet time."

Time for what? Mustard wondered, but to his surprise found himself curled up in the bulk of Mu Mao's great belly, and falling into a deep and this time dreamless sleep until a lick on the nose awakened him again. "It is time, my son," the older cat said.

There were tears in Jeannette's kind brown eyes when she lay the bundle down beside the Master. "It's Susan's second loss," she said. "And there have been others in that neighborhood, too. The woman down the street, Diane, lost one of her cats to the same thing."

"Looks like we have a serial cat-killer on our hands," Dr. Tony said grimly. He was gently opening the bundle. Mustard's tail lashed angrily, and his ears laid back flat against his skull. Would he see now that the Kitten had been crying to him before her death, that her black curly underside would no longer vibrate with her purrs, her bright intelligent eyes that had watched so attentively while he told his hunting stories would be glazed with death before she had a chance to catch her quota of vermin?

He cried out as the tip of a black ear came into view. The eyes were shut, the whiskers stiff—her under-whiskers were so very long they curled under at the tips. The black nose. His worst fears confirmed.

But then he saw that the fur was short and coarse and the body much larger than the slight little female's. As the bundle was further unwrapped he saw the once powerful muscles slack under the sooty fur and the long sleek tail, which had been so expressive, now hung limp. "Boston Blackie!" he cried. This was the grown male companion Susan had brought home from the pound with the Kitten. Her protector, until she had charmed all but the old girl into loving her. With Blackie dead, or here, which would be all the same to Susan and the Kitten, he could only hope the kitten would grow quickly and manage to keep out of the old girl's way in the meantime.

Mustard had resented Blackie, of course, but not as much as some others. The big black cat, so massive and tough-looking, actually had been a decent sort who realized the Kitten's play with him had convinced Susan to bring the adult cat home too. The big boy had looked after his small companion, protected her from the others, taken the heat for her, as if he were her mother. He also had been decently respectful of Mustard's seniority.

"Poor fellow," Mustard said to the Master, Paddy, and Paka. "A real softie for such a big palooka, you know? That must be why the Kitten was sending me those dreams. She was mourning the big guy."

"Either that or she's next," Paka said grimly.

"Never fear, my son," Mu Mao said, giving Mustard's flat ears a lick. "He will soon be reborn into his new life, and a very good one it will be. He was a very old soul indeed and we have need of such a brother among our fold."

"That's great for *you*," Mustard said. "But what about Susan? And the Kitten? And Diane? And even that cantankerous old girl? Are the little one and the old biddy going to come here too and leave Susan all alone and afraid to have any more friends for fear of the same thing happening to them? And Diane, who is so kind and comes to feed us or finds someone like that nice Drew fellow to come stay with us when Susan is gone, she's sick all the time, you know. She depends on her cats to be there when she's too ill to move and lonely and afraid. She told me so."

Mu Mao surprised him by flipping his tail and saying, "That may be, but our kind have problems enough to concern us. Until they come or are brought within our walls, the companions of human beings are not within our protection."

"You can't dislike *people*?" Mustard demanded. "What about Tony and Jeannette?"

"Both were cats in their last lives, and of our order," Mu Mao said. "That is how they know to bring others to us. Like myself, they are bodhisattvas, not the ordinary sort of person that abandons a cat who is no longer small and cute, or has become inconvenient. Why should you care? This male and others, like Brother Paddy's former self, take from you the attention that is rightfully yours. If you return to your Susan and find the others all dead, should you not rejoice? Surely you will not make the same error twice and die again of the same poison? With no competition, your Susan will love you and only you."

Mustard didn't argue. Master indeed! This old cat obviously

didn't understand Susan. Mustard had always hated it that she was always bringing home other cats, true, but he had also licked away her tears for the cats she had to leave at the shelter. He never had to be in a shelter. She had picked him out of his mother's litter, still in a good home with loving people. He'd always felt entitled to love but he knew from what the others said they had no such hope, and getting a home with someone like Susan was a big break for them.

He hopped in the van before Tony and Jeannette left and rode in back. He desperately wished to be petted, but felt too restless and anxious to lie quietly. They didn't seem to notice him. They got a call and drove past the turnoff for their clinic back along the route he recognized from his own visits to the vet. He thought maybe old Mu Mao had asked them to give him a lift, but no, they were stopping at another house, not too far from his own.

Mustard thought it interesting that they had a phone in their van. He liked Susan's phones. She sat still to talk and he could usually curl up in her lap for a nap. He was good at doing it and staying so still and relaxed that she didn't even notice until she hung up.

He jumped out of the van after Jeannette and trotted the single block to his house. No one was in the yard and he approached the catflap so confidently that he nearly banged his head on the rectangle of board that barred entrance to or exit from the house. He scratched at the door and meowed until he noticed that Susan's car was gone as well. Of all the nerve. Here he had taken the trouble to return from the dead and she couldn't even bother to be home. Just like a person.

Then, from behind the front door, he heard an answering scratch and a small mew. "Let me out! It's a pretty day. I don't want to be in here. Where's Boston Blackie? I want him to come and play!"

"Now now, young lady, this is no time for tantrums," Mustard said. "I don't think Blackie will be coming back but I dreamed of your danger and have returned to save you."

He meant to be reassuring but she gave a chirrup that was the kittenish equivalent of a giggle. "Uncle Mustard? Is that you? Where have you been? Do you feel better? Susan said those ashes she sprinkled on the roses were you but they didn't look like you. Weren't even orange."

"Stop prattling, child, and let me think. Why is the catflap closed?"

"Susan said so we wouldn't go outside and get into whatever killed you and Blackie." Her voice turned plaintive. "Is Blackie *really* gone forever? I don't like the old girl. She is not nice to me at all and I'm going to scratch her face if she keeps saying those mean things. I miss you and Blackie. I want to come too."

"That's just what you mustn't do," Mustard said. "My—er— illness, was long and very painful and far too much for a mite like yourself to bear. Or even a battle-ax like the old girl. About Blackie, I can't tell you anything else. But we need to make the neighborhood safe for our kind again. Especially our yard. Have you noticed anything different?"

"No, nothing. And everyone has been looking out for us. Susan, Diane, Drew, Debbie and Dennis, Janice and Theresa, Mary and Michael Ann. Even Steinway barks very fiercely if he sees anything suspicious."

She was referring to Mary's and Michael Ann's dog next door. "Steinway must have a really suspicious mind, then," Mustard said. "He barks at everything all the time."

"No, I think he's trying very hard to help. Merlin is very scared." Merlin was the black feline in charge of Mary and Michael Ann and Steinway and Chopin, the junior cat of the house.

"Hmm. Merlin never struck me as a scaredy-cat. Maybe I should go have a word with him."

"Yeah, okay. I gotta jump now. The old girl is coming."

"Who is it?" the old girl's voice demanded in a growl. "Who's out there and who were you talking to, you little . . ."

"Lay off her and pick on someone your own size," Mustard growled back through the door.

"What the . . .? *Mud Turd?* Is that *you*? You're dead, ashes, gone, kaput, and you can't have the warm place on the video back. It's mine forever now."

The thump of paws came from inside and he could see through the lace curtain across the glass door panel that she had hopped up on a high shelf so she could, as usual, look down on him. He glared back up at her and shouted, "Yeah, sure, until you eat the wrong thing and end up with the grandfather of all bellyaches and writhe in agony till you're a ghost too, just like me and good old Blackie."

"A ghost?" she leaned so far forward she fell off the shelf. He heard the kitten titter from somewhere high and the sound of a cat giving herself a brisk shake before coming to the closed cat-flap to sniff. "There's no such thing as cat ghosts."

"Oh, that's rich. A cat who doesn't believe in ghosts. Well, there are, and I've seen them. I are them, in fact. And like it or not, you too can be in the same situation if you don't stop bullying and try to help out here. Do you know what killed me? How I died? Or what got Blackie?"

"Of course not. Can I help it if the dumb beasts around here eat any poison thing they come across? I survived loose in the neighborhood for two years on my own after those *people* went off and left me when I was only a little kitten, no bigger than Miss Burnt Pop-Tart, here . . ."

"Yeah, yeah, we all know how tough it was for you out in the neighborhood, taking handouts . . ."

"Hey, smart guy. You asked. I'm trying to tell you. The point is, in my two years I made the rounds of all the neighbors and I tell you, there's not one of them, not even one of the kids, who would hurt a cat. In this neighborhood, kids and dogs are brought up to have the proper adoration for our sort. I could have had a real home any time I wanted but I didn't want any of them. I wanted my house back and the minute I asked Susan, she displaced all of you who came with her from her old house and invited me in. She *knew* this was *my* home."

"Sure it was, old girl," Mustard said with a comforting purr this time. She was right of course. The only people who had changed houses since the time the old girl was on the streets were the renters in the back, and they had been there a good year and a half and were wonderful people who loved cats. "Thanks. But listen, I know you want to be top and only but I gotta tell you, the other side, over here where us ghosts are, it's not what you think it's going to be. I miss you and the kid too . . ."

There was a huff of air as she sank to her chest onto the floor and she said grudgingly, "Yeah, I miss that terrified look on your yellow face when I chased you, and watching you stand on your hind feet to stretch. How in the world did you *do* that anyway?"

He didn't answer but just said, "I'll be back. Just take care of the kid, you hear me? Remember, too, that she's going to be a strong young adult by the time Susan brings in the next strays and you may need someone to protect *you*. It's never too late, old girl."

"Shove it, Mud Turd," she growled, but softly, regretfully. "It's dull around here without you. You're coming back, you say?"

"At least for a little bit. I have to figure this out. The kid thinks Steinway and Merlin might have seen something."

"I'm sorry I can't tell you more about Blackie. One minute I see him out rolling around like an idiot on the picnic table, the next thing I know the big galoot can hardly talk for the sores in his mouth . . ."

That was how it started with himself, Mustard realized, though he hadn't known what was happening to him at the time. He tried to remember just when he had begun to feel uncomfortable but the whole experience was blurred by the fact that he had slept through as much of it as he could manage. He left the old girl to ruminate and sauntered next door to see Merlin and Steinway, who of course barked his few brains out when he saw Mustard.

"Cat ghost at two o'clock!" he yelled. "Cat ghost! Cat ghost!"

Mustard put his face right up to the fence and spat his nastiest at the bouncing, barking black Lab, who backed off, hunkered down, and whined.

"Nice dog," Mustard said. "Hi, Steinway. Good to see you again. Can we talk?"

The dog whimpered and a black cat as sleek as Blackie, though not as well-formed, suddenly appeared, followed closely by a gray-and-white spotted longhair prancing officiously behind. "Hey, there, you. That's *our* dog. If he needs spitting at, we'll do it," the black one said.

"Merlin!" Mustard said. "Just the guy I wanted to see."

"So, rumors of your demise were highly exaggerated, eh?" Merlin asked. For a musicians' cat, he had a pretentious penchant for literary misquotes.

"No, I think I pretty well bought it, okay. I'm sort of between lives at the moment, I guess. Can't seem to get on with number two until I figure out how I snuffed number one. Boston Blackie apparently died the same way."

"Not Blackie?" Merlin asked with genuine regret. "That is one fine specimen of my particular color. Poor guy. And he was so happy yesterday, just rolling on the picnic table, purring. I think he'd just had a visitor."

"Any idea who?" Mustard asked, looking first from one cat to the other and then to the dog, who covered his nose with his paws and whined. "Anybody unusual around?"

Steinway whined again. "You know how it is in your yard. Your mistress lets everyone walk through to get to the houses in back. Much too sloppy to keep proper surveillance on, though I try. A lot of thanks I get though. 'Shut up, Steinway,' people say, and uppity neighbor cats, who ought to be dead, hiss at me."

"You're breaking my heart," Mustard said. "You should know most of the people who go through the yard by now. Anyone you didn't know?"

"Nope. Just the usual residents and the usual guests. Of course, I think someone may have been through as I was chowing down—even I take a break once in a while. Because right after I got back was when I saw old Blackie rolling on his back on the picnic table."

"Well, thanks, I guess," Mustard told them. "I seem to recall something about the picnic table too. Guess I'd better check it out. Could be the scene of the crime."

A recent rain had washed the table clean, but the sealant on the wood was old, and so maybe small particles of the poison might have sunk into the cracks.

He trotted back to the door and asked into the room beyond. "How long ago did Blackie start getting sick?"

The old girl was just beyond the door. He could hear her scratching the bald spot on her head against the sill. "I dunno, let me see, I saw him rolling around yesterday afternoon. Susan noticed he was sick last night and took him to Tony's. Er—unless my memory fails me."

There was the sound of light, delicate paws landing on the floor beside the door. "No, that's right, okay. I asked him when he came in what was wrong. I could tell he wasn't himself right away. He was grumpy and kind of groggy and he smelled funny."

"Funny in what way, Kitten?" Mustard asked.

"Like that nasty stuff Susan sprinkled all over the floor at Christmas—that stuff that made you all act crazy. I was scared."

"You're always sc—" The old girl's growl began. At a warning hiss from Mustard she moderated it to "Always scared. That was nothing to be scared of. Just catnip."

Catnip! Of course! He raced to the table and sniffed—the rain had done a good job. And there might be fine particles of nip in the cracks, but he couldn't see them. He jumped under the table and put his paws on the supports and sniffed the undersides. His lips curled at the edges. 'Nip yes, and another smell, a smell he had not really noticed except as one of the subtle vintage differences in 'nip, but now that particular difference made him feel nauseous.

He streaked up the street to Diane's house, to the cabin at the back of it, the one Diane rented to Drew.

Sadie barked a warning, but Mustard ducked past her and over to a window where he scratched at the glass. No response. Then he looked through the pane. The inside of the cabin no longer contained Drew's books and bed, the little arrangements of Christmas lights he made, or Moonshadow's dishes. It was to-tally empty and almost odorless.

He was about to ask Sadie where his friend had gone when he heard the sound of Dr. Tony's and Jeannette's van pulling into the driveway. Diane met them at the door and ushered them in-side. Sadie kept bouncing and barking.

"Shut up!" Mustard hissed. "What happened?"

"It's Moonshadow. He's been laying in the cabin for the past two days while Diane was gone."

"Dead?"

"No, but close. Oh poor Moonshadow! He's been so lone-some since that Diane made Drew leave."

"Why did she do that? Drew was nice."

"I don't know. Maybe he peed on the rug."

"Has he been around the last couple of days?" Mustard asked.

"Yes, Friday the thirteenth it was, day before yesterday. He came to pick up his things. I heard him yelling through the door to Diane but she wasn't here. He petted us, gave Moonshadow some catnip, and left."

"Catnip!" Mustard exclaimed, and bolted out of the house and back down the street again, to the front door. "Kitten! Old girl! Are you there? Where is Susan anyway?"

The Kitten's voice answered in a plaintive mew. "She went to get Drew to come and stay with us while she goes to visit her friends in Copperton. She doesn't want us left alone with all this cat-killing going on."

Mustard twined back and forth across the ridges that held the catflap. He was agitated and had no idea what to do now, ex-cept to say, "Look, don't either one of you let him near you. Don't eat food he puts out or touches, or even water. And don't take any catnip from him."

"Ick," the Kitten said. "That nasty stuff. I am not one of the youth with a drug problem, Uncle Mustard. I think that stuff sucks."

"Just keep thinking that way," he said, noticing she was al-ready falling into the teenage vernacular.

He was about to run back down the road to check on Moon-shadow when Susan drove up. She got out of the car on one side. Drew emerged from the other. "Thanks for coming to get me, Susan. With Diane's car broken down again, and me taking that job out of town, I had no way to get here. But it will be good to see the kitties again. I'm sure going to miss Blackie and Mus—" He stared straight at Mustard, who walked calmly over and sat down in front of him and stared right up at him.

"Returned to the scene of your crime, eh, murderer?" he asked, but Drew didn't understand that much. He did, however, recognize Mustard for who he was. Which unfortunately was more than Susan did.

"What's wrong? Oh, look at the pretty white cat. Hello, honey. You better be careful around here."

White cat? Was she nuts? He looked down at his own orange stripes and back up to her. Well, Mu Mao had said this was a second life and he wouldn't seem the same to Susan. But *white?* So impractical.

He returned his attention to his murderer, who certainly looked guilty enough. Mustard was certain that somehow Drew saw his victim for who he really was. There had always been something uncannily catlike about the big man—leonine, really. It was what the cats liked about him. Had he been a cat in his last life like Tony and Jeannette? But he was no bodhisattva, even though at one time Mustard would have said so. Drew was wonderful with animals, he had often heard Diane and Susan say. But Diane had thrown him out. And Mustard doubted it was for peeing on the rug. She must have found out something about him to make her run him off, and hadn't told Susan yet. No wonder, really. Right after Susan met Drew, she and Diane had had a fight, though they'd been the best of friends for years. But why would he poison the cats? His friends? Because now Mustard was sure it was Drew who did him in. You could still smell the tainted catnip on him. Probably had a bag in his pocket to feed the old girl and the Kitten.

Well, no way was that man going near them! Or any other cat, or Susan, not if Mustard had his way. He did the only thing within his power and sprang for Drew's throat, biting and clawing his way up as he went while Drew swore and tried to tear him off.

"The damned thing's rabid!" Drew screamed to Susan, who tried to pull Mustard away from his murderer. "Kill it!"

"No! I have it, see?" she said, pulling Mustard spitting from his victim. "But you need a doctor."

"No, I—"

"Don't be silly. I saw Tony's van up at Diane's. He can look at those scratches and test the cat for rabies. Just let me pop him into the carrier in the trunk. I still have it—" Her voice broke and she looked very haggard. "From taking Blackie in, you know."

Of course, Mustard, white or not, was gentle with Susan and only hissed over his shoulder at Drew, who surprised him by sticking his tongue out at him and making a neck-breaking gesture with his big hands just before Susan tucked Mustard into the carrier.

They drove down the street in a split second, just as Tony was leaving. Moonshadow, bundled into Jeannette's arms, mewed plaintively and Drew pretended to make over her.

"Don't let him near you, Moon!" Mustard cried. "He tried to kill you!"

As Drew stuck out his hand to stroke Moonshadow, she crouched back against Jeannette, laid her ears back, hissed, spat, and tried to rip his hand open, despite her illness.

Drew pulled his hand back just in time, then hissed back at her, *"Traitor,"* he spat, and then tried to look wounded. "She must be delirious. Doesn't seem to know me," he said to the others.

It was Mustard's good luck that Tony and Jeannette were who they were. *They* didn't think he was white and recognized him, too. Furthermore, they seemed to understand him. While Tony was examining Drew's scratches right there in the driveway, Jeannette called Susan and Diane over to look at his shirt. The pocket was ripped and a small bag of the tainted catnip sprinkled its contents down to mingle with the still-wet blood.

"Just what is this?" Jeannette demanded.

"A treat for the cats," Drew said. *"Ouch,"* as Tony washed out a scratch.

"It smells funny. You don't mind if I analyze it, do you?"

"It's a special kind and it cost me a lot. But hey, nothing's too good for my kitties, huh?"

"Is that why Moonshadow is afraid of you?" Jeannette said. "Because you gave her this?"

"Afraid of me? Why should she be afraid of me? When *Diane* wouldn't let Moonie in the house because Rasta gave her too much shit, I took her in. But when Diane threw me out, did Moonie so much as catch me a mouse to get by on? Hell, no! And Susan—she wouldn't even hold my hand but she treated those cats of hers like royalty and wanted me to do it too! She wouldn't even pay for me to go to a movie with her but she spent thirty bucks every two weeks on food for *them.*" His eyes, which had always seemed blue, were now blazing green with jealousy. Yep, no doubt about it. The guy was one jealous dude—even of the cats. And if Mustard was right, he had *been* a cat himself. But then, cats were jealous of other cats. Mustard himself, for instance. He began licking his right front paw in embarrassment while the questioning continued. It didn't take long to wring a defiant confession from Drew.

As he had already said when he let the cat out of the bag, he had poisoned Mustard, Blackie, and Moonshadow because he was angry with Diane for throwing him out and with Susan for breaking up with him—which Mustard actually hadn't realized happened. Human mating habits weren't of particular interest to him, after all.

Mustard told all of this to Mu Mao and the others later, as they kept vigil over the still body of Boston Blackie.

"But why did he hurt the cats he had taken such care to befriend?" Paka asked.

"Well, I guess he had a long record as a con man who got nasty when his victims turned. He was nice to us because that was a good way to get him close to single, cat-loving, independent ladies like Diane and Susan. He tried to go back on what he said about trying to punish them for rejecting him and said he was just trying to upset them so they'd turn to him in a crisis because they thought he was sympathetic to their love for us."

"And with your Susan, it almost worked," Mu Mao said.

"She's sweet, but not always real bright," Mustard admitted. "But at least the neighborhood should be safe from that particular danger now."

"You've done good work, my brother," Mu Mao said, and Mustard noticed that he said "brother" instead of "son." "Will you be returning home to Susan again, even if she thinks of you as a white cat?"

"I've thought about it," he said. "But I'd like to know a little more about this place, and there's a shelter full of kittens who've never had a good home. Susan will fall in love with some, the Kitten will play with them, and the old girl will have her usual tantrum. But she'll be okay."

"It isn't just that Susan didn't know you and it hurt your feelings, is it?" Paka asked.

"No, no," he said, though perhaps that was part of it. "I was never her top cat. I think I see why now. I always hated all of the others—even hated her for loving them. But, you know, it took all of us to figure it out."

"You're too modest," Mu Mao said. "You overcame your jealousy of your housemates to save their lives. You are evolving very quickly, my brother, and growing in enlightenment."

Brother Paddy licked Mustard's ear affectionately and for once, Mustard didn't mind. "Not only that but he's smart. Mustard was always the smart one. Why, now he's a real detective, just like in those books of Susan's."

"Or on TV," Blackie mumbled, stirring and sitting up. The other cats surrounded him, licking and purring and he responded with a weak purr himself.

"The Mystery series," Sister Paka said. "That's right. Oh, Mustard, you have to stay now, won't he, Master Mu Mao?"

"If he wishes, of course. It's entirely up to him. But it would add very much to our order to have our very own Brother Catfael among us."

Elizabeth Ann Scarborough

Veteran fantasy writer Elizabeth Ann Scarborough is edging into mystery with more than short stories. Her newest novel, just out, is The Lady in the Loch, *a Gothic mystery set in eighteenth-century Edinburgh and featuring the young Walter Scott as a protagonist. She has written the best-selling* Powers That Be *with Anne McCaffrey and is the solo author of twenty-some fantasy novels, including* The Healer's War, *which won the Science Fiction and Fantasy Writers of America Nebula Award, and her Godmother series, the latest of which is* The Godmother's Web. *She lives in a forties-vintage log cabin in Washington state with four cats: Kittibits, a fluffy orange Maine Coon–type; Trixie, a fluffy black kitten; Treat, "a large, sleek Midnight Louie lookalike"; and Popsicle, a grumpy old calico.*

Mr. Ed Gorman is a Renaissance writer. He does so much so well that it is hard to keep up with him. This tale of man's inhumanity to man—and woman—and the species' own institutions of law and order and the public good (reminds me a little of Ibsen, a seriously philosophical cat-pal of mine, and a Norwegian Forest Cat by trade) cuts the hair very fine indeed. And at the heart of it is a rescue operation, for creatures animal and, alas, all too human.

—M.L.

The Cage
Ed Gorman

I LOVED HER. If you grew up in this small town of ours, I guess you pretty much know that. Back when there was still a theater downtown, this would be back in the eighties, then you would always see me walking her to the movies on Saturday nights, tenth-grade boy, ninth-grade girl. This was before the four-plex out at the mall chased the Rialto out of business.

Jane, her name was. Jane McCoy. She was the smartest girl in the class, and the third prettiest. This wasn't my ranking. It belonged to Davey Thornton, who was always ranking girls by various body parts. Personally, I didn't care if she was first prettiest or sixteenth prettiest. I loved her, and had loved her since second grade when her family moved to town and her dad opened up the paint store right across the street from my father's pharmacy.

By senior year in high school, people started saying things like, "Well, when are you and Jane going to get married?" and

"When will you and Jane have your own family?" It embarrassed me when people talked this way—I'm basically a shy and private person, but it also made me feel great because it confirmed my deepest desire: that as soon as we both graduated from the University of Iowa, we'd come back to town here and get ourselves married. Dad wanted to open a second pharmacy, an operation three times the size of the original store, and he wanted me to run it. Jane was going through nursing school and planned to work at the town's only hospital.

She loved animals. The summer before senior year I'd built her a large cage in her backyard and she filled it with distressed animals of all kinds. One day I counted a robin, a wren, a opossum, and a raccoon. There was a weathered wooden pole standing a few feet from the cage. Jane was once visited by an oposum who loved to climb that pole over and over again. He fit right in. All her animals were strange enough or sick enough or damaged enough to leave one another alone. She tended them with fierce maternalism.

The one thing I hadn't counted on was Bob O'Day. He was the class heartbreaker. I don't say that sarcastically. Other boys excelled at sports, music, academics. Good-looking Bob excelled at winning girls. He usually spent his time breaking hearts in the grade ahead of us. Somehow it was more impressive to break the heart of an older girl. But then we were seniors and there were no older girls left so he concentrated on our grade. His wealth didn't hurt, either. Six years ago, his father had saved the town, moving his avionics plant from outside Chicago to our little town. He put a good share of our people to work at good-paying jobs. Now the town depended on him utterly. If he ever decided to move the business away, the town would for all intents and purposes fold up. And everybody knew this. And treated him accordingly. There were two O'Day boys. The youngest, Ken, was a total waste. At least Bob never rubbed your face in his money. But all Ken had was his father's money, he wasn't smart, good-looking, or pleasant. All he could do was pull rank.

One afternoon early in senior year, the gym smelling sweetly of fresh wax, the sun streaming warm and golden through the long narrow windows, the Homecoming colors of black and orange looking bright and crisp draped about the gym, Bob O'Day started dancing with Jane. And when I saw them there on the dance floor together, I had a terrible sense that my life was about to change.

At first, my friends said I was just being paranoid. Because I was looking for signs, they said, I was finding them.

But the signs were there. No doubt about it. Everybody gets his heart broken at some time in his life. And this was going to be my time.

I had to kind of talk her into making love now. And she didn't laugh much when I tried to be funny. And when I held her hand, she always found an excuse to ease it away after a few moments.

The first time I caught them together was at the Pizza Hut out on Highway 149. It was a chilly late October evening and everybody was pretty much psyched-up for a basketball game. She'd been very vague about her plans that night and when I decided to just stop by and see her, her dad answered the door and said she was gone. He didn't say where. He looked kind of sad. He'd always liked me, even though I suspected that his wife had always thought Jane could do better for herself. "She's kinda goin' through somethin', I think," he said. He'd done well for himself in the retail paint business but he'd always be a lot more blue-collar than white-collar and I guess that's why we got along. Despite my dad's standing in the community—he was an elder in the Lutheran Church, and a town council member, and the head of the library board—I'd always been blue-collar myself.

There wasn't any big scene that night at the Pizza Hut. Or the next day when I walked up to her locker and she gave me my ring back. She changed; and then I changed. When I knew it was over, I started drinking a lot of beer and borrowing my older brother's Harley and writing her a lot of angry letters I had the good sense not to send. I tried other girls but I just ended up talking about Jane, and they just ended up feeling sorry for me and wanting to go home early. I spent a few months of raising hell too, landing in jail one night for being drunk and disorderly, and then having to pay $250 in fines from the college money I'd earned the summer before. I'd smashed out windows in a vacant warehouse. I don't know who felt more ashamed, me or my parents.

And then one rainy day a few weeks after graduation, I stumbled out of bed, all jittery and hungover from too much beer and marijuana, and went down to the army recruiting office and had the black corporal there give me the spiel. I suppose it was the midwestern equivalent of joining the Foreign Legion. My folks got really pissed, needless to say, but I'd done well on my tests, my health checked out, and I was eighteen and old enough to be legal, and legal I was. I spent four years in the army, ending up a Military Policeman.

During those years, I got back home three times. On my first visit, I heard that Jane and Bob had gotten married; on my second visit, a year and a half later, I heard that they'd had their first kid, a girl; and on my third visit, a year after that, I heard that she was pregnant with their second kid. And I heard that he beat her a lot.

After the army, I came back home. The town looked pretty small to me. I felt superior, I have to say, having spent a year in England and a year in Germany. My folks expected me to either work for my father or enroll at the U of I, which was sixty miles east. I did neither. There was an opening on the police force. I took the exam and passed it. I was a cop. This did not greatly please my parents. They had a sense of themselves in the community. Cops weren't in their social group.

I saw Jane a number of times, my first year back. Nothing dramatic. I saw her and spoke to her and knew that I was still in love with her. There was pain and loneliness but they were tolerable. I was a big boy now. No more smashing out windows.

Bob had built them a mansion on a hill, complete with a white fence that ran for nearly a quarter mile. Against the green summer grass, the fencing was beautiful. His thoroughbreds ran here.

Jane didn't see any of her old friends. She had herself a sleek little red BMW. One afternoon I saw her and the car in the supermarket parking lot. She was standing beside it, letting the bag boy put the groceries in the trunk, when I walked up to her.

She'd aged a lot in the six years we'd been out of high school. Her luster was gone. The first time I noticed this, I'd felt good. Served her right, losing her luster that way, dumping a fine fellow like me. But now when I saw her, the too-thin body, the too-wrinkled face, the sad, dead eyes, I felt real sorrow. I wanted to hold her, hold what she'd been, all that joy and fine sharp intelligence and sweet little face, hold her tight and never let time take her. But it was already too late for that. Even in her expensive jeans and white silk blouse, even in her red BMW convertible, it was already too late for that.

Then she turned and faced me fully and I saw her nose. Broken. Right at the bridge. A faint mark remained, alongside a yellowing bruise under her eye. The nose had probably been broken three or four weeks ago. I had no doubt at all as to how it had been broken.

She saw where I was staring and said. "I tripped and fell against the fence."

"It's usually a doorway."

"A doorway?"

I waited until the freckled bag boy got his tip and walked away. "The domestic abuse calls we get. When the wives change their minds about pressing charges, they always say that their husbands didn't do it, that they tripped and stumbled into the doorway."

Embarrassment touched her cheeks with color. They needed it. "Don't believe all those stupid stories about Bob. People hate him because he's rich."

"So he's never hurt you?"

Now it was her turn to stare. All these years later, in a moment I would not have been able to even imagine with my high school mind, we stood close to each other in a summer parking lot on a lazy butterfly afternoon, adults now, or at least sort of adults anyway, and I realized that I was in love with an utter stranger, somebody who'd once existed but existed no more. And yet I was still drawn to her, or the ghost of who she had been, and I still wanted to touch her in the way you touched something unimaginably precious. I don't know what she hoped to find in my face. Maybe she found it; maybe she didn't. She said, "No, he's never hurt me. It's just gossip, Ted. Honest."

"I guess I'll have to take your word for that, won't I?"

She seemed defiant suddenly. "I love him, Ted. He's got his faults the way we all do."

"Hitting your wife is more than a 'fault,' Jane."

"Maybe his life isn't as easy as most people think. Having money doesn't solve everything, you know."

I tried to end on a happier note. "I hear you've still got that cage I built you?"

Somebody had told me that the other day. If you had a sick stray animal, you brought it to Jane and she'd make it well for you. Maybe this was the nursing side of her personality she never got to express.

For the first time, she smiled. Not much of a smile. But at least a bit of one, anyway. "They're good friends of mine, those animals." Her voice was sad, then. She didn't try to hide the sadness at all. "Sometimes, I think they take care of me as much as I take care of them." Then, standing there with her black eye a swirl of discoloration, she said, "You know the funny thing?"

"What?"

"He's a great father. He's very gentle with them. And they love him."

"They're not old enough to understand what he's doing to you. Not yet. But they'll learn soon enough."

"They love him more than they do me. If he ever went away—"

A few weeks later, over lunch at Henry's restaurant, Bill Hastings, the town banker, said, "You ever see Jane much anymore?"

"Not much."

"Well, she isn't having an easy time of it."

I expected to hear another abuse story. I wondered what bone or bones of hers he'd broken this time. But Hastings said, "Some of his investments went bad last year. And now his stupid little brother wants to sell out to some big firm back East. Close the company here. You have any idea what that'd do to this town?"

"He's got a lot of money. He can ride it out."

Hastings smiled coldly. "And that's just what he's doing. Riding it out."

"Oh? You mean a horse?"

He shook his graying head. "I mean a lady. You know that new dress shop opened out at the mall?"

"I guess so."

"It's a chain store. Gal from Chicago came out here to manage it. You should see her. She's about the sexiest thing that ever hit this town, that's for sure."

"And he's seeing her?"

"Seeing her a lot."

All I could think of was Jane's broken nose. And now he was cheating on her besides. And what she'd said about the girls loving him more than they loved her, and how distraught they'd be if he ever left them. The Jane I'd known would never have tolerated any of it. But then she was long past being the Jane I'd known.

Summer came. The Chief talked of retiring—something he did periodically—and said that those night courses in criminology I was taking at Iowa would come in handy someday, the implication being that he'd recommend me to take his position when the time came. I always had Sunday dinner at my folks'. The Sunday I told them what the Chief had said, all I got was (Mom) "That's nice, dear" and (Dad) "You know, it's not too late to go back to pharmaceutical school." They still didn't understand that I enjoyed my work. I think they saw me as a confused twenty-seven-year-old who was playing a grown-up version of cops and robbers. When a man could be a pharmacist, being a cop wasn't a real respectable occupation.

That was the summer I started dating a lot. And that was the summer, a half dozen different women sitting next to me in my new Firebird, that I realized how much I still loved Jane, the old version of her anyway. There was sex with a few of these women, and there was even tenderness, and one of them I started to have real feelings for. But none was Jane. And none would ever be.

I got the call late one night early September night when the aroma of autumn was on the breeze coming down from the piney hills to the north of town. I didn't sleep much and hadn't even tried this particular night. I'd been on a Steinbeck kick lately. I was rereading *Of Mice and Men* and really appreciating it.

"Ted."

"Yes."

"Tom Wolverton."

Dr. Wolverton. The new intern at the hospital. A small hospital like ours, it was possible for one man to run the ER and cover the hospital beds.

"What's up, Tom?"

"Think you could run over here for a couple of minutes?"

"Sure."

He lowered his voice. "I understand you know Jane O'Day."

"Yes, I do."

"Well, I'd appreciate it if you'd talk to her."

Dr. Wolverton looked like a high-schooler masquerading as a very young adult. The white medical jacket was a nice touch, and so were the black horn-rimmed glasses. He led me through several white-tiled rooms to a small room where Jane lay on a gurney. A nurse was finishing up with a cast for her left arm. Jane had a fresh black eye. Her lower lip was bulbous and bloody. She looked even older than the last time I saw her.

"I didn't ask you to come over here," she said.

"I asked him," Dr. Wolverton said. "I'm supposed to report cases like these to the police."

"Cases like what?" she snapped. "I fell down the stairs."

"Why don't we leave them alone?" Dr. Wolverton said to the nurse, who nodded.

They left the room. I dragged a stool over next to the gurney. The glass faces of two cabinets reflected the brilliant white fluorescent light from above. The smell of medicine reminded me of my boyhood. There'd been a doctor named Riley, dead now, and if you were a boy and you complained about getting a shot, he'd pinch you harder than you'd ever been pinched before. Girls could complain—my sisters gave Academy Award performances—but not boys.

"I don't want you here."

"I don't want to be here," I said.

"Good. Then leave."

"He's going to kill you, you know."

"You don't know what the hell you're talking about."

"Don't I?" The word on Main Street, and Main Street was still where everything important got discussed, was that she was still very much in love with him and wouldn't give him a divorce, no matter what kind of settlement he offered. He loved his new girlfriend. He had a bad problem with the bottle and he had a lot of debt he couldn't handle and he had a wife he didn't love and the only way he could deal with any of it was to smack her around.

"You're still angry that I dumped you back in high school."

"I probably am."

"He's just confused right now. And scared. His brother is really pushing him to sell the company. I think Bob thinks he owes it to the town to stay here. But things'll be all right for us again. I know they will."

I changed the subject. "How's your animal cage doing?"

The subject always seemed to soften her. "I've just got one bird there now. A robin. I never could figure out what was wrong with it. It was just dying. But now it's starting to get healthy again. Maybe in a couple of weeks it'll be able to fly."

The back of the gurney was up so she was sitting as much as lying down. She wore a yellow blouse and jeans. A brown suede car coat hung from a hook in the corner.

"You've got to get away from him."

"I'm sorry about what I said. About dumping you. I really was in love with you, Ted."

"He's going to kill you."

"I'm sorry for all the pain."

"Listen to me."

Her eyes were damp with tears. She glanced away. Looked at her car coat. "I can't help loving him, Ted. I can't. And I can't give him up."

"I know the pattern here, Jane. I see it every day. He won't stop drinking and he won't get help to stop the abuse. Too proud. So it'll happen again and again. And each time it'll be a little worse than the time before. Do you understand that?"

She snuffled up her tears and said, "Sometimes I wonder what it would've been like if I'd married you."

"I wouldn't have been exciting enough for you, Jane. When I look back, I can see that the signs were there pretty much all the time. You wanted me to be exciting, which I wasn't and wouldn't ever be; and I wanted you to be the same kind of homebody I was. It wouldn't have worked."

She watched me carefully for a long moment. "Would it hurt your feelings if I said you were right?"

I laughed. "Well, I guess I'd rather hear that I'm wrong, that we would have made a lovely couple. But I guess I know better. And I guess you do, too."

"How about a little kiss?"

"My pleasure."

"I'd better warn you. My breath probably smells like a kitty litter-box."

"Now there's a romantic thought."

I kissed her gently on the lips, which is all she wanted. This was about friendship and fear on her part; and on mine, it was saying good-bye to my dream, to putting it away forever, like something that goes up in the attic never to be seen again. All this right here in a cramped little ER room. After all these years, because of the chasteness of the kiss, and because of the circumstances that had prompted it, I was free of the dream of her.

"The next time he even shoves you a little," I said, giving her a fatherly admonition, "you call me. Hear?"

She nodded. Tears wet her eyes again. "I'll be fine, Ted, I really will."

But she wasn't fine. On May 2 of the following year, Bob O'Day called the Chief and reported his wife missing. Said she'd been gone twenty-four hours. Said he was afraid she might have done something foolish. Said they'd had a fight and they'd both said stupid, angry things and then he'd gotten up in the middle of the night and she was gone. He'd called all her friends and relatives. Nobody had seen her. The funny thing was, her red BMW was still in the garage. The Chief said he'd be out in an hour or so. I asked him if I could go along and he said no. He said, "You two have an issue between you, Ted. I don't think that makes for very good police work." What I wanted to say was that despite all his financial troubles, he was still the richest man in town and the Chief didn't want to piss him off. But I liked the Chief and I liked my job even better.

The Chief went out and the Chief came back. He said it was damned strange the way she'd disappeared and I said she hadn't disappeared, she'd been killed by her husband, Bob, and he said, "That's the kind of talk that could get you and me in a whole lot of trouble. And that's the last time I want to hear you say that to anybody, you got that?" Like I said, I liked my job. I knew when to keep my mouth shut. But in order to do that I had to leave the office and walk around the downtown area. Or what was left of it.

Now that a leg of the new Interstate swung near town, two new malls had opened up. A lot of the downtown store windows had been painted black. The closed movie theater was the saddest of all. If you listened closely, you could still hear all the giddy Saturday afternoon laughter and Friday night date talk in the dark air inside.

I went over to the last dime store in this part of the state, Kronin's. It looked and smelled comfortably of the past. I wanted to say hello to a young woman there named Teresa Conners, who'd recently moved back here from Chicago. She'd been a cute little college kid when she'd left; now she was a woman with a divorce and a miscarriage behind her. I wouldn't say I was in love with her exactly but it was a good sign that I couldn't seem to stay away from her. And she couldn't seem to stay away from me, either. She had a ribbon in her hair this day, a festive ice-blue ribbon, and it was sweet and sexy at the same time. I wanted her to stop me, and I told her that, too, as we stood at the cash register (she was hoping to find a better-paying job soon), but she said, "You know he killed her, Ted. And you know how the Chief gives in to political pressure. You need to get involved in this. You don't have any choice." She paused and then said, "You loved her, Ted. You owe her this."

The mansion was two-story redbrick with white Colonial columns out front. There was a three-stall garage, and a vast backyard that ran into heavy forest. The air was piney and sweet, the breeze gentle and warm. Near the forest was a green gazebo that had been repainted recently. You could smell the paint. And near the gazebo was the cage where Jane had tended to her ailing birds. The cage was four feet high and built of heavy plywood on three sides and wire fencing, with a door, in front. One bird had the entire cage to itself, a rather large robin. It looked at me momentarily and then started to walk away with a kind of limp. I wondered what might be wrong with it and wondered if it had anything to do with the small stain on its light reddish breast. I was still wondering when a voice behind me said, "The Chief told me you were staying out of this."

The booze hadn't been kind to him. He had the old swagger but not the old hail-fellow good looks to go with it. He looked pasty and heavy. He also looked angry. He wasn't used to having riffraff up to the family manse, not unless it was riffraff that could help him in some way. I definitely didn't fit into that category. He wore a blue button-down shirt loose outside his Levis to conceal his burgeoning gut, and a pair of moccasins. A Rolex rode one hairy wrist.

"Just thought I'd look around."

"You don't have any right to look around."

I looked at him and smiled. "A man with a wife missing, I'd think he'd want all the help he could get. Unless he had something to hide."

"I'm not pretending I miss the bitch. She walked off and left our three kids."

"Don't call her a bitch any more, all right?" We stared at each other, boys on a playground. He was bigger than me, but soft. Sure, he could have my job with one word, but not before I'd had the pleasure of doing some damage. And right now it was a pleasure I was having a hard time resisting.

He smiled suddenly. "Still have the hots for her, huh?"

"Maybe so."

"Well, any woman who'd run off and leave her kids this way—"

"Can it, O'Day. You killed her. I know it and you know it and the Chief knows it. The thing is, I'm the only one who's going to do anything about it."

I walked over to the birdcage. If my suspicion was correct, I'd already figured out how he'd done it. The thing was, I had no idea how he'd taken the body away or where he'd hidden it.

He dug a cell phone out of his back pocket and angrily punched in some numbers. He said, "Chief. This is Bob O'Day. Your assistant chief is up here without a warrant and without my permission. He just accused me of murdering Jane." Beat. Then he handed me the phone. "Chief wants to talk to you."

You can guess what he said, starting with, "Get your ass back here. I didn't tell you to go up there and I don't want you up there. You don't belong on this matter and you know it."

I handed the phone back to O'Day. "If I see you up here again, I'll kill you. You understand?"

I drifted over to the birdcage. "How long's the robin been in here?"

"How the hell would I know? A couple days, I guess. Now I want you the hell off my land."

I got the hell off his land.

I went back there at 11:15 that same night. I came the back way, through the woods. Branches slapped my face, prickly vines bit my legs and arms, and any number of small holes caused me to stumble forward like a bad novelty act. Moonlight was wan and broken into golden patterns as it tumbled through the canopy of budding leaves and angled branches and touched the damp dirt path I'd taken. Leaves still smelled wet and musty from winter snow and spring rain. Much as I liked to think of myself as a he-man outdoorsman, the forest at night was a world I didn't know anything about, filled with shiny mysterious nocturnal eyes in

the bushes, and animal cries alternately plaintive and angry. Outdoors to my mind was sitting on a sunny bank fishing, Pepsi in
hand, headphones blasting a Garth Brooks tune. This was an
alien world.

The mansion was dark except for a lone downstairs light. The
grass was dewy and soaked my shoes. I'd been afraid of a security light going on but apparently I was out of range of the system. A place this big, more an institution than a home, looked
wrong on the prairie. This was something you would see on the
East or West Coast but not out here.

The robin didn't give me any trouble. I did just what my
friend Lisa in the State Crime Lab had told me to do. I cut away
a good slice of the stained breast feathers and then I put them
carefully into a white envelope. I was a little too conscientious, I
guess. While I was doing everything Lisa had told me to, I'd forgotten the possibility that O'Day might see me out here. Well, not
only had he seen me; he'd decided to do something about seeing
me. He came bursting out of his back door with a hunting rifle in
his hands, a rifle aimed right at me. He wore a football jersey,
jeans, and no shoes.

"I've already called the Chief," he said. "So stay right where
you are."

By this time, I had the robin back in the cage, and the cage
locked up. The envelope was in the pocket of my windbreaker.

Before I could say anything, a small figure in pajamas appeared in the rear door. She was sleepily rubbing her eyes. And
then rushing toward us across the dewy grass.

At first, O'Day looked as if he didn't know what to do, keep
the gun trained on me, or lean down and pick up his youngest
daughter, Tandy. He fixed the gun under one arm and scooped
her up with the other.

What I saw shocked me. The tenderness. She was crying
pretty hard by this time, those precious choking sobs that only little girls are capable of, and saying, "You weren't in your bed,
Daddy, when I went in to find you."

"I'm here, honey. It's all right."

"Niki and Michelle are scared, too."

"I'll be right back inside, sweetheart." He kissed away her tears. "Now you be a good girl and go back inside."

But she didn't go back inside. She clung to her father with clawing desperation, her face lost in his neck. He touched her with great care, almost as if he was afraid to touch her. I wanted to think he was putting on a show for me. Trying to make me think he was a good daddy when he was anything but. But then I remembered what Jane had said, about how they'd kept the truth about his abuse from the kids, and how much the three girls loved him.

We want our villains pure. We don't want them to spoil everything by doing anything against type. I resented him for being a good father at a moment like this. I resented knowing that he was capable of this kind of dutiful parental concern. He was a killer. He didn't have any right to be acting this way.

The Chief was there suddenly, stalking across the lawn, leaving his headlamps on to spear across the grass, all the way to the gazebo. By this time, Tandy had fallen asleep against her father's shoulder.

"You're not supposed to be out here, Ted."

"So O'Day was just telling me," I said. I didn't lean back on the sarcasm.

"I'm sorry about this, Bob."

He looked at me as he spoke, O'Day did. "I want him fired, Chief. Do we understand each other—"

"But Bob—," the Chief started to say.

"Fired. Do you understand?"

Tandy, waking and troubled, muttered something. "This young lady needs her sleep," O'Day said, holding her tight against him so there'd be no chance she'd fall. "And you've got your job to do, Chief." He glared at me briefly again, and then went back inside.

I started to say something as O'Day walked back to the mansion. The Chief said, "Shut up, you stupid bastard." Then he said, "Meet me at the Hawkeye in ten minutes."

Then he was walking away, too.

The Hawkeye had once been a workingman's tavern. Lunchboxes had gleamed in the gloom along the bar and most of the men had steel-plating in the toes of their work shoes. They were the old roughneck working class that went all the way back to early railroads. No more. O'Day Avionics had a cafeteria for its employees, and the shoe of choice seemed to be Reeboks, and if you were having difficulties on the job, you went to see the company shrink. And thus, the Hawkeye was no longer merely a bar; it was a sports bar, which meant a satellite dish out in the backyard and two huge TV screens inside. The waitresses, most of whom had driven to Chicago for discount boob enhancements, wore nifty little miniskirts and sweaters in the black and gold colors of the U of I.

We'd just been served our Buds, the waitress no more than three steps away, when the Chief leaned over and said, "Leave it alone, Ted."

"He killed her."

"You can't prove that. Like I said, leave it alone."

"You know he killed her, Chief."

"What I suspect and what I know are two different things. I don't have any proof and you don't have any proof."

I didn't tell him about the stain on the robin's breast.

He sat back and said, "Look around."

"At what?"

"The people."

I looked around. A pretty wide variety of faces for a small Iowa town. White, black, brown, yellow. And they all drank comfortably in the same place, too.

"We've got a good town," the Chief said.

"I know."

And we did. On average, we had a murder about every six years, there were virtually no robberies, and though highschoolers were constantly experimenting with drugs, we as yet had no hardcore problems.

"We arrest Bob O'Day," the Chief said, "and that's all gonna change."

"What the hell are you saying?"

"I'm saying that the minute his brother takes over the company, O'Day Avionics moves down South. And takes all the jobs with them. And everybody knows that."

"So we don't arrest him?"

He sighed. "You ever hear of the greater good?"

"I've heard of it. But I don't believe in it."

"A lot of families would be destroyed, Ted. A lot of them."

I remembered my run-in with O'Day earlier. "Well, I guess I don't have to worry, anyway. I'm no longer on the police force."

He waved a dismissive hand. A hockey team had just scored a goal. The bar had come alive. "Aw, hell, he's always threatening people like that. I'll talk to him." He looked at me carefully. "But you think about what I said, all right?"

"That we just let him go free."

"I never said that."

"That's what you meant."

"Is it?"

I'd been wondering why he'd gone so easy on O'Day and now I knew. The greater good. It was a terrible way to look at things when you were in the business of law enforcement.

"Tomorrow's supposed to be a nice day. Why don't you drive around town? Think back to what it was like to grow up here. Think of what's happened to some of the other towns around here when the major industry moved out." He pushed himself out of the booth. The way his gut was getting, it took some doing. "I know you don't see me the same way now, Ted. I think you used to have at least a little respect for me. But that's gone now, isn't it?"

I just kept staring at my glass of beer.

"It isn't just O'Day we've got to worry about, Ted," he said. "It's the whole town. A whole lot of lives, Ted. A whole lot of them."

Then he left.

I didn't drive around the next day, or the day after. I didn't have time. There'd been a domestic shooting out at the trailer court on the east edge of town and I was assigned to investigate. It was a three-way sort of thing, husband–wife–her lover, complicated by the fact that none of them would talk. The husband had taken the bullet in the shoulder and had been forced to spend one night in the hospital. But he wouldn't talk and there wasn't a hell of a lot we could do until he did. The lover, you see, was his brother. The town loved this sort of thing, even if it was out at the trailer park, which barely qualified for city limits.

Summer came three mornings later. It happens that way in Iowa. One night you go to bed and it's a drizzly forty-two degrees and then you get up in the morning and the sun blinds you when you open the curtains, and the birds fill your ears and your soul with their golden music. The temperature is in the high seventies. For girl watchers—and, I imagine, for boy watchers—the streets are filled with ladies wearing the bare legal limit of clothes.

Three days after that I got the call from my friend Lisa at the crime lab. I heard just what I wanted to hear and I took it right to the Chief.

"Let me understand you here, Ted."

"Understand all you want."

"You cut a piece from a robin's chest."

"Right."

"And sent it to the crime lab."

"Right."

"And they confirmed that this stain was blood."

"Right."

"And you're sure it's Jane O'Day's blood."

"I am."

"What makes you so sure?"

"For one thing, it matches her type."

"A, you said."

"Right."

"That's a pretty common type."

"He came up from behind her and struck her with something. And some of the blood got on the cage and some of the blood got on the breast of the robin."

"So where's the body?"

"Wherever he buried it."

"The DA won't be impressed."

"He will be after she's missing for thirty days or so. There won't be any way to explain her absence except foul play. And there'll be only one person to look at for foul play. Bob O'Day himself."

"You take that ride yet?"

"What ride?"

"Around town. Looking at what a nice little town we've got here. Damned near full employment. And good employment, too. No minimum-wage crap."

"It won't work on me, Chief. He killed her and I want him to stand trial for it."

"Then there's the kids."

"What kids?"

"His kids. Her kids. You think she'd want their father in prison?"

"It's where he belongs."

"It may be where he belongs. But it sure as hell isn't going to do those kids any good, him up at Fort Madison for the next ten years. So just go and do me a favor. Take that ride."

"It won't work on me, I'm telling you. Even if you let him go, he'll drink himself into a hole so his brother'll have to take over. And then the jobs'll move away anyway."

"Just knock off the next couple of hours and drive around town. That's an order."

"He's guilty."

"Just take the ride, for God's sake, and quit sitting there tellin' me how guilty he is."

So I took the ride.

Our town came to be because of the Civil War. Before then, it hadn't been much more than a stage stop. But because of our proximity to the Mississippi, the governor felt that building a small hospital here for our wounded would be very helpful. Then, when the soldiers were feeling better, they could be transported by stage to their hometowns. That was the beginning. A few years later, merchants realized that there wasn't a good central shopping point for the surrounding farmers, and so they moved in behind the hospital. And we suddenly had ourselves a town. There are still places where you can see hitching posts along the sidewalks, and the deeply embedded tracks of the first electric trolley, and the old barn where the blacksmith plied his trade, and the tavern John Dillinger shot up when he felt he'd been cheated at poker. That's the old town. The new town is family vans and the new county consolidated high school and the redbrick hospital extension and the big mall that seems to be crowded seven days a week and the new public library and the airport that's being expanded next year.

And the Chief had put it all on me. He wasn't exaggerating, that was the thing. If O'Day Avionics was pulled out of this town, the town would slide into turmoil soon after the company left. There'd be a brave scramble on the part of the Chamber of Commerce types to replace O'Day, of course, but here had been a unique set of economic circumstances that had brought it here in the first place. And those circumstances no longer existed. We might get one or two small manufacturing plants to move out here if we could offer the right tax breaks and make a gift of certain parcels of land, but we'd never replace O'Day.

I drove. I knew what he wanted to me to think and I was thinking it. Looking at all the nice middle-class houses; looking at all the lovingly tended lawns; looking at all the merry faces of summer children. Knowing how this would all change if O'Day moved. It had happened to other one-industry towns. You could bitch all you wanted to about how unsafe it was for a town to be dependent on a single manufacturer for employment. But it's a predicament a lot of small towns find themselves in these days with so many factories moving down South or out of the country entirely.

Around dusk, I stopped in at a tavern and had a Bud. I was off-duty and I needed to cut the dust in my throat. I'd ended up in the bluffs above the river, up where Jane and I used to walk down dusty trails, trails we used to follow back in high school.

I was halfway through my Bud when he sat down next to me, the Chief. He was off-duty now, too. He'd kick your ass if he ever caught you drinking when you were supposed to be working. He also had a strict policy about drinking and driving off-duty. Two beers or one mixed drink. Any more than that, you got yourself a designated driver. If you didn't, and you got caught, he fired you on the spot.

"You go for that drive?"

"I did."

"And?"

I leaned in close to him. "He killed her."

"Tell me something new."

"I just want to hear you say it once."

"What difference does it make?"

The bartender brought the Chief his bottle of Bud and a glass. When the bartender went away, I said, "You gonna say it?"

"You're like a little kid, you know that?"

I just watched him.

"You sonofabitch," he said.

I just kept watching him.

He sighed. "All right, you prick, he killed her. Now that didn't do us a whole lot of good, did it?"

"It did me some good. I just wanted to make sure you weren't trying to rationalize anymore."

He shook his head. "I've been thinking about what you said. Even if he does stay here, his brother could still take the company over, if Bob keeps on drinkin' and whorin' around. They throw him in a detox program one more time, brother Bill can take over legally. Either way we move, we're screwed. A whole lot of people're gonna be out of a job real soon."

"Maybe not."

"Oh?" he said, sounding skeptical. "You come up with some kind of idea or somethin'?"

"I didn't. But Jane did."

"Jane?" he said. He then gave me a most peculiar look, the same kind of look he'd given me the day he'd seen me reading a book on near-death experiences.

"Yeah. I went up to her gravesite today and talked to her."

I thought he might laugh. Instead, he said, "Yeah, I do that, too. With my wife, I mean. Go to her grave and talk to her all the time, in fact." He swung his head up from his drink and said, "So what did Jane tell you?"

I shook my head. "I'll let you know how it works out. Then I'll give you all the details."

He raised his beer glass. I raised mine. We clinked them together. "Good luck."

"Yeah," I said. "I'm sure I'll need it."

I called him from the car. He wasn't happy to hear from me.

"I told the Chief you could keep your job as long as you didn't pester me anymore."

"That was damned nice of you."

"This is pestering me."

"Is your maid there?"

"Our maid? What the hell you want to know about her for?"

"Is she there?"

"Yes, she's here. And I'm hanging up."

"Be out on your steps in ten minutes. I'm picking you up."

"By the time you get here, you'll be out of a job."

"If you're not out there, I'll come in and get you."

He didn't hang up. I did.

The mansion was all lit up when I got there. I thought of how small Jane had always looked when she was here at home, engulfed by a terrible marriage that seemed to shrink her even more as the years went on. And yet there'd always been that unfathomable loyalty to him, an almost childlike clinging. For the hundredth time in the past few days, I wanted to kill him. My

hands could feel the pleasures of his throat, the trachea collaps-
ing beneath my thumbs, and his useless gasps for breath.

Then he was there. On the porch. He wore a dark windbreaker and jeans. He had a gun in his right hand.

He came down the steps and over to the car. I reached over
and rolled down the window. He pushed the gun inside. "I wasn't
able get hold of the Chief. He's supposed to call me back. In the
meantime, I want you to give me your gun and your badge."

"Don't be any more of a jerk than you usually are, O'Day."

"You think I'm afraid to kill you."

"You weren't afraid to kill Jane. I guess you probably aren't
afraid to kill me, either."

"Get out of the car."

"You'll have to shoot me right where I am."

"Get out of the car. And right now."

"I'm not moving, O'Day."

He leaned his gun and his head inside the car. "I'm going to
count to five."

"You've been watching TV again, haven't you?"

"Four."

The maid interrupted his little drama, coming to the edge of
the steps. She wouldn't be able to see his gun from where she was,
his body blocking it.

"The Chief is on the phone, Mr. O'Day."

"Thanks, Brenda. Tell him I'll be right in."

She nodded, turned around and walked back through the
gleaming rectangle of doorway.

"You're in luck. Now I don't have to take your badge and
gun. I'll let the Chief do it."

I didn't say anything.

"Just get the hell off my property and right now. You
hear me?"

I stared straight ahead.

"You hear me, you sonofabitch?" He expelled a great whoosh
of whisky breath into the car.

I stared straight ahead. Silently.

But the Chief was waiting. He had to get inside.

He called me another name and then he turned and started back toward the steps.

I had to move fast. I burst out of the car, got my weapon in my hand, and fired.

I got him once, right below the back of the knee. The effect of the shot was such that he completely forgot about the gun he was holding. It clattered to the flagstone.

He was down on his good knee, holding both hands to his wound. He was shouting curses up to the stars.

I ran around the front of the car and got him. I wasn't gentle. I got my hands in his hair and dragged him around the back to the trunk. I was mad enough that lifting his two hundred and twenty-some pounds wasn't as tough as I'd anticipated. He started to yell again but I clipped him hard with the handle of my weapon. He stopped yelling immediately, banging his unconscious head against the tire jack as he slipped deeper into the trunk that smelled of tire rubber and gasoline.

I closed the trunk and drove away. The maid was just then appearing in my rearview mirror.

When we got out of town, I let him out of the trunk and marched him up to the front seat.

The fishing cabin belonged to my uncle. It sat isolated on a bluff above a leg of the Cedar River. Crickets and coyotes and barn owls were just now, in the purple-gold star-sprinkled dusk, warming up for the concert they'd be giving when the moon reached its zenith.

O'Day wasn't doing too well. He'd called me every name he knew twice over. Now he was given more to groans and grunts than intelligible speech. He kept his hands wrapped tight around his leg wound.

"Look at all the blood I'm losing," he said, sounding half-hysterical.

"Yeah, and it's getting all over my car."

"You're gonna go to prison for this."

"I guess we'll see, won't we."

A deer ran with great muscled speed across the angle of my headlights as we pulled up to the dark and shuttered cabin. The windows showed grime and cobwebs. Nobody had used it for a long time. A new dam upstream had diverted what had been good fishing waters. That and the fact that the cabin had no electricity and no plumbing left it unused.

I got him inside and tied him to a chair. I went back to the trunk and got a Coleman lantern and brought it back inside. I dusted off a place on the wobbly kitchen table and sat both lantern and tape recorder down. A big plump rat haunched down on a chair in the north corner and watched us.

"Why don't you shoot the sonofabitch?" O'Day said.

"He isn't hurting anybody."

"He's a rat."

I smiled at him. "So are you."

The cabin was a single room. There were two cupboards above a counter for preparing food. One of the cupboard doors hung at an angle. A dirty word had been spray-painted on one of the cupboard doors. The cabin smelled of must and heat and an infinite variety of critter feces. The dust was awful. Both of us were sneezing constantly.

"I need to go to the hospital."

"Yes, you do."

"Then you'd better damned well take me."

"I will," I said. "As soon as you tell me what I want to know."

"You really will wind up in prison. You know that, don't you?"

"Right now, I don't give a damn. And that's the truth, O'Day. You better keep that in mind."

"I keep losing blood." The half-hysterical note was back in his voice.

I turned on the recorder. The Coleman lantern played red-yellow streaks across his face. I could smell his salty sweat suddenly, and the high tangy odor of his blood.

I used my usual interrogation process, identifying myself, the date, the time, the place, and the person being interrogated.

"This is all bullshit," he said. He leaned toward the recorder and started shouting, "I've been shot in the leg by this man and now he's got me tied up in a chair! He's going to force a false confession out of me! I want you to understand all this! I may be forced to make a confession!"

He slumped back in his chair, silent, exhausted. In the flickering light of the lantern, his face was glazed with sweat.

I reached into the pocket of my windbreaker and took the lab report out. I let the tape roll. I had a ninety-minute cassette in it. I pushed the report toward him. "This came in from the lab. I cut a little piece off the breast of the robin Jane had in her cage and had the crime lab analyze it. Type A. Same as Jane's."

Between wincing from the pain, and glancing again and again at the door and all the wonderful freedom that lay on the other side of it, he was preoccupied. He didn't seem to understand the import of what I'd just told him.

"The way I see it, you came up from behind her and struck her on the head with something heavy. Heavy enough, anyway, that the blow sprayed blood in the cage and on the robin. I was lucky, by the way. The lab told me that the blood had dried and not rotted. If it had rotted, they wouldn't have been able to take any DNA samples. Interesting, huh?"

"You can't do this." he said, gripping his leg.

"I can't?"

"You haven't read me my rights and my lawyer isn't present."

"We're just having a nice little conversation."

"I'm starting to feel dizzy. You've got to get me to the hospital."

"Is that pretty much how it happened?" I said. "The way I described it to you?"

"I don't know what you're talking about."

"You know, you coming up from behind and hitting her with something."

He screamed, then. I would have screamed, too. I'd kicked him hard in the leg. The wounded one.

"You can make this easy, or you can make this hard, O'Day.

And believe me, I'm hoping you make it hard because it'll be a lot more fun for me."

I kicked him again. This time he put his head down on the table the way a child would have, and started softly crying.

He said, in tears, "It won't work. The court'll throw this whole confession out. Even if I say I killed her, it won't matter."

"True enough," I said. "If all you tell me is that you killed her. But you're going to tell me something else, something only the real killer could know."

"What the hell're you talking about?"

"You're going to tell me what you did with her body."

It took me an hour.

I had to kick him several more times, and once he fell out of his chair and I stepped on his hand pretty hard, too. But it wasn't the pain that got to him. It was the blood loss. It got to me, too. I was afraid I was going to have a corpse on my hands, and that wouldn't help anybody.

He said, finally, "It was an accident."

"Right."

"It was. It really was."

"Tell me about it."

"I was carrying some bricks from a birdbath we'd torn down. Jane said something argumentative to me and I just dropped the bricks and hurled one in her direction. I didn't mean for it to even hit her. But it did. Right in the back of her head. Blood sprayed everywhere. It was one of those freak accidents. It really was. I don't expect you to believe me. But it's the truth. And I panicked." He was sweating. Cold sweat. His whole body was shaking. I suspected he'd also wet his pants. There was a certain stench. He said, "I've got to get to the hospital. I'm going to die pretty soon if I don't." He was licking cracked lips.

"I'm going to do you a favor, O'Day."

"What? What favor?" He was starting to sound vaguely dazed.

"I'm going to make you into a model father and a model citizen."

"I don't understand. I'm too weak to understand."

"Very simple. You're going to quit drinking and drop the bimbos and start paying attention to your company again. And make sure all these jobs stay right here in town."

"I don't know what you're talking about," he said. "You're not making any sense."

I kicked him again, a lot harder than I had before. Then I grabbed him by his hair and pulled out a thin handful. "Now what did you do with Jane's body?"

"You're not gonna get away with this."

"Tell me where you put her body."

"You're going to prison."

I kicked him again in his wound. Hard. He started crying.

"Where is she?" I said.

"I'm not going to tell you anything."

"Sure you are," I said. And kicked him again.

It took a couple of more kicks, which I didn't mind at all inflicting, and then he told me. I got hold of the Chief on the phone and told him to go alone to a certain place and see if he found a recent small excavation there. He phoned back twenty-five minutes later and said that the body was there, all right. I told him to keep it buried and that I'd meet him at the hospital, where I'd be taking our good friend Bob O'Day.

By this time, O'Day was unconscious, pale, unmoving, and breathing in fitful little gasps.

There was a lot of explaining to do and on all sides. O'Day had to explain how he'd been shot (an accident) and we had to explain to skeptical townsfolk why we weren't pursuing O'Day (not enough evidence). There was a lot of doubt (and all sorts of theories, the most popular being that O'Day had bought us off), but as the months passed, the public mind found other things to tantalize itself with: there was the robbery at the county fair, a couple of good old boys getting pretty badly shot up for their troubles; the bank scandal involving the staid president and his secretary; and the hospital troubles, where some of the nurses tried to hook up to a union, to the great dismay of nearly everybody in town. People died, babies were born, seasons changed. O'Day belonged in prison, and I could never quite let myself forget this. So I went at least twice a week up in the clay hills where he'd buried her and I sat and talked to her for long periods of time. Even when the snow came, I went up there. I believe she spoke to me one day, and I believe she said that what I'd done was all right, considering what O'Day's company meant to the town. I also believe she told me that I should go ahead and ask Teresa Conners to marry me, which I promptly did. We were married last month and moved into the house I grew up in. I put a small addition in the back, the cage that I'd built for Jane all those years ago. Now I'm the one who takes care of stray animals.

As for Bob O'Day, so far so good. It's been two years now. He's become a prime mover in the local Alcoholics Anonymous chapter, and he spends most of his free time with his kids. I see him at church every other Sunday or so. He seems interested in the new choir leader. She's a nice, sensible woman.

O'Day Avionics is doing well, too. With Bob sober and paying attention to his work, in fact, the company has hired an additional seventy-five people. Good jobs, good benefits.

I saw O'Day on the street lately. He knows I'm always checking up on him. I can't say he ever seems happy to see me.

But yesterday he stopped me—a bright but very windy early autumn day—and said, "For what it's worth, I really didn't kill her on purpose. I doubt you'll ever believe me. But it's the truth."

"But all those other times," I said, "all the black eyes and broken bones. Those were on purpose."

He smiled bitterly. "I guess you're never going to like me much, are you?"

I kept my eyes right on him. "No," I said, "I guess I'm not."

I went home, then. Teresa was out shopping. I went to the cage and looked in on the baby raccoon. She'd hurt her paw somehow and was limping badly when I'd found her in the backyard. She couldn't have weighed three pounds. I'd taken her to the vet and he'd worked on her and told me to let her take it easy in the cage for a while. And then to let her go.

I guess that's one thing you learn the older you get, how you have to let go of people and things you care about, even though you know you'll be the lesser for their leaving.

I gave the raccoon some food and then went in and opened myself a beer and popped in a videotape of a football game I'd wanted to see last Saturday. And then I just sat there feeling old and bleak and very, very lonely.

Ed Gorman

As a prolific multi-genre novelist and short story writer, Ed Gorman always has his fingers on the pulse of the Mystery Scene, *especially since he was cofounder of that magazine. His suspense and crime fiction has been selected by several book clubs and his work has won the Shamus, the Spur, and the International Fiction Writer's Awards. He's also been nominated for such mystery awards as the Edgar, the Anthony, Britain's Golden Dagger, and the Bram Stoker horror award. In recent years he's concentrated on suspense novels. New this year was* Harlot's Moon, *third in a sequence that includes* Blood Moon *and* Hawk Moon. Black River Falls, *another recent suspense title, was a best-seller in England. He lives in Cedar Rapids with his wife, Carol Gorman, who writes young adult novels. Their cats are the strays Tasha and Crystal, and the purchased Tess, who isn't a purebred. Says Ed, "they're all mutts."*

AFTERWORD
CAROLE NELSON DOUGLAS

Most writers put animals in their novels and stories because they like them.

Dig beneath that liking, and you'll find personal stories much like J. A. Jance's account of Mandy. Writers, because of the empathy their very nature encourages, identify, quite literally, with the "underdog." Mystery writers, especially, identify with those given short shrift by blind Lady Justice. This could be the murder victim, or—if the victim was destructive to others—with the victims of the late unlamented one.

Companion animals, whom our legal system regards not as life-forms but only as "property" with a shockingly low dollar value considering the roles they play in most peoples' lives, are often the most helpless victims of all.

That's why the eighteen-year-old high school "boys" who broke into a shelter to maim and club dozens of cats to death with baseball bats couldn't be charged with a felony. The court valued each dead cat at $32; even the multiple carnage didn't add up to the $500 necessary to sentence the perpetrators of the boyish "prank" to more than a few days in jail. Life, when it is furred, feathered, or scaled, is cheap in our legal system.

While visiting animal shelters during the Midnight Louie Adopt-a-Cat program, which combines bookstore signing events with cat adoptions, I heard the many needs and complaints dedicated shelter workers voice. One frustration was that when severely abused and neglected animals are seized, often the case doesn't come to court until the shelter has rehabilitated the animals (that live) to a semblance of health. Often the judge will return the animals to the abusive owners.

I had a suggestion: Why not require judges to accompany an-

imal control officers on at least one seizure raid involving a severe animal abuse case? Shelter people looked at me aghast. You
don't "require" or even ask a judge to do anything, apparently
not even seek insight on matters of animal life and death. So
some animal-ignorant judges, bowing to "property" rights, sweep
abused animals back into the custody of their abusers.

Yet the social price of ignoring animal misery is high. Recent
research proves that animal abuse is a precursor to human abuse;
many serial killers practice first on insects, then wild birds, then
domestic pets, moving up to children and finally adult human
beings.

It strikes me as odd that our culture encourages every child to
identify with animals through books, animated films, and stuffed
lions and tigers and bears, oh my, yet much of that empathy is expected to vanish when the playthings of a child are put away.

The boy who hugged a bear at three may be encouraged to
shoot a bird or a squirrel at twelve. The only way he can do that
is to destroy his empathy for the animal, a facility that is even
more useful when that same boy at twenty is required to shoot at
a human enemy in a war. Girls are not expected to learn to destroy life, although that is coming, but the girl who loved classic
stories like *Winnie the Pooh* and *The Velveteen Rabbit* at nine
may grow up to be ridiculed for reading or writing about animals
as an adult.

What are the animal-disparagers afraid of? Of being perceived as immature? Or of being perceived as compassionate? Is
adulthood a state of indifference to the pain and needs of others,
including animals?

I've written in several fields, daily newspaper journalism as
well as science fiction/fantasy and mystery fiction, and in each
field I've written about animals, although I've known that writing about animals is the lowest-status thing to do and is often
ridiculed.

In my experience, it's mostly boys and men who disparage
writing about animals, as if caring for animals undercuts their
very notion of manhood. And hurting animals is a way some

preadolescent boys (and, later, certified abusers) seek to attract female attention, and fear and revulsion.

I'm reminded of the twenty-year-old boys/men working for the summer at a Montana lodge, who shot a beaver and installed it at midnight in the girls' dorm, or who later took a litter of abandoned kittens, got them drunk on beer and threw them into the girls' bedrooms at night.

One landed on me, and became my charge for the rest of the summer. The kitchen workers and waitresses, who each gained at least fifteen pounds that summer snacking on kitchen foods, begrudged me a few scraps for the kitten even as they stuffed their own faces. My dormmates were irritated by it, so when we moved cabins, I chose a single bedroom with the kitten rather than a common bedroom with my own species.

The kitten was tiny, terrified, and too young to eat well, or even to live long. When I took it outside and it heard a distant dog bark, it climbed me like a tree, up to my shoulder. At night, it kept wanting to sleep on my face for security, but I found it far finer company than the spoiled and callous young adults around me.

Why do I write about animals? Because, after a lifetime of helping a few survive the human world's cruelty, I find they always help me find the humanity in myself. And because, at times, I have found far more humanity in them than I can find in some of my own "higher" species.

As long as people write about and read about, and empathize and identify with animals, the animals will be better off, and so will we.